Fallen Unchained

STATE OF GRACE: BOOK ONE

CASSIDY REYNE

STATE OF GRACE BOOK ONE
FALLEN
Unchained
CASSIDY REYNE

Copyright 2024 By Cassidy Reyne

All rights reserved.

No part of this book may be reproduced in any form or by any electronic or mechanical means, including information storage and retrieval systems, without the written permission from the author, except for the use of brief quotations in a book review. Licensed material is being used for illustrative purposes only and any person depicted in the licensed material is a model. This book is fiction. Names, characters, and incidents are the product of the author's imagination or used fictitiously. Any resemblance to any actual persons, living or dead, events, or locations are entirely coincidental.

Till min mamma.
Du var min trygghet, min förebild, min idol, min ledstjärna, en grundsten i mitt liv. Nu har din mjuka musik tystnat och min värld har förlorat något av sin lyster. Du fattas mig i livet men förblir för evigt i mitt hjärta.
Jag älskar dig.

For my mom. You were my comfort, my role model, my idol, my guiding star, a cornerstone of my life. Now, your gentle music has stopped sounding, and my world has lost some of its glow. You're gone from my life but will forever remain in my heart.
I love you.

Head up, heart open;
sail on, sail on,
like it's your last sunset.
(Poem by Heather Grace Stewart)

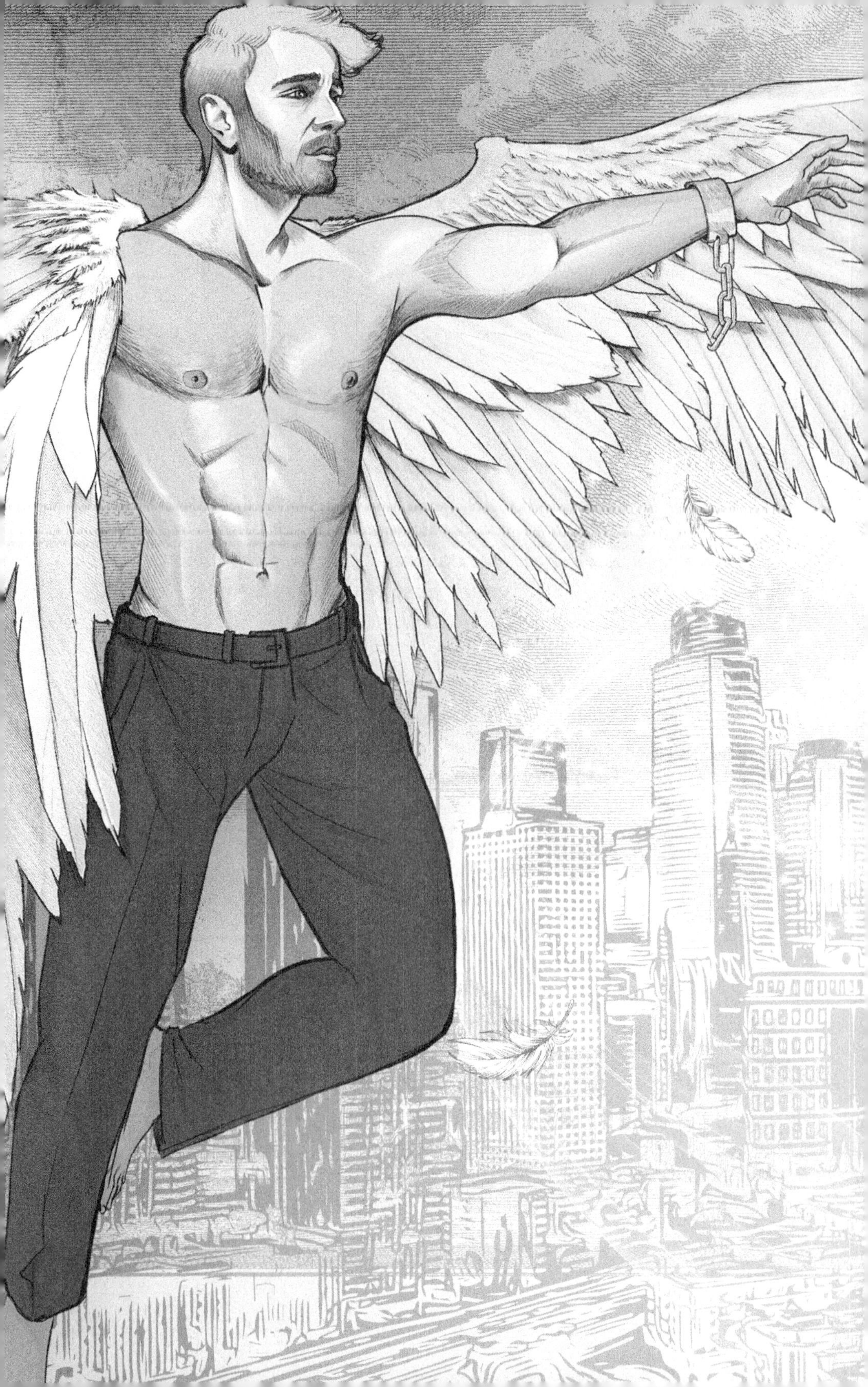

Prologue

Pain.
Excruciating.
Agonizing.
Torturous.
Pain.

It was both devastating and paralyzing. The flesh on his back tore into strips, blood dripping as it ripped him apart. A scream tore from his lungs, piercing and unearthly, but the dark vacuum surrounding him swallowed every sound he made. Still, he screamed into the quietude until his throat bled and burned. Overwhelmed by the deafening, dead air, his senses switched off one by one, until there was nothing left, and he drifted aimlessly in a vast nothingness.

Having always been surrounded by bright lights and familiar, comforting sounds, the forbidding darkness and complete absence of everything terrified him. It burrowed under his peeling skin, like a parasite searching for a vulnerable spot to sink its claws into, penetrating the emptiness of his core. He begged for relief, cried for someone to take him away from the hellish existence into which he'd fallen. His only reply was more of the empty, suffocating silence.

How long he floated there, he didn't know and didn't want to contemplate. It seemed eternal. The pain in his back gradually faded, the fires on his skin dying out and turning into a dull ache. It was bearable. Barely. Although, any relief was better than the agony he'd experienced for so long. If only the dark would withdraw and the silence ease its death grip on his sanity. He no longer believed salvation was possible for him, but he still held a glimmer of hope that there was something more for him out there than just this... nothingness.

Drifting through the emptiness, he kept his eyes closed. What was the point of having them open when he saw nothing but an impenetrable black void? As he pulled memories out of his head and kept replaying them on a loop, his heart ached for his loved ones — his family. He'd almost stopped asking himself why. Why had this happened to him? Was there a purpose to his agony? He had to believe there was. That somewhere, somehow, there was a reason for his miserable existence.

Floating, drifting on this endless sea for what felt like eons, he once again forced his unwilling eyes to open. Blinking hard, he stared around. Nothing there, still. Yet, there was something. The black wasn't quite so black. The silence was no longer as silent.

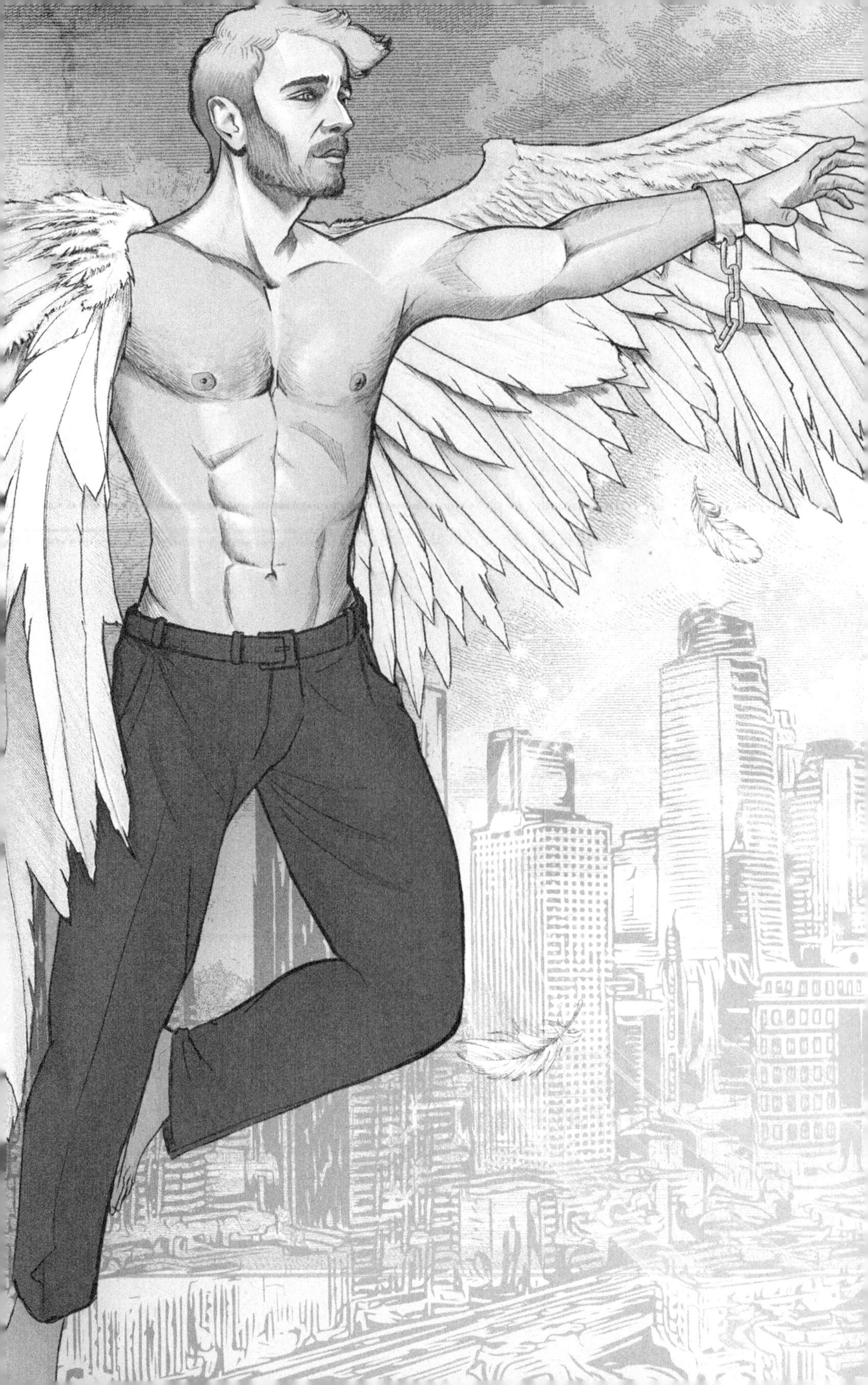

One

ALINA, 2010

It was a beautiful spot. Almost too beautiful. The grass was lush and green, sloping down toward the cliffs with the deep blue ocean beyond sparkling as if diamonds had been scattered by the handfuls across its surface. The light was blinding, and yet all she saw was darkness.

She turned her gaze away from the stunning view, attempting to focus on the people around her. Her eyes swept across their familiar faces, all with serious expressions and many with tears staining their cheeks. Staring at each person in turn, recalling little details about them, she tuned out the voice that spoke about being called away too soon, taking the most beloved before those around them were ready to give them up.

Her gaze flitted from the people gathered to the trees and the grass under her shoes. It danced from the perfect feather-shaped cloud on an otherwise clear sky, to the birds taking flight, soaring ever higher on warm winds — anything to keep herself from seeing what was right in front of her.

One large box, flanked by two smaller ones, containing her life, her heart, her soul.

She didn't need to look to know every tiny detail about them. The exact shapes, sizes, colors…

Lowering her gaze, she stared at the specks of dirt on the side of one shoe. A heavy rain had swept across in the night, washing away the dust from the dry weather of the last few weeks, leaving everything refreshed, cleansed, as new. All except her future.

The soft notes of a hymn played on a flute floated through her fraught mind, gently soothing her torn nerve endings. Looking up, she steeled herself and fixed her eyes on the coffins before her.

Her entire family, her life, her reason for being, lay in those simple caskets. A light wooden one for her husband, powder blue for her boy, and the smallest, doll-sized one, the palest, the creamiest pink for her tiny baby girl. All ripped from her in the blink of an eye. With all her heart, she wished she was lying next to them, holding her husband's hand in death as she'd done countless times in life in the last eight years.

Fate was a cruel mistress. In that split second, she'd gone from living a happy, fulfilled life with a man she adored, and two wonderful, bright, and gorgeous children, to facing a bleak and joyless future. The memories of that day burned in her mind, angry, searing, and ferocious. They ate at her sanity, piece by piece, and she knew they would soon consume her.

Carefully rolling her shoulders to ease the throbbing pain across her shoulder blades, she fought against the tsunami of despair and torment threatening to engulf her. Her mind scrambled frantically to find the blessed numbness she'd languished in for weeks after the… Abruptly, she stopped her train of thought. That day needed to stay buried. Forever.

"Alina? It's time to go, sweetie."

A voice from behind ripped her away from the swirling blackness she'd stumbled toward.

"No, I can't leave yet. They need me." The voice coming out of her mouth sounded alien, a mere shadow of how it used to sound.

"They're at peace now. There's nothing more you can do for them. You need to look after yourself."

"I'm staying. You go. I'll be fine on my own. Tell everyone goodbye for me."

"Don't do this to yourself, Lina. You need people around you, and everyone is expecting you back at the house."

The use of her nickname sent another stab to her heart. Her husband had had his own nickname for her, always saying she was so special to him he wanted something that was just theirs. He'd called her Li. No one else was ever allowed to call her that. All her friends and family only ever said Lina if they didn't use her full name. A gray and rainy morning three weeks ago was the last time she'd heard that name spilling from his lips.

"Okay, I'll see you back at the house. Please, don't be too long, or I'll have to come and get you. If you won't look after yourself, I'll do it for you."

"I won't take long, I promise. I just want... they need... I need to be with them."

Near-silent footfalls on the grass disappeared somewhere behind her. She didn't care where to, as long as she was left alone.

On stiff, painful legs, she dragged her feet closer to those wooden caskets that held her entire existence. Standing before them, the tenuous hold she'd had on her emotions and the brave face she'd put on broke with an almost audible snap. She sank to her knees, an anguished cry rising from her throat, spiraling toward the skies, as her heart shattered into a million pieces again and again. Despair, anguish, rage, sorrow, and unbearable pain crashed through her like the deluge from a broken dam, and she was caught in the maelstrom swirling inside her.

With her hands on each of the pastel-colored coffins, she rested her forehead on the larger casket in the middle. Closing her eyes, she tried to sense their presence, feel their love, the joy they'd brought to her life, but there was nothing — only cold, hard wood and wetness from the ground seeping through her pantyhose. She crumbled to the ground, fists grasping clumps of grass for something to hold on to while her heart tore apart and her mind fractured.

She lay still, not hearing the birds twittering in the nearby trees, or the bees buzzing among the flowers, nor did she feel the soft breeze with its tang of salt from the ocean, or the gentle caress of the sun's rays on her cheek. Feeling as though she was standing on the edge of a precipice, she hesitated, waiting for either fear or calm to set in, but all she felt was a blank nothing.

After an eternity, Alina pushed herself to her feet, swaying on unsteady limbs. She swung her gaze away from the trio of caskets. They were no longer there. She was alone.

Turning, she took one small, agonizing step away from her once so joyous and beautiful life. She made her way back toward the car, where the driver waited patiently for her. A tall, older man in a dark suit with a kind face and deep crinkles at the corners of his eyes opened the passenger door and offered his hand to assist her into the backseat. Without a word, he got behind the wheel and drove her away from the last earthly remnants of her soul.

With a final glance out the rear window, she shifted to face forward, closed her eyes, and inhaled a sharp breath. As she let it out, a darkness spread through her core, followed by numbness. Every emotion, every thought of what was and any hope for the future was snuffed out. All that remained was a shell — a mere shadow.

PULLING up to the curb outside a two-story house with a large front yard, white picket fence, and a riot of colorful flowers, the driver sat quietly, waiting for her to decide whether to step out. He seemed to understand her hesitation and reticence to face the world outside the little cocoon the town car afforded her.

Alina wasn't sure how long she sat there, staring at the house. Vehicles filled the street and driveway, and she could see people moving about in the living room through the picture windows. They were all waiting for her, she knew, but her head was screaming at her to flee, to run anywhere as fast as she could — *to be anywhere but here* — but she knew she couldn't do it. Those people inside had come to support her, pay their last respects, and remember.

Plastering the best imitation of a smile she could muster, she forced her feet to move along the familiar paving stones of the driveway, purposely ignoring the garage, which was missing its metallic occupant, and entered the house that had until only recently been full of happiness and laughter.

"There you are. You okay?" Kate slapped her hand against her forehead. "Sorry, that was a stupid question. Is there anything I can do? Let me get you something to eat and a cup of tea." Her friend wrapped an arm around her shoulders and steered her into the kitchen, which was thankfully empty.

"I'm fine. Just tired, I guess. And I ache a little. I still have plenty of bruises."

"That's not surprising. You only need to say a quick hello to people. No one expects anything more from you. Then I'll help you get rid of them while the caterers clear up."

"Thanks, Katie. I don't know what I would have done without you. The last few weeks have been..." Her voice trailed off.

"I'm so sorry, Lina." Katie paused, clearing her throat before continuing, "I can't even imagine what this has done to you. I wish I could have helped more."

Alina allowed herself to be enveloped in a hug. Katie had been there for her since they were old enough to stand and had been her rock ever since—

Remaining still in the embrace, she searched for a response to the touch. A feeling of comfort, warmth, or... something, but more than anything, she felt uneasy. No amount of hugs would bring her comfort. In fact, it made her uncomfortable. Her friend's touch on her skin sent a shudder down her spine, making her want to jerk away, but she resisted, not wanting to hurt Katie's feelings.

It would pass, she decided. She hoped. In time, she would find a new normal. A normal without her loved ones. She didn't want to think about it. Her normal was gone, and she desperately wanted it back. She'd do anything to have it back, but it was impossible.

"You've already done so much. I'll be okay. I'm not the first person to go through this and" — she glanced toward the living room and sighed — "unfortunately, I won't be the last."

Katie squeezed her hand.

Closing her eyes for a moment, Alina took a deep breath. "I'd better say thank you to everyone for coming. Never realized so many would turn up." Injecting some much-needed steel into her backbone, she put that grimacing mask back on her face and marched into the other room, bracing herself for platitudes, more hugs, and sympathetic smiles.

Looking around, Alina saw the faces of their friends, but they seemed more like strangers now. It was weird. The faces were familiar, but there was also something false about them, as if they were wax copies of the real things. Behind their benign expressions was a vacuum, a void, similar to what she sensed inside herself.

One by one, her guests trooped out the door, disappearing back to their own lives, probably drawing sighs of relief that it was over for them. They could go home to their families and their loved ones and put all this behind them. They'd done their duty, showed up, cried a few tears, and now they could move on. Not so for her. Somehow, she had to put the pieces of her fractured existence together and form them into something new. If only she knew how. It was a problem for tomorrow, however, as right now, she just wanted to be alone.

"Lina, I'm leaving now. Unless you want me to stay for a bit?"

The quiet voice startled her out of her thoughts. Alina took a deep breath, schooling her features before she turned around. A pair of warm brown eyes met hers, concern swirling in their depths. Katie's face, normally so bright and relaxed, looked worn and tense. Her dark skin, pulled tight over her cheekbones, held a tinge of gray, and sharp lines formed in the corners of her mouth. Her black, glossy hair still held its chic style but had lost some of its usual shine.

A sting of shame pierced Alina's heart. Katie had taken care of everything for her, answered every phone call, liaised with undertakers, arranged flowers and caterers, and organized a myriad of other details, all so she wouldn't have to do it while recovering from her injuries and drowning in grief. Katie deserved more from her, but right now, Alina didn't have it in her. As soon as she'd pulled herself together and could think clearly, she'd make sure Katie knew just how much she loved and appreciated her.

"No. Thank you, though. You've been amazing, and I couldn't have gotten through any of this without you."

"As if I wouldn't have been here for you. We're best friends, sisters, and you would have done the same for me."

"Yes, of course. Still, I am grateful and appreciate everything you've done."

"I'll call you tomorrow just to check in, okay?"

"No, don't, please. I think I need some time to myself with no interruptions. I might sleep all day, I'm that exhausted." Alina tried to sound reassuring, but her voice sounded shrill, even to herself.

She met Katie's gaze and, once again, the fake smile swept across her lips. So far, it seemed to have worked, but Katie knew her better than anyone and could usually read her like an open book. A frown appeared on Katie's brow, but she didn't protest, just gave a brief nod and hoisted her bag on her shoulder. With a final, quick hug, she walked down the steps of the porch toward her car parked in the driveway.

Alina stayed in the doorway, waving as Katie pulled out onto the street, heading back to her house, her normal, her life. With yet another deep sigh — there had been too many of them recently — Alina waited until the taillights had disappeared around a corner before closing the door behind her, shutting out reality, if only for a little while. Heading up the stairs, she hesitated outside the master bedroom. The desire to fill her nose with the scent from his clothes and his pillow warred with the knowledge it would all dissipate, and she'd be left with only a few photographs and fading memories.

Swinging her gaze to the two doors opposite, their wooden nameplates burned into her mind. A tidal wave of despair engulfed her, shredding her heart for the millionth time, leaving destruction and havoc in its place. The urge to flee rose from her gut, searing its way up to her throat. Spinning on her heel, she stumbled back down the stairs and collapsed on the couch in the living room.

THE HOURS TICKED BY, but Alina barely moved. Night had fallen when she finally stirred. Blinking rapidly, her eyes stung and felt full of grit and sand, struggling to penetrate the darkness of the room. It was better this way, she decided. At least in the dark, she didn't risk seeing the photographs scattered around the room, the box of toys in the corner, or the baby blanket thrown over the armrest of the squishy armchair.

Blindly, Alina felt her way through the room toward the stairs, dragging her feet up to the second floor again. Without stopping, she padded on silent feet along the hallway as if making a noise would awaken memories she was trying to lock away. Out of habit, her step stuttered outside their — her — bedroom, and she snatched her hand back before it pressed down the handle, a burning sensation on her palm and fingers. A sharp gasp escaped her lips. Quickening her step, she moved farther down the hall to the guest bedroom, closed the door behind her and let out the breath she'd held in without realizing.

She flung herself on the bed, inhaling the scent of freshly laundered linen to chase away any remnants of other, so very familiar smells. Those that were already fading, turning into a whisper on the wind. Curling up in a ball, she wrapped herself in the quilt and closed her eyes, hoping for some rest.

A bridge.
So high they felt like they were traveling through the clouds.
Bright lights. Too bright. Too close.
Metal crashing, grinding against metal. Screeching tires. Whining brakes.
Spinning, somersaulting, thumping, crunching.
Lightning bolts. Stabbing pain. Glass shattering.
Screaming. Oh, God. The screaming.
A shuddering halt. Silence. Hideous, terrifying, ominous silence.
Colors. Red. Blue. Flashing, swirling. Wailing sirens.
Tinny voices.
"Ma'am, are you all right? Ma'am, are you in any pain?"
The voice was indistinct and came from far away. She tried to form words, but her tongue wouldn't cooperate. A metallic taste flooded her mouth, and her face felt wet. Something dripped into her eyes, but her lids stayed open, fixed on the hypnotic dance of colors in front of her. Movement by her side jerked her head toward it. Shards of black and white filled her vision. Indistinct and disjointed images and sounds filled her mind, telling her there was something she needed to remember. The same voice as before broke through the fog in her head.

"One female, conscious but unresponsive, one male non-responsive, two children—"

It moved away. She couldn't hear what it was saying. Who was unresponsive? Why was she here? She grasped at the images in her mind, but they were like ice floes on a dark sea, floating away as she reached for them. Another voice. This time, it was inside her head. Children's laughter.

A heavy weight slammed into her chest, crushing her lungs and squeezing her heart.

"My babies! Where are my babies? My husband? Daisy? Theo? Jonas? Jonas! Jonas! Where are you? Answer me, please!" *she screamed, struggling to force enough air in and out of her lungs.*

"Ma'am, please calm down. We're going to help you. Just calm down and let us make you more comfortable."

She couldn't breathe. Where was her family? Her children? Her husband? What was happening? Movement, jostling, pulling, tugging.

Then nothing.

A darkness enveloped her in its icy embrace as torment and despair spread through her veins.

BRIGHT LIGHTS, *stark white above and to the sides, beeping machines. She'd seen this before — several times — but she couldn't seem to stay here. The black void returned each time, dragging her away to nothingness.*

Voices spoke to her. This had also happened many times, but it seemed different this time, as if she could finally understand some of it. Sounds came out of her mouth, but she couldn't work out if it was in response to whoever was talking. Blinking, a face came into blurry focus, and she could see the mouth move, but the words filled her with fear. They made no sense.

"I'm so sorry to have to tell you, but your husband and children didn't make it. We did everything we could, but they died on the scene. You are lucky to have survived. When you're a little stronger, someone will come and talk to you about what happened and answer any questions you may have."

"No, no, no. You're lying. I want to see them. I want to see my husband, my babies! Why are you telling me this? I know they're here. I can feel them! Please, don't take them from me! Please!"

Hands held her down as she struggled to move, to go find her family. They were close. Their presence was weak, but she could still feel them. It was fainter than before, but she'd always been able to sense them wherever they were. She searched frantically in her heart and her mind. Their lights were fading, diminishing with every frantic beat of her pulse.

SHE JOLTED UPRIGHT, sweat pouring down her face and back. Her heart beat in her chest at an impossible speed, and her throat closed up, preventing the air from reaching her lungs. An overwhelming wave of grief and despair swept through her, forcing an agonized scream from her chest. They were gone and were never coming back. She'd lost them. She'd lost her reason for living. Her life was a gaping abyss, and she wanted it to swallow her, to take her to her husband and children. Without them, she was nothing.

Alina leaned back against the headboard, exhaustion seeping through every cell in her body. The anvil sitting on her chest still made breathing difficult, and somewhere inside her ribcage, the shriveled remains of her heart burned white-hot with fear. She needed rest, but the nightmare of what had happened haunted her every time she closed her eyes, just as it haunted her every waking moment.

Why was her family taken away from her? It should have been her who was removed from this earth. Not her children. She'd change places with them in a heartbeat, without a moment's hesitation. She'd already lived a wonderful life filled with joy, love, and happiness. Theirs had barely begun.

The image of the bridge hovered in her mind. There was something about it that felt wrong. It had spanned high above a gorge with a raging river below. Her fraught mind mulled it over. It didn't fit with the other horrifying pieces of images ricocheting through her head.

That was it! They'd never crossed a bridge. She couldn't even think of one anywhere near them that was that high or with a river beneath it. What did it mean? Was her brain trying to tell her something? That she was the one who'd put them all at risk? She already blamed herself for being alive when her family wasn't, so this only reinforced her self-condemnation.

The guilt of surviving ate away at her soul, spreading its poison, turning her thoughts bitter and resentful. She needed someone to blame, and the only person within reach was her. The driver of the other car had been drunk and never stopped at the red light. He'd hit their car side-on, crushing both Jonas and Daisy immediately. Theo had been sitting behind her and lasted a little while longer but passed before the first responders had managed to cut him out of the wreckage.

Physically, she'd gotten away with a severe concussion, a couple of cracked ribs, and a riot of deep-tissue bruises covering most of her body. Mentally, she bore the brunt of the entire incident. The drunken driver hadn't worn a seatbelt and was thrown through his windshield, catapulted through the air into oncoming traffic. His life had ended under the wheels of a garbage disposal truck. There was no one else left to blame.

If only rolled like tumbleweed through her mind on a constant loop.

THE DARK outside her window slowly gave way to the muted colors of dawn. The familiar features of the room came into focus. A few paintings hung on the white-painted walls, landscapes mostly, and sage green curtains framed the windows. Staring at the ceiling, her body shook and trembled. Deep sobs worked their way into her closed throat, forming a large lump she couldn't remove. Her chest felt tight, and she could barely fill her lungs with enough air to breathe.

Behind her ribs, her heart raced frantically, causing pain to shoot through her body. Her limbs tensed until her muscles screamed in protest, the sound increasing in strength in her mind as her skull threatened to split apart. Agony exploded behind her eyes, setting them on fire, and all she wanted was to burn. Burn in the fire of her grief and sorrow, burn until nothing more than ashes remained. She'd even accept spending an eternity in the fires of Hell if it meant the pain of her loss was erased. She couldn't take much more of the anguish. It was driving her insane.

Slowly, the fires died down. The pain in her body receded, and the pounding in her head turned into a muted, throbbing ache. Sweat covered her skin. Her clothes and bedding were damp, but she was too exhausted to care.

The stress and exertion of the last few weeks took their toll on her body, and Alina fell into an uneasy slumber. The faces of her husband and family spun through her mind, their laughter a soothing balm to her soul. Gradually, the images and sounds faded, and a new voice took their place. She strained to hear what it said, the words floating toward her like the soughing of the wind in a copse of trees.

He will find you.

It sounded firm and decisive, benevolent and compassionate even.

A different voice curled around her mind, soothing, comforting, whispering.

Just take one small step.

Two

KIRAN, 1948

Kiran suppressed a sigh, looking out the grimy window of the interstate bus. He was back where he began his last journey. What drew him here, he wasn't sure, but something inside told him he needed to return. Not that he had any choice in the matter. He never did.

The place had changed while he was gone. How long had it been? He shook his head. Time was a strange thing, and he still hadn't worked out how people experienced it. For him, it was fluid, ever-changing, and all-encompassing, and the town he remembered was now a city where the rich and famous were lauded and put on pedestals, and the poor were just as poor as they'd been before.

The war had only been over for a few years, and the after-effects were still visible, with men in uniform mingling with civilians on the streets. In the harbor, warships were still tied to their moorings, ready to steer their bows toward the open ocean and defend the homeland.

After the attack at Pearl Harbor and America joining the war, the war machine had sent him to England to care for their troops fighting the Nazis in Europe. Trained as a surgeon, his skills had come to good use more times than he cared to remember. This hadn't been his first war, but he sincerely hoped it would be his last. He'd never been able to understand the reason people went to war with one another.

Looking back, there'd been so many of them, each bloodier and deadlier than the last. At least, with the invention of planes and tanks, the soldiers were slightly more protected than before, but the fighting also spread to the far ends of the earth.

Once he'd reached the end station, he stepped off the bus and strolled down the sidewalk, relishing the fresh air after hours in the stuffy confines of the vehicle, once again wondering what his purpose was. The war was over. Now what? He'd spent several years stitching pilots back together, only to send them out for more of the same. He'd lost count of the men he'd saved from death's clutches, seen them walk out of his hospital, brought back not long after with life leaving them as he fought a hopeless fight to keep their hearts beating. It had been soul destroying.

MUSIC FILTERED OUT from a nearby club as the door opened to let some revelers out. Smoke and laughter followed in their wake but were abruptly cut off when the heavy doors slammed shut behind them. He smiled. Fun and laughter was exactly what everyone needed after the tough years of fighting a war.

Without thinking, he headed for his apartment. How he knew where it was or how to get there, or even how he had an apartment in a city he hadn't lived in for many years, he no longer reflected on. It was the same thing wherever he found himself. He had somewhere to live, enough money in his pocket, and a job — or at least an interview lined up, which inevitably led to a decent job. It was just how it was, and no matter how much he searched for answers, he always came up empty-handed and disappointed. Not thinking about it made his existence somewhat easier.

The loneliness was the worst part. He'd had no close relationships with anyone for... he didn't even want to think how long it had been. The most recent wars were only partially to blame, but most of the guilt lay elsewhere. Somewhere, or someone, he could no longer reach.

With a deep sigh, he entered the apartment building and climbed the stairs to the fourth floor. Giving the door a shove to force it open, he entered the small hallway. He hung his coat on the hook behind the door and dropped the keys in a bowl on the little table before walking through to the living room. The kitchen was at one end of the surprisingly spacious area, and at the opposite end were two bedrooms and the bathroom. Why he needed two bedrooms, he wasn't sure. The extra space was a luxury he hadn't enjoyed before.

He changed out of his clothes in the bedroom and washed up before pulling on a clean shirt and a pair of comfortable pants. Standing before the mirror, he pulled a comb through his wavy blond hair, examining the extra lines around his eyes and mouth that war, no doubt, had bestowed on him, despite only being in his early thirties. To be honest, he was only guessing at his age. He'd never been told exactly how old he was meant to be. In fact, he'd never been told anything at all. But whatever identification documents he found in his pockets seemed to indicate he was in his thirties at the start of every new phase. The exact age varied, and a couple of times, he'd been much younger. Once, he'd even been an old man, but that life had been mercifully short.

It also seemed as if the people he met either didn't notice that he never aged, or maybe saw what they expected to see, or he did age, but his mirror reflection only showed how he always saw himself. He'd never been able to work out which was true and had added it to the multitude of questions he wanted answers to when he finally returned home.

Padding back to the kitchen, he opened the refrigerator and stared at its meager contents. Some eggs, a few slices of luncheon meat wrapped in paper, and a carton of milk were all the refrigerator contained. The pantry revealed a box of cereal, a bag of potatoes, and some apples.

Oh, well, he thought to himself. It was better than nothing. Rummaging through the cupboards and drawers, he found a frying pan, flatware, and some silverware. With his stomach rumbling, he quickly set to making a simple omelet with the eggs and meat. He'd leave the cereal for breakfast but might treat himself to an apple for dessert.

In no time, he slid the omelet onto a plate and carried it into the living room. Settling on the sofa, he turned on the radio to a music station and cut into his food. Songs by Frank Sinatra, Bing Crosby, and Cole Porter followed each other, filling his head and drowning out the questions constantly swirling in his mind.

In front of him on the coffee table lay some papers with typed writing on them. He turned them over and found an employment letter for a position as a surgeon at Los Angeles County General Hospital. His start date was the following day. With a sharp huff, he flung them down, sending them skittering across the table and onto the floor. Kiran stared at them for a long time before sighing and gathering them into a neat pile again. No one was around to see his little temper tantrum, and no one cared.

He was lonely. He'd been lonely for a very long time, but when the war ended, and he watched families, friends, and lovers reunite, their displays of unbridled joy and affection, he'd felt it like sharp jabs in his chest. That kind of connection with another being was something he would never get to experience. Not because he didn't want to, but because he wasn't capable of it. It was the way he'd been created.

He'd been here for a long time, but he had yet to feel anything more than camaraderie for another being. Animals elicited more affection from him than people did. That didn't mean he couldn't relate to others or create friendships, but even that was something he avoided.

Knowing he'd lose them no matter what he did, had made him cautious and forced him to keep most people at a distance. He'd put on a show, fit in, create a facade of being the good guy, the trusted friend and close confidante, but he kept his own heart — if he even had one — well protected with thick armor plating and long lengths of heavy chains holding everything in place.

Rising from the couch, Kiran put the dishes in the kitchen, washed everything, and placed them back in their right places. Keenly aware that he could be ripped away at any time from where he currently found himself had amplified his naturally tidy tendencies to a near-compulsive behavior.

He wasn't sure what happened after he shifted, — whether his presence was wiped from people's minds and all records of him ever having existed was erased. However, from what little he knew, the reason most of them Fell was to have some form of impact on the human world. Perhaps after their work was done, they became just a vague memory, leaving behind the effect of their existence.

The thought of simply fading from the lives of those he'd known, his friends, was disconcerting, but he was, if not at peace with it, then at least used to the idea.

He was tired. Not just the it's-been-a-long-day tired, but a bone-weary, nothing-matters-anymore kind of tired. He could only hope it would pass with the new job and new challenge awaiting him. Slipping into bed, he curled up into a ball under the sheets, determined not to allow his dark thoughts to overwhelm him.

Tomorrow was another day, and he would make the best of it, as he always did. He owed himself that no matter what he'd done to be left adrift without a reason for existing. It happened so long ago he barely remembered how it had been before. The sense of belonging, of kin, remained, however, and he would do anything to feel that again — if only for a fleeting second.

He felt himself longing to see the splendor of a new dawn. His sister, Eos, was the one tasked with creating every new day on Earth. She took great care and pleasure in blending the colors and making them blaze in new combinations every day. Thinking of his sister once again made him wonder how the humans would react if they knew their ideas of religion and paganism were miles away from the truth.

All deities, whether Greek, Roman, Norse, or from Ancient Egypt, were all part of the same fabric of faith. Eos and Nyx, the Roman goddess of the night, were as much his siblings as Thor and Loki of the Viking beliefs. Above them all was their Father — He who oversaw them all and ultimately decided the fate of every civilization and every living creature.

Kiran clenched his jaw and took a deep breath. He missed them. He missed his serene existence. His solitary life was hard to bear, even after all this time.

Somewhere deep inside him, the chains rattled, as if something was trying to break free — or simply breaking.

As the sun's rays colored the bedroom in hues of pale pink and gold, he stretched his arms over his head, a wide yawn cracking his jaws, and dropped his feet to the bare floor. Resting his forearms on his knees, hands clasped, his head bowed, he sent his thoughts out into the wide unknown, asking for guidance and strength.

In the beginning, he'd demanded answers and raged at the silence, but even his tenacity and stubbornness had fallen to the wayside after so many centuries. It was only with great effort he could recall how the world had looked back when he first Fell and awoke in such a strange, but wondrous place. Confusion, bewilderment, and fear had enveloped his senses until he'd found his bearings, and there was no getting away from it despite the incredible events he'd borne witness to.

He used to try to commit to memory everything he'd seen and experienced, but too much time had passed, and he'd endured his life more than experienced it. For now, it was what he had to deal with, and he could only hope he'd get an answer one day, a reason, for everything that had happened to him.

Huffing at his own morose musings, he stomped into the bathroom to take care of business, shower, and shave. After dressing, he grabbed a bowl of milk and cereal, making a mental note that he'd have to go grocery shopping after his shift, before heading to the hospital.

"Dr. Mitchell, I'm glad to have you with us. I look forward to working with you." Dr. Radford, the Chief of Staff at County General, greeted him with a firm handshake.

"Thank you, Sir. I'm pleased to be here." Kiran looked around as Radford took him on a brief tour of the emergency room, operating theaters, and general surgical wards.

"As you can see, we are a fully equipped and modern facility accepting patients from all over the city. Of course, service personnel were our priority for a long time, but in the last few years, we have seen fewer of those cases, naturally."

"Naturally. I'm sure it must be both a blessing and a relief not to have the victims of a war pass through the doors as frequently," Kiran said.

Los Angeles had been relatively fortunate, especially compared to Pearl Harbor and the European countries. The Japanese had refrained from attacking the city, although they'd had an action plan put in place to do so. Oahu and Pearl Harbor had drawn the short straw in that regard, but all things considered, they'd gotten off lightly.

"Of course, you must have seen some terrible things while stationed in London, I imagine. It was actually one of the merits that persuaded me to offer you the position. We could benefit from your experience and expertise in the trauma surgery department. As I mentioned during our interview, you will be responsible for any emergency surgery that may come in on a daily basis. Planned surgery is dealt with in the General Surgery department, but of course, you will work alongside them as well to the benefit of our patients." Dr. Radford looked at Kiran expectantly, and he realized he'd barely said a word in the last ten minutes.

"Yes, of course. It will be a privilege to get to know them."

"Right. Well, I shall leave you in the capable hands of Dr. Martin here and let you settle in. Any questions or concerns, please do not hesitate to make an appointment to see me." With a sharp nod, Radford pivoted and strode back down the corridor toward the administration offices.

Kiran stared after him before turning to the other man.

"Dr. Martin, it's a pleasure to meet you."

"The name's Andrew." The man stuck his hand out and shook Kiran's. "Kiran. That's an unusual name. Don't think I've ever heard it before. Is it British?"

Kiran laughed. "No, my parents lived in India before they had me. My father was a consultant to the Brits on the railroads, and my mother fell in love with the name. It's Hindi and means 'beam of light'. She always said I was the light of her life." It was a total lie, of course, but very useful to explain his unusual name and satisfy people's curiosity.

"Huh. Interesting." Andrew nodded. "Well, it's a nice name wherever it comes from."

"Thank you. It's kind of you to say so," Kiran replied. "Many people find it strange and often end up calling me Dr. Mitchell, or just Mitch or Mitchell, as they seem to be confused by a Hindi first name. I must admit, the combination is rather unusual." Kiran gave an embarrassed laugh, but Andrew smiled and didn't seem perturbed at all.

"We don't stand too much on formalities here in Trauma. By its nature, we all work closely together, and the more we keep the hierarchal stuff out of the department, the better we get along. Being on a first-name basis helps with all that."

"That sounds like my kind of working environment. I'm not a very formal person and prefer an easy-going camaraderie as far as possible."

Andrew gave him a friendly slap on the back and put him to work getting to know the routines and meeting the nurses and the other physicians on staff in the department.

THAT EVENING, Kiran returned home to his apartment exhausted but satisfied with how his first day had turned out. He looked forward to returning the next day to fully integrate himself as the newest, but highly competent, member of the Trauma and Emergency Surgery Department.

It would be a welcome change to work in a modern hospital with access to equipment and medicine with a simple scrawl on a request form. During his time in London, everything had been in short supply, and he couldn't even begin to remember the times they'd been forced to improvise. Yet a surprising number of his patients had walked out of there — more or less — even those deemed lost causes when they arrived on his operating table.

Somehow, he seemed to have a sense of what needed to be done to each man, or woman, who was left in his scalpel-wielding hands. He sought out the bleeding arteries, the perforated lungs, the fragmented bullets, and worked his 'magic' as someone had once called it, leaving the patient as healthy as he was capable.

Not everyone could be saved, though. The ones that didn't pull through, whose bodies were too damaged even for his skills, were the ones he remembered. Every. Single. One. His mental logbook containing all the names was heavy to carry, but he had a compulsive need not to forget any of them.

It was as if he was searching for someone, and by remembering the names of those he'd lost, he knew the one he was searching for was still out there. Who it was and where they were, he didn't know. Hell, he wasn't even sure he was meant to search for anyone. Maybe this was all he was supposed to do. Wander the earth for eternity and do what little good he could manage.

As long as he stayed in one place, he was good with it. It was the sudden rips through time that he struggled with. New people, new places, and most of all, leaving the familiar behind. He had to believe it was all for a reason, or he would go crazy from the uncertainty. Even he had a need for stability, friendships, and a sense of belonging.

THE NEXT MORNING, he arrived early for his shift so he could take a few minutes to observe the routines of his co-workers and the rhythm of the Trauma Department. They worked closely with the Emergency Room, but also received patients from the wards who had developed problems needing immediate attention. The main surgery unit took care of any planned procedures but would step in and take on cases if Trauma was busy.

Many of the nurses nodded to him as they passed by, usually with a smile, but some with a puzzled look, as if they'd never seen a doctor observing them go about their duties. He introduced himself to those who weren't scurrying to and fro, and to the ER staff before starting his shift.

Within minutes, he'd scrubbed in to perform an appendectomy on a young woman who'd arrived in the ER with severe stomach pains. He needed to move fast, before the appendix burst and contaminated her abdomen. Once that happened, it was much harder to prevent a systemic infection. Antibiotics would help, but they didn't always do a good enough job.

His day passed quickly, and the dedication of the staff and the efficiency of the entire department impressed him. On his walk home, he mulled over his new life. The shifts were exhausting and confusing, but at least he was moving forward in time. He'd been on a boat traveling back from England after the war ended, so it hadn't been a big jump. Only three years or so.

Waking up on that interstate bus had been disorienting, and it took him a little while to get his bearings as it always did. His shifts were always forward in time, never back into the past. He wasn't sure why, but he'd always figured it was because it would upset the timeline and possibly have huge implications for the future. Of course, He was always able to ensure nothing too disastrous occurred, but Kiran knew He rarely, if ever, got involved in the minutiae of humankind.

Not for the first time, he wondered why he'd been discarded and what he was supposed to do or accomplish. He had no direction, no advice, and no guidance of any kind. How long before he finally found the true meaning of his lonely existence? He'd seen so many people come and go, seen joy, sadness, tragedy, and overwhelming horrors.

At times, he'd been worked to the bone, and other times stood in the spotlight. He'd suffered great loss, watched exceptional events unfold from afar and been right in the middle of some of them. Occasionally, he'd felt free as a bird but also spent decades wearing the shackles of an indentured slave. Kindness and brutality had relieved one another — not enough of one and too heavy a burden of the other. How he endured, he'd never know. Kiran rubbed his wrists as if steel cuffs still encircled them.

Three

KIRAN, 1948

"Dr. Mitchell, we need you in Trauma One," the nurse overseeing the patients sent from the ER called out.

Kiran had just finished a late lunch, or maybe it was early dinner, and was on his way back when she came toward him.

"Why? what's the matter?" he asked.

"A nasty crash on the Parkway with several vehicles involved. It looks bad, Dr. Mitchell," the nurse puffed out, breathless from running through the hospital corridors to find him.

He lengthened his stride, marching into the Trauma department and heading straight for the double doors leading to the operating theaters. Orderlies had already wheeled two patients into separate rooms to be prepped by the nurses and anesthesiologists.

"Dr. Martin is scrubbing in right now and will take the patient in OR Two," she said, having regained her breath.

Kiran replied, "Thanks, Mary. I'll be in as soon as I'm gowned up."

He began the vital routine of meticulously scrubbing his hands and forearms before slipping them through the sleeves of the surgical gown a young assistant nurse was holding for him. She tied the strings around his waist and across his shoulders and fixed the mask in place. Nodding a brief thank you, he used his back and shoulders to open the doors and entered the surgical area where an older man lay on the raised bed, just slipping into a pain-free, induced sleep.

After taking a deep breath, Kiran rolled his neck to relieve the fatigue of an already too-long shift, cleared his mind of anything but the task in front of him and focused on what he did best.

Many hours later, he hung his coat on a hook in the doctor's lounge, bracing a hand against the wall with his head hung low to take a breath and allow the strain of complicated surgeries to drain out of his mind and body. He'd spent almost an entire extra shift dealing with the severe injuries sustained by the victims of the pile-up, and it was the third doctor's coat of the day he'd used up, along with several sets of surgical scrubs. He'd had to toss the other two coats in the hospital laundry after various bodily fluids had sprayed all over them. It was a normal work hazard, and being single entitled him to use the hospital's laundry facilities for his scrubs and white coats, which made his life a little easier.

He'd found a lady in his apartment building who took in clothes for washing, so that saved him from attempting to launder his normal clothes. She didn't charge much, so instead, he'd pick up some fresh fruit or vegetables for her whenever he did his grocery shopping as a thank you.

Kiran left the hospital, needing some fresh air, and headed for a park near his apartment. A small playground was tucked up in one corner where little boys and girls milled around with adults supervising them. He settled on a bench nearby and watched the activities with interest. He found it fascinating how young people could find joy in the smallest things.

This particular playground was brand new with swings, slides, and climbing equipment. The squeals of the children racing down the metal contraptions rose in the air, and Kiran shook his head. It looked precarious, but they were heedless of any danger, wide smiles shining on their little faces.

He sat on the bench for over an hour, breathing in the fresh air and soaking up the sunshine. His mind wandered as he turned his face to the blue sky. With no indication of what he was doing here, he'd searched every day for answers, prayed for guidance, but all he got was silence. Today was no different.

His thoughts turned to the last time he'd taken a jump forward in years. He'd been working as an assistant to a Dutch topographical engineer. Following orders to investigate Krakatoa, a volcano west of Java, he'd huddled in a small hut near the base of the cone with his instruments, hoping against hope it wouldn't erupt before he'd finished his assignment. Leaving early hadn't been an option, as his employer would have fired him on the spot, leading to Kiran having to find and pay for his own voyage back to Europe. His meager savings would at the most have given him passage in a rowboat to the next rocky outcropping.

The lush, isolated tree-covered island was uninhabited, so Kiran had been alone there for nearly two weeks. It wasn't surprising, as it mainly consisted of an active volcano on the verge of a cataclysmic eruption, although his employer had assured him nothing would happen for months yet and sent him off in a small boat with a local man at the oars.

He'd watched while the man had turned his barely seaworthy skiff around as soon as Kiran had grabbed his bag and equipment, leaving him with a few rations of food and some flasks of fresh water. Just enough to survive for the next three weeks, if he was cautious enough.

Kiran had made a small shelter out of a tarp and poles he'd brought with him. He set out his equipment and spent the next ten days monitoring the readings and making notes in his journal. After only a few days, he'd realized his situation was extremely precarious and survival uncertain.

The earth beneath his feet had shuddered and rumbled constantly, black plumes rising high in the skies, blotting out the light from the sun. The air had filled with ash and noxious fumes, making it difficult to breathe, and the heat from the ground itself had been unbearable, but his ride out hadn't been due for another week.

How he'd survived the first twenty-four hours of eruptions he'd never know, but the main event — four explosions, he'd found out later on — had signaled the death knell. He'd heard and felt two of them. The third had been loud enough to make his ears bleed, and his brain got so scrambled he no longer knew who he was. Unfortunately, he'd been sheltered from the terrifying shock wave the eruption created, or it would have squashed him like a bug, which would have been preferable to the hell he'd had to endure.

After the eruption, all he remembered was a heat so intense his skin crackled and peeled from his body. Caught under the weight of pumice and ash, he'd slowly burned to death as lava flowing from the vents engulfed everything in its path.

It was the only time he'd begged for mercy, for salvation, for death.

Kiran blinked as the sound of a child screaming at the top of her lungs from a climbing frame yanked him out of his horrifying memories. Sweat ran down his back, and he was glad he was sitting or he may have fallen. His legs had turned into jelly from remembering the horrors of his past. He had plenty of them, but that day back in 1883 was the worst. Not even the spectators' thumbs waving for the coup de grâce in the mighty arena in Rome had been as frightening as that final day in Sunda Strait. The emperor's decision had been more of a blessing after surviving the games for so many years. He'd lost more friends and acquaintances in that time than at any other time in his long existence.

He took a few deep breaths to steady himself before rising to his feet, carefully ensuring his legs would carry him, and slowly ambled back onto the street. According to his watch, it was still early enough to buy some food from the grocery store to have for dinner and headed in that direction.

A few cars rumbled by as he strode down the sidewalk. Gas was still an expensive commodity after the war, so only those well-off could afford to buy and run an automobile. Personally, he had no hankering for them more than occasionally wishing he was in one when his legs were worn out from too many hours in surgery, or the rain was coming down by the bucket load as he made his way home.

The little grocery store was almost devoid of people. Only one other customer, a man in his mid-twenties of medium height and light brown hair, stood searching the confectionery shelf, clutching a bunch of flowers in one hand. Kiran ignored him and picked up a few items to make a light meal for himself. He was no gourmet cook but had learned enough over the years to make a decent and satisfying meal. The modern equipment available, like stoves and ovens, made cooking considerably easier than what he'd experienced over the centuries.

By the time he'd finished and reached the cashier, the younger man was walking out the door, presumably having found what he was looking for. Kiran paid for his groceries, hefted the paper bag into his arms, and left the store to return to his apartment. Stepping out onto the sidewalk, something caught his eye, and he bent to examine it closer. It was a man's wallet containing a few dollars and a military identification card. He realized it belonged to the man who'd just left, and Kiran swiveled his head in all directions to spot him. There! The sandy-haired head came into view farther down the street. Kiran lengthened his stride, grateful that the man seemed to be in no hurry wherever he was going, and closed in on him after half a block.

"Excuse me, sir! I think you dropped this!" he called but got no reaction.

Several passersby stared after him as he half ran down the sidewalk to catch up. The man suddenly crossed the street, and Kiran swore under his breath before dashing across to keep up.

"Sir, please stop! Sir! You dropped your wallet!" Finally, the young man stopped and turned, staring at him with concern in his eyes.

"I'm sorry. Were you talking to me?" he asked.

"Yes, I'm so glad I caught up with you." Kiran panted. "I was in the grocery store, and when I left, I found this wallet right outside. I'm sure it belongs to you."

The man patted his pockets, his face falling as he found them empty. Holding out the wallet, Kiran nodded at him to take it.

"Oh, my goodness," he exclaimed. "Thank you ever so much. I'd have been completely lost without it." The young man grabbed Kiran's hand in his and pumped it several times in gratitude.

Kiran grinned, pulling his hand back and flexing his fingers, relieved the man hadn't squeezed harder. "You're welcome. I'm just glad I found you."

"You really have no idea how much this means to me." The man wiped his brow. "I keep the address of the girl I'm taking out for a date tonight in here." Opening the wallet, he showed Kiran a slip of paper with an address on it. "It's the only place I have it written. She doesn't have a phone, so I wouldn't have been able to get a hold of her. You're a lifesaver."

"So that's who the flowers are for," Kiran stated with a smile.

"Yes, the lady deserves only the best. That's what I was in the store to buy. These flowers" — he held out the colorful bouquet of chrysanthemums — "and some Junior Mints. It's our very first date, and I want to make a good impression."

The confused look on Kiran's face prompted an explanation. The man showed Kiran the box of candy.

"Junior Mints have a soft, minty center covered in chocolate. They're my favorites, and they keep my breath fresh." A bashful smile curled up the corners of his mouth. "Since they're also chocolate, I hope it will be a pleasant treat for Clara. That's her name," he added eagerly. "The girl I'm escorting to a concert on the pier in Santa Monica, I mean. Tommy Dorsey is playing at the bandstand, and he's Clara's favorite musician."

"That sounds wonderful. I hope you have a lovely time together." Kiran nodded, and after a brief handshake, the two men parted ways, each with a different evening ahead.

While Kiran prepared his supper later that evening, his mind wandered back to the young man and his excitement over a first date with a woman. He had yet to wrap his head around the mating rituals of humans. After all the time he'd spent among them, it still baffled him.

So far, he'd had no desire to get himself involved in any kind of relationship beyond friendship. He'd had offers, of course, and been pursued by a female or two and even a few men over the years, but he'd mostly rejected their advances gently but firmly. A few times, he'd succumbed to his body's urges and found release in a woman's arms, but he'd never felt any more than friendly affection toward them. He'd long since accepted that he'd never know what true love felt like. It was a mystery he didn't feel inclined to unravel and always thought he should be content with what he had. Things could be a lot worse.

MONTHS PASSED, and Kiran went to work every day, socialized some weekends with colleagues, and occasionally visited a bar for a beer with friends. Summer was over and fall had set in, but he couldn't really tell the difference. The temperatures were a little cooler at night, but the sun still shined brightly most days. It was something he both liked and disliked about California. Instead of the usual four seasons, you really only had two, and sometimes he missed the cold winters of the East Coast. He shuddered slightly at the memories of his time there. The persecutions, the accusations, the so-called trials of women, and even a few men, who'd done nothing wrong. The name Salem still sent chills down his spine.

He'd just arrived in Trauma when Dr. Radford called his name.

"Is there something I can help you with, Sir?" he asked.

"I'm glad I caught you, Kiran. I need you to do me a favor." Dr. Radford placed his hand on Kiran's shoulder. "A medical supply company we often use is sending someone over to discuss the hospital's requirements for surgical implements and other devices we may need." He waved a stuffed folder in the air. "They always listen to any suggestions we have for improvements and have recently started a new department focusing on developing modern techniques and tools." Kiran's boss opened the folder and showed him several drawings of surgical equipment with notes, arrows, and hand-drawn figures. "Apparently, this man has a background in electronics and mechanics and is keen on hearing what issues we may have and if there's anything they can do to better what we're already using."

"Yes, of course. I'll speak with him." Kiran nodded. "But am I the best person for this? Wouldn't someone like Andrew Martin be better suited since he's worked here much longer?"

"Andrew is in surgery already, an injury on a building site, and I'd rather someone talked to this man today," Radford explained. "We had that problem with the oxygen masks the other day, and I was hoping you could bring that up with him."

Kiran accepted the folder Radford held out to him, flicking through some of the pages. "Right, well, it's not a problem. I'd be happy to talk to him. Let me ask the staff if they have anything else they want the company to look at," he said. "I'm sure there's plenty of equipment that could do with improvements or just an update."

"Good man. I knew I could rely on you." Radford patted his shoulder. "His name is Edward Miller, and he will be in the reception area at eleven this morning." The doctor gave Kiran a sharp nod before striding down the corridor back to his office.

Kiran stared at him, wondering what he'd gotten himself into, but it was too late to back out now. Besides, he was only meeting this man to discuss possible improvements, not ordering new and expensive equipment without permission from the hospital's management.

Glancing up at the clock on the wall behind the nurses' station, he saw he had a couple of hours before the meeting, which meant he had time to check in on the patients he'd recently operated on. Although it wasn't customary for trauma surgeons to visit with their patients, Kiran had made a point of looking in on as many of them as he could. It was heartwarming and satisfying to see them on the road to recovery after performing emergency surgery on them.

Kiran spent an hour on the surgical ward, addressing any concerns his patients still had, and graciously deflecting any thanks toward the emergency personnel who'd brought them in and his staff who'd been in the theater with him. They were the ones who did the heavy lifting, he claimed. His job was just to put a few stitches in here and there. Of course, the patients all knew he was being modest and thanked him even more for it.

Afterward, he checked with his colleagues if they had any ideas for changes or tweaks to the equipment they used on a daily basis. He wasn't surprised to find they had plenty of suggestions, and he went back to his office to make comprehensive notes and add his own ideas.

AT A QUARTER TO ELEVEN, he made his way to the main entrance of the hospital to meet Mr. Miller. Stepping out into the open lobby, he looked around for anyone who might be waiting for him, but there were too many people bustling about. He approached the reception desk and asked if anyone had arrived yet to see him. The receptionist smiled and pointed toward a row of benches near the front doors, saying Mr. Miller was waiting for him there.

Kiran turned and did a double take when he recognized Edward Miller. He realized now why the name had seemed so familiar as the man rose and came toward him.

"Mr. Miller. I'm Dr. Kiran Mitchell." Kiran held out his hand and grasped Joseph's in a firm grip. "We meet again. I hope your date went well."

"Please, call me Edward. I didn't know it'd be you I'd be talking to." Edward beamed. "Then again, I didn't know you were a doctor." Grinning, he continued, "Our date went splendidly, and we've been out several times again since." His voice lowered, a flush of red spreading across his cheeks. "I guess you could say we're going steady."

"I'm glad to hear it." Kiran waved toward the doors leading to the Trauma department. "Shall we go to my office?" Being a surgeon meant they afforded him his own office. It wasn't fancy, but it was spacious and had a window overlooking the street. It wasn't much of a view, but it was better than some of the other windowless, cubbyhole offices in the building.

Kiran settled behind his desk, and Edward perched himself on the chair facing it. His shoulder bag was filled to bursting with folders, notebooks, and drawings, and he pulled out a sheaf of papers, handing them to Kiran.

"This is the purchase order from the surgery department for the past six months. It includes all requests for improvements or changes to the implements we make." Edward pointed to where he'd made notes in the margins. "I have looked them over and would appreciate your input on the ones marked in red. It's where I feel we can improve them further, but I need a surgeon's input."

Excitement shined in his eyes, and Kiran smiled to himself. The enthusiasm in the young man was obvious and refreshing to see. The war had taken its toll on everyone, but people were beginning to get over the lingering fear of more fighting and were looking toward the future with hope and joy.

A COUPLE OF HOURS LATER, Kiran leaned back in his chair, amazed at the ideas Edward had come up with. The man had a sharp mind, an eye for detail, and a vision for how tools could be changed to perform better and more efficiently. Some of his suggestions could even revolutionize the way surgeons operated if they were able to manufacture the implements to the exacting specifications.

"This is fantastic work, Edward." Kiran studied the multitude of papers in front of him, tapping his fingers on the diagrams Edward had produced. "I'm excited to see these tools in action. Of course, we have to try them out on cadavers first, but I firmly believe you have come up with something incredibly useful here." He glanced at Edward again. "I look forward to more of your ideas."

"Thank you, Dr. Mitchell. I'm excited about working with you."

"Please, call me Kiran. I think we're past the formalities, don't you?" Kiran smiled. "How did Clara like the mints and flowers?"

"She enjoyed them very much." Edward grinned. "I even think Junior Mints may have become her favorite as much as they are mine."

Kiran tilted his head to the side. "How did you two meet? If you don't mind me asking?"

Edward put an ankle over his knee. "We met early in the war. It was back in 1943, and I was working as an engineer at the Naval Shipyard in Long Beach. Clara was a trainee nurse, but since it was all hands on deck, so to speak, she got her training while taking care of sailors fighting the Japanese in the Pacific. She's a surgical nurse, so she knows what is needed in an operating theater and has helped me with some of these ideas." He paused, smiling. "We first met at a tea dance organized by the Navy in Long Beach. They invited all personnel from their facilities there. I saw her walking in and immediately knew I wanted to ask her to dance." Edward lifted his coffee cup and took a sip before continuing. "It took me a while to find her again inside, but then I spotted her sitting with her girlfriends, and I went over to invite her to the dance floor. She's a lovely dancer, you know."

"So what happened after that? You said when we met that day that you were taking her out on your first date."

"The war, I suppose." Edward shrugged. "We were working long shifts at the shipyard. She was working just as much at the hospital, and we never got the chance to meet again. Then there was a reunion, of sorts, at the shipyard, and some of the staff from the hospital were also there. That's when I saw her again and asked her out. We've been courting for nearly six months now, and I'm soon going to ask her to marry me."

"That's a wonderful story," Kiran said. "I hope it all works out for you. And let me know when the wedding is, so I can buy you a drink."

Edward waved a hand. "You will come as our guest, of course. Without you, we might have never had our first date."

"Thank you. That's very kind. I look forward to it."

Kiran ushered Edward back to the main entrance, and they shook hands before saying goodbye. They'd already scheduled another meeting so Edward could show Dr. Radford his ideas.

Kiran strolled back to his office, deep in thought. Meeting Edward the way he had, he wondered if there was something else behind it. Not that he'd ever find out. He shook his head.

The people they met in life and learning from the experiences they had always had meaning behind it. That was the natural and predestined order of things. He knew better than to read more into it than there was. Still, more than ever, it made him long for a sense of direction and purpose. It was what his mind always came back to. He wanted his life to have purpose — all his numerous lives. So far, he'd seen nothing that would show he'd impacted the lives of the people around him. Except for maybe Edward, but he and Clara were sure to have connected, even if Kiran had never found that wallet.

Shoving his morose thoughts aside, he headed toward Surgery to see if they needed him. He wasn't scheduled in theater today, but another pair of hands was always welcome.

Four

ALINA, 2011

As Alina walked to the front door, she hesitated, as always, before putting the key in the lock. She closed her eyes and said a quick prayer before pulling it open and stepping into the hallway, pausing just inside. With black desperation in her heart, she listened for any sounds in the house, listened for the noise of her son playing with his favorite cars, her tiny girl babbling in her own baby language, and Jonas chatting to both of them while he made them a snack. She listened for their laughter, their tears, their heartbeats.

Silence.

Steeling herself and shoving her emotions into the deepest parts of her heart, she hung her coat up, put the keys on the hook in the wall cabinet, and continued into the kitchen. Opening the fridge, she stared at the nearly empty shelves. An apple from the fruit and vegetable drawer would have to serve as dinner tonight. She wasn't hungry, anyway. Grabbing an empty glass from the draining board by the sink, she filled it with water and took it into the living room, dropping onto the sofa.

She grabbed the remote and flipped on the TV, searching the channels for the noisiest show she could find. The house was too quiet. If she didn't have the TV or the radio on, the walls started closing in, and the panic that always lurked inside her spread like black poison through her veins.

She couldn't carry on like this. Living in this house was killing her, but how could she leave? This was where she and Jonas had planned their future, made love in every room, brought Theo home for the first time, followed not long after by Daisy. Their hopes, dreams, and prayers were infused into the very fabric of this house.

After living in an apartment in the city for several years while they built their careers and enjoyed life as a young couple, they'd finally taken the plunge and bought a plot of land. A year later, their dream home stood ready, and they had moved in, filling every space with the essence of their love and adoration for each other.

Alina held back a sob. Her eyes burned with unshed tears before one broke loose, spilling down her cheek. She swiped angrily at it. Crying helped no one. It only made her feel even more miserable and wretched. Biting down hard on her cheek, a coppery taste filled her mouth. She fought for control until the storm in her heart calmed, and she could push it all back down where it belonged. It no longer had a place in her life. With a shuddering breath, she forced all emotions into the giant-sized furnace in her soul, together with all the memories, hopes, dreams, and the once so beautiful future with her little family. They burned with a fire so ferocious it scorched her very cells, but it was better than giving them free rein in her mind.

She stared unseeingly at the screen, the screeching of a heavy metal band filling her head, an emptiness consuming her soul, and began making plans for the rest of her existence. Or at least for the next few months.

She refused to call it a future. A future was what she and Jonas had had together with their babies. What she had left was nothing more than getting through each day until they were all together once more. Something she hoped would happen before too long. Not that she would do anything stupid and irreversible because Jonas would only scold her when she finally saw him again. However, until that happened, she would go through the motions of living her life and being a part of society somehow.

She left the TV on, washed her glass, and threw away the remnants of her apple before trudging up the stairs. Walking past her and Jonas' bedroom, she paused briefly. With a shaky hand, she pushed the door open an inch and put her face close to the crack. Inhaling deeply, the air from the room filling her lungs, she savored the familiar scents. They were fading. Soon, all that would be left were stale air and dust.

After slamming the door shut, she leaned her forehead against the wooden barrier to the heart of the house to steady herself. Then she backed away and scurried into the guest bedroom, which she'd made her refuge in the past twelve months.

Another week and an entire year would have passed since she last felt his arms around her. One year since she kissed her children. One year since her heart died together with her family in that horrific split second when the drunk driver lost control.

The man's wife had written her a letter, apologizing for his actions, hoping she wouldn't hate him and praying for Alina and her family. She'd ignored it. Hating the man would only add to her misery, but she had no energy to spare to make the woman feel better about something she'd not been responsible for. The man was dead. He'd already paid his price.

She slumped on the bed, curled up in a ball, and allowed three images to float through her mind. One each of Jonas, Theo, and Daisy. Their faces were a little blurry, their voices a little indistinct. Bit by bit, she was losing all she had left of them. Soon, only photos, videos, and vague memories would remain. No, she wouldn't, couldn't let that happen. She had to keep them alive. They deserved not to be forgotten, to live on in her memories with bright faces, clear voices, and sparkling energy.

One day, she'd be brave enough to look at all the photos and video recordings she had on her old phone. She'd bought a new one after leaving the hospital because she couldn't bear to use her old one. There were more on Jonas' phone as well. The police had returned it to her after ascertaining he hadn't been using it at the time of the accident. She kept both of them charged to preserve everything stored on them but still hadn't switched either back on. No matter what, she would cling to everything that had been her family until she had nothing left and could join them in their new existence.

Alina closed her eyes and resumed her planning for the immediate future. Step by step, as options and choices were considered and rejected, she decided on what the next few months would entail and how she would accomplish her intentions. Her biggest worries were how her friends would react and what Katie would think. She didn't want to hurt her best friend. Katie had been her rock, her calm in the raging storm, and her sanity when everything else tilted and spun like an out-of-control fairground ride. Her friendship was the only thing that had kept Alina going throughout the turmoil, and Katie's opinion and approval were important to her.

By the early hours of the morning, with her mind set and a plan of action mapped out, she fell asleep, making way for dreams and nightmares.

As she walked down an unfamiliar street, Alina heard music playing. She recognized Dean Martin's Return To Me. It seemed fitting to how she was feeling, somehow. She looked around, but nothing gave away where she was, although everything appeared to be old, like something out of the fifties. All she could really see was a few feet in any direction, however, so she couldn't be sure, but the cars gliding past in the haze and the style of clothing on the few people visible in the cottony mists seemed to hint at a past long before she was born.

She moved slowly forward, treading carefully in the strange fog swirling around her. A fresh breeze chilled her skin, and she shivered in her thin shirt and cotton pants. Looking down, she noticed her feet were bare. Her brow furrowed as she puzzled over her attire. It seemed completely unsuitable for the temperatures and out of place with what little she could discern of her surroundings.

A murmur of voices reached her ears, and when the wisps of mist lifted slightly, she found herself standing at the edge of a cemetery. In the far distance, a high bridge rose, the top of the supports disappearing into the fog, and the sound of rushing water accompanied the scene unfolding in front of her.

Nausea slithered in her stomach. A funeral. She hated funerals. Yet she couldn't keep her gaze away from the group of mourners dressed in black standing around a coffin covered with white and pink flowers.

A tall man stood out from the rest of the group. With one hand resting on the casket, he bowed his head as if in prayer. As Alina watched, a gentle, shimmering glow surrounded him like early morning sunlight. His blond hair shined like pale gold, and there was something eerily familiar about him.

The minister finished, and as one, the mourners turned and walked away, leaving the grieving man on his own. She couldn't see his face clearly, but she somehow knew he was beautiful. Not handsome, but beautiful in a classical sense.

As she quietly watched him, his eyes lifted and caught her gaze. A frown stole across his brow, followed by a widening of his eyes, as if he recognized her. For a long moment, they stared at each other, neither able to look away. A paralyzing sadness gripped Alina's heart, but it wasn't the grief she carried for her family — it was sorrow for the stranger.

She was astonished to see a ribbon of light emanate from the center of her chest and float toward him, reaching out, soft and gentle like the caress of a hand on her cheek. As the translucent tendril touched him right above his heart, binding the two of them together, a sharp pain erupted across her shoulder blades, making her gasp, but it disappeared as quickly as it came.

The mist thickened and began to well in, obscuring the scene, and she had just enough time to see the shimmering man flinch and take a step back while a look of wonder and longing swept across his face. Then she was alone once more. From far away, a whisper floated across the swirls of white gauze, curling around her heart in a soothing embrace.

Just take one small step.

Alina bolted upright in bed, her heart beating in her throat. Her back throbbed for several minutes before finally fading away, and she rolled her shoulders to ease the tension. It was only a dream, she told herself. It may have felt real despite the fog, but it was only a dream conjured by her frazzled mind and the events of the past year. In her head, she could still hear the smooth voice of Dean Martin singing about being lonely and wanting his love to return to him. The ache in her chest pulsed with every soft note drifting through her mind.

Clutching her pillow to her chest, she pressed her face into its softness, willing the tears to go away. Once the burning behind her eyelids receded, she dropped it back in her lap, picking at a tiny white feather sticking out of the fabric from its downy filling. With a sad smile, she remembered Katie telling her white feathers were left behind by angels visiting. It was a message, a sign that they were watching over her.

She'd always laughed and dismissed Katie's interpretation of the innocuous-looking feathers. If she was right, Alina would have to have an army of celestial beings watching over her as the pillows in her bed alone had to contain thousands of them. No, there was no angel standing guard over her, or she'd never have lost her family to begin with. Any angelic creature would have known she'd have preferred joining her little family in death rather than suffer through the hell of the last twelve months. Surely God wouldn't be so cruel as to let one of his guardians stand by and watch while her husband and their two precious babies were ripped away from her? It was bad enough he'd allowed it to happen in the first place.

It was early morning and time to get up to start her day, no matter how much she'd have preferred to hide under the covers. Dropping her feet to the floor, she walked into the bathroom to take a shower. The hot water sluicing down her body washed away the sweat covering her skin from the dream — or was it a nightmare? She toweled off, dried her hair, and dressed before venturing downstairs for some coffee, the one thing she always made sure her pantry was stocked with.

Cup in hand, Alina wandered out onto the rear patio and settled in a chair. Pulling her cell from her back pocket, she drew a deep breath and called her best friend.

"Katie, it's me. Are you free to chat?"

She could hear Katie's two boys in the background and her husband Bryce telling them to go outside to play. Her heart clenched, and the pit in her stomach deepened.

"Hi, sweetie," Katie replied. "Of course. I always have time for you."

A rustling sound and the abrupt quiet told her Katie had closed the door to the rest of the family. She was probably in her study trying to get some work done. Bryce would take the children to school while Katie got a head start in the office. They owned and ran a large events company, which they'd started ten years ago. Until the accident, Alina had worked for them as well, running the marketing and booking side, while Katie and Bryce took care of client contacts and the actual planning of the events. They'd grown to be one of the biggest in California and needed to expand out of the home office and into some larger premises. They also needed to hire more staff since it was too much for the three of them to handle. Well, the two of them, as Alina had only done the bare minimum for the past six months.

"Are you sitting down? I have some stuff I need to talk to you about." She gripped the phone tightly, her heart beating like a jackhammer.

"Sure, sweets. What's up? I mean, I think I know what this is all about, but lay it on me."

"Okay, well...." She cleared her throat. "You know what? Can we meet instead? I really need to see you, and I can't do this over the phone."

"Sure, honey. Do you want to come here?" Katie asked. "Bryce has a client he's meeting with in an hour after he's dropped the kids at school, and I can put the phones to the messaging service."

"Yeah, that sounds great. I'll see you in a little while."

Alina hung up. It wasn't fair to drop this on Katie over the phone. It was the kind of stuff you did face-to-face over a cup of coffee. They'd known each other since high school and had been inseparable since the first day. When Katie's dad passed away from a sudden heart attack at the young age of forty-two, it was Alina who'd held her together while her mom had been busy arranging the funeral and adjusting to a new life as a single parent. Katie had been fifteen at the time, and losing her father hit her hard. Now, Alina was here herself with the most important man in her life ripped away by fate's cruel hand.

THE DRIVE over to Katie and Bryce's house took just over twenty minutes. She pulled up at the curb and got out, taking a moment to gaze at their home. Everything about it screamed 'happy family' with colorful flowers in the beds under the windows, a neatly cut lawn, and two small bikes leaning against the garage door. A football lay deserted on the grass with a lone sneaker next to it.

Alina's heart clenched, remembering a similar scene in her own front yard, the image cartwheeling through her mind before she swatted it away. Swallowing past the lump in her throat, she blinked back tears as the front door opened and Katie waved her in.

"You want coffee? Or tea?" Katie asked, opening a cupboard to get the cups out.

"Coffee, please. It's not a tea kind of day." Alina gave her a tiny smile.

Katie furrowed her brow but refrained from asking any questions until they were settled.

"How are Bryce and the boys?" Alina was stalling.

She knew exactly how they were and what they were doing since Katie kept her updated several times a week.

"They're great. The boys are running us ragged with their antics, and I'm debating whether to bribe their teacher not to throw them out of class. She must be tearing her hair out."

"Milo and Troy can't be that bad. Besides, the teacher is already paid to handle boisterous boys. But I'm sure she'd appreciate the odd bottle of wine snuck into her bag to enjoy once she gets home."

"Ooh, that's a good idea. I knew there was a reason we were friends." Katie's braids bounced as she nodded, giggling.

Alina grinned, settling on a stool by the island in the comfortable kitchen. Sitting and chatting with her best friend over a cup of coffee felt comfortable and easy, even if it only lasted for a short while.

"I'm your best friend because no one else would have you, and I introduced you to Bryce."

Katie nodded. "That's true. Not the first part. It was the other way around, but you did introduce me to Bryce, and I can't thank you enough for that. I wouldn't be where I am today if it wasn't for you. Now, come on, Lina." She leaned forward, her arms on the counter, hands folded around her cup. "Enough stalling. What did you want to talk about? Don't get me wrong, we can sit here and chat all day, but I can tell something big is coming."

Katie's dark brown eyes bore into hers, and Alina squirmed. She wriggled in her seat to get comfortable and drew a deep breath.

"I'm leaving," she murmured. "As in leaving California. And I don't know when or even if I'm coming back. Please, don't hate me." Her head dropped between her sagging shoulders.

"Leaving? To go where?" Katie stared wide-eyed, worry deepening the lines around her mouth.

"I'm not sure." Alina's shoulder rose in a half-shrug. "I'm gonna have the house packed and everything put in storage after I leave, and then put it up for sale." She looked at her friend, tears burning at the back of her eyes. "Katie, I can't stay there any longer. It's killing me. I haven't been able to touch any of their things. The guest room has become my bedroom because I can't go into Jonas and my room. All his things are still exactly where he left them. I can see him and hear him and smell him everywhere. When it's quiet, at night, I hear—" She swallowed past the huge knot in her throat. "I hear their voices. I hear Theo come running into the kitchen. I hear Daisy twittering new words and mixing them with her baby babble."

Alina swiped at the stubborn tear that refused to be held back before she continued, "Whenever I come home, after running errands, or from the shops or whatever, I stop outside the door and say a prayer before I go into the house. I pray it was all a horrendous nightmare, and they'll be waiting for me inside."

"Oh, Lina. I'm so sorry." Katie's warm gaze filled with sadness and sympathy. "Of course, you can still feel them. They'll always be with you, in your heart and your soul. Jonas and the kids will never leave you."

"It's been a year, and it feels as if it all happened yesterday. I'm not living, just existing and going through the motions. If I don't get away, I'll end up doing something really stupid." Alina peered at her best friend from under her lashes, praying she'd understand.

"I get it. I do. But I'm gonna miss you so much."

"I'll miss you too, but we'll keep in touch. And when I feel stronger, I'll come back and see you all."

"You'd better, or I will hunt you down." Katie poked her in the arm. "When are you leaving, and where will you go?"

"I'm heading to Yellowstone next week to go hiking for a little while. After that, I'll go to Chicago to see my folks. We haven't spoken properly since the... accident. I know my mom can't wait to look after me for a little while, and as much as it smothers me, I think she and I both need it." Her face scrunched. "But she's not been well, which is why they couldn't come to the funeral, and my dad has enough on his plate with looking after her. I have a job lined up with a small convention hall there. It's only temporary, but it'll do until I can find my bearings again. Which reminds me, I quit." She grinned weakly.

Katie's face scrunched. "I figured. As much as I hate to lose my best friend and employee at the same time, I understand why you have to do this."

"Thanks, hun. I don't know what I'd do without you." Alina squeezed Katie's hand. "You've been my rock this past year, and if you hadn't been there, I wouldn't be here today. I know that much. I love you, Katie. You will always be my best and closest friend. You're my sister."

Nodding, Katie replied, "You know I feel the same way." She wiped away a tear. "Which is why we won't ever be apart — even if we're on opposite sides of the continent. Or the world, or even the universe." Katie wrapped her in a hug as the tears escaped and dripped down her cheeks. "So, what can I help you with?"

"I'd really appreciate if you would be there with the moving company? I just need to know everything gets packed away securely and nothing is lost or broken."

"What are you going to do for money?" Katie asked. "You'll get a severance pay from us, of course, and I'll add your bonus to that instead of at Christmas."

"Financially, I'm fine. Jonas had a... generous life insurance that I didn't know about. It came with his job, I gather. So I have no worries there." Alina paused. "I just wish I had Jonas instead of all the money in the world. And my babies."

"I know, sweetie." Katie's voice hitched with emotion. "We all wish for that. It was cruel and unfair for them to be taken away from you that way, but they are still with you. I can feel and hear them in you. Marrying Jonas and having the kids changed you into an even better person than you were before. That is still in you. *They* are still in you, in your heart and in your soul."

"I guess." Alina shrugged. "It's hard to tell anymore. I don't feel like myself. I walk around the house like a wraith, afraid to touch anything in case I disturb something of theirs. I eat and sleep, but not very well." She rubbed her face. "And really, I'm like a ghost with no one to haunt and no purpose to my existence. It has to stop. If I'm to have any kind of life again, it has to be away from here where all I see and hear is my family. I don't even know why I bother praying for them to be returned to me." A note of anger crept into her voice. "No one can bring them back. They're gone, and I won't ever see them again." Alina clenched her fists, tears gathering behind her eyelids as she squeezed them together.

Katie stayed quiet and just hugged her tighter.

After waving farewell to her oldest and best friend, Alina drove back to her house to finalize her move. It would be difficult to leave California, where she'd lived all her life, but it was time for something new, to leave things behind and restart her life, no matter how hard it would be.

It was time she started living.

A week later, her SUV was packed, a set of keys to the house were with the moving company, and she'd said goodbye to Katie, Bryce, and the boys. She'd only taken her most precious mementos from the house — a few photos of Jonas, Theo and Daisy, their favorite stuffed toys, a bracelet Jonas had given her on their fifth wedding anniversary, and hers and Jonas' old phones. Everything else would be packed in boxes.

She threw the last bag into the trunk and closed it with a firm thunk. Before locking the house, she took a final look around, her chest tight, eyes dry and burning. Her entire life had been contained within these four walls, and now it was all gone. All that was left were memories, and even those were too painful to be given any space in her mind.

She got behind the wheel, started the ignition, and after casting one last glance at what was meant to have been her forever home, she stifled a sob and eased the car out of the driveway. Before long, she was heading North-East toward an uncertain future.

Five

KIRAN, 1964

Life had settled into a steady rhythm, but Kiran still waited for the other shoe to drop. Being catapulted into a new life was inevitable, and waiting for it was exhausting. He was happy with the way things were now. He'd lived in Los Angeles for sixteen years, his longest spell yet, and even got married, but he still expected to be shunted forward at any moment.

With his wife by his side and a great job with fantastic colleagues, he wanted to live out his final days here in Los Angeles. Maybe this was his final existence? Maybe this was what he'd been pushed toward this entire time?

He certainly hoped so, but something in the back of his mind told him this wasn't it, and that he had a lot more living to do before he could finally rest. The thought sent shivers down his spine. Juliet was a kind and loving woman, and even if he didn't quite have the same feelings toward her as she did for him, he appreciated her company and was content to spend his life with her.

A smile lit up his face as he thought of the woman he'd married so many years ago. She worked part-time as a secretary at a nearby accounting firm. When they first met, he wasn't sure he could have a relationship, or if he even wanted one, but as they got to know each other, a warm affection grew between them. After a year of courting, he'd gotten down on one knee and proposed. It felt right, somehow, as if it were what he was meant to do. Did he love her? He honestly couldn't say yes or no, as he didn't know what love felt like.

A warm feeling bloomed in his chest whenever he thought of Juliet, and her touch always comforted him. Was that love? If it was, then yes, he loved her — in his own way. Their wedding had been a simple affair, with colleagues and friends attending. Juliet was an only child, and both her parents had passed away. Her father died in Normandy and her mother only a few years after the war had ended. The few relatives she had lived too far away to make the long journey to California. Of course, he had no family at all, so he'd only asked a few people from work to attend. Some he considered friends, and others more like close colleagues.

His contentment with life did nothing to stop him from longing for his true home, however. It was nothing like the humans imagined. Even their name for his kind was entirely their own construct. He and his family were just... Well, they didn't even have a name for themselves. That was something only His creations were afforded. They just *were*. Their existence was infinitely longer than time, and he wasn't even sure where the humans got the name from. They were celestials, but never thought of themselves as angelic the way they were depicted. They didn't wear white, flowing robes or have halos, and certainly didn't look like chubby little babies playing miniature harps.

KIRAN THRIVED in his job at the hospital. Still working as a surgeon in the Trauma department, he was now also responsible for gathering improvement requests from the ER and General Surgery Department. He also collated suggestions for all manner of implements used within operating theaters and in the care of patients and passed them on to Edward Miller and his staff.

Every so often, he and Edward met to discuss new innovations and forward strides in the medical equipment division where he worked.

Edward never ceased to amaze him with his knack for finding improvements, understanding the intricacies of surgery, and the exacting adjustments needed on the implements. He'd already redesigned some of a surgeon's most-used tools, including adjusting the shape of the handle on the scalpels to better fit their hands.

After every shift, Kiran came home to the apartment he and Juliet had made their home. If it was in the middle of the day, she'd be at work, but it was never long before she walked in the door, smiling and asking how his day was. Within minutes, she'd have a meal prepared, and they'd sit talking about their days.

They'd been married for nearly ten years now, and despite Juliet desperately wanting children, it had never happened for them. They'd both gone through tests and examinations, but no one had been able to pinpoint anything wrong with either of them.

Juliet was bitterly disappointed and had struggled for a long time to come to terms with their barren life, but Kiran had showered her with affection and tried to make their life as joyful and fulfilling as possible. He'd only wanted children for her sake, so he didn't suffer as much from not being graced with them as she did.

For a long time, he'd believed it was the pinnacle of a relationship, of being human, but he'd found himself doubting his commitment while they'd tried to get pregnant. It wasn't so much a relief as it was a lightening of the burden he carried on his shoulders. Who knew how a child from his seed would turn out? There was a term for them as it had happened several times over the millennia, but he'd never bothered finding out anything about the offspring.

Human.

If it was something he was absolutely certain of, he was not human. Not entirely, at least. He acted and bled human, but none of them lived as long as he had, or rather had as many lives as he did. It was simply impossible. He was a good imitation, performing the same tasks and made somewhat human relationships while dressed in ordinary clothes.

He huffed a mirthless laugh, shuddering at the memory of the ridiculous togas he'd worn so long ago. Mediolanum had been freezing in winter, and centuries later, Ravenna had been little better. The warmer months had been bearable, but the constant rain showers combined with high temperatures created the perfect conditions for biting insects. Absentmindedly, he scratched his thigh as a prickly sensation erupted all over his legs at the thought of the bites that had covered them back then. With an irritated sigh, he shoved the memories back into their box. All they did was emphasize the passage of time and his solitary existence.

"Kiran? I'm going to bed. I feel so tired, and I'm working tomorrow." Juliet kissed him on the cheek, a wan smile on her pale face.

She'd been tired a lot recently, and if she didn't rally soon, he'd take her to see the doctor. As a surgeon, he could tell when someone wasn't feeling well, but diagnosing ailments that weren't surgical was not his forte. A prickle of worry settled in his chest. Juliet had barely had so much as a cold in the decade they'd been married.

Their anniversary was coming up in a few months, and he'd already bought a gold necklace to give her. They were also hoping to take a few days vacation and go away somewhere nice. Most likely, they'd both be too busy and would have to settle for dinner in a fancy restaurant.

"Are you feeling all right?" He cupped her face in his hand and studied her pale skin and the circles under her eyes.

She'd lost weight as well, he noticed, and resolved to make an appointment for her with a colleague at the hospital if their normal doctor couldn't see her in the next few days.

"Yes, I'm fine. I just need a good night's sleep. It's probably just a bug or something. There's been a lot of them going around the office lately. You know how it is in winter."

Kiran nodded, gave her a kiss and watched her disappear into their bedroom, his eyebrows knitting when she could no longer see him. He didn't think this was some kind of virus. She'd been tired and listless for too long. A cold or the even flu would have come and gone by now and didn't make someone lose this much weight. Hopefully, a full night's rest would do her good, and he made a mental note to pick up some vitamins for her in the morning.

With heavy steps, Kiran entered the living room and slumped on the sofa. Turning the radio on low, he leaned his head against the back cushion and closed his eyes. The soft notes of Cole Porter filled the room, the music wrapping around his mind, giving him a few minutes of peace.

THE NEXT MORNING, Kiran woke up early to an empty bed. Juliet was already busy making him breakfast. After taking a quick shower, he shaved, dressed in his usual suit, shirt, and tie before following his nose to the kitchen.

"Good morning, dear. Did you sleep well?" Juliet asked without turning away from the stove as she took the boiled eggs out of the pan.

Placing them in egg cups sitting ready on the counter, she poured him a cup of coffee, handing it to him with a smile. Kiran watched her bustle about the kitchen with her usual efficiency — almost, at least. She still looked pale, and he thought he detected a slight trembling in her hands when she took the toast out of the toaster and placed it on a small dish.

"There, breakfast is ready. Sit down, dear. You'll be on your feet for hours soon enough." Juliet sounded bright and cheerful, and her cheeks seemed to have more color in them than a minute ago.

He shook his head. Maybe he was imagining things. Or it was a trick of the light.

"Thank you," he replied with a smile. "Are you sure you have to work today? Maybe you should take the day off and rest?"

She shook her head. "No, I'm fine. Sleep was just what I needed, and I feel back to normal. Don't worry, there's nothing wrong with me."

Kiran let the subject drop, and they moved the conversation to Christmas, which was just around the corner, and the plans for the festive season.

"Is there a department Christmas party again this year?" Juliet asked. "And what about the hospital? Last year, they did that benefit gala on New Year's Eve. Do you think they'll do that this year as well?"

"As far as I know, we're having a party again." He took a sip of coffee, grimacing. "I think Andrew is in charge of the planning, so goodness knows what we'll get."

"I'm sure Andrew will do a fantastic job," Juliet said, looking amused. "Please tell him I'll be happy to help any way I can."

"I'll let him know." Kiran wiped his mouth with the napkin, having finished his egg and toast. "The hospital is definitely having another benefit after the roaring success of last year, but I think they're looking to book one of the larger venues in town since it was so popular." His lips pursed, and his brow creased. "They've asked me to give a speech."

"They have? That's wonderful," Juliet exclaimed. "You're obviously highly thought of by the board."

"You know what it means, though? We will be sitting at the top table with all the board members and other specially invited guests." Kiran's mouth twisted slightly. Having to smooch hospital donors and members of the board wasn't his idea of fun. "You'll have to put on your best frock and let that gorgeous smile grace your lips all evening."

"I think I'll manage. Oh, this means I'll need to buy a new dress." She clapped her hands in excitement. "And maybe new shoes as well. How exciting!"

Kiran smiled at her exuberance, happy to see a little of her usual sparkle back in her eyes. He looked forward to seeing her in a new evening gown, her hair done in a fanciful way, and maybe even some makeup. She only wore a tiny bit of lipstick usually, and he'd never felt she needed anything else. For a special occasion, however, she'd add some more, and he knew she'd look even more beautiful than usual.

THE WEEKS LEADING up to Christmas went by in a blur. Kiran spent many long hours in the operating theater, and when he wasn't in surgery, he did his rounds on the wards, caught up on paperwork, and filled in when they were shorthanded in the ER.

Juliet seemed to have gotten over whatever had ailed her and kept busy at the accounting firm. Some weeks, they felt like ships passing in the night, barely seeing each other for days. By the end of the holiday season, they were both exhausted and in need of a break. Kiran decided they should take that vacation they'd talked about and booked them a long weekend in a small hotel in Santa Barbara for their wedding anniversary.

He resolved to tell her as soon as she got home that afternoon. It was a sunny but cold January morning, and he had a rare day off. Reading the newspaper at the breakfast table, he was horrified by the war in Vietnam, which had been raging for nearly ten years. Every time he read the reports from Southeast Asia, relief washed through him, knowing America only had military advisors involved in the conflict.

He sincerely hoped it would stay that way, as he'd already served through several wars during his long existence, and he had no desire to get dragged into another one. The last time, he'd not seen combat, but patching up pilots well enough to send them out in their planes again to fight the German Luftwaffe had been almost as bad.

Countless times, he'd seen their names on the killed-in-action sheets, knowing his efforts had been wasted. Of course, if you asked the pilots, they'd tell you it was all worth it. The longer they'd stayed in the air, the more Jerrys they'd been able to shoot down, and the greater the chance they'd had of winning the war.

The war in Vietnam was different. Most of it was fought in the jungles where not only could you be killed by the enemy but all sorts of tropical diseases lay in wait for the unsuspecting soldier as well.

Kiran spent most of his day off tidying up their apartment, vacuuming, and putting clothes away. He differed from most men his age that way. Doing a little housework didn't bother him, and he enjoyed lightening the load for Juliet. She was still more tired than usual, but her doctor had found nothing wrong with her. It had been a relief to get his verdict, and he'd only prescribed vitamins, plenty of fresh air, and light exercise — all of which was easy enough to accomplish.

He resolved to organize his schedule more, not take on so many shifts, and spend more time at home with his wife. It wasn't as if they needed the money. They had plenty on just his wages, and Juliet's pay packet was a bonus they could use for things like a weekend away.

1965

THE DRIVE back down to Los Angeles from Santa Barbara along the Pacific Coast Highway was stunningly beautiful. The ocean sparkled in the late winter sunshine, crashing against the jagged rocks along the shoreline. Juliet sat quietly beside him, gazing out the window. Kiran was glad he'd arranged this weekend away for them. They needed a little time to relax and just be together.

They'd only bought the car eighteen months ago, and this was the first longer trip they'd made. It rolled smoothly along the blacktop, the engine growling under the hood. Their previous car had been an older, secondhand model Chevrolet, but they'd traded it in and upgraded to a brand-new car. It had been a proud moment for both of them when they picked up the gleaming vehicle from the dealership.

Kiran glanced over at his wife. Her face was a little pale, her skin almost translucent, but she had a serene smile on her lips, and her eyes were bright. Occasionally, she'd let out a contented little sigh or point out a boat skimming across the surface of the water. They'd had two wonderful days together, staying in a little Spanish-hacienda-style Bed and Breakfast right across from the beach.

They'd taken long walks along the sprawling expanse of white sand, relaxed on the front porch of the motel, and taken in the glittering sights of Stearns Wharf. On a Saturday night, they'd enjoyed a sumptuous meal in the Harbor Restaurant, once owned by James Cagney. Juliet had been disappointed to find out he'd sold it nearly ten years ago since she'd hoped to catch a glimpse of the famous movie star. They'd had a lovely time even so and walked back the short distance along the beach to the motel.

Kiran had never felt so contented and relaxed in his life before. Spending every day with a person he truly appreciated and felt comfortable with was something entirely new, and he prayed he could live out his existence with Juliet by his side. She was sweet, caring, and always brightened his day.

"Are we nearly home, Kiran?" Juliet's soft voice pulled him from his thoughts.

"Yes, we are, sweetheart. Something wrong?" He glanced at her, and his brows furrowed at the gray sheen on her face and the tightness around her mouth that had replaced the gentle smile. They'd been driving for an hour and a half and were only another half hour away from home.

"I — I don't feel good," she said between shallow breaths. "I'm sorry,"

"What do you mean? Do you want me to stop the car?" Kiran slowed down, frantically searching for a place to pull over, but the road was narrow with a granite rock face on one side and a steep drop on the other.

"No, don't stop. I just want to go home and lie down. I have a terrible stomach ache." She curled up in her seat, clutching her abdomen.

"Which side of your stomach?" he asked, biting back his worry.

"In the middle. All over. I don't know, but it's not in just one place," she gritted out between clenched teeth.

That made it less likely to be appendicitis, which was normally localized on the lower left side of the abdomen.

"I'm taking you straight to the hospital, sweetheart," he stated firmly. "You don't look good, and I don't like how suddenly this has come on. Could it be something you ate?" He thought back to what they'd had over the last few days, but they'd both eaten the same foods, and he felt fine.

"It's —" Juliet started to say something but stopped again.

Kiran took his eyes off the road for a second to look at her.

"What? Juliet, please tell me." Frowning, he focused back on the highway as a chill spread through his veins.

"It's just that... This is not the first time. I've had these stomach pains for a while now, but I didn't want to say anything over the holidays." She sounded breathless, and the knot in Kiran's stomach grew. "Then I started feeling a little better, and I've been fine this whole weekend, but now it's back. And it's worse than before."

He pressed his foot down on the accelerator as much as he dared. "We're going to the ER. Now. No arguments."

A cold sweat broke out on his back, and he fought to swallow back the nausea churning in his gut. Thank goodness they weren't far from the hospital where he worked, and he could get some answers from doctors he trusted.

Pulling up outside the Emergency Department, Kiran drew a sigh of relief when he spotted Andrew Martin standing outside the doors, talking to a nurse. Beside him, Juliet whimpered, still hunched over. A feeling of dread settled like a rock in his stomach, and his nerves vibrated under his skin. Behind his ribcage, his heart pounded, sending shock waves through his chest.

Six

ALINA, 2011

N<i>early there</i>, Alina thought to herself as the tires of her SUV rolled through West Yellowstone, a small township of around a thousand residents, right outside the entrance to the famous national park. It was late afternoon, which gave her plenty of time to check into the little inn she'd found on the internet.

Following the instructions on the car's GPS, she swung into a small parking lot in front of a rustic-looking building. The sign out front welcomed her to the Grizzly Bear Inn.

Leaving most of her stuff in the SUV, she grabbed her overnight bag and strode up the steps to the front door. Stopping inside, she looked around and took in the simple but comfortable decor. Behind a desk, a nice-looking man looked up expectantly, smiling as she approached.

"Good afternoon, ma'am. You must be Mrs. Montgomery. We've been expecting you." His voice was deep and gravelly.

"Yes, that's me. Nice to be here." She politely returned his smile.

The man pushed an old-fashioned, leather-bound register her way. "Have you had a long journey?"

She nodded, picking up a pen to fill in her details. "I left California a few days ago, so I think I've done about a thousand miles since then."

"Wow, yes, that's a long way to come, but Yellowstone is worth it.

I'm guessing you're here to sightsee?" The man tapped on his computer while talking to her, passing her another form to fill in with her car registration.

Pushing the ledger back to him, she replied, "Hiking, actually. I have backcountry permits to stay for thirty days, and I intend to use every single minute of it."

The man's eyes widened slightly. "Is anyone joining you this evening?"

She shook her head. "No, I'm on my own. I needed to get away from everything for a little while, and hiking through some backcountry seemed like the perfect idea."

A raised brow and pursed lips told her he was either surprised or concerned by the idea of a woman hiking through the wild country on her own. Her dad had taken her camping many times since she was little, and she'd gone many more times with Jonas before the kids came along. She had several cans of bear spray and would use it if she encountered any intrusive grizzlies, coyotes, or cougars. She knew what she was doing and would take as many precautions as needed.

Her route was planned, and she'd lodge it with park officials before she left, together with the dates she expected to enter and leave the area. Even though she wanted to get away and be completely by herself, she wasn't stupid enough to think nothing could happen to her while she was out there.

After settling into her room and washing up after the long drive, she got behind the wheel again to find the sporting goods store where she'd pick up the last of the supplies she needed. West Yellowstone was a tiny place, and after consulting a map on her phone, she soon found what she was looking for.

Entering the warehouse-size store, she took in the array of tents, bicycles, sleeping bags, and every paraphernalia a hiker could want. She wandered past the colorful displays, mentally going through the list of things she needed. A new camping stove was a must as their old one had fallen apart when she took it out of the box in the garage.

She'd planned on eating military style MREs — Meals Ready to Eat — for convenience and only cook on the stove if she caught a fish and wanted a change in her diet, but she needed it for hot water if nothing else. MREs weren't the tastiest of foods, but she didn't really care about the flavor. Most meals tasted like cardboard to her, anyway. She hadn't enjoyed a decent meal since... she lost them.

"Did you find everything you need?" the cashier asked as Alina pushed the cart to the checkout.

"Yes, I did. Thank you."

"Hiking the trails?"

Alina didn't feel like getting into a long conversation about her plans but didn't want to be rude either.

"Yes, I am." She gave a slight smile and changed the topic of the conversation. "Where can I get a decent cup of coffee around here?"

"There's a great place just a block down the road. Great coffee, fresh donuts, pastries, and the best pies in the state. Take a right and don't stop until you see The Fountain. You can't miss it."

"That sounds perfect. Thank you."

The woman smiled. "No problem."

Alina nodded her thanks and walked out of the store with a wave, stowing her new gear in the trunk of her car. Leaving it in the parking lot, she strolled down the sidewalk toward the diner the cashier had suggested.

A few bistro chairs and tables underneath a bright green-and-white stripe awning told her she'd reached the right place. When she stepped inside, it was cool and airy, with plenty of seating and several customers waiting to be served. While waiting in the short line, she gazed at the multitude of sweet treats on display behind the glass. Pastries, donuts, macaroons, and cupcakes in a riot of flavors and colors sat in neat rows, just waiting to be devoured.

She sighed. None of it appealed to her, but she felt as if she should want something to go with her coffee. It's how it was done. What was expected. When it was her turn, she asked for their largest and strongest coffee, a couple of donuts, and two slices of their huckleberry pie. She didn't care if she didn't eat it all. She'd made the effort, and that would have to be enough. Then she realized. No one would ask if she'd eaten anything, or if she'd left the house at all in weeks.

She had an entire month of being on her own, with only wild animals, birds, trees, and the whispering winds for company. She'd be free to think, be quiet, and just breathe for the first time in over a year. That's if she could get rid of whatever had tied itself around her lungs and wrapped around her heart, slowly squeezing both so hard there would soon be nothing left. Maybe out here, away from the reminders, she'd finally be able to begin healing.

"Here you go, one large coffee and your pastries. Enjoy!" the older woman behind the counter said, her eyes crinkling in the corners from the bright smile on her face.

"Thank you." Alina smiled back and took the go-cup and the paper bag in one hand while handing over the cash with the other.

She walked out into the bright sunshine and groaned when the lid of her cup popped off and fell to the ground. She stared at it, frowning, then glanced back at the diner, debating whether to go back in for another lid, but there was now a long line of customers waiting. How was she going to get back to her car without spilling the coffee? A muttered curse fell from her lips.

"You need a hand?" a voice at her elbow called out.

Alina looked up, startled, nearly dropping the cup. A young man stood before her, a brow quirked at the sight of her uncovered coffee and crumpled pastry bag.

"No, I'm all right, thanks. I think." She stared at the cup in her hand.

"Really? That coffee is gonna spill if you're not careful. Here, have this. It's much better than one of those flimsy things." He held out a metal travel bottle.

"No, I can't take that. I wouldn't know how to return it." She shook her head.

"There's no need. Someone gave that to me many years ago, and that man's kindness and encouraging words helped me stay on track after my life had imploded," the young man said.

"Really? He must have been an amazing person," she said, feeling uncomfortable.

She wasn't used to people being so frank and open with a total stranger. It never happened in California.

Shrugging, he explained, "If it weren't for that man and what he did for me, I wouldn't be here. I stayed in school, worked hard, and now I'm at college studying architectural engineering with a focus on bridge construction. I've never forgotten him and always hoped I'd be able to pay it forward somehow — no matter how small a gesture it would be. This feels like the right time." He held out the bottle. "Please, take it."

Hesitantly, Alina's fingers closed around the worn and dented bottle. Some kind of logo was printed in silver on the front, but she couldn't make out what it was.

"It's a souvenir from somewhere." — his finger lightly traced a worn print — "but I've never tried to work out what it is. It looks a little like wings, don't you think?"

"Yes, I guess it does..."

It was strange. The metal almost hummed in her hand, a tingle spreading up her arm. It was as if it belonged there. It felt comfortable, familiar, and somehow comforting.

"Thank you. It's very kind of you. But are you sure?" Strangely, she found herself reluctant to give it back and secretly hoped he'd say no. "If this man meant so much to you, shouldn't you keep it?"

"No, it's time it has a new home. Here, let me help you." He unscrewed the cap from the bottle and poured in her coffee. "There. It'll keep that coffee hot for a lot longer, and you can use it for water afterward."

He passed it back, gave her a wide grin, then turned on his heel and strode off with a quick wave over his shoulder. Alina stared after him. Then she looked at the bottle, a smile forming on her lips. Inside her chest, a tiny crack deep in her heart knitted together from the simple but kind gesture of a complete stranger.

THE FOLLOWING MORNING, Alina entered Yellowstone National Park through the West Entrance just as the sun breached the horizon.

She was glad to get in ahead of the crowds and hoped to be well away before the trails filled up with families, couples, and other hikers. She'd be following the official paths for only a short while before setting out with just a map and a compass to guide her.

Her plan was to make her way toward a large lake and follow its perimeter before veering off toward another, smaller lake. Then she'd stick close to the shoreline until she could head back along the opposite side of the first lake, before returning to where her SUV would be parked for the duration. If she hiked a minimum of one-and-a-half miles a day, which would be easy for the most part, she'd make it back with several days to spare for quick trips to the famous geysers and hot springs.

By the end of the month, she'd head east to Chicago, where her parents lived. Her mom had been ill for a long time and had been unable to make the journey to California for the funeral, so it'd been nearly two years since Alina had last seen them. While she got herself set up, she'd finally be able to spend some quality time with them.

She was looking forward to a new place of her own and starting her job in corporate events. It was the boost she needed and hopefully, it'd be a fresh start. God knows she needed it.

The small parking lot at the head of the trail came into view, and she pulled in, parked her car near the exit and got out, stretching her legs after the hour-long drive.

After making sure she'd put any valuables in the glove compartment and locked it, she engaged the central locking system and alarm. Grabbing her backpack from the trunk, she hoisted it onto her shoulders. It was a little heavy, but no more than she could handle. As she went through her food supplies, it would lighten anyway.

From a side pocket, she pulled out the metal bottle and took a sip of the coffee she'd filled it with at the inn before she left. After savoring the strong, hot drink, she took a deep breath and headed into the forest on the well-worn path.

The air was still cool and the light dim between the tall spires of pines. A rich scent of damp earth, pine needles, and moss filled her nose, almost making her head spin. It was so rich and primal, she felt it trickle into her soul. As she tramped along the trail, winding its way between rocks and trees, her mind seemed a little clearer, and the dark cloud surrounding her lifted for a second. Somewhere in the deepest recesses of her mind, a faint voice whispered.

Just take one small step.

She'd heard it several times before and put it down to her subconsciousness telling her to keep moving forward, whether it was a fraction of an inch or a foot. At the moment, that was as big a step as she could take. She knew she had a life to live, even without her family, and they wouldn't have wanted her to waste it all, buried in grief, but she didn't know *how* to live without them. Not yet, anyway.

She followed the marked trail for a couple of hours, heading due south, and by the time the sun had risen above the tree line, a sparkling blue hinted between the tall trunks. She'd reached the lake, her first goal. It was a popular spot for families to hike, so she wouldn't be stopping for long. From here on, she'd make her way through the backcountry, avoiding any marked trails, and hope no one else had decided on doing the same thing. She'd also have to be even more careful where she put her feet, and who she shared the forest with. A moose cow protecting her young wasn't something to mess around with, and she had no wish to come face to face with a grumpy grizzly, either.

ALINA BLEW out a big puff of air when she trudged the last few steps of the hiking trail and saw her car sitting by itself, with all four tires and no shattered windows. She'd made it back. Several bruises, some scratches, a sore ankle, and a few blisters adorned her body, but she counted them as battle scars and wore them with pride.

It had taken her twenty-nine days to hike thirty-five miles through sometimes rough terrain. Elation surged through her chest as she dropped the backpack from her shoulders and dug out the car keys from a waterproof pouch at the bottom of the bag. Dumping the pack on the backseat, she climbed behind the wheel and started the engine. It caught right away, and she fist-pumped to celebrate.

It hadn't all been smooth sailing. Fighting her way through dense forests, clambering over giant boulders, and cursing every mosquito trying to suck her dry had felt like an impossible task at times. At night, the tears she'd held back for so long would be held back no more. She cried rivers, screamed out her pain, cursed God, the Heavens, Fate, Destiny, and Mother Nature for ripping out her heart and taking her loved ones away from her.

Some days, she'd only made enough headway to cover the necessary daily distance, spending the rest of the time going over every moment she'd had with Jonas from the day they met. Every conversation, every text message, every smile, every touch. Once she reached that last fateful day, she'd go back and do the same with her babies. The moment she knew she was pregnant, the morning sickness, the flutters, the kicks, and the first time she laid eyes on them. That feeling when they put their little arms around her neck and clung to her, telling her how much they loved her and planting sloppy kisses on her cheeks — it was all still in her head. What she wouldn't do to hear, see, or feel any of that again.

Not a single moose or even a squirrel had crossed her path, and the cans of spray were still tucked into the pockets of her pack. Maybe the ruckus she'd caused at night when her grief became unbearable had scared off even the hungriest grizzly. She was grateful, whatever the case.

Being on her own for so long had done her good. She felt a little lighter. The grief was easier to bear. A few days ago, for the first time when she heated one of her MREs, she'd actually been able to tell what she was eating. Sort of, anyway. She'd guessed at some beef stew, which hadn't been entirely unpleasant. It still had cardboard as the dominant flavor, but there had been other ones lurking around on her tastebuds as well.

BEFORE DRIVING SOUTH through the park, she changed her socks for a fresh pair and the hiking boots for her favorite, most worn-in sneakers. They felt like heaven on her feet, and she wriggled her toes inside them for a while. Wearing the same pair of boots for a month was hard on your feet, no matter how comfortable they were.

With a contented sigh, she placed her now favorite water bottle in the cupholder, settled back in the seat, and pulled onto the blacktop. From here, she'd spend a few days sightseeing in the park before she headed east to Chicago.

The sun blazed from a cloudless sky as her SUV trundled along the highway that wound its way through the incredible scenery. It was late in the afternoon, and she hoped she could find a room in one of the motels dotting the tourist areas. It was nearly September, and Labor Day weekend was still five days away, so there was hope the crowds hadn't descended yet.

It felt strange moving along without using her legs and at a much higher speed. The road was nearly empty of other cars, and she could allow her mind to wander. The sun shined brightly, the sky was cerulean with fluffy cotton clouds dotting the expanse, and little lakes and meadows broke the dark green of the forest lining her route. She was tired, but relaxed and content,

Just take one small step.

The voice floated through her head like on a breeze, always from far away but never completely silent. It was comforting and always warmed her heart a tiny bit.

Pulling into one of the larger visitors areas, she stopped outside the nearest decent-looking motel and jumped out. Stretching her legs, she looked around, shuddering at the number of RVs and overloaded cars rolling in from the highway. She dug through the backpack to find her purse containing her credit cards and pushed open the entrance doors.

Five minutes later, she found her room — a suite, actually, as it was all they had left — dumped her pack on the floor and stripped off her stained and muddy clothes. A hot shower was her first priority. There weren't many bathrooms in the backcountry, and she'd made do with washing in streams and lakes. She didn't mind roughing it while she was out there, but a hot shower felt like heaven right about now.

After a few days of playing tourist, Alina had had enough of traipsing down narrow paths, hanging around for others to finish taking a million selfies and watching families enjoy themselves. So she packed her SUV again and mapped her route to Chicago.

She'd spend a few weeks with her parents while she decided on a course of action. The new job was at the top of her list, and if it didn't work out, with no ties to anywhere, she could go wherever she wanted. She could even go abroad if something exciting came up.

Her skills as an event planner and project manager were transferable to many industries and professions, so finding a new challenge shouldn't be too difficult.

Driving out of Yellowstone, she murmured a goodbye to the incredible park. A little sadness tinged the contentment in her chest at having to leave its majestic beauty behind, but she had a life to live, and she needed to rejoin the human race.

Seven

KIRAN, 1965

The beeping and whirring of the machines had merged into a background noise Kiran no longer noticed. He'd lost all sense of time as days and nights passed in a blur of sympathetic words, endless tests, and whimpers of pain. The still form under the white sheets no longer belonged to him. It belonged to the cruel disease eating it from the inside. After months of scans, medications, treatments, and intensive prayers, they'd reached the end. They'd run out of options.

Juliet had asked for everything to stop, to let her go. When Kiran had pleaded with her to keep going, to keep fighting, she'd smiled her serene smile, caressed his cheek, and told him she was happy and wanted to die in peace. Anger had blasted through him at her words. He didn't understand how she could give up, could stop trying and leave him behind. Yet he knew why. It was futile. The cancer ran rampant through her body, having reached her bones and her brain. Soon, there would be nothing left of the woman who'd become so important to him.

The day her oncologist had given them his final verdict — a death sentence — was the day Kiran said his last ever prayer. He was finally convinced no prayer of his would ever be answered. If not now, when he needed it most, then when?

He remembered that day with excruciating clarity. Dr. Zimmerman had called them into his office to give them the results of the latest round of tests. Juliet had been so calm and relaxed, whereas he'd been a bundle of nerves. In hindsight, he'd realized she'd probably known what the outcome would be and had already accepted it.

He scrunched his eyes shut and tried to block out that entire day, but it wouldn't be held back.

"Mrs. Mitchell. Dr. Mitchell. Thank you for coming in so promptly." Dr. Zimmerman shook their hands, his expression neutral, but his gentle brown eyes held their usual kindness.

"Not at all, doctor. We're anxious to hear what you've found." Kiran's stomach was tying itself in knots, and it was only Juliet's fingers interlaced with his that stopped him from demanding immediate answers.

Clenching her hand, he inhaled through his nose and slowly counted to five before releasing his breath. This wasn't about him, so he needed to get a grip on his nerves and calm down.

"Please, sit down." The doctor waved at the two chairs facing his desk as he sank into his plush leather seat and opened a thick manila folder on the blotter in front of him.

Steepling his hands, he pursed his lips and tapped his fingers against them. He fixed his eyes on the stack of papers, a frown creasing his brow. Kiran's heart squeezed as he watched the oncologist surreptitiously take a deep breath.

"Now, I've had your test results, Mrs. Mitchell" — *he paused, turning over a couple of sheets covered in typed words and numbers to more of the same on the pages beneath* — *"and I've discussed them with several of my colleagues."*

Black ink on white paper. Notes scribbled in the margin. Kiran had seen it all before and had held countless similar folders himself, with his own notes scrawled over them. It was what doctors did every day. Patient notes. They wrote them all down by hand, and then a secretary typed them in neat and tidy paragraphs before tucking it into a manila folder with the patient's name in bold letters on the front. The scribbles were added later when the patient was seen again.

The typed script was too small for Kiran to read upside down, and he wanted to reach across the desk, snatch it out of the doctor's hand and see for himself. The only reason he didn't was Juliet tightening her grip on his hand. He glanced down at her. She smiled and mouthed at him to take a breath and be patient. For her sake, he tried to do just that, even as his heart screamed to take action. To do something. Anything. The waiting was torturous, though less than a minute had passed.

"Yes, doctor?" *Juliet asked, her tone light and gracious, but Kiran noticed the fear biting through her words.*

"Right, yes. As you know, these were the last in the battery of tests we have performed on you over the last few weeks, and I'm so very sorry to tell you that there really isn't anything more we can do." *He blinked, a sympathetic expression settling over his face.* "We've come to the end of the line, I'm afraid."

"What do you mean? Where do we go from here?" *Kiran already knew the answer, but he wasn't ready to accept it.*

There had to be something else they could do, some new drugs they could try. Until they'd exhausted every single avenue of treatment, no matter how experimental, he wouldn't let them give up. They had to keep trying. Juliet deserved it, and he needed her. Never before had he actually felt that about someone, but he needed *her to live, to share her life with him, to smile her serene smile that filled him with such warmth and comfort. Without her, he'd be on his own again — alone, like he'd been for so long before they met. Only this time it would be worse because he'd know what it felt like not to be alone, and it would gut him. She was his shield against that crushing, devastating loneliness that always hovered at the back of his mind. The one thing he feared more than anything.*

"Dr. Mitchell, I think you know just as well as I that we've tried everything." *Dr. Zimmerman leaned forward.* "No options have been left unchecked, no available treatments or drugs not considered or used. This is it." *He gave them a gentle smile and waited for them to digest what he'd just told them.* "I am truly sorry to have to be the bearer of such devastating news, but all we can do now is keep Juliet comfortable and in as little pain as possible."

Kiran stopped breathing. His lungs closed, cutting off all oxygen to his brain. Black spots danced in front of his eyes, and his vision narrowed.

No, it can't be true! Not my Juliet! Not her! She has to stay with me!

He swallowed hard, shoving his panic and despair down deep inside him. He couldn't fall apart now. Juliet needed him to stay strong. He was her husband, and she depended on him to be her rock and her safety net. Dragging in a raspy breath, he put his arm around her shoulders and held her while she composed herself.

"How long, Dr. Zimmerman? I mean, how much time—" Juliet's voice broke, and a sob wracked her thin body, making her shoulders shake with held-back emotion.

"It's hard to tell, as I'm sure you can imagine." The doctor's voice lowered. "With a little luck, maybe three or four months. But it's so advanced now that it could be a matter of a few weeks. Of course, we will give you as much help and support as you need, and a bed will be made available in the hospice next door."

"No! I don't want to be in the hospice," she cried. "I want to stay at home where I'll be comfortable."

"Mrs. Mitchell, you realize we won't be able to help you if you... encounter any trouble if you're at home?" Dr. Zimmerman frowned. "A hospice would have the necessary equipment for the medical staff to utilize in case of anything happening before you—"

"I don't care," she interrupted him. "I won't go to the hospice. I will stay at home, sleep in my own bed, and if there's something we don't have that I may or may not need, then so be it." She turned to Kiran. "Please, my love. I can't bear the thought of spending what little time I have left in some sterile, depressing medical ward where everyone is just waiting to die." Juliet's eyes brimmed with tears, punching Kiran in the gut. "Please, don't do that to me."

"I would never do that to you," he murmured. "If you want to stay at home, then that's where you shall be. We'll hire a nurse and anything else you need for your care while I'm at work, and the rest of the time" — he lifted her hand and pressed his lips to her knuckles — "it'll be just you and me. Like it's always been. You and me together."

Juliet kissed him. It was so full of love, gratitude, compassion, and warmth it nearly broke his heart into a million pieces. He had a feeling there wouldn't be much left of it by the time she took her final breath.

Anger spread through his veins, but he was careful not to let it show. He focused on his breathing while the doctor told Juliet in more detail what she could expect in the coming months. He'd wanted to wait and have some time to process before going through all the nasty details of how her last few months — or weeks — might look, but Juliet wanted it all out of the way now so she could sort through it in her mind and prepare for her life to end. Kiran knew he would never be prepared to lose her.

It took just six months for Juliet to change from rosy-cheeked, energetic, and smiling, to pale, gaunt, and listless. She'd carried on working for a few weeks after her initial diagnosis, but it didn't take long before the endless doctor's appointments, hospital visits, and grueling rounds of chemotherapy took their toll, and she'd had to resign.

They'd tried everything without the slightest improvement to give them hope. Not even the most recent combination therapy — using several drugs at once — had any effect on the mutating cells. If they'd known sooner, before the cancer spread, radiotherapy might have worked, but by the time Juliet's pain was more than just the occasional, mild stomach ache, it was too late.

Once they'd had the final verdict, it had been the end of the hospital stays, and Juliet had been confined to her bed at home. Kiran had worked enough shifts to ensure he had plenty of money coming in to pay for her care, but other than that, he'd sat by her bedside. They'd talked, he'd read to her, told her stories of his past lives — of course, she thought they were just something he made up to distract her from her pain — and he'd waited. Week after week, day after day, hour after hour, he'd waited. Waited for her to die.

His rage still simmered with glowing embers in his stomach, ready to flare into a volcanic eruption, but it wasn't aimed at Dr. Zimmerman, or even at the cruel disease, and certainly not at Juliet. He couldn't be angry with the woman who'd given him nothing but love, kindness, and joy. This wasn't her fault, and fighting a war she could never win was useless. He would let her go peacefully with him by her side, where he belonged.

He watched her chest rise and fall in shallow, labored breaths under the pristine white sheet that was tucked tightly around her. The moans of pain had receded after the doctor had increased her pain medication. Her thin, frail hand rested in his, no longer gripping it tightly the way she'd done only a couple of hours ago. They'd talked for a few minutes, and he'd made sure she knew what she meant to him, how she'd graced his life with her gentle demeanor and kindness, and her ability to find pleasure in the smallest things.

Juliet had asked him to carry on with his life without her, but he wasn't sure how he'd be able to do that. Not that he'd have much of a choice. No matter what happened, he always came back, never knowing the time or the place in advance. Of course, she knew nothing of the millennia he'd spent wandering the earth. It wasn't something he could ever explain or share with anyone. It was his burden to bear for a reason he would probably never know.

He sat quietly by her bed like he'd done for so many days and weeks now, barely leaving her side other than to work the minimum hours at the hospital required to keep his job. Dr. Radford had given him as much leeway as he could, and Andrew covered as many of his shifts as possible, coming in early or leaving late to allow Kiran a few more hours with Juliet.

His gaze wandered around the room, seeing it as if for the first time. Juliet had chosen the color scheme in here as well as in the rest of the house. The walls were a gentle cream, the carpet a soft beige, and the curtains were pale blue with a faint trace of swirls and spirals in a light brown. She'd gone against the trend of garish colors, often orange, red, and yellow together, and crazy, psychedelic patterns, in favor of more muted tones in simple designs. It had suited her personality — calm, kind, and comforting with a light and breezy air.

Kiran tightened his grip on her hand, squeezing it gently when her eyelids flickered open. He cupped her cheek with his free hand, despairing at the dry, burning hot, paper-thin skin. She stared unseeingly for a moment before focusing and finding his gaze. A thin smile tugged at her chapped, flaky lips as recognition sparked in their depths.

"There you are. I was hoping I'd see your beautiful eyes again."

"Hi, my love," she whispered, coughing from the effort.

"Don't talk. Save your energy. I'm here, and I'm not leaving you." Kiran leaned forward and kissed her forehead.

Her lips moved, her eyes darkening with the effort. "Kiran, I love you. Be safe, be happy, find love again."

He had to strain to hear her words, fear thrusting his heart into his throat.

"I'm happy with you, my darling. You've made me feel so loved, and you never lost your faith in me." His voice broke, and he cleared his throat. "I don't want you to go."

When she spoke again, she sounded a little stronger, a flush of crimson staining her pale cheeks.

"It's time. I just wanted to tell you one last time how much you mean to me." Her words came out in a wheeze. "You are the perfect husband and my best friend. Just promise me one thing?"

Kiran swallowed hard past the tears in his throat. "Anything. I'll promise you anything except to be happy that you're gone."

"Promise me you won't forget me, not because I'm gone, but because I lived. Promise me you will try to be happy again." A single tear trickled down her cheek, and Kiran wiped it away with a knuckle.

"I promise I'll try. But my life will be so empty without you. I don't know what I'll do when you're no longer with me." He bowed his head, unable to contain the sob fighting its way up from his chest. "You are my home, my comfort, my happiness."

"You will be fine, Kiran. It might take some time" — Juliet coughed, a few drops of blood staining her lips — "but one day, you'll look back on this and know that you've survived, that you are living your life the way you're supposed to. I want that for you."

Carefully and as gently as if she was made of the finest porcelain, he wiped her mouth with a cloth.

"I'll try." Pain and misery sliced through his words, despite his best efforts to prevent it. "That's all I can promise you. I will try."

"Kiran?" she whispered.

"Yes, sweetheart?"

Juliet's gaze bore deep into his soul, and she must have seen something there, for her eyes widened, and her mouth formed a small 'o'. Then she nodded as if her question had been answered.

"Your true love awaits..." Her voice trailed off, and she sank lower into the pillows.

His brows knitted and furrows appeared on his forehead. "I don't understand. You are my true love."

What did she mean? This was not something he wanted to go through again, so another relationship was out of the question, no matter what happened to him in the future. The pain and sorrow of losing her was too much. His heart was being ripped apart and would never be the same. From this moment on, friendships and acquaintances were as far as he would go. No further. Ever.

Kiran searched her eyes for an explanation of her words, but she was already fading. Turning her cheek into his hand, she gently pressed her lips against his palm. Then she whispered a few words before a final breath of air left her lungs in a gentle puff.

"Just take one small step."

Kiran stared at her, but Juliet was no longer there. Her soul had left her, leaving behind an empty shell. Agony exploded in his chest, a muted roar bursting from his lips as he gathered her body in his arms one last time. He couldn't breathe, couldn't think, couldn't do anything but hold her tight and cry out his anguish. Tears ran in rivers from his eyes, drenching them both, but he didn't care.

She was gone.

COLD, hard anger filled his veins as he listened to the minister droning on about being taken too early, and God wanting his favorites by his side. It wasn't true. None of it was. It was cruelty, plain and simple. Or indifference to people's suffering. Worse, he had a nagging feeling it was done — to him at least — out of sheer enjoyment just to see him fall apart again and again. This time, however, was the worst. He'd never created such a bond with another person. Not as deeply, anyway. He'd had close friends and companions, fought alongside men he considered brothers and protected women with his life, but none of them had held such a place in his heart as Juliet or a bond like the one they'd formed. With everything in his soul, he wanted it back. He wanted Juliet with her sweet smile, tender hands, and sparkling laughter.

It was impossible. He knew that. But it didn't stop him from raging at the heavens and shouting out his demands. No one listened. No one had ever listened since he first awoke on cold, damp earth at the dawn of civilization.

The day was beautiful, but it could have been freezing cold and pouring rain for all Kiran noticed. The grass was green and lush under his feet, and birds twittered in the nearby trees. In front of him, Juliet's casket rested on poles laid above the rectangular hole in the ground. Flowers covered the simple but beautifully carved wood. Behind him, their friends and colleagues had gathered to pay their respects and say their final farewells.

Out of the corner of his eye, he saw Andrew Martin, his close friend and co-worker from the hospital, step up to the little lectern to speak. With half an ear, he listened to the heartfelt words, the catches in his voice as he spoke and saw the moisture in his eyes.

Andrew had been a great support these last six months, taking on every shift when Kiran had to be somewhere else or simply couldn't function from the tiredness and stress. He'd never complained or refused, just smiled, patted him on the back and told him to go do what he needed to do. Andrew's wife, Maryan, had also been a godsend. She'd sat with Juliet when he needed to leave to go to the hospital for a shift and the nurse hadn't come in yet, and she'd brought him homemade treats, flasks of coffee, and books to read as he waited by his wife's bedside.

Guilt ate at him. He was a doctor, a surgeon. It was his job to make people better, but he'd been powerless to help his own wife. What did he miss? Were there signs he'd dismissed as something else? He couldn't remember, but he was sure there had to have been something, and he'd failed to notice. Juliet had suffered because of his failings, because he hadn't been observant enough, hadn't been good enough.

She'd died because *he wasn't enough.*

Juliet had been a popular and cherished friend and co-worker. He'd introduced her to some of the doctors he worked with, and he'd met her colleagues from the office. They'd even had regular dinner parties with a few of them.

Dragging himself out of his self-recriminating thoughts, he could hear the muted sobs of their friends behind him and their comforting words to each other. All he wanted was for everyone to go away so he could be alone. The best thing that could happen was for him to be taken away from here to start anew in a different place and time. It had happened so many times before, so why not now?

Kiran stepped forward and placed his hand on the casket, hoping to feel Juliet's presence, her soul — anything. He felt nothing. Only cold, hard wood. The scent of the large mass of roses and lilies filled his nose, choking him. They were all wrong. Juliet's favorite flowers were daisies. She'd always said their delicate petals and sunny faces filled her with simple joy. Kiran had bought them for her every birthday and their wedding anniversaries.

Ten years.

That's how long they'd been married. It wasn't anywhere near enough, but he would cherish every single one of those years he'd had with her. She deserved to be remembered and celebrated, and he would ensure she was never forgotten.

To his relief, the minister had stopped talking and was solemnly walking away. Kiran had asked for the casket not to be lowered while they were still there. He couldn't bear the thought of seeing it sink into the gaping hole in the earth. It was so final, and he didn't want his last memory of Juliet to be a wooden box covered with damp, sticky dirt. She deserved better. It was the least he could do after having let her down in such a terrible way.

Both Andrew and Dr. Radford had told him so many times there was nothing he could have done. Juliet's symptoms didn't show until it was already too late. On an intellectual level, he knew they were right, but nothing they or anyone else said would ease the viselike grip on his heart.

Everyone else turned and followed the minister back to where the cars waited. He didn't bother saying goodbye as he'd see them all back at his and Juliet's house for the wake.

He scoffed. It was no longer his and Juliet's house. It was his and only his. She no longer existed in this world. Once again, he was alone. He could only hope she was at peace and free from the excruciating pain that had gripped her in the last few months of her life.

Was there a Heaven? A very long time ago, he'd been able to say yes with absolute certainty. Now, he wondered if it had all been an illusion, an elaborate ruse to lull him and others into a false sense of security. Or was it just him? Was he the only one enduring this Hell on Earth? What had he done? It must have been such a heinous crime he didn't even deserve to be confronted with it, and not knowing was part of his punishment. Grief and despair replaced the anger. What was the point of being angry when there was no one to vent his rage on?

He bowed his head, his hand still on the gleaming wood, as a gentle warmth wrapped him in a soft embrace.

Juliet.

No, it felt different. It was a kind and loving presence, but not quite that of Juliet. It was something or someone else. He lifted his eyes and scanned the grassy expanse in front of him. In the far distance, an ethereal figure stood watching him. A woman, he was sure. He couldn't make out her face or anything at all about her, but he was certain it was a female.

He frowned as he searched his memories for anything similar having happened before, but he drew a blank. Unable to tear his gaze away, his eyes widened when a sense of recognition flooded his chest, sending his mind into a tailspin since he was sure they'd never met. How he knew that without being able to see her clearly, he didn't know, but he was absolutely certain.

As his gaze locked onto hers, he felt more than saw a tendril of her sorrow and empathy for him reach across the space dividing them. As it touched the spot above his heart, he staggered back at the sudden onslaught of emotions erupting in his chest like an exploding star. It was overwhelming and dizzying, forcing him to a knee. To make it worse, pain broke out in two separate spots on his shoulder blades, sending nausea roiling through his gut. He breathed heavily, swallowing hard to force it away.

Kiran looked back at the woman, and the pain and overwhelming anguish washed away, replaced by a wondrous feeling and a sharp longing. Was it for her? The ethereal woman he could barely see? No, it had to be for Juliet. The woman he'd just lost. The woman resting in the casket before him. Mists swirled in his eyes and when they cleared, the spot across the grass was empty. From far away, he heard Juliet's last words to him, and grasped on to them, holding them to his chest and letting them sink deep into his heart.

Just take one small step.

Eight

ALINA, 2011

Alina was relieved. After driving five hundred miles a day for three days, seeing the signs for Welling where her parents lived put a smile on her face. The roads were unfamiliar until the very last minute, since she'd never approached from the north before.

Since her parents left California to relocate for her dad's job, every time she'd visited them, she'd flown in to O'Hare Airport, west of the city, where one of them would pick her up. Thankfully, the GPS in her SUV hadn't steered her wrong so far, and once she exited the freeway into the little town north of Chicago, she no longer needed it.

She slowed down when she entered familiar territory. Passing the little café on the corner of the intersection on Main Street, memories of her mom taking her there floated to the surface in her mind.

Her younger sister had moved with their parents, albeit with a lot of moaning and grumbling, but after settling into a new high school and making a few friends, she'd been happy enough and began looking at arts courses at the University of Chicago.

Alina flipped her turn signal to swing left onto a road running alongside the shore of Lake Michigan. Finally, she saw the street sign she'd been looking for. Turning onto the short dead-end lane, she soon pulled into the driveway. It was a two-story family home with five bedrooms and five and a half baths. Painted white, the clapboard siding was offset with gray shutters and a black-tiled roof. A two-column porch framed the black door, coach lights lining the stone path from the wide driveway. The backyard stretched all the way to the shoreline with a magnificent view of the water. They'd justified the size of the house by saying both Alina and her sister would bring boyfriends home, and they needed space for their grandparents to visit for the holidays as well.

Once she'd switched off the engine, she released a breath, relishing the silence. The hum from under the hood had become her constant companion since she left Wyoming and frankly, she was sick and tired of it.

The tall front door swung open, and a petite, slender woman hurried out toward her. Alina smiled. Her mom hadn't changed at all. Maybe a little thinner and a little paler, but her warm and loving smile was the same, as was the way her eyes crinkled at the corners when the smile widened.

"Alina, darling. You're here," she gushed, pulling open the car door. "We weren't expecting you until later."

"Hi, Mom. I guess my foot got a little heavier on the accelerator the last few miles." Alina stepped out of the vehicle and took a deep breath of fresh air, the nearby lake adding a touch of brine and reeds to it.

"Let me see you. Oh, honey. You are much too thin." Her mom looked her up and down with a critical eye before enfolding her in a warm embrace. "I bet you haven't been eating properly lately."

"I'm fine. Just a little tired. Where's Dad?" Alina asked, unwilling to get into a conversation about the state of her health, and glanced toward the house just as an imposing man came striding around the corner from the back of the house.

"There he is." Her mom beamed. "I told him I heard a car in the drive, but he wanted to finish tidying up his tools in the shed. He's spent the last couple of days preparing the yard for the fall and winter."

Alina gave her dad a warm hug before he helped her into the house and upstairs with her baggage. Her room was ready for her, and she eyed the bed longingly. She was exhausted after a week of driving the thirteen hundred miles from Wyoming to Illinois.

"Sweetheart, why don't you take a nap first?" Her mom waved

toward the bed. "I'll make a start on dinner, and we can have drinks first out on the terrace. I'll cook for seven, so you've got plenty of time to rest and freshen up."

"Thanks, Mom." She stifled a yawn. "I could really do with some sleep, but make sure you wake me up in time to eat. I don't want to sleep all afternoon and evening, or I won't sleep tonight."

"Sure thing, darling." Her mom patted her cheek. "You'll find fresh towels in the bathroom and extra pillows in the closet if you want them."

Closing the door behind her mom, Alina sank onto the bed. Its billowy softness tugged at her tired body, but she wanted to clean off the road dust first. Letting out a deep sigh, she was grateful her mom hadn't asked any questions about how she was feeling or wanted to know how she was coping. All she wanted was to rest and get her bearings after so many days of being on the road.

After washing her hands and face and grabbing a pair of pajama shorts and tank top to sleep in, she set an alarm on her cell, slid beneath the cool sheets, quietly moaning with pleasure, and closed her eyes.

THE AFTERNOON SUN bathed the back deck in a golden glow. Alina sat curled up on the lounger with an empty wine glass, staring sightlessly over the sparkling blue lake peeking from behind the trees. If she didn't know better, she'd almost think she was back in Northern California enjoying the views of the Pacific.

The last few weeks with her parents had been good for her. She felt more at ease with herself and finally had hope she could move forward with her life without Jonas and her babies. The pain of losing them would never go away, but it had dulled to a persistent ache with the occasional sharp stab. Breathing had become easier, and the nightmares were not so devastating. They'd changed as well, becoming dreams rather than instruments of torture.

Since that first time she'd dreamed of the blond man at the funeral, he'd been back in her sleep-induced visions several times. Always at a distance but getting a little nearer each time. She still couldn't see his face, but there was something warm and comforting about him. He had an aura that wrapped around her, soothing her fraught mind. She still couldn't work out why she was dreaming about a man other than Jonas, but if it helped her deal with her grief, she'd take it. It was probably her bruised and fragile mind using a disguise for Jonas to ease her pain.

"Hi, sweetheart. How're you doing?" her dad asked, settling in a chair next to her.

He held out a cold beer for her, and she took it with a grateful smile.

Twisting off the cap, she returned her gaze to the shimmering blue waters of the lake, a small sigh escaping her lips. How was she doing? To be honest, she wasn't entirely sure. Her moods had gone from yo-yo-ing every minute of the day to shallow swells with longer distances between the peaks and troughs. She still had days when everything was bleak and dark, but a lot of the time, she felt more balanced and leveled. However, she also had no real highs. There were no days, or even hours, when she felt happy. Mostly, she just felt... numb.

She shrugged. "I'm okay, Dad. Still taking one day at a time, you know?"

Her dad nodded slowly in agreement. "I guess that's all you can do. I can't even imagine..."

Alina glanced over at her normally stoic dad when she heard the catch in his voice. His eyes were glassy, and his lips had formed a tight line.

"I know, Dad. I wouldn't wish it on my worst enemy."

"I'm so sorry we couldn't be there. Your mom—" He paused for a moment. "Well, she's better now after the operation, but I couldn't take the risk of letting her on that plane. She wanted to go so badly, and I had to forcibly stop her from driving to the airport. I couldn't bear the thought of—" He stopped again.

Alina put her hand on his, squeezing it gently.

"Dad, don't worry about it. The last thing I would have wanted was for Mom to get worse because of me. I'm glad you stopped her from coming. Katie was there and helped me through everything."

He squeezed her hand back. "Your sister wanted to come as well, but her boss wouldn't give her the time off. I would have wrung his neck if I'd been able to get my hands on him."

"I'm sure you would have, Dad," she said reassuringly. "Sophia called me several times, you know. It was nice to hear her voice, but with California nine hours behind Paris, it was hard to find a time when we were both free." Alina kept her voice neutral so he wouldn't catch onto the fact that she wasn't particularly looking forward to seeing her younger sibling.

Sophia had been working in France for several years after finishing her Master's degree in Fine Arts at the University of Sorbonne. She was a talented artist and photographer and was finally coming back to Chicago for good after landing a job at The Art Institute of Chicago.

It was true that Sophia had called after the accident, and then again after the funeral, but it had seemed more out of obligation than anything else. She'd even started the conversations with 'Mom said I should call'.

Alina had just been in a serious car crash, lost her husband and children, and had to bury them while still recovering from her injuries. All her sister could say was, "I'm sure you'll be better soon." That was when Alina swore she'd never rely on her sister for anything.

"Well, she'll be here soon, and you'll have all the time in the world to catch up." Her dad smiled. "When do you start this new job of yours?"

A slight buzz cartwheeled through her stomach at the thought of getting stuck into something new. It would be a distraction from the dark thoughts that still prodded and stung her mind.

"I'm not sure. They're supposed to call me in the next few days to set things up."

She thought she was looking forward to it, but even the prospect of a new job couldn't conjure more emotion than a slight flutter of excitement. Once she was settled in and kept busy, she was sure she'd be more enthusiastic and upbeat about her future.

"Can I ask how you're feeling? I mean, not just at this very minute, but how you're really feeling. Your mom and I have both been so worried," her dad murmured, his eyes carefully studying her face. "And I know you. You like to pretend everything is all right, and you're coping just fine, but I can't imagine you're anything more than just okay."

Alina shifted in her seat, her hands clenching into fists, while she gathered her thoughts. Was she just okay? How far in her grieving process had she really come? While she was in Yellowstone, she'd thought she was sixty percent on the way to a new normal, but coming back here and spending time with her parents had made her doubt her progress. Beside her, her dad waited patiently for her to respond, but she wasn't sure how to explain how she felt.

"To be honest, Dad" — she took a breath and unclenched her hands — "some days I feel I'm getting better, and other days I just want to hide in a dark place and cry. And some days, though they're getting fewer and farther apart, I want it all to be over. I'm sorry. I know that's not what you wanted to hear."

"Sweetheart, I asked for the truth, and that's what you gave me. I never thought you were in any way over what happened and ready to just move on and leave it all behind. Jonas, Theo, and Daisy will always be with you, and them having been in your life will shape your future." He took a breath. "What I don't want is for you to walk around and hide your feelings because you think it's what we want. Both your mom and I want you to feel exactly how you feel, and if you want to scream and shout or cry all day, then that's what you should do." He dragged a hand down his jaw. "We're here for you, but if you're not honest about how you're getting on, day to day or even hour to hour... We want to support you" — he leaned over and took her hand in his, giving it another squeeze — "or leave you alone if that's what you need instead. We love you, and we are so, so sorry this happened to you. We miss them too, and we'll always keep them in our hearts."

Alina held back a sob, blinking away the tears brimming in her eyes. She looked across the lawn and the water beyond. Taking a deep breath, she rose and leaned against the railings.

"Thanks, Dad. I know you and Mom worry, but I'm mostly okay. I have my ups and downs and probably will for a long time, but at least I can breathe now. It's taken me a full year to get to this point" — she turned back around to face him — "but I'm finally here. Leaving California was the right thing to do. It held too many memories and too many broken dreams and hopes. This new job will hopefully be my next stepping stone to a different future than the one I wished for, but life is cruel, and I have to roll with the punches, right?" She smiled at her dad, who came to stand next to her.

She cast a glance at him and said, "I think I'll go for a walk before dinner if that's okay? Will you tell Mom I'll be back soon?" She kissed him on the cheek and headed across the lawn to the tiny path that meandered along the shoreline for a couple of miles.

The fresh air and solitude would do her good. She needed a clearer head to deal with her sister arriving soon. Where Sophia had been quiet and mousey as a teenager, she was now loud and brash as a twenty-five-year-old. Alina wasn't sure if it was France and Paris that had brought it out or if she'd always been like that and had hidden it well all these years.

ALINA SETTLED FARTHEST AWAY from her sister, who insisted on having their parents on either side of her. She'd arrived in a cab with her boyfriend, Frederic, only a few minutes earlier and already Alina was wishing she could escape to her room. The last few days with her parents had been blissfully quiet and serene. Sophia's entrance had shattered that peaceful existence.

She'd stepped out of the taxi with an air of arrogance and snootiness, sounding the way you spoke to an acquaintance and not your closest family. Alina had already felt the sting of her sister's barbed words and new-found superior attitude.

Frederic had seemed nice enough. He'd been polite if not overly friendly, and apologized for not letting their parents know he was joining Sophia for a few days. Sophia had clung to his arm possessively and with a triumphant gleam in her eyes.

While they waited for dinner time, they gathered on the lounge chairs on the back deck. Sophia and their mom chatting animatedly — or rather, Sophia using grand gestures and dramatic pauses while she spoke about her adventures in Paris, dropping French words and expressions into her monologue. Frederic sat mostly quiet, interjecting a word here and there, but not taking an active part in the conversation. Alina got the impression he was bored and would rather be anywhere but here.

She studied him for a minute. He was slim, medium height, with reddish hair and pale, freckled skin. His chin was weak and his eyes too far apart to call him handsome, but as long as Sophia loved him, it was all that mattered. The clothes he wore looked expensive, and Alina had glimpsed the logo of a famous fashion house on his sports jacket. She knew of his family. Frederic's father had made his money in the advertising business, and they were among Chicago's wealthy elite.

Alina dropped her head back on the cushion, raising her eyes from the tree-line with the glitter of the lake beyond. The vaulted sky was cerulean. The sun's rays playing with the leaves on the trees, creating a dappled pattern on the wooden boards of the terrace. She closed her eyes and listened to the excited prattle, nearly dozing off when a high-pitched squeak pierced her ears. One word sounded louder than all the others, sending stabs of pain and sorrow through her heart.

Engaged. Sophia is engaged.

She squeezed her eyes shut, focusing on her breathing.

In. Out. In. Out.

I can do this. I can be happy for my sister. She's engaged and in love. I'm happy for her. So happy. Definitely happy.

Sophia waggled the fingers on her left hand, the diamond ring sparkling in the afternoon sunshine. "Aren't you gonna say something, Ali? Won't you congratulate me? You must see my ring. It's so gorgeous. Three carats set in platinum. Yours was one carat in white gold, wasn't it? I suppose Frederic has a little more money than Jonas has. Had." She put her hand over her mouth, rolling her eyes. "I mean had. So sorry. It was a slip of the tongue. Freddie comes from old money, and there are certain expectations on things like engagement rings." *Ali?* Since when had Sophia ever called her Ali? She'd always been Alina or Lina to everyone, except for Jonas, who'd called her Li. And when did her sister turn into such a mean girl? It didn't matter how many diamonds you had. It was a symbol of love and commitment. Why was Sophia deliberately trying to upset her? Hadn't she suffered enough?

"I'm going to be Mrs. Frederic Howland," Sophia continued, "and will need to look the part. Isn't that right, Freddie?"

"Yes, of course. You'll be the talk of the town soon, I'm sure," Frederic replied, looking uncomfortable with Sophia's outpouring of glee.

Sophia stared at Alina, an eyebrow raised and her lips in a thin line.

"Well? Aren't you happy for us?" she asked.

"Of course, congratulations. I'm thrilled for you." Alina rose, smiled stiffly at her sister and her new fiancé and gave her mom a quick kiss on the cheek. "Mom, will you excuse me? I have some stuff to organize with the house sale."

A whispered 'sorry' in her ear from her mom told her she wasn't alone in thinking Sophia was being insensitive, which in itself was a vast understatement.

With a sigh of relief, she closed the door to her bedroom behind her, her shoulders sagging. Curling up on the bed, she pulled out one of Jonas' shirts and two soft toys — one pink and one blue — from under her pillow and crushed them to her chest. Tears spilled freely down her cheeks. She swiped angrily at them, but then her dad's words echoed in her ears to remind her she could feel however she felt.

Alina gave in to the rush of emotions and sobbed into her pillow, making sure she did it silently, or her sister would probably hear and have a snide remark at the ready. What Sophia had said was cruel and uncalled for. What had she done to deserve that? They hadn't been close in years — if ever — but she'd always put it down to her being a few years older and then living in California and Sophia in France. Sophia had only been back twice in the last three years and each time, Alina had been unable to travel to Chicago to see her. Once was because of work, and the other time she was heavily pregnant with Daisy.

Dark thoughts rolled around in her mind, churning and grinding against each other like rocks in a landslide. Everything was in turmoil, and the relative calm she'd achieved in the last six weeks had gone in an instant. Grief and loss tore at her heart, and the black hole in her chest ripped open where she'd so carefully tacked it together with sticky tape and determination.

By the time she fell into an exhausted sleep, it was dark outside, and a wind had picked up, making the branches of the tree by her window tap and rustle against the glass.

Nine

KIRAN, 1965

Mindlessly stirring what passed for coffee in the doctor's lounge, Kiran stared unseeingly at the wall behind the counter with its cracked plaster and stains of unknown origin. He was beyond tired, taking on every shift the department would give him. Anything to avoid going back to the house he'd shared with Juliet. She'd been gone two months, and he just couldn't get used to the emptiness her passing had left him with.

A radio on the small table suddenly squawked, and a news bulletin interrupted the music program that had been playing. The war in Vietnam raged on, and the president had been increasing the number of American soldiers in Southeast Asia ever since the first ground troops had deployed in March.

Kiran abhorred war. He'd seen so much fighting during his time, in all its various, horrifying forms. There was no such thing as a good war. They were all appalling. Innocent people were hurt, lives were lost by the thousands — if not millions — and for what? A few square miles of extra land? More power over people who never wanted you in the first place? In his opinion, war was the purest form of idiocy.

He glanced at his watch, realizing his break was over and that he had to get back to work. He'd finished a night shift in the ER, slept for a few hours in the on-call surgeon's bed, and then started his afternoon shift in the Trauma department. He wasn't scheduled for surgery today, just assessments and follow-ups, for which he was grateful. Operating on a patient in the state he was in would have been ill-advised and dangerous.

What he really needed was a few days off to recharge and rest, but that would mean going home, the thought of which made him sick to his stomach. Maybe he could book a weekend away somewhere. Las Vegas, Reno, anywhere with plenty of people and lots of noise. Silence was his enemy, and he avoided it as much as he could.

"Earth to Kiran? Are you all right, buddy?"

The voice from behind jerked him out of his dark thoughts.

"Huh? Yeah, sure. I'm fine." Kiran tried to smile reassuringly at Andrew, but the man was much too perceptive to be deceived by a bright voice and a fake smile. "Just a little lost in my own head. You know how it is."

Andrew rolled his eyes but chuckled and squeezed Kiran's shoulder to show he was kidding.

"Of course you're fine, because God knows the most excellent Dr. Mitchell wouldn't be anything else, right?"

"You know me too well." Kiran's smile was brittle, but he stuck it firmly on his face, nonetheless. "But I promise I'm okay. I'm tired after a long shift, but I'll go… home… tonight and sleep for twenty-four hours."

Andrew pursed his lips. "Still can't bear to be in that house? Can't say that I blame you. Maybe it's time to look for something else?" he said. "So you don't have to live with the constant reminders of Juliet. You have your memories. You don't need the visuals as well."

Kiran dropped his gaze to the floor. The truth was, he'd considered moving, but it felt as if he'd be betraying Juliet's memory. All her things were exactly as she'd left them, even her toothbrush next to his in the bathroom.

He could no longer sleep in their bed, or even enter their bedroom for fear of disturbing her belongings. He could still hear her sweet voice, smell her scent, and feel her presence in every room. The guest bedroom had become his sanctuary for the few hours he did spend in the house.

The guest room didn't contain any of her things or any special memories of her, so it was a safe place for him to be.

The strange thing was that he still couldn't say if he'd ever actually loved her. He didn't even know what love was, but he knew he missed her terribly, and there was a hole in his chest where her warmth and comfort had found a home. Yet when he'd watched a movie with a romantic plot or read a book with a similar theme, he hadn't recognized the overwhelming feelings the characters seemed to experience. Maybe it was exaggerated for the storyline, but he didn't think so.

All his married friends talked about how much they loved their spouses and how they felt when they first met. It was all butterflies in the stomach, sweaty palms, and racing hearts, but he'd felt none of that. They'd enjoyed each other's company, found happiness and mutual respect with each other, and that had been enough for them.

"Listen, Kiran," Andrew began. "Why don't you come over to our house tomorrow for dinner? Maryan would love to see you, and we could just relax, maybe have a brandy in the library after we've eaten. You could even stay the night in the guest room if you wanted. To be honest" — he grasped Kiran's shoulder, squeezing gently — "you look terrible, my friend."

"Jeez. Thanks, pal. I knew I could count on you to be my biggest supporter." Kiran laughed. "But I hear you. I know I haven't been taking care of myself much lately, and I need to get straightened out." He dragged a hand through his hair, only succeeding in making it look even more mussed. "Thanks for the offer, but I think I need a little more time before I try to be sociable. Thank Maryan for me and tell her I'll take you up on the offer soon."

"Sure thing. It's an open invitation." Andrew patted him on the back. "Come over whenever you feel like it, all right?" He walked out of the lounge, leaving Kiran with his thoughts.

It was a kind gesture from Andrew, but Kiran couldn't force himself be around people unless he was at work. He was still angry, and there was a real risk he'd open the lid to Pandora's box and spill all his secrets. It would probably mean the end of their friendship, and Andrew would have him measured for a straitjacket within minutes.

How could he ever explain his existence without sounding like a lunatic? It was impossible, and he couldn't take the risk. No, he needed to stay away from any heart-to-hearts for the foreseeable future. He was an anomaly and didn't belong in this world, yet here he was, wishing every day that he wasn't.

The things he'd seen and lived through would have broken a normal man halfway through the first lifetime. For him, there was no choice. He was shoved back into a new world every time he was ripped from the previous one. Even though the shifts were smooth and usually barely noticeable physically, they were still mentally jarring and disorienting.

Since he had no way of preventing them, he could only try to make the best of each life he lived. This one had gone on too long, but he'd finally learned his lesson. No more close friendships, no more attachments, and absolutely no more relationships. It was just too hard, too heartbreaking, too devastating.

After another glance at his watch, he sighed and poured the rest of his now-cold coffee into the sink. Before leaving, he washed the mug and placed it back in the cupboard. He liked things neat and tidy and wouldn't leave his dirty dishes for someone else to clear up.

On leaden legs, he returned to his post in Trauma for an afternoon of assessing patients for surgery and following up on post-operative care. At least he had a chair and a desk where he could do the paperwork, but for the majority of the next ten hours, he'd be on his feet, moving from room to room in an endless cycle.

By the time he was forced to go home by both Andrew and his department chief, his feet were numb, and his brain had decided to shut down. He'd tried to protest, saying he could nap for a few hours and then cover triage in the ER where they expected to be short-staffed for the first few hours of the early morning shift, which also happened to be one of the busiest times of the day there. They refused to let him stay and sent him home despite his protests.

HE PULLED into the driveway and sat motionless for several minutes, staring at the little house that had once been so warm and welcoming.

Now it was dark, silent, and forbidding. Steeling himself, he stepped out of the car, staggered to the front door, and reluctantly let himself in. Without turning on any lights, he headed straight for the guest room, passing his and Juliet's bedroom without sparing it a glance, and closed the door behind him.

Toeing off his shoes and pulling off his clothes as he went, he left them in a trail on the floor. Then he stumbled into the bathroom to wash and brush his teeth. His head spun, nausea curled in his stomach, and his movements were shaky and uncoordinated as if he'd spent a weekend drinking heavily. Rushing to finish his bedtime routine, he pulled on his pajamas and slumped onto the bed, barely able to pull the comforter over him before he fell asleep.

Kiran propped himself up on one arm as he slid his fingers gently across her skin, whispering sweetly in her ear, and lightly brushing a kiss over her lips. She let out a quiet moan, urging him to explore more of her heated skin. With the pads of his fingers, he traced a path along her jaw, down the sensitive skin of her neck and along her collarbone, planting gentle kisses in their wake.

Lowering his head farther, he nuzzled the soft swell of her breast, grazing his teeth against the tender skin underneath before swirling his tongue against it to soothe the sting. He smiled when her fingers threaded through his hair, gripping it tightly as he took a taut nipple into his mouth and sucked hard, nipping it with his teeth. The whine escaping her mouth when he pulled off with a soft pop stoked his desires, and he raised his head, gazing at her while a fire burned in his loins.

Pressing his painfully hard shaft against her hip, he caught both her hands in his and trapped them above her head before returning to her tantalizing mounds with their rosy buds, ringed by dusky skin. She arched her back, the motion pressing her soft curves against his shaft, sending jolts of electricity down his spine. He couldn't hold back a growl of lust, which seemed to spur her on.

She pulled her hands from his grip, and he reluctantly let them go. Her fingers threaded through his hair, nails scratching against his scalp, making him hum with pleasure and need.

To hold himself back, he returned his attention to her breasts, sucking each nipple in turn and grazing the sensitive skin with his teeth.

Then he switched position to hold himself above her, exploring her arms down to her hands, giving each fingertip a gentle suck, sending his imagination to places he'd love her to put her mouth on, but that was for another time. He moved across to the other arm, sweeping his lips over her chest as he went, placing wet kisses wherever he could, and then worked his way up from her fingers to her slender neck. Her gasps and moans were like music to his ears, making him smile with his mouth still against her tender flesh.

A thin glimmer of light lit the air around him and the woman by his side. She was familiar, yet also not. Something about her was different from what he'd expected, but not enough to make him stop. He recognized the shape, scent, taste, and touch. It was all etched into his memories as if they'd always been there. This was his love, his joy, and his comfort. The first woman he'd been with in centuries, and the only woman he'd taken into his life. How could it be anyone else?

As he explored every inch of her skin, leaving a small mark behind her ear, he licked, nibbled, and kissed his way down her body, worshiping her like a goddess. He wedged himself between her slender thighs, so the treasure he'd been seeking lay bare in front of him. After feasting his eyes on her slick sex, he placed a gentle kiss right above where the folds met and lowered his head to flick his tongue against—

KIRAN SCRAMBLED TO SIT UPRIGHT. His shoulders heaved as if he'd run a marathon, his pulse a roaring thunder in his ears. What had just happened? Where was he? Behind his ribs, his heart beat crazily in a staccato rhythm. Was he having a panic attack? Or a heart attack? Surely not. He was a doctor and would know the difference.

Surrounded by velvety darkness, he stared with wide eyes at the shape next to him. The woman was barely discernible, but her gentle curves and shiny tresses glimmered in a strange, pale light.

His rock-hard erection throbbed and pulsed, and without thinking, he gripped it in one hand while the other cupped his sac. As he pumped up and down, the images came roaring back and with them, the taste of her skin, her lips, her sex.

With a muted shout, Kiran came so hard red and white spots erupted in his vision. Spurt after spurt of thick, creamy liquid splashed onto his chest and stomach, creating a sticky mess. His climax seemed to go on forever, but when it finally waned, his head fell back against the headboard. He closed his eyes for a few seconds before prying them open and once again seeing the beautiful woman lying next to him. He was sure she had a contented smile on her face. It was the smile of a woman sexually pleasured and satisfied.

Juliet.

He squeezed his eyes shut, savoring the moment. It had to be her, but he'd never had this kind of experience with his wife. It had always been wonderful, but much more restrained. He looked at the pillows next to his, but she was gone. It was as if she'd never been there in the first place.

A dream.

It was just a dream.

He grabbed a few tissues from the box by his bed, wiping away the mess he'd made, feeling disgusted with himself for having so little self-control. He shook his head to dispel the last of the visions and impressions of the woman from his mind. It had felt so real, so familiar, so... exquisitely sensual.

Without warning, a wave of despair washed over him. The grief of losing Juliet mixed with something else. No longer able to feel the touch of the woman in the dream made him feel bereft and even lonelier than before. Sorrow and despair filled his chest, tearing at his heart, and bleeding his soul dry. The agony left him gasping for breath, and he curled up in a ball with his arms wrapped around his stomach as if trying to hold himself together.

Across his back, the old pain returned in full force after having been absent for nearly ten years. The searing ache was too much for him to withstand, and a gut-wrenching roar erupted from his throat. He screamed until his lungs burned, and a blessed darkness overwhelmed him, sweeping his consciousness away to another, kinder place.

A SHRILL RINGING jolted Kiran out of his unconscious state. Throwing a hand out to grab the receiver off the phone on his nightstand, he put it to his ear and croaked a gruff hello.

"Kiran, it's Andrew," the voice said. "Are you awake?"

"No, I'm not. What time is it? Please, don't tell me I've overslept." Kiran pushed up on one arm and peered at the alarm clock by his bed.

It showed just after eight, and judging by the light outside, it had to be morning.

"No, you didn't miss anything. I was just calling to tell you we've got a cover for your shift this afternoon. We don't need you until the evening shift starts tomorrow at three."

Rubbing the sleep out of eyes that felt full of grit, he tried to focus and recollect his allotted shifts. "What? I didn't think I was due in today at all. I was supposed to have thirty-six hours off. Did I mess up my schedule?"

"Wow, you sure have lost track of time." Andrew chuckled. "You left the hospital a day and a half ago and were due back this afternoon. Have you slept this whole time? You imitating Sleeping Beauty or something?"

Kiran groaned. "That's impossible. There's no way I could have been asleep for thirty hours."

"Sorry, my friend, but I think that's exactly what happened." Andrew took a moment before continuing, "I'm not surprised. You've been working yourself to the bone and then some." He sighed. "I understand why, but you were about to become a liability, so I'm glad we sent you home for some rest."

"Yeah, I guess so. I'm sorry. I didn't mean to become a burden." Kiran gripped the back of his neck.

Andrew huffed. "Wait. Stop it right there, pal. You're not a burden. You're going through a traumatic time, and we all understand and want to help you as much as we can."

"It's just that..." He swallowed hard. "She's gone, Andrew, and there's nothing I can do about it. She's gone, and I'm left here alone in this house. Not to be too dramatic, but it feels as if the walls are closing in, inch by inch." Kiran fell silent, suddenly worried he'd shared a little too much.

"I'm sorry, buddy. It must have been devastating to lose her like that. Us physicians always think we should be able to save everyone, but when it comes to those we love" — Andrew cleared his throat — "we have this idea that it's somehow our fault they become sick in the first place. I've never told you this, but I had a brother who died from a congenital heart defect. He was only twenty-two. I was doing my residency at the time, and for a long time, I blamed myself for not being able to cure him. On tough days here, I still think that way, even if most of the time, I know there was nothing I could have done. We didn't even know he had this defect."

Kiran nodded, even though Andrew couldn't see him. "I'm so sorry, my friend. And yeah, you know exactly how I feel. I'll get past it eventually, I guess, but for now, I just have to deal with it the best I can."

Kiran said goodbye to his friend and replaced the receiver in its cradle. Slumping back on the pillows, he flung an arm over his eyes, still not quite believing he'd been asleep for a whole day and night. It was crazy, but Andrew wouldn't play that kind of joke on him.

Frustrated, he pushed the covers aside and rose gingerly from the bed, stretching his arms over his head and scratching his jaw. Padding into the bathroom, he showered and shaved before dressing in a shirt and casual pants, then descended the stairs to pick up the newspaper from the porch. Opening the door and finding both yesterday's and today's editions confirmed Andrew's claim he'd slept for nearly two days.

With the refrigerator door open, he stared at its meager contents. A few eggs, an onion, a couple of slices of ham and some wilted green beans. Nothing very exciting, but at least he could make an omelet with it. Making a mental note to go out later and buy some groceries, he set to making some breakfast.

With the coffee percolating, he chopped the onion, sliced the ham, and steamed the beans before whisking the eggs and adding them to a pan. The smells wafting to his nose suddenly made him realize he was ravenous. Having had little to no appetite the last few months, it was an unfamiliar feeling, but welcomed, nonetheless.

Once the omelet was cooked, he slid it onto a plate, filled a mug with the coffee, and settled at the little kitchen table. Eating slowly, he scanned the front page, frowning at the reports coming in from the war. Rumors abounded that President Johnson was about to send thousands more US troops to the battle zone.

Kiran's stomach soured at the thought of how many more soldiers and innocent civilians were about to die. Memories from the last time he'd served as a surgeon during a conflict resurfaced, and a pit opened in his stomach at the same time as an idea formed in his head.

Checking to see the time on the kitchen wall clock, he folded the paper, drank the last mouthful of lukewarm coffee, and took his dishes to the sink to wash. Ten minutes later, he locked the door behind him and headed to the grocery store to fill his refrigerator and pantry. Juliet would have been horrified had she known how bare the cupboards were. She'd always kept them well-stocked and ensured they never ran out of anything.

I'm sorry, my love. I'm not very good at doing this without you, but I promise I'll try harder. I'm—

He swallowed the lump in his throat instead of finishing his thought.

There was no reply. Of course, there was no reply.

He was alone.

Again.

Ten

ALINA, 2011

"I see. Yes, I understand. I'm sorry, too. Well, thank you for letting me know." In a daze, Alina pressed the 'end call' button on her cell, letting it drop to the cushion beside her. Tears prickled behind her eyelids, but this time, she refused to let them fall. The job she'd meant to start the following week was no longer available. The company that had offered her the position of corporate events manager had decided to outsource it to a specialist firm instead and no longer needed her.

It was supposed to have been her new start, her chance at building a different future and becoming a productive member of society again. Now, the opportunity was gone, and she'd have to go job hunting all over again.

She pushed up from the couch where she'd been sitting and ambled through the house. Her parents were out for lunch with friends, and Sophia was... somewhere nearby. Alina didn't know and didn't care. She headed toward the stairs but paused as she passed her father's office. Voices trickled through the door, which was slightly ajar. It was the mention of her name that had made her stop. Sophia was clearly having a conversation with someone on speaker phone.

"You should have seen her face, Sasha." Sophia giggled. "She was so jealous of my beautiful ring. Hers was paltry in comparison. I've been wanting to wipe that smirk off her face for ages. She was so smug about her perfect husband, her perfect kids, and her perfect life. I couldn't stand it. I'm sorry about Jonas and those kids, but in a way, she deserved to know what it feels when your life is flipped upside down."

"What happened? Did he leave her and take the kids away or something?" A tinny voice asked over the speaker.

"No. Didn't I tell you? There was an accident, and Jonas, Theo, and Daisy all died. Alina survived without a scratch, of course, and I think she was the one driving. She was probably drunk or something."

"Oh, my God. That's awful, Sophia," the voice gasped. "Alina must be devastated. Did it happen recently?"

"No, it was more than a year ago. You'd think she'd have gotten over it, but she mopes around the house as if her world has ended," she drawled. "She couldn't even be happy about my engagement, Sasha. How rude and inconsiderate is that?"

Alina stood frozen to the spot, one hand covering her mouth, her heart pounding in her chest. Was this really how her sister felt about her? What had she done for Sophia to be so nasty and spiteful? They'd barely seen each other in the past ten years.

With her pulse roaring in her ears, she wanted to run, but also felt a morbid fascination with the vitriol her sister was spewing.

"Soph, that's not very long when you've lost your husband and children," Sasha admonished. "Don't you have any sympathy for her?"

"You're supposed to be my friend, Sasha, and be on my side!" Sophia's voice turned shrill. "If you want to cry for my sister, then we might as well hang up now."

Sasha quickly backtracked. "No, that's not what I meant. I just thought you'd feel a little more sorry for her, that's all."

"It's all Alina's fault. She was allowed to stay in California, and I had to come here and start a new school, try to make new friends, and have no one to talk to for months." Sophia's voice took on an unpleasant whine. "She was always the popular one and never stood up for me. It was only when she wanted to impress someone that she included me in her friend groups. She was so perfect, with perfect grades and perfect friends, and everyone loved her. I had to live in her shadow, and it was suffocating."

A sound like a fist banging on a table made Alina jump.

Sophia continued her rant, "Now she wants to take the attention away from my engagement as well with her stupid grief and sadness. It happened more than a year ago. Get over it, already! It's my turn to shine and have everyone want to talk to me, to congratulate me, to see how well I've done. I'm just as perfect as she is!" Her voice took on a high-pitched squeal. "Freddie's parents are going to introduce me to their friends at the country club. Alina never had that. I'm more than good enough to fit in with that set, and in any case, Freddie loves me and says everyone at the club will as well. I will finally be more popular and more admired than Alina." Sophia breathed heavily after her monologue, but Sasha stayed quiet on the other end.

Alina had heard enough. She felt nauseous and needed to sit down. On silent feet, she bolted up the stairs to her bedroom and closed the door behind her with a quiet snick. She pressed her hand to her chest, her heart hammering under her palm. To calm herself down, she stepped into the adjoining bathroom and splashed cold water on her face.

She had to get away from here, from Chicago, from Sophia. Her parents would be upset, but she couldn't stay with her sister hating her the way she did. All she'd ever tried to do was be a good sister and a friend to Sophia. It wasn't her fault her dad's company had relocated him. Sophia had still been in Middle School and Alina had been accepted into the University of Southern California and was ready to leave home.

What was she supposed to have done? Change college at the last minute? Everything had already been arranged with a room on campus, who she was sharing with, and what she wanted to study. It had been too late to change it all. Besides, she'd had no idea her sister had been so distraught over the move.

She slumped on the small sofa by the window, her mind swirling with snippets of her sister's conversation, the disappointment about the job failure, and not knowing what to do or where to go next.

As she stared across the wide backyard, it took her a few minutes to let go of the tension, but she finally relaxed. Her eyes lost focus, and she drifted away to memories of happier times.

Alina rubbed her face, leaning back in the high-backed leather chair and stretched her arms over her head. Her shoulders ached after sitting hunched over her laptop for several hours. Scouring the internet for a job was wearing her out. So far, she'd found nothing that seemed even reasonable. She was willing to go anywhere in the country except back to California. Nothing was tying her to Chicago even if her mom wanted her to stay close, and she couldn't wait to get away from her sister.

Sophia had spent most of her time with friends ever since Alina had overheard her conversation with Sasha. Alina had said nothing to her about it but made no attempt to be more than civil. Her mom had asked what was going on, but she'd refused to upset her by revealing Sophia's true feelings.

She looked around her dad's den, smiling at the familiar books and mementos dotted around the room. He was an avid reader and loved the old classics, filling the shelves with copies he found in second-hand bookshops. Alina had inherited his love for reading, and hoped she'd have her own little library at home one day, where she could curl up in a comfortable chair and read to her heart's content.

A knock on the front door brought her out of her reverie, but on hearing her mom's footsteps, she ignored it and returned to the lists of recruitment agencies on the screen.

"Alina?" her mom called out from the entry hall. "Where are you? There's someone here to see you."

Frowning, Alina slowly got to her feet, confused as to who could possibly want to talk to her. She didn't really know anyone in the area, and none of her friends from California had said they'd be taking a trip east. Padding out of the office, she quietly approached the front door where her mom was chatting with someone on the stoop. The voice was deep, male, and vaguely familiar.

"Aaron? What are you doing here?" She stared at the tall, broad-shouldered man, who looked up, smiling at her appearance.

"Hi, Twinkletoes. How are you?" His eyes sparkled with mirth.

"Seriously? Are you ever going to let me forget that?" She laughed and rolled her eyes at the moniker she'd earned in college.

During a drunken night out, she and a friend had danced on top of a table in a bar to the entertainment of Aaron and his buddies, who'd also been there. Ever since, he'd called her Twinkletoes and seemed to have no intention of ever letting it drop. After that night, the two of them had become close friends and spent a lot of time together just hanging out.

Aaron tapped a finger against his lips as if deep in thought. "Let me think. Uhmm. Nope. Not in this lifetime. It's way too much fun watching you squirm and blush. As for what I'm doing here, I heard you were visiting your folks, so I thought I'd stop by and say hello."

"Of course, I'd forgotten you live around here." She smiled apologetically. "I'm sorry. That sounds awful, but I've had a few things on my mind lately."

Her mom smiled and waved Aaron inside. "Aaron, why don't you come in and have a cup of coffee? I was just about to make some. Alina, show him out to the deck, and I'll bring it out for you."

His cologne wafted into Alina's nose as he walked past her, and a warmth settled in her chest. She breathed it in and studied his wide shoulders, tapering to a narrow waist and hips over long, firm legs.

His jeans fit snugly over his a—

She blinked and stopped herself from finishing the thought. What was she doing? Aaron was an old friend, and Jonas had only been gone for a little over a year. She had no business checking out Aaron's anything.

She took a deep breath and straightened her shoulders, releasing a little of the tension, and followed him out into the backyard. He knew where he was going as if he'd been here many times before. Her eyebrows knitted at the thought. She tried to remember if her parents had mentioned Aaron ever visiting them since he'd moved here after grad school.

"Alina? Aren't you going to sit down?" His smooth voice jolted her out of her thoughts.

"Yes. Yes, of course I am." She lowered herself into the chair across from him and glanced at his face from under her lashes.

Feeling a little uncomfortable, she shifted in her seat, waiting for Aaron to speak.

"You're wondering why I'm here, aren't you?" Aaron chuckled quietly as he leaned back, resting an ankle on his knee.

Alina looked at him, pursing her lips. Was she that easy to read?

"Yeah, I suppose. You seem to feel at home here. Have you visited my parents a lot?"

He nodded. "Over the years, yes. It's been a while though, but when I ran into your dad at the hardware store the other day, he mentioned you were home."

"Oh, I see."

"My parents told me about the accident." A deep vertical crease split his brow. "I'm so sorry, Alina. I can't imagine what you must have been through."

"Thanks, Aaron. It's been a rough year" — she shrugged — "and I'm not sure I'm over it yet."

Aaron studied her face for a long moment before responding. "To be honest, I don't think it's something you ever get over. You just learn to live with it."

Alina dipped her head, thankful when he didn't seem to expect a reply. He was right, though. She was learning to live with it, little by little, but the pain would always be there.

LATER THAT EVENING, she mulled over her conversation with Aaron, surprised at how she'd been able to laugh and joke with him. It had felt comfortable and familiar. He'd asked her to join him at a lakeside café the following day, and even though she'd said yes, she was now half-regretting her decision. Her time was better spent continuing her job-hunt than drinking coffee and eating cake. Too late now, though. She'd already agreed and couldn't back out for no good reason. At least it would get her out of the house for a while.

In need of a distraction, she turned on the TV, chose the noisiest, most action-filled film she could find and made herself comfortable on the bed, using the pillows to prop her up. Staring at the screen, she let the sound of warp engines and loud buzzing from lightsabers fill her mind, leaving no room for dark thoughts, regrets, or her sister's catty and vicious remarks.

Toward the end of the movie, she felt her eyelids drooping, and her mouth started aching from yawns wide enough to crack her jaw open. Fighting the tiredness, she soon admitted defeat and clicked the remote control button to switch the TV off.

She slid her feet to the floor, and then padded into the bathroom to brush her teeth and wash before bed. She changed into her pajamas, closed the curtains, and set an alarm on her phone before she curled up under the comforter with Jonas' shirt and her children's favorite cuddly toys in a tight embrace. After only a minute, her eyes closed, and she fell into a deep sleep.

A gentle caress on her arm. A soft whisper in her ear. A tender kiss feathering across her lips.

Her eyes fluttered open as a quiet moan floated past her lips. She wasn't alone. He was here. The way he was supposed to be. She gasped as his fingers caressed her jaw, skimmed down her neck, and across her collarbone. The sensation was exquisite, her skin tingling beneath his touch. She held her breath while he planted kisses where his fingers had just set her senses alight, her skin burning from their touch, and heat pooled in her stomach, rushing south to create an inferno between her legs.

He moved above her, propping himself on one arm. His head bent to tease her nipples, switching from one to the other until they were throbbing. She felt the lust surge through her core as he nipped the tender skin underneath one breast. He licked away the sting, sending more shards of lust to every cell in her body. She grasped his head, threading her fingers through his soft hair, to move his mouth to where she needed it.

A gentle chuckle and a quick shake of his head told her he would do things his way, and all she needed to do was lie back and enjoy. It was impossible. Her body shook and trembled from his assault. No one had ever made her feel this way.

The flat of his tongue licked a wide strip from the underside of one breast. The sensation made her quiver. She'd never realized how sensitive that area was. When his lips closed around her nipple again, she nearly jumped off the bed. A moan left her mouth at the intense feelings erupting in her body when he sucked hard on the tightened bud, swirling his tongue around it and grazing it with his teeth. He pulled off with a wet plop and raised his head, staring down at her with eyes darkened with desire.

The heat from his hardened length against her hip burned her skin. She desperately wanted to touch it, but he caught both of her hands in one of his and trapped them above her head. Instead, she had to make do with arching against his stiff erection and enjoying the stifled moans her actions elicited from him.

She freed her hands from his gentle grip, her nails scratching against his scalp, making shivers run down his body that she felt against her own. He worshiped her breasts, leaving one wanting while the other enjoyed his loving attention. Each tug and nibble sent jolts of electricity down to her core and back up again, as if the two were interlinked. Was it possible to come from just him caressing her nipples? Right now, it certainly felt like it. God, she wanted more.

He lifted over her. His mouth traced a path down the inside of one arm, floated across the top of her chest and then worked its way up the other, kissing each finger in turn, setting her skin ablaze once more. Her breath turned into pants, and she was powerless to stop moans that spilled unhindered from her lips. It was delicious torture, and she didn't ever want it to stop, but she also needed more. Much more.

As she shifted in his arms, she felt his smile against her neck, right behind her ear where it was so incredibly and delightfully sensitive. She drew in a sharp breath when he sucked hard on her skin as if he wanted to mark her as his. It was bound to leave a bruise. There was no need. He was infused into her very cells, and she felt addicted to his touch.

She floated on a cloud of sensations, feeling him all over her as his mouth and tongue licked, tasted, and kissed across her entire body. It was as if he were touching her everywhere at the same time. When he blew gently at her skin, she squirmed from the tickling sensation. The skin on *her stomach alternated between a fiery heat and a cool breeze, sending her every receptor into a renewed frenzy, her muscles contracting and releasing in waves.*

In the velvety darkness of the room, his skin and hair seemed to emit a pale golden glow. For a second, she could have sworn his hair was blond and not dark brown, and his eyes a piercing blue where they should have been green. Then the light faded, and she was back in the comforting blackness. It was just her imagination, fueled by the exquisite pleasure the love of her life was bestowing on her. What else could it have been?

She held her breath when he lowered further, his tongue leaving a wet trail across her mound until he finally reached where she needed him most. He placed a gentle kiss right above where her folds split, his tongue flicking to—

Alina bolted upright in bed. Sweat trickled down her skin, her breath coming in great heaves. The sheets were soaking wet and tangled around her legs, and the blanket had slid to the floor.

Her mind spinning out of control, she swung her head from right to left, checking to see if she was alone. Where was her lover? Her *love*. Heat pulsated between her thighs, and shards of lust sliced through her core like flaming arrows, making her body quiver.

What's happening?

She could still feel his lips on her skin, his tongue licking and sucking, his hands gently caressing and revealing her most sensitive areas. His scent lingered in her nostrils, and his voice soothed her overwrought mind.

Gradually, her heartbeat slowed to a heavy beat, and her head cleared enough for her to realize it had all been a dream. Only it had seemed so real. She'd wanted it to be real. In fact, she was desperate for it. It felt as if her heart had been ripped apart again, and she wasn't sure she could take any more.

A sliver of moonlight eased through the partially drawn curtains, highlighting the edges and corners of the furniture in the room. The soft glow sent an image of a man with hair that shined like gold through her mind. With a gasp, Alina realized she'd seen that man before. That time it had also been in a dream. She'd watched him at a funeral, with his head bowed and a hand on a casket, while Glen Porter sang Return To Me.

She shook her head to dispel the vision. It had to have been Jonas she'd dreamed of. There was no other man in her life, and she doubted there ever would be. At least not someone who would capture her heart the way her husband had done. It was impossible.

She dropped her feet to the soft carpet and tiptoed into the bathroom to splash some cold water on her face. Her body was still heated and glowing embers had taken up residence in her core, ready to be fanned into flames once more. No, she couldn't allow it. If it wasn't Jonas she dreamed about, then she'd rather not dream at all.

Rather than suffering the damp sheets, she wrapped herself in the blanket and curled up on the little sofa by the window. She pulled the drapes slightly apart, leaning her head against the cushions and staring across the backyard. It was still dark, but the moon reflected off the lake's still surface, creating a kaleidoscope of shimmering silver shards.

Unable to resist the tiredness tugging at her eyelids, she let them fall shut and drifted into a light slumber.

Eleven

KIRAN, 1965

Andrew Martin hid his head in his hands. Then he looked up at Kiran, who sat opposite him.

"Are you sure about this? I'd hate to lose you, and with this, there's no guarantee you'll ever be back. Please, don't rush into it." Deep concern swirled in his eyes. "Think it over before you sign up."

"I have thought about it, Andrew. I've thought about it again and again, and I just can't stay here." Kiran grimaced. "Going back to the house is painful, but I can't bear to sell it and live somewhere different. Knowing someone else is in there would just feel like a betrayal of Juliet. I'm stuck. I can't go forward, but going backward isn't an option either. So, tell me. What do I do?"

The devastated look on Andrew's face cut Kiran to the quick. They'd become close friends over the past seventeen years, and Kiran would miss him.

Andrew sighed dejectedly. "I understand, my friend, I really do. That doesn't mean I'm happy about it. I will miss you terribly."

Kiran leaned forward in the chair, his elbows on his knees, and his head low between his shoulders.

"I don't know what to tell you. I just know I'm not living at the moment. I'm existing. Juliet would give me a swift, hard kick if she knew what my life has become." His mouth twisted in a cynical smile. "I've tried to bury myself in my work and look how that turned out. Every morning, I wake up and turn over, expecting her to be there next to me. Nothing has changed. I haven't changed. I can't come to terms with her not being in my life anymore. Despite promising her I would carry on and live life to the fullest, I'm slowly wasting away. I even told her I'd do my best to find someone new to share my life with. Who does that?" He threw up his hands. "We were married for ten years. I can't just leave it behind and pick up with another woman. I don't have it in me."

Andrew regarded him for a brief moment. "I'm so sorry, Kiran. I understand, and I'll support whatever decision you make. I just wish it wasn't a suicide mission." He rested his arms on the desk and leaned forward. "When are you telling Radford? He will be irate. He hates losing great staff, and you've been the best addition to this department since it opened." A mischievous glint lit his eyes. "Can I be a fly on the wall when you tell him?" Andrew chuckled.

Kiran glared at him. Telling his boss was next on his list, but he was putting it off as long as he could. This afternoon was the latest he could delay it.

He knew signing up for a field hospital in Vietnam was a risky, foolhardy, but honorable thing to do, but staying in Los Angeles was even more hazardous to his health. The number of times he'd contemplated ending it all was too numerous to count. Not that it would do him much good since he'd only be thrown back to where he was or catapulted into the next cycle, neither of which was particularly appealing.

This was the end of the road for him in Los Angeles, though. If he ever came back here, there was no telling when or if anyone he knew would still be alive. It was the curse he was living with, and he should have known better than to begin a relationship and even marry. He'd tempted fate, and it brought him to his knees, with Juliet paying the ultimate price for his conceit.

Later that afternoon, Kiran left Dr. Radford's office with a heavy heart. The Chief of Surgery hadn't been pleased to hear Kiran's news, but it was done now, and there was no going back. Tomorrow, he'd hand in his formal resignation and after that, it was only a matter of formalities before the hospital released him from their staff rotations.

Walking back to Trauma, he passed Andrew's office, his steps slowing, and gave him a brief nod as his friend looked up. His expression was one of sadness and despondency, sending a sting of regret to Kiran's chest. Clawing back his earlier determination, he continued down the busy corridor until he reached his own office.

He stopped just inside the door and looked around. Although spacious, it seemed drab and bare, with its white walls and gray carpet. Before he lost Juliet, it had been a place of calm, an oasis, the eye of the storm that was the Trauma department, and he'd relished coming in here for a few minutes of peace and quiet whenever he'd had the chance. The worn wooden desk gleamed from the polish the cleaners had heaped on it, and a couple of bookshelves stood along the walls. Behind the desk, two large filing cabinets nestled in the corner, and a large window overlooking a small grassy area took up almost a whole side.

He sank heavily into his chair, staring at the picture of a smiling Juliet. He'd taken it in Santa Monica on their first wedding anniversary, where they'd gone for lunch and a walk on the beach. They'd been happy and looking forward to spending their lives together. Back then, Juliet had still held hope of them having a child, maybe even two, to complete their little family, but it hadn't been in their future.

He switched his gaze to the second photo. It was encased in an ornate silver frame, the metal gleaming in the light streaming in from the window. Juliet had asked a passerby to take a picture of the two of them on their last trip to Santa Barbara. She'd been relaxed and laughing, enjoying exploring the little town with its Spanish colonial heritage.

Like he'd done too many times before, he thought back and studied the photo, yet again noticing the little signs on her face of what was to come. He'd berated himself every day for not realizing before it was far too late. With great effort, he shoved his deep regrets and self-recriminations to the back of his mind.

He rubbed his eyes, rolled his shoulders, and tried to clear his mind of what had just transpired between him and the Chief. It hadn't been an easy meeting and more than once, Radford had tried to change his mind, but he'd stood firm. In the end, his boss realized there was no use arguing the matter and signed Kiran's request without further discussion.

Sighing, he pulled a stack of medical files toward him. They were all follow-ups on surgical patients who'd undergone treatment in the Trauma department. He had a lot to get through before he was scheduled for a shift in the OR. Grateful for plenty of work to keep his mind from going into the darkness, he opened the first folder and began scanning its content.

STARTLED, Kiran looked up when a rat-tat-tat sounded on his door and one of the nurses came in.

"Dr. Mitchell, you asked me to remind you before you're due in surgery. You have another fifteen minutes before you need to scrub in, but I'm going on a break, so I thought I'd give you the heads up now."

"Thank you, Phoebe. I'll go over there immediately." He rose and followed her part-way through the department until he reached the surgical section. It was out of bounds for anyone without the necessary permissions, so the usual hustle and bustle of the hospital rarely reached inside the white-painted walls of the operating areas.

He pushed through the double doors, striding down another corridor before entering a quiet preparation area. It was where patients due for surgery were moved across from their beds to the operating gurneys and readied for anesthesia.

All was quiet, which meant the orderlies had yet to arrive with the patient. Grabbing a clipboard off a hook on the wall, he read the patient's name and what type of operation she was here for. According to the chart, she'd broken her leg in a car accident and needed pins inserted to stabilize the bones.

Kiran hoped it would be a routine procedure and the woman could eventually regain the full use of her leg, but he wouldn't know for certain until he'd taken a proper look at the x-rays, which would arrive with the patient.

As he stood by the stainless-steel sinks in the sterilizing area, Kiran thoroughly scrubbed his hands and forearms with the special soap they used for this purpose. It smelled strongly of iodine — an odor that was permanently stuck in his nose. Behind him, Andrew entered to scrub in as well, since he was assisting Kiran this afternoon.

The doors to the operating theater whooshed open, and a nurse strode in to help them gown-up to keep everything as sterile as possible. She placed cloth caps on their heads and tied the gowns behind their backs before holding out the latex gloves. Masks covered their faces, nothing but their eyes showing. Nodding to say she was done, Kiran and Andrew entered the OR where the patient was just counting down from ten, falling asleep with the mask on her face before she reached six.

When the anesthesiologist settled on a stool by her side, Kiran caught his first glimpse of the woman whose leg he'd be taking care of. He froze mid-stride.

Juliet.

A cold sweat broke out on his brow. It was his wife lying on the table. Here was his chance to save her, to bring her back, to spend the rest of his life with her the way they'd planned.

She's alive. She's come back to me!

Kiran stared at her, unable to move. His head spun, and everything around him faded into the background. All he saw was Juliet covered with a white sheet, one leg exposed where it had broken in two places.

Voices sounded from far away, but he couldn't hear what they were saying with the thunderous roar in his ear. He focused all his attention on the woman in front of him.

"Kiran? Kiran! Are you all right, Kiran?"

With a whomp, the surgical room slammed back into focus, Andrew's worried voice breaking through Kiran's strange vision. He blinked furiously and shook his head to dispel the disturbing images. Looking back at the patient, he saw the woman bore a strong resemblance to Juliet, but it wasn't her. Of course, it wasn't her. She was gone, and he was still here.

A hand squeezing his elbow got him moving again, and he stepped up to the surgical table.

His chin dipped once. "Yes, I'm fine, Andrew. I just — I'm sorry, something went through my mind, that's all. Shall we get started?"

"If you're sure you're okay, then yes, let's get on with it." Andrew took his position by his side while two nurses stood opposite.

With a scalpel in his hand, Kiran sliced open the skin where the break had occurred on the leg and began the task of fitting the pieces together again, using screws and pins to secure them in place.

An hour and a half later, the patient was wheeled out of the OR and into recovery, where she would stay until they transferred her back to a ward. Kiran and Andrew returned to the scrub room, removing their caps and gowns and placing them in the bins by the door.

Andrew still had several hours left of his shift, but Kiran's had ended. Saying goodbye, he headed out of the hospital toward a different institution where he would completely alter the direction of his life.

It was time.

He needed the change after everything that had happened in the last year.

By the time he returned home, he had a pile of papers to look through, and several appointments to make after he'd worked his last shift at the hospital. That day was only two weeks away. The thought filled him with a great deal of sadness mixed with trepidation about the challenges ahead. Only time would tell if he was strong enough to conquer them.

THE NEXT MORNING, Kiran woke to bright sunshine streaming through his windows. The heavy rains were over for now, and Los Angeles showed off its usual bright and warm demeanor.

After breakfast, he decided to go for a walk. The exercise would do him good and give him time to think about his future. More importantly, it got him out of the house. Stepping onto the front porch, he turned his face to the sky and soaked up the warmth of the sun's rays. It had been much too long since he'd felt sunshine on his face and breathed in the fresh air. Since Juliet's death, it had seemed as if it was something he shouldn't enjoy. Not without her.

He started walking down the street aimlessly, nodding and saying hello to a few neighbors, but he was soon in unfamiliar territory. Head down, he trudged on while his mind turned his thoughts and decisions over and over in his head. Barely aware of where he was going, he crossed street after street, occasionally turning down a different one just because he could.

He'd been wandering around for hours when his stomach reminded him it was long past midday, and he'd only had coffee for breakfast. Looking around for somewhere to eat, he spotted a diner across the street and went inside.

Behind the counter, a woman in her early thirties smiled cheerily at him. Her yellow waitress dress and white apron complemented her dark blonde hair and hazel eyes. A spark of interest lit in them, and her smile grew wider as her gaze raked across his body. He kept his expression friendly but neutral since he had no wish to engage with her more than to place his order and maybe ask for a slice of pie later.

"What can I get you, Sir?"

"Coffee, please. And a menu." He slid into a booth and opened the stiff, tattered card folded lengthways. No longer feeling hungry, he decided to order a burger and fries, nonetheless. Fueling his body with food wasn't optional, even though he'd been treating it that way recently. His clothes hung on him after losing more weight than he could afford, but he'd lost his appetite along with everything else in the past many months, and even if it was slowly returning, it was still very hit and miss.

The waitress sashayed out from behind the counter with a coffeepot in one hand and a pencil and notepad in the other.

"Have you decided what you'd like?" She poured him a cup and then waited with the pencil poised. "Our burgers are delicious, and the pies are the best within a ten-block radius, I promise."

"In that case, I'll have your regular burger with a side of fries, please."

She beamed at him. "Sure, no problem. You won't regret it. Can I tempt you with some pie as well? We have blueberry, cherry, and pecan."

Barely affording her a glance, he handed her the menu. "Maybe later. I'll let you know."

The woman's smile faltered for a second but was soon back, if a little stiff. "Okay, great. I'll put this in for you. Should only take about five minutes. Give me a shout if you want more coffee."

Kiran settled back against the vinyl padding and lifted the cup to his lips. Blowing on the steaming hot liquid, he took a careful sip. It wasn't the best he'd ever had, but certainly not the worst either. It felt strange to be doing something so normal as drinking coffee in a diner. Since Juliet had deteriorated past the stage where she could still go out and live a normal life, he had been nowhere except the hospital and his house.

The waitress — Sally, her name tag said — brought out his burger and after attempting a little flirty small talk, which he declined to engage in, she disappeared back behind the counter to serve customers who'd just walked in.

Once he'd finished his lunch, he wiped his mouth with the paper napkin and pushed the plate away. He'd eaten nearly the entire meal, only leaving a few remaining fries on the side, having been even hungrier than he thought.

The little diner had slowly filled with customers and the sounds of people chatting and laughing, silverware clattering against china plates, and the cook calling out the orders ready for collection. It was comforting and gave him a sense of normalcy.

After a little while, he tuned out the noises around him and stared out the window. His mind returned to the decisions and preparations he had to make in the coming two weeks. Compiling a mental list, he felt a little apprehensive as it grew longer and longer the more things he realized needed sorting out.

A droning sound, like bees in a hive, penetrated his churning thoughts, bringing him back to the little diner. The buzz grew louder by the second, and Kiran realized it was the noise of hundreds of people marching up the street outside. As they grew closer to the diner, shouting and chanting rose above the din of feet stomping along the paved surface.

He quickly established it was an anti-Vietnam protest with not just hundreds of participants, but thousands. In a matter of seconds, the previously empty street filled with people shouting, waving placards, and singing demonstration songs. Many of the young men held their draft cards high in the air, calling out their objections against being sent to a war they believed had nothing to do with them.

Walking alongside the protesters was a veritable wall of police officers, accompanied by more on horseback. They swiftly rebuffed any attempt to move in a direction other than right down the street with firm grips on collars and arms wrenched behind their backs.

Suddenly, a loud crash was followed by a high-pitched scream. Kiran flew up from his seat and craned his neck to see what was going on. In the middle of the street, right next to the diner, a melée involving a mounted police officer and several of the demonstrators was in full swing. As he watched, more officers arrived to break up the fight, but his heart jumped into his throat when he noticed they were using batons to beat back the young men and women. When one woman sank to the ground, dangerously close to the horses' dancing hooves, Kiran sprang into action. Without thinking, he dashed out of the diner to where the woman was lying unmoving in the street. Another protester tried to get to her, but a policeman held him back.

"I'm a doctor, let me help!" he called out, but his words barely carried over the cacophony assaulting his ears.

Another policeman attempted to push him back, but he grabbed hold of his arm and shouted into his ear that he just wanted to help.

"Officer, just let me help her. She's unconscious and about to get trampled by the horses."

"Back away, Sir, or I'll have to arrest you." The uniformed man glared menacingly, but Kiran wouldn't be deterred.

He pointed at the prone woman where one horse pranced nervously, its hooves just avoiding clipping her head.

"She needs help!" he shouted. "I'm a doctor. Please let me get her away from here."

Understanding swept through the officer's eyes, and he nodded, striding past the horses and calling out orders to their riders. Kiran followed in his wake until he could kneel next to the still form. A trickle of blood ran down her cheek from a cut on her brow, but there were no obvious signs of injury.

With the river of protesters flowing on either side of the little group in the middle, Kiran lifted her into his arms and gestured for the police officer to create a passage through the swift-moving stream so he could get her to safety. Behind him, other participants helped some of their comrades get out of the way of what was beginning to resemble a stampede.

Kiran headed straight for the diner and was relieved to see the waitress holding the door open for him. Once inside, he lowered the young woman to the seat in a booth where someone had moved the table out of the way to make more room.

Pushing her hair away from her face, his fingers prodded her cheekbones and around her eyes, but nothing seemed broken. On the back of her head, he found a lump the size of a goose egg, which hopefully explained her unconsciousness.

When the door to the street opened again, the angry roar of the protesters swept inside like a tsunami. Kiran looked up as a voice pleaded for help. Several more injured people had entered the little diner, one bleeding heavily from a gash on the leg, and Kiran paled at the task facing him. He had no supplies, no assistance and no way to properly help these people.

He scanned the people peering down at him until he saw one he recognized.

"It's Sally, right?"

The woman nodded, her face pale and eyes wide with worry.

"Call County General and warn them there will be casualties flooding in any second. Tell them Dr. Mitchell asked you to call."

Sally nodded her head vigorously and raced behind the counter, where a phone hung on the wall. The officer Kiran had spoken to outside made his way through the crowd that had sought refuge inside the diner.

"How is she? Can you help her?" His voice was gruff and authoritarian.

Kiran ignored him and continued his physical exam of her back, arms, and legs. Thankfully, he found nothing else wrong with her.

"Well?" the man grunted.

Kiran's eyes swung his way, his brows forming a v-shape.

"She's unconscious. That's all I can say with no equipment or x-rays."

A commotion outside drew everyone's attention, and the door flew open, slamming into the wall behind it.

"Someone help! He's been stabbed!"

Kiran rushed to help with the man, who staggered in, leaning heavily on two others. He was holding a rolled-up shirt pressed to his stomach, already coloring scarlet. Instructing the bystanders to assist, Kiran got them to push some tables together to lay the man down so he could examine the wound closer.

Wiping a hand across his brow, Kiran got to work, wishing he'd stayed at home that day, but also grateful he was in a position to help. Maybe with his assistance, these injured protesters would go back to their families soon enough.

IT WAS WELL past midnight when Kiran finally left the hospital. What had started as a minor scuffle had soon turned into a mass brawl, with both civilians and police officers injured. When the ambulances arrived at the diner, he'd gone with the last one to continue helping at the hospital. More victims had poured into the emergency department all evening, and every pair of hands was needed.

He exited through the glass doors and stopped out front of the hospital and breathed in deeply, filling his lungs with the cool night air. It had been a frantic afternoon and evening, and all he wanted was to go home and get some sleep.

His legs ached, and his feet felt numb after several hours of standing in the OR, stitching stab wounds, repairing broken limbs, and removing glass and other bits of shrapnel from backs, abdomens, and heads. Two people had died — one of them under his hands on the operating table — and his heart ached for the families that would never see their loved ones again.

It was such a waste of lives. And for what? All they'd wanted was to protest against being sent to fight in a war on the other side of the world in which they had no stake. Kiran tended to agree with them, but he also wanted to believe their government had its reasons for participating in the conflict. It had to serve some higher purpose they, as civilians, knew nothing about. Didn't it?

Twelve

ALINA, 2011

The little bell above the door jingled when Alina pushed it open. She stilled just inside, inhaling the tantalizing smells of freshly ground coffee, baked goods, and sugary treats. Memories of her and Jonas taking Theo here only a few years ago swept through her mind like a song on a soft breeze. She'd been pregnant with Daisy at the time. The morning sickness had passed, and she'd finally been able to stomach the smell of coffee — even if she stuck to the decaffeinated stuff for the baby's sake.

The coffee shop on Main Street was exactly as she remembered it, if a little brighter and cheerier. It still had the polished hardwood floors, matching counter, and glass displays filled with every kind of cake, pastry, and pie one could imagine. The only additions were a fresh coat of paint, some colorful accents in artwork on the walls, and what looked like brand-new tables and chairs in gleaming wood and chrome.

Looking around the room, she spotted Aaron in the corner by a window and waved as he smiled at her. She tugged off her jacket and slid into the chair opposite him. A server appeared to take their order, and Aaron asked for a large black coffee and a piece of cherry pie. Alina wanted a cappuccino, having trouble choosing between a vanilla Danish or an apple strudel to go with it. In the end, the Danish won, and the server scooted back behind the counter to fill their order.

"You came." Aaron smiled again, making a dimple appear on his cheek, his eyes crinkling at the corners.

"Of course. Did you think I wouldn't?" She looked at him, her brows drawing together slightly.

"When I saw you the other day, I could see the hesitation in your eyes. You were questioning my motives for dropping by. I promise you, I'm only here as a friend."

"Am I that easy to read?" She let out an embarrassed chuckle.

"Only because I've known you for so long. We're friends, nothing more. Good friends, I hope."

Alina studied his face for several seconds, then nodded. "Yes, of course we are. Even if you do call me Twinkletoes."

"Aw, come on. You know it had to be after that little performance on the table." Aaron laughed at her mock scowl.

"Whatever." She waved a hand. "So, tell me everything you've been up to since I last saw you. How long has it been?"

"Probably around six years, I think."

"That long? Really?"

Aaron nodded, taking a long sip of his coffee.

Alina picked at her Danish, breaking off soft flakes covered in sweet, gooey cream cheese.

"Are you... are you seeing anyone?" She cringed at how her voice came out shaky and at a higher pitch than normal.

He hadn't mentioned dating someone, and she didn't like to pry, but she also didn't want some girlfriend or fiancée to get the wrong impression.

"No, not for a while now. I was with someone for several years, but when I wanted to take the next step, she bolted. I haven't seen her since." He shrugged as if it was no big deal. "In hindsight, we weren't right for each other, but I couldn't see it then. I was ready to settle down and maybe start a family, and she wanted to go clubbing every weekend."

"I'm sorry. Sounds like you're better off without her," Alina murmured.

"I think so. I'm taking it easy now, working my way up in the company" — he took a bite of his pie and chewed slowly before swallowing — "and occasionally dating. When I find the right woman, hopefully we'll both be ready for more than overpriced dinners at the latest trending restaurant or chugging tequila slammers at some private club in the city."

Alina nodded. She'd found Jonas soon after leaving college, and they had both known immediately they were perfect for each other. Theo had come along shortly after they got married and Daisy not long after that. Having two children in diapers had been hard, but they'd enjoyed every precious moment of their lives. She understood Aaron's longing to settle down and have a family.

"Are you still with the same company?" she asked.

"Yep, I'm now VP of Sales and hope to get my own department soon. My boss will retire in the next year, and unless I do something stupid" — a wry smile tugged at his lips — "they should appoint me as his successor. When do you start your new job? Is it downtown or closer to here?"

Alina's shoulders dropped. She knew he'd ask eventually, but she wasn't sure she was ready to talk about it. The disappointment stung, and on the job front, she felt like she was being swept along a raging river with no land in sight.

Aaron leaned forward with concern on his face, placing his hand on hers and squeezing gently.

"What happened?" he asked.

"They called yesterday to say they were outsourcing the events and conference jobs to some company instead of keeping it in-house." One shoulder lifted in a small shrug. "I'm back at square one and don't know what to do. I spent all of yesterday evening and this morning scouring the job ads, but no one is hiring in my sector at the moment."

Aaron blinked. "I'm sorry. That's awful news. So you do corporate seminars, meetings, that kind of stuff?"

"Yes, but I can put together pretty much any kind of event. Back in LA, we did fancy weddings, birthdays, company team building events, and all other types of large meetings. We even helped with some of the trade shows in the area."

"That's pretty impressive." Aaron fell quiet, staring into space for a moment.

Alina said nothing. She wasn't sure her voice would hold, and the last thing she wanted was to break down in front of her friend.

"What else is going on in that head of yours? I can tell there's more." Aaron interrupted her glum thoughts.

"Oh, nothing, really. I'm fine—" She stopped when Aaron pinned her with one of his 'don't give me that crap' looks that he'd perfected during their years at college.

She sighed. There was no use trying to hide anything from this man. He was much too perceptive.

"Fine. If you must know, my sister is being a bitch, and I don't know why she suddenly has a problem with me. And by problem I mean she hates me." She glanced defiantly at Aaron, hoping he'd back off and be satisfied with her answer.

He cocked an eyebrow and leaned back in his chair, arms folded over his chest.

She sighed again, even deeper this time, and gave him the whole ugly truth. When she'd finished, Aaron stared openmouthed at her.

"And you haven't confronted her?" His brows knitted. "You can't let her get away with it."

"I will try to talk to her. She doesn't know I overheard her conversation with Sasha, though, so she'll probably have a hissy fit over that first." Alina rubbed her eyes tiredly. "Maybe it's best to leave it be. If that's how she feels, then nothing I say will change it. In fact, I'll probably make things worse."

"It's up to you, I guess." He pursed his lips. "But she's completely out of line and needs to be told."

Alina nodded. She knew he was right. Sophia would only get worse if she didn't say something. She just didn't have the energy to deal with her little sister's tantrums on top of everything else.

LATER THAT EVENING, Alina had just taken a long, hot bubble bath and was brushing her thick hair after blow-drying it when her phone chimed with an incoming message. Glancing over at the nightstand where she'd left it on charge, she decided to ignore it.

Her head felt heavy and tired after a long dinner, listening to Sophia and her wedding plans. Her parents had tried to curb the flood of excited chatter to spare Alina the hurt, but there was no stopping her sister once she got going.

Alina had stayed quiet throughout, only nodding occasionally to avoid an angry outburst and accusations of not being supportive enough. As soon as she'd gotten the chance, she'd disappeared to her bedroom to rest her tortured ears.

Again, her cell chimed, but she refused to check the text. She didn't feel like talking to anyone, not even through text messages. Padding over to the dresser, she pulled out a pair of pajama bottoms and a t-shirt to be comfortable in. It wasn't late enough to sleep yet, but she wanted to curl up on the bed and read a book she'd just downloaded on her tablet. It was the latest release from her favorite author, and she couldn't wait to get lost in the pages.

Once more, she was interrupted by her cell making a noise. This time, it was someone calling her, and she blew out an irritated huff. Grabbing the phone from the nightstand, she swiped the screen to answer.

"Yes?" she growled, annoyed with whoever was interrupting her evening.

"Alina?" Aaron's voice rumbled across the line. "I'm sorry if I'm disturbing you. I tried texting, but you didn't reply, and this can't wait."

"Sorry, Aaron." She swiped a hand across her forehead. "I thought it was some telemarketer or something. What's up?"

"I have some good news for you," he replied. "At least, I think they're good, but you might not be so happy with me. Please, don't think I'm interfering. I saw a chance to help you and do a favor for a friend of mine at the same time."

"Are you gonna tell me what you've done so I know whether to be upset with you?" Alina couldn't help the small giggle slipping past her lips.

Aaron sounded apologetic, but also as gleeful as a kid at Christmas.

"A buddy of mine owns an event and conference planning business. He told me the other day his chief event planner had suddenly been forced to quit after being diagnosed with some kind of chronic illness. After our chat today, I called him and asked if he was still looking for someone for the position, which he was, and if you're okay with it, he'll call you tomorrow morning for an interview." The words tumbled out of his mouth as if he were worried she'd stop him from talking.

"Are you serious? Oh my God, Aaron! That's incredibly kind of you!" Alina squealed with excitement. "Of course, it's okay for him to call me."

"That's great. Phew, I was a little worried you'd resent me for interfering. There is a catch, though." Aaron paused. "They operate out of New York City."

Alina heard him draw in a breath and hold it.

"New York? That's fine." Her voice squeaked a little. "I have nothing holding me here in Chicago, and my parents are used to me living far away. Now that Sophia is back, they'll have her and her fiancé for company, and it gives me an excuse not to be here. You're such a lifesaver!"

"Whoa, hold on." Aaron laughed. "You haven't gotten the job yet, although I talked you up a little, and I know my friend will hire you on the spot."

After giving Alina as much detail about his friend, the company, and the job as he could, Aaron hung up, and Alina slumped back against the pillows. Clutching the phone to her chest, a huge smile broke out on her face. Her body zinged with exhilaration. This could be the answer she'd been looking for.

Maybe losing out on the job here in Chicago had been a blessing in disguise. She'd never have gotten this opportunity if she hadn't told Aaron about the job.

Wait, I haven't gotten the job yet.

She hadn't even had the interview. This was not the time to get ahead of herself and risk another huge disappointment if she didn't get it.

No matter what Aaron had said about his friend, if she didn't come across as someone he could work with, or they had no rapport, the whole thing would fall flat, and she'd be back to scouring the internet listings for job openings.

WAKING UP EARLY, Alina was ready when the call came in from New York. Aaron's friend, Stephen De Vries, was friendly, down to earth, yet very professional. After asking Alina to tell him about her qualifications and experience in the business, he'd described his company, what they did, how they operated, what the vacant position entailed, and wondered if that was a set-up she felt she could work with. They talked for nearly an hour, with questions from both sides, finding familiar ground and mutual respect. When they finally cut the connection, Alina bounded down to breakfast, surprising her parents with a huge smile.

The interview had gone even better than she'd hoped, and he had offered her the job on the spot. In less than two weeks, she'd leave Chicago for New York and move into a company-owned apartment around the corner from her new office until she could find a place of her own to rent. They'd even offered a small relocation bonus and help with finding an apartment as soon as she was ready.

Sophia came down not long after, stomping through the kitchen and slamming the cupboard doors after grabbing a mug. She had dark circles under her eyes and wore a scowl that would frighten Lucifer himself.

Alina couldn't help herself and asked sweetly if everything was all right with her and Frederic, receiving a death-stare in reply. Sophia's bedroom was just across the hallway from hers, and she'd overheard a one-sided argument between the lovebirds while she was getting dressed earlier and felt not a small amount of glee that not everything in her sister's paradise was as glorious as she made it out to be.

She slid onto a stool by the center island, watching her mom make pancakes just like she'd done when Alina was little.

"Alina, what are your plans for today?" her mom asked.

She thought for a moment. "I have a couple of phone calls to make this morning, but after that, I should be free. Do you need me for anything?"

Her mom slid a stack of hot, golden-brown pancakes onto her plate. "Yes, I was hoping you'd help me run some errands. My car is in the shop, and your dad needs his for a lunch meeting with friends."

Alina nodded, her mouth full of pancake, blueberries, and maple syrup, childhood memories bouncing through her head as the flavor hit her tastebuds. "Sure, mom. It'll be nice to have some time together. Why don't we grab lunch somewhere while we're at it?"

"That sounds wonderful." Her mom beamed. "I agree. We've had little chance to chat since you got here."

"I can take you, Mom. I have a few things I need to get this morning as well. Wedding stuff, you know." Sophia threw a haughty glance at Alina, which she promptly ignored.

"That's all right, Soph." Her mom patted Sophia's hand. "Alina and I can manage. You get on with your wedding planning, and then you can tell me all about it later tonight. I'm sure I'll have plenty to do once you've got the basics figured out."

"Is Frederic going with you?" Alina asked her sister.

"No, he has a meeting this morning." Sophia's tone was curt.

"That's right. I thought I heard him up and out the door at the crack of dawn Was that him on the phone?"

Her sister didn't reply but glared daggers at her, realizing Alina must have heard their argument. Alina mentally rolled her eyes.

With breakfast finished, Alina filled her mug with more coffee and then went out on the back porch to make a few calls. She sank onto the swing hammock, sipping slowly from the bitter brew. Her dad had left the morning paper on the table, so Alina picked it up and scanned the headlines. It was the usual articles on political brawls, famine in the developing world, and threats to the Amazon rainforest. It was all pretty depressing, and she wanted nothing to spoil her good mood, so she flicked past the headlines to the less sensationalistic news.

A brief article about a teenage girl caught her eye, and she stopped to read it properly. A sixteen-year-old girl who'd been missing for six months had finally contacted her parents and, with the help of the police, returned home. The teenager hadn't wanted to give any interviews, but she had said a guardian angel had helped her see sense. He had injected her with the courage to contact her parents and given her a hot meal and access to a phone.

The girl didn't know who he was since he hadn't told her his name, and all she knew was that he had blond hair and the most beautiful and kindest blue eyes she'd ever seen. She'd never forget him and asked the journalists to mention him so he might know she'd always be grateful for his help and compassion.

As short as the item was, it brought tears to Alina's eyes. At least two parents had had a lucky ending to their ordeal, and a young woman was safely back where she belonged and able to get on with the rest of her life. She'd been fortunate, since there was no telling what could have happened had she met someone other than the stranger with blond hair.

The description of the man made her think of the blond haired man in her dreams. The one in the graveyard and in her bed. Her cheeks heated. That dream still sent conflicting emotions cartwheeling through her chest. She'd felt so much desire, passion, and love in his arms, but guilt overwhelmed her as soon as she woke up. He was also blond, with mesmerizing blue eyes.

It wasn't the same man, of course. How could it possibly be? Hers was a figment of her imagination, and the teenager's savior had been a real flesh and blood human being. Still, she allowed her mind to drift and imagine the possibility of him being out there somewhere.

Shaking herself out of her silly dreams, she picked up her cell and got started on her calls. Thirty minutes later, she'd gotten most of it done and felt prepared to make the move to New York.

Alina had a long chat with Katie, who promised she'd drive over to the storage company to oversee the packing of some of her belongings and make sure she got what she wanted.

ALINA's last week in Chicago flew by, and the closer she got to leaving, the more excited, nervous, and apprehensive she felt. This was a chance she had to take, but it was a huge step and fear of not being up to the task in the cutthroat New York environment was a constant companion. She'd felt safe and like a more balanced version of herself since staying with her parents, but she knew she'd get too comfortable if she didn't forge ahead on her own.

Finding a new, steady, and solid normal was the only way she'd be able to keep living while still holding the family she'd lost close to her heart. For over a year, she'd been surviving. Now it was time to take a step toward living.

On her last night, her mom cooked a wonderful meal for them all — even Sophia and Frederic were there — and Alina invited Aaron as well since he was the one who'd introduced her to Stephen, her new boss.

It didn't take long before Sophia started asking what Aaron's plans for the future were, and if he was considering a move to New York as well. Making little snide remarks and insinuating comments had become her forte recently, and Alina was sick to the back teeth of it all.

"Won't you miss Alina when she goes?" Sophia asked sweetly. "I'd have thought you'd be planning for a little reunion in the Big Apple before Christmas. Seeing as you've become so close recently." Sophia smiled insincerely at Aaron, who frowned, his jaw clamping shut in annoyance.

"Of course, I'll miss her, but we'll still be friends even from a distance, same as we were before," he muttered. "And I've no intention of moving East. I have a job and a house here. Why would I leave?"

"No need to be coy. You looked very cozy at the café the other day." Sophia tittered. "I was a little surprised how quickly Alina seems to have gotten over losing her entire family, but I suppose we all deal with grief in different ways." She waved a hand in the air. "I'm not sure I'd ever be able to start seeing someone else if that had been me, but I guess she and I are very different that way."

Everyone stared at her.

"Sophia! Why would you say something like that? She's your sister!" Frederic hissed at her, loud enough for everyone to hear.

"What? We all know she has a thing for Aaron." Sophia rolled her eyes. "I never thought she and Jonas were right for each other, but after the kids came along, I guess he had no choice but to stay with her."

"That's enough, Sophia!" their father thundered. "What on earth has gotten into you? Why are you deliberately trying to hurt Alina? This has gone far enough. I've put up with your cattiness for too long. It ends here" —his hand slammed down on the table — "and now! Jonas loved your sister and their children more than you could even imagine, and leave poor Aaron out of this. He doesn't deserve to be dragged into your nasty little schemes. They are friends. Period." He pinned Sophia with a hard stare. "And if they were ever to become anything more than that, it's their business, not yours. Concentrate on your own relationship with Frederic, who clearly adores you despite your constant whining about him not paying enough attention to you. He's working hard to support the two of you until you start your new job, so give him some slack and appreciate his efforts." Their father's words sliced through the thick tension around the table.

Sophia's face scrunched, but she clamped her lips together and didn't respond.

Alina had been ready to give her sister a piece of her mind when their dad had stepped in. She was glad she wasn't the only one who'd noticed Sophia's behavior, but she was sorry Aaron and Frederic had both been pulled into the fray.

The dinner conversation resumed, slowly at first, but soon became animated and lively again, with Aaron providing much of the laughter with his recounting of his and Alina's college exploits — much to her embarrassment. Sophia stayed mostly quiet, only talking quietly with Frederic and her mom. She avoided speaking with Alina and their dad altogether.

That night, as Alina curled up in bed under her comforter, she thought about Sophia's outburst and wondered if they could ever mend what was broken between them. She felt sorry for her mom and dad having to see their daughters at odds with each other.

Despite the flutter of butterflies in her stomach, Alina fell into a deep sleep. Her subconscious mind swirled with images of wings, arching bridges, rushing water, and a tall, blond man whispering words she could only just make out.

Just take one small step.

Thirteen

KIRAN, 1966

As November arrived with heavy rainstorms and high winds, Kiran said goodbye to his friends at the hospital and packed the house, getting it ready to be sold. Andrew and Maryan invited him over for a farewell dinner, which was marked by both joy and sadness. The bond Kiran had formed with his friend was stronger than any he'd had before, and it was depressing to think it was highly unlikely they'd ever see each other again.

It was only days after that he took one final look around the house he and Juliet had shared before walking out and locking the door behind him for the very last time. He didn't look back.

Later that week, he sank into the narrow seat on a chartered airplane with several other doctors and a few nurses seated nearby. The rest of the passengers were draftees, enlisted men, and commissioned officers.

Once they left Travis Air Force Base, their first stop was Pearl Harbor, Hawaii. From there, they headed to Johnston Island, then Wake Island. After that, they flew into Andersen Air Force Base on Guam and hopped over to Clark in the Philippines before reaching their final destination — Tinh Nang Hue Air Base in Saigon, Vietnam.

FALLEN UNCHAINED

KIRAN CLIMBED out of the Pan Am 707 with everyone else — almost two hundred of them. The humid heat slapped him in the face like a wet blanket. Within minutes, his shirt was soaked through from sweat, and when they finally stepped inside the large shed being used as a receiving terminal, a collective groan sounded from his fellow passengers as it was even hotter and more humid inside.

After a long wait, they were finally processed and given their assigned duty stations. Kiran was being sent to a base just south of the demilitarized zone. The Air Force had set up a mobile field hospital there, and Kiran, three other doctors, and five nurses who'd flown in with him were tasked with running it.

He collected his papers, nodded to the officer in charge and steeled himself for yet another flight. The plane wouldn't take off for a couple of hours, so he and his new colleagues went in search of something to eat and drink. Behind the metal shed stood a smaller tent with cooking smells emanating from it. Ducking inside, they found rows of makeshift tables and long benches, with men and women occupying about half of them. Apparently, they'd arrived just in time since lunch was being served from behind a long counter.

They each grabbed a meal tray and shuffled forward in the long line until a cook could dish out beans, rice, and a few tinned vegetables. It didn't look very appetizing but tasted surprisingly good. In any case, he'd better get used to it quickly, since it was probably the best meal he'd get for a long while.

As soon as they'd eaten and rested, they were called to board the plane. It was a military transport plane, so the seats were made of canvas webbing, which weren't comfortable for a fly to sit on, but he'd chosen to come out here, so it was no use complaining.

The flight took just over two hours, and by the time they landed, Kiran had had enough of planes and traveling. Getting to Vietnam in the first place took over twenty-four hours with all the stops they had to make to refuel. Apparently, they'd been lucky to go by plane as the military sent most personnel by ship, which took nearly three months to arrive.

It was even hotter and more humid in Son Tai — if that was even possible — and Kiran couldn't wait to get some water to drink. He also needed sleep. With all the stopovers on the way to Saigon, he'd only catnapped along the way.

If his memories from WW2 were anything to go by, sleep would be a rare commodity from now on. He didn't mind. Being busy meant less time to dwell on things, and right now, he couldn't think of anything better than not having any spare time whatsoever. Dwelling would be a thing of the past from now on.

He would focus on his work and forget everything else. Almost everything else. Juliet was not someone he ever wanted to forget, but having lost her was best left in the past. Keeping the two separate was next to impossible, of course, but he'd become pretty good at compartmentalizing.

IN THE YEAR Kiran had spent here, he'd become accustomed to the distant sounds of battle. In the beginning, he'd gone on full alert with every little bang, adrenaline nearly replacing the blood in his body with the amount it was producing, but after a few months, he'd become accustomed to the sounds and knew when he needed to be prepared for casualties.

He'd just finished ten hours of surgery after a battalion had come under attack while defending a nearby hill. Earlier, they'd heard the loud booms of heavy artillery and the drone of enemy aircraft followed by enormous explosions and had immediately gone into readiness. Kiran and his fellow surgeons scrubbed in while the nurses received the injured, triaged to determine who needed what treatment, and sent the most severe cases for surgery.

"Hey, Doc! We have those supplies for you. They're being unloaded now," a young corporal called to him.

"Thank you," Kiran shouted back. "Will you make sure they go into the supply store for me?" Yawning heavily, a grateful wave to the young soldier was as much as he had the energy for.

The operating room had had revolving doors with one injured soldier after another arriving on the table in front of him, and they'd worked through the night. He'd barely had time to finish stitching one patient before they were moved to the side for the next one to take his place. They'd lost some. In fact, they'd lost several patients today alone.

Kiran had seen every type of injury imaginable in the twelve months he'd been here, and today was far from the worst of it. Shrapnel wounds, burns, and head trauma had become as mundane as sprained ankles and dislocated fingers were back in Los Angeles, but having a patient die on the operating table would never become mundane or ordinary. If it did, then Kiran would hang up his stethoscope and look for another profession.

He and his team worked well together, which was a blessing as they were under constant pressure, with skirmishes and battles happening all around them on a daily basis. Son Tai was a strategically placed base, close to the demilitarized zone, which meant they received injured soldiers day and night.

The team worked in shifts to make sure someone was available whenever needed. Luckily, the higher-ups had sent two more doctors and another three nurses, so they were able to get the work done without stretching themselves beyond their limits.

Turning his face to the sun, he closed his eyes, swaying slightly from exhaustion. After an unseasonably cold winter, he was glad to feel the heat of the sun penetrate his core. The hustle and bustle of the base disappeared in a haze of tiredness as he stood there, soaking up the warmth and letting the smells of the operating room evaporate from his skin and clothes. The odors of disinfectant, iodine, and body fluids tended to cling to the insides of his nose, but with spring in the air, they were replaced by fresher, greener scents.

At the sound of an aircraft rumbling down the runway ready to take off, his eyes flew open, following the huge shape as it picked up speed. The transport plane lumbered sedately into the sky, turning southward in a slow bank, and headed away from the base. A few months ago, a smaller cargo plane had crashed shortly after takeoff, killing everyone onboard. Since then, he kept an ear out every time a plane took off, just in case.

He pivoted and headed for the small metal hut he shared with another doctor. As much as he needed food, sleep was a much more demanding master. He'd nearly made it to the door when a voice called out behind him. Kiran groaned, and his shoulders hunched.

Please, don't let it be more injured coming in, he prayed as he turned to see the woman the voice belonged to.

"Kiran, you haven't eaten yet. You can't go to sleep before you've had some breakfast."

It was Susan, one of the nurses, who beckoned him over.

"Thanks, but I'm not hungry." He attempted a smile, but even that was becoming too much.

"Nonsense." She tilted her head to the side. "You won't sleep properly on an empty stomach. Come on, I'll sit with you and keep you awake until you've had at least a few bites. But no more coffee!"

This time Kiran did smile. She knew him too well. Coffee was a lifesaver around these parts. Being so close to the demilitarized zone, fighting was always going on somewhere around them, and the stream of casualties was never-ending.

Taking his first bite of what was supposed to be scrambled eggs, he realized Susan was right. He was ravenous and wouldn't have slept long enough without filling his stomach first. Toast appeared on a plate next to him, and he'd soon devoured everything he'd been given.

Eyeing the coffee, he gave a start when a mug of milky tea was plonked down on the table in front of him. He peered under heavy lids at the culprit, who wouldn't let him have his favorite morning drink. Okay, so it was his favorite drink any time during the day or night, right along with water. Another nurse stared down at him, eyebrow raised in challenge.

"I wasn't going to have any coffee! I promise." He glared at the woman, who was clearly in cahoots with Susan sitting across from him.

"Sure, you weren't, doc. And now you won't. Drink your tea and smile. Nurse's orders." Margaret, a thirty-something woman from

Texas, stared pointedly at the milky liquid in the cup in front of him, a smile tugging at her lips while she attempted to look stern.

Kiran sighed dramatically and took a long sip, making no attempt to hide his distaste for the hot but weak drink. He hated tea, but out here, you drank and ate whatever they gave you. This close to the North, there were few luxuries, and the weekly supply drop was a much-anticipated event because the people on the other end of the chain sometimes sent them a few extras, like bars of chocolate, or fresh fruit.

He drank the last drop of the tea, held it up so both nurses could see and pretend-scowled when they gave him their best you've-been-a-good-patient smiles. Dropping his tray on the pile of other dirty ones to go back into the kitchens, he gave Margaret and Susan a quick peck on the cheek each and left the mess hut.

He rubbed his eyes in the bright sunshine, his legs feeling heavier than ever, and a vicious headache was forming behind his temples. Once in his quarters, he stripped down to his undershirt and boxers, crawled in between the sheets and pulled the scratchy blanket over him. He was asleep within seconds, dreaming of a woman with chestnut hair and soft gray eyes.

IT WAS one of those rare moments Kiran had learned to make the most of. The base was quiet, and the hospital ward was nearly empty. Taking a much loved and well-thumbed book, a canteen of water, and a sandwich with him, he hiked the short trail up a nearby hill with views over the base and the sparkling blue waters of the South China Sea. Behind him, mountains rose, clad in lush green trees and vegetation.

This was as close to the jungle as he'd gotten. Between him and the enemy he knew was hiding amongst the vines and tree trunks only a few miles away stood Camp Pinner filled with fearsome, trigger-happy Marines. So far, every attempt by the Viet Cong to get past them had failed spectacularly.

Making himself as comfortable as possible, he hunkered down

behind a large boulder, leaning his back against it. Through a gap in the tall grass in front of him, he could see the runway and the beach beyond.

Mostly hidden on all sides, he relaxed and opened his book. He'd read it many times before, but Hemingway's The Old Man and the Sea never failed to keep him enthralled. There was something about the elderly man's fight for the fish and for survival that spoke to him.

Juliet had bought the book as a Christmas present over ten years ago, and inside the front cover, she'd written him a brief message.

Just take one small step.

The same words she'd whispered to him on her deathbed when she took her final breath.

It made him treasure the book even more, and he wished he could keep it when he started his next life. It was impossible, though. Each time he was thrown back, all he had were the clothes on his back, a fresh change in his cherished duffel bag he'd somehow been allowed to keep after WW2, some means of identification, keys to somewhere to live, and the memories in his head.

Carefully sweeping his fingers across her neat handwriting, he resolved to buy himself a new copy wherever — whenever — he went next. It wouldn't have her writing in it, but it was better than nothing.

A rustling sound nearby drew his attention, and he sank lower to the ground. Holding his breath, he waited for whoever it was to pass. Most likely, it was a shepherd boy looking for his goats, but he could never be too sure.

"Kiran, what are you doing here?" a voice muttered.

He looked up and saw his friend Henry, one of the doctors he'd flown out with, standing peering down at him.

"Reading. Or at least I was until you came stomping up the hill." He got to his feet and brushed the dust off his pants.

"Why aren't you packing?" Henry asked. "Our flight leaves for Saigon in a couple of hours."

Kiran lifted his head and stared up at the sky while gathering his thoughts. Lowering his gaze, he looked at the man who'd become such a good friend in the year he'd spent in Vietnam.

"I'm not going." Pressing his lips together, he rubbed the back of his head, making his hair stand on end.

"What are you talking about? Are you taking a later flight? I thought our replacements were coming in on the plane we're hopping on to get us out of here?" Henry stared at him, confusion written all over his face. His hazel eyes darkened as realization hit. "You're not going home at all, are you? Dammit, Kiran! You can't stay here! You've done your duty. Now it's time to get back to safety. You'll only get yourself killed if you stay."

Kiran swung his gaze to the sparkling waters beyond. "I signed up for another year. They need experienced doctors here, and I have nothing to go back to."

"Seriously, buddy, this is crazy!" Henry exclaimed. "You can go anywhere, work anywhere, back home. If you have nothing to tie you down, then the entire country is wide open for you. They need doctors in every hospital all over America. They'll be clamoring for you, and you'll have your pick of positions at the best hospitals on either coast and everywhere in between."

With a shake of his head, Kiran murmured, "I'm sorry, Henry. I can't leave. My time here isn't over yet. It's only another year, and then I'll think about what to do next. The new guys coming in can do with someone who knows the ropes. Remember how we scrambled about in the beginning?" He turned to his friend. "I can show them how things work and prepare them for what's about to become their entire existence."

"Are you sure about this?" Henry asked, his brows pulled into a line in consternation.

Kiran nodded solemnly. This would most likely be the last time they ever saw each other. He was happy to see his friend go back home to his life. He had a family, a job waiting for him, and friends who'd be happy to see him. Kiran had none of that, so he might as well stay here where he could make sure more young men could go back to their families, or were sent back for another round of fighting an enemy they could barely see.

Henry's shoulders dropped. "I'm gonna miss you, my friend. I'll leave you my contact details, so when you do get back to the States, look me up, and we can go out for a beer or something."

"Sure, I'll do that." Kiran smiled.

"At least come down and wave us off, will ya?" Henry squeezed Kiran's shoulder. "I know I'm not the only one who'll want to say goodbye."

Kiran promised he would, and then watched Henry make his way back down the hill to the base. A tight feeling in his chest made him breathe in sharply as his friend disappeared out of sight.

AN HOUR LATER, Kiran followed the dusty trail back down the hill. As much as he'd have preferred to stay in his peaceful bolthole, he'd promised he'd see the others off and didn't want to disappoint them.

"Kiran, I hear you're staying?" Margaret called out to him as he passed through the gates into the rear of the compound.

"Sure am. My stupidity knows no bounds, or so I'm told." He turned and smiled at the pretty brunette. She was a bright spark, always happy, and as professional and competent as they came.

"In that case, I'm just as stupid." She laughed. "I signed on for another year a week ago, but I thought everyone else was leaving. I'm kind of glad you're not. A familiar face around here will make it more bearable. And it's one less doctor I have to train to look after themselves." An impish grin pulled at her mouth.

Kiran rolled his eyes but smiled back at her.

Together, they watched as the passenger plane came in for landing and taxied to its parking spot. Crew rolled out the stairs and as soon as they were in position, the doors opened, spilling its contents of young men drafted to fight in a war thousands of miles from their homes. A few women were dotted in among the men — mostly nurses and support personnel.

One by one, their friends came to hug them goodbye before disappearing inside the aircraft. Kiran felt a sting of regret but squared his shoulders and reminded himself there was nothing left for him back home. Margaret held on to his arm, tears running down her cheeks as she waved to the faces looking out the little windows.

They watched while the plane taxied to the end of the runway, the whine of the engines strengthening as the pilot increased the power. After a few seconds, the aircraft rolled forward, slowly at first, then gathering speed as it hurtled down the wide strip of tarmac. The nose tilted up, and it rose gracefully into the air, slowly banking over the sea to head south. Kiran put his arm around Margaret, squeezing gently in friendly support, while sobs wracked her lithe body.

From the opposite direction, a different whine reached their ears, like a mosquito buzzing in their ears. Within seconds, chaos broke out all over the air base when the air raid klaxon blared, and pilots ran for their aircraft, trying to get up into the skies as quickly as they could.

Kiran and Margaret stared in the direction of the noise, holding their breaths in worry, and soon spotted a small plane flying low over the hill behind the base. It buzzed right above their heads as a rat-tat-tat followed in its wake from guns mounted around the airfield. The blood in Kiran's veins turned to ice, and he felt rooted to the ground, unable to move or even take his eyes off the scene unfolding before him. Fear engulfed him, and he knew disaster was about to strike.

The little fighter plane headed right for the passenger craft still doing its turn over the blue ocean, its guns never going silent. Suddenly, a loud boom reached their ears, and the large plane turned into an enormous fireball in the sky. Kiran gasped.

"No! Please, no! Oh, God! Help them!" Margaret cried out, covering her mouth in horror.

Immediately after, the enemy craft turned into a smaller ball of fire as fighter pilots from the base chased after it, shooting it down before it had a chance to escape, but the damage was already done. Large chunks of scorched and still-glowing metal fell to the sea in great big splashes. None bigger than a suitcase.

Kiran stared in disbelief, his mind numb.

They're gone. Every person on that plane is gone. All our friends and colleagues. Gone.

Kiran wanted to scream. Grief and anger spread like a wildfire through his system, lodging somewhere deep in his soul, making it writhe in pain. People who had survived a year of fighting a dirty war had been turned into dust in an instant. They'd survived injuries, broken or torn limbs, dehydration, and being exposed to the heat and humidity of the jungle for days on end, or just being far away from their loved ones in a hostile environment.

He couldn't tear his eyes away. Margaret hid her face against his chest, and he wrapped his arms around her as she sobbed hysterically. Deep inside him, something broke, joining the already broken pieces he'd hidden away for millennia. This time, it felt like he was crumbling from the inside out.

Fourteen

ALINA, 2011

Alina felt the prickle of tears behind her eyelids, waving a last goodbye to her parents before walking through security at O'Hare. It had done her good spending these last few weeks with them, despite her sister's antics. She would miss them, but it was time to take the next step.

Once in the departure hall, she went to a café to have breakfast before spending a little time browsing the shops. After waiting in line for a few minutes, the barista handed her the blueberry muffin and coffee she'd ordered, and she made her way past the throng of customers to an empty table in the far corner. Settling down, she people-watched for a few minutes, slowly sipping the hot liquid, then she picked up her magazine and began flicking through the pages.

An article by a medical journalist caught her eye. It was a biography of a famous oncologist who'd been active in the fifties, sixties, and seventies. It described his devotion to cancer research and attempts at developing a cure. His findings had been the basis of many treatments long after he passed away, and even today, his work was lauded among his peers.

The writer described how the wife of one of Dr. Zimmerman's colleagues had developed stomach cancer, and after exhausting every treatment and medication, there'd been nothing more he could do to help her. The impact of seeing a happy young woman, whose husband was also a doctor, change into a shell of her former self, had hit him hard.

Standing helplessly by and watching someone you know live her last days on earth in agony had changed something in Dr. Zimmerman, and after Juliet Mitchell passed away, he'd switched career from treating patients to trying to find a cure.

His work was interrupted when he signed on for the Vietnam War as a surgeon for two years. Despite his age, the US Army had welcomed him with open arms, and he returned relatively unscathed, picking up where he left off to work a few more years before retiring. He passed away in his sleep at the age of eighty-five.

Alina was engrossed in the story, tears brimming in her eyes over the woman's passing, and she nearly forgot where she was. She loved reading about pioneers in any field, and Dr. Zimmerman had made so many advances with his research that still helped cancer victims today.

As she mulled over the article, she wondered who this Juliet Mitchell was and how her husband had coped with her death, being a doctor who saved lives himself. Did they have any children? Did Dr. Mitchell go on to do something equally amazing?

She couldn't explain it, but the story fascinated her, and she felt a connection to Juliet Mitchell. It was silly. She'd never heard of the woman before, and probably never would again. Millions of people got cancer every day, and many didn't survive. So why did Juliet's fate make her cry? And why did she feel an urge to find out what happened to her husband?

Like an echo from far away, she heard a voice whisper, *"Just take one small step."*

The sharp cry of a child jolted her out of her thoughts, and she looked at her watch. She still had time to check out some shops before boarding her flight. Stuffing the magazine in her carry-on, she slung her purse over her shoulder and meandered along the concourse, perusing the many stores with their colorful displays, but in the back of her mind, the Mitchells' story left a lasting impression.

Before long, her flight to New York was announced, and she made her way to the gate. It was full of passengers by the time she got there, so her hope of having a middle seat free, or better yet, an entire row to herself, quickly diminished.

She crossed her fingers she'd at least get someone nice next to her, or someone really quiet. She had the aisle seat, so having two people wanting to get up and go to the bathroom or just take a wander down the aisle was frustrating. However, she wasn't keen on the window seat either when she flew alone as she always felt a need to get into the aisle as soon as the fasten-seatbelts sign was switched off after landing. It was a touch of claustrophobia talking each time. Strangely, before and during a flight, she had no trouble at all. It was only after they'd landed.

Her seat was at the front of the plane, which avoided the traipse along a cramped aisle full of people finding their seats and trying to stow too-large carry-ons into the overhead lockers.

Once settled and the plane was on its way to New York, she pulled out her laptop, cell, and earbuds to deal with her emails and other paperwork waiting to be finished. She'd inwardly cheered when no one had claimed the middle seat, after all, and the young man by the window had gone to sleep before they'd even left the gate.

After finished on her computer and slipping it back into its case, she put her earbuds in and closed her eyes. The music allowed her to switch off for a while and lose herself in her thoughts.

By the time they neared New York, she felt ready to start the next chapter of her life. She had a new job, a place to stay until she found somewhere more permanent, and a new challenge ahead of her.

Stephen De Vries, her new boss, was sending someone to pick her up from La Guardia despite her assurances she could just take a cab to the condo they were letting her borrow. He had insisted, however, saying it was the least he could do since she was taking the position on such short notice.

She had great hopes for this job. The company was small but growing steadily and had plans to expand in the near future. She'd be working with a team of four, focusing mainly on smaller multi-media and technology seminars and conventions. It was something completely new and different for her, and she was looking forward to it.

The music filled her mind, and she let herself drift off. As her surroundings disappeared, her mind wandered, and she found herself soaring like a bird over an unfamiliar coastline. Lush jungle fringed powdery white beaches, and sparkling blue waters glittered in bright sunshine, and the farther she traveled, the more details she noticed. Planes zooming through the skies, shooting at other planes, violent explosions going off on the ground, and the sound of bullets zinging through the air forced her to descend and float just above the surface of the ocean.

Then the scene changed, and she was suddenly standing in tall grass on a hillside. A man sat nearby with a book in his hand. His hair shined like gold in the bright sunlight, and a melancholy aura surrounded him, dulling the shimmering light that seemed to emanate from within. She could only see him from the side and at a distance, but somehow, she knew his eyes were a startling blue, and his smile so gentle it wrapped around her heart.

It was him. The man from her dreams.

Heat rose from her core, parts of her body tingled, and strange emotions filled her chest. She watched as he opened the book and read something on the inside of the cover, gently brushing his fingers over the words. A deep sense of love and devotion filled her heart, and tears fell from her eyes.

Once more, the scene changed. Again, she flew like an eagle, soaring on air currents above the vast, sapphire waters. On a nearby beach, buildings were scattered on a flat plain, and a small landing strip for planes ran along the edge of the shore. A larger plane was just taking off, and people the size of ants stood watching as the aircraft rose gracefully into the sky.

The plane turned gently, and a bolt of fear stabbed through her heart. Unable to turn away, hovering mid-air, she stared at the gleaming craft rising higher, banking in a slow arc. Suddenly, the plane disappeared in a reddish-gold fireball, the shock wave sending her tumbling. Struggling to right herself, horror, fear, and anguish made her very cells contort and writhe. She screamed. Her throat burned, and her head pounded from the agony and heart-wrenching sorrow she felt from the blond man standing near the beach watching the tragedy unfold.

The sense of loss and pain was so intense, her breath was sucked out of her chest, and she began to fall. Smoke, burning debris, and chunks of metal whizzed past her. With a soundless splash, she broke the surface of the blue ocean, sinking until darkness surrounded her. Her lungs ached from the lack of oxygen. Black spots danced on the edge of her vision, and closing her eyes, she embraced her fate.

Jerking awake, her eyes flew open, and she drew in a gasp of air. In the seats nearby, she saw the other passengers putting away their belongings and fastening their seatbelts. They were about to land in New York.

Her heart thumped in her chest from the strange dream. She must have been asleep for over an hour, as they'd only been in the air for thirty minutes when she drifted off. None of the other travelers gave her funny looks, so maybe she hadn't cried out or thrashed about as she'd done in the dream.

Her stomach was still in knots and her heart filled with despair from what her mind had conjured up, making her hands tremble while she ensured her seat was upright and her tray folded away. Pushing the remnants of the dream out of her head, she forced herself to focus on getting off the plane with all her possessions and finding her way to the arrivals hall where the driver would be waiting for her. She had the weekend to settle in, and on Monday, her new challenge awaited.

2013

WITH A DEEP SIGH OF RELIEF, Alina slipped out to the rear terrace of the large country estate, glad to find it empty. She walked down the steps to the manicured lawn, recessed lighting casting a soft glow over the paths winding through clipped shrubs and tended flowerbeds. A small bench beckoned in the semi-darkness, and she sank onto it, almost moaning with the pleasure of taking the weight off her feet. She reached down and pulled her high heels off, wiggling her toes to get the blood flowing again.

It felt strange being back in Chicago, even if it was only for a few days for her sister's wedding. The city hadn't changed as far as she could tell, although she didn't know it all that well, but she had gone through a huge transformation. Some of the heavy weight of grief had eased off her shoulders, and she felt more in control of her life.

She'd been living and working in New York for two years now and had enjoyed every minute. Her boss, Stephen, was a sweetheart to work for, and he had recently promoted her to Vice President of Event Sales and Marketing. She'd gone from organizing the events on-site to marketing, selling, and planning everything from medium-size seminars to international conventions.

The company had grown from a small operator to a large-scale leader in the business, had recently opened a new office in Atlanta and was about to open several more across the country in the next couple of years. They'd taken on more staff every six months and had to rent an extra floor in the building to accommodate everyone. Luckily, the one below had recently been vacated, and Stephen had jumped at the opportunity to add more space to the company's offices.

Alina loved everything about her job and living in New York. She spent nearly every waking moment in the office, even weekends sometimes, and finally felt she was living again. It had taken her almost a year to feel comfortable in her own skin, but day by day, she'd found her bearings and could enjoy things again. Jonas and the children were never far from her thoughts, but the sharp pain she used to feel whenever she thought of them had turned into a dull ache.

She'd been back to visit her parents several times, and they'd come to see her in New York as well, but she'd rarely ventured into Chicago proper and mostly stayed in Welling at her parents' house. This time was different, however, and she honestly wished she could have spared herself the ordeal the long weekend presented.

Sophia and Frederic had gotten married that afternoon in a lavish affair with a five-course dinner following the ceremony. Sophia had chosen this venue purely because it was lauded as *the place* to hold any social event if you were or wanted to be anyone in Chicago's upper societal circles. Of course, that was where Sophia felt she belonged and now, having married into one of Chicago's most prominent families, she'd reached the heights she'd aspired to for many years.

Most people in and around the city had heard of or knew someone who knew Frederic's parents. They were involved with many charities and other worthy causes as donors, supporters, or organizers and had their names displayed on boards at schools, shelters, and museums everywhere around Chicago. Sophia clearly felt her marriage would now mean her name would also be included when anyone talked about the Howlands.

Alina shook her head but instantly regretted it when the headache that had been brewing between her temples gave off a painful twinge. It had been an exhausting day, and it wasn't over yet. Why Sophia had wanted such a huge wedding was beyond her. Most of the guests barely knew Frederic and had never met Sophia. They were only invited because they were someone, either in the corporate world or in Chicago society, and the main reason for attending was for the chance to be seen on the gossip pages of the local newspapers and women's magazines, and to satisfy their curiosity about the woman who'd just become a part of their social circles.

Alina couldn't think of anything worse than the false smiles, the insincere compliments, the snide, muttered remarks behind a turned back, and the subtle comparisons of wealth being not-so-subtly used for quiet conversations that she'd seen and heard all day.

Everything from the style and wording of the invitations, the designer wedding dress Sophia had worn, the vows she and Frederic had spoken, the temperature of the champagne, the table decorations, the speeches, the extravagant meal, to the choice of music for the first dance, had been discussed, pulled apart, commented on, and chewed over by nearly every single one of the more than three hundred guests that were attending.

Okay, so that might have been an exaggeration, but to Alina, it certainly felt like everyone was overly critical. Fortunately, she didn't think Sophia had noticed the way people were talking. She was too busy enjoying the spotlight and showing off her new diamond-encrusted wedding band.

"Alina, there you are. I was wondering where you'd gone," Aaron called from the terrace above her.

Alina looked up. "I just needed a break from all the festivities. Want to join me?"

"Yes, please." Aaron blew out a breath. "If I have to answer one more question about my financial future, I will deck the nearest person. I swear, I've never met a bunch of people more conceited and arrogant. Who cares how much someone earns or how far up the corporate ladder they're able to climb in the shortest time?"

Alina scooted over on the bench to allow Aaron to sit next to her.

"Ugh. I know what you mean," she replied. "I'm so glad I don't live here. I don't think I could take it with Sophia throwing her new-found wealth in my face all the time."

"She really loves bringing out the claws around you, doesn't she?"

"Yep. Not that I care. She's got some weird jealousy going on when it comes to me, but I refuse to engage. She can live her happy life here, and I'll have mine in New York."

"I'm glad you're enjoying it over there. Stephen is a great guy, and he talks about you constantly." Aaron gave her little nudge with his shoulder, a big smile on his face.

Alina grinned. "He's amazing, and I love working for him. I can't thank you enough for putting us in touch."

"I must admit, I kind of regret telling you about the job with his company."

Her head flew up, her gaze meeting his in the dim light. "Why? You didn't want the job yourself, did you? I'm sorry, I didn't realize you felt that way."

"No, no. Please, I didn't mean it that way." Aaron waved his hands back and forth. "I only meant that I'd have loved having you closer so we could see each other more. We were great friends in college, and I feel we still are."

"Okay. Phew. You had me worried there." Alina shook her head, a wry grin playing on her lips. "You could always move to New York and find a new job there. Then you, me, Stephen, and Carl could have tons of fun together."

"You'd love that, wouldn't you?" Aaron laughed. "Thanks, but I'm happy here. My job is great, and I might have met someone."

"Oh, really? Who is she? How long have you been dating?" Alina turned to face him, a warm glow in her chest at the thought of her friend finding a new love.

Aaron pursed his lips. "I don't want to say too much yet. We've only been on two dates, but her name is Faith, and she works as a nurse at a private clinic in Welling."

"I hope it works out for you, and keep me posted. I want to know everything. Well, almost everything."

"Enough about me, what happened with your invitation for this little shindig? You mentioned something about it arriving really late?"

Rolling her eyes, Alina took a deep breath. "I only received it in the mail three weeks ago. Sophia said it was sent out with everyone else's, but I overheard one of Sophia's friends talk about it at the rehearsal dinner. She didn't want me here at all and hoped that by sending it out late, it would be too short notice for me to get the time off and book flights." She shrugged. "I wasn't bothered one way or the other, but Mom really wanted me to be here."

"I can't believe your own sister would do that," Aaron said, incredulous. "Is that why the seating plans were changed at the last minute as well?"

"What do you mean? What was changed?"

Aaron looked uncomfortable and shifted in his seat. "Well, I came down early this morning and walked through the dining room. The staff were just setting up, and I saw your mom and Sophia arguing over something, and then your mom started to change some of the place cards around. I'd already checked on the board outside who was sitting where and saw you and I were seated next to each other on the table up in the far corner."

"Of course. I should have known." Alina rolled her eyes again. "And was I seated as far away from the main table as possible? With my back to everything?"

A grimace pulled at Aaron's mouth. "Actually, yes, you were facing the far wall... with your back against a pillar."

Alina could only sigh. "So, not only did Sophia not want me to come at all, but when I RSVP'd yes, she decided to give me the worst seat possible."

Aaron nodded. "Doesn't family usually sit as close to the top table as possible? I mean, I've always seen the parents of the bride and groom with the couple, and then siblings, grandparents et cetera on the next nearest table. I thought that was kind of an unwritten rule."

"It usually is, but Sophia has a mind of her own. I honestly don't care. I only came because my parents wanted me here." She huffed a brief laugh. "Total waste of time, but I'll do anything for my mom and dad. The bonus was you being able to come as my plus one. I'm sure Sophia hadn't counted on that one. My guess is that the table she'd originally place me at was for all the single people she had to invite but didn't actually want there."

"Your parents are good people." A smile stole across his features. "I'm very honored to be your plus one. Maybe one day, you can return the favor."

"Of course, but if things go well, you'll have Faith on your arm and won't need me."

"We'll see, but I have a good feeling about her. You'd really like her, I'm sure."

The door on the terrace flew open, and music from the live band streamed out, mixed with the voices and laughter of the guests in the ballroom.

"What are you two doing out here? You were making out, weren't you? I knew it! Always trying to spoil things for me." Sophia leaned over the balustrade, her voice an octave too high. "Come inside right now! You've already missed us cutting the cake, and I won't have you not being inside when I throw the bouquet. All the single girls have to be there. It's my day, and everyone should do what I want. Don't ruin things for me the way you always do." She pivoted, threw her hands in the air, and marched back inside.

Alina looked at Aaron, a giggle bubbling in her chest. He bit his lip, obviously trying to hold back laughter as well. A second later, it burst from his chest, and he threw his head back, laughing uncontrollably. Alina couldn't contain hers either. The situation was so ridiculous. Her sister was annoyed they'd missed her and Frederic cutting their swanky, designer, seven-tier cake that looked like someone had thrown every piece of costume jewelry they could find on it, and insisted she took part in the bouquet toss even though she never wanted Alina at the wedding in the first place. And on top of all that, she thought Alina and

Aaron were making out in the dark like a couple of teenagers. Go figure.

Once they'd stopped laughing, which took a minute or two, they wiped their eyes and headed back inside. No one would be able to say Alina hadn't done her best for her sister.

LETTING the door slam shut behind her, Alina gingerly felt her way down the steps of her front stoop, testing each one with a booted toe before stepping on it. She'd sanded the stoop only the other day, but more snow had fallen and turned into ice since then.

Once she'd made it to the sidewalk without incident, she began her twenty-minute walk to the office. It was only a mile to the building by Bryant Park, and even in bad weather she preferred walking to taking the subway.

She'd even started dating again. A friendship with one of her colleagues had turned into a relationship almost a year ago. It was different from what she'd had with Jonas, not as exciting and passionate. However, she'd figured it was because she was a little older and more world-weary.

Warren had been very patient and understanding when she told him what had happened in California and asked for them to take it slow. Recently, however, he'd become more demanding and self-centered. She wasn't sure what had gotten into him but was worried it had something to do with her promotion. He hadn't said anything, but she had a feeling he'd hoped to get the VP position.

Stephen had told her in confidence that Warren wasn't the right fit for the job and had never been in the running. He was good at what he did, but his leadership skills were lacking, according to her boss. Alina felt a little bad for her boyfriend, but she had no say in who got a promotion and who didn't.

Trudging along the slippery sidewalk, avoiding the puddles of gray, icy sludge, she kept her head down against the biting wind. The sky was leaden, casting the morning in a murky twilight, and the forecast had predicted another heavy snowfall by evening. If she was totally honest, she could do with a Californian winter right about now — maybe even Southern California style.

She pulled her coat tighter around her, redirecting her thoughts to what she needed to get done in the office today and her evening with Warren. He was coming over to her place for dinner and maybe a movie. With the risk of heavy snowfall later, they'd decided to stay in rather than go out to a restaurant like they usually did.

Keeping a brisk pace kept her warm, but she was glad when she turned the corner onto Sixth Avenue, and the tall glass and steel building came into view. She hurried her steps, wanting to get into the warmth as quickly as possible. The wide doors swung open when she neared, and a blast of warm air hit her on entering the marble-clad lobby.

She nodded a greeting to the security guards on duty, swiping her ID card at the turnstiles before pressing the call button for the elevators. Suddenly too hot, she pulled her scarf and gloves off and unbuttoned her coat. Her office was on the forty-eighth floor, with a wonderful view across the park and Midtown South. She could even see the Empire State Building peek up above the adjacent buildings.

"Morning, Alina. You made it okay, then? The streets are pretty treacherous right now," Stephen called out from his office as she walked past.

She stopped in the doorway to say hello.

"Yes, I was fine. If you're careful where you step, it's not so bad." She tucked her gloves in her pockets and the scarf in her bag. "Not sure what it'll be like in the morning, though, if we get as much snow as the forecast predicts."

"If you can't make it, don't worry," Stephen replied. "Just work from home until it's safe. That goes for Warren as well."

"Thanks. We'll see what it's like on Monday." She gave him a quick wave before continuing to her own office.

Several hours later, she finally came up for air after dealing with a cancelation, a change of venue for a national seminar, and a double booking for a large convention center in the city. That one had required getting the managing director of the site involved and insisting they retained their original reservation. It had been on their books for over a year and the other event — booked months after theirs and much smaller — would have to move.

Alina had offered to give them some suggestions for locations and put in a good word, but this close to Christmas, most places had no availability. It wasn't her problem, though, and she was fully focused on their own agreement being honored.

"Hey, Cupcake. Are you ready to go home?" Warren rapped his knuckles on the doorframe to her office.

Alina looked up, resisting an eye roll, and smiled at him, despite disliking the use of the nickname. She especially bristled when he did it at work and had asked him to keep it professional while in the office, but he still hadn't stopped. She'd have to tell him again.

"Yes, I am." She reached for her bag by the side of her desk. "Let me just shut down my computer and grab a couple of files."

A scowl passed over Warren's face. "Do you have to work over the weekend?" he grumbled.

She stopped what she was doing and glanced at him, frowning. "Yes, you know I do. This car tech convention won't run itself."

Warren sighed dramatically. "I was hoping I'd get you all to myself this weekend. Are we still going to my parents' house for lunch on Sunday? They're expecting us."

"Of course we are," she replied. "I wouldn't just pull out of that. It'll be nice to meet them." Alina's heart sank.

She wasn't ready for a meet-and-greet with Warren's country club parents. They lived in North Hills, Long Island, and spent most of their time playing golf or socializing with their friends. She and Warren had promised they'd be there, though, and she didn't want to disappoint him or his parents.

She stuffed her briefcase full of the files and folders she needed to work on, slid in her laptop, and slung her purse over her shoulder. She wouldn't look at anything tonight, and just spend some time going over things tomorrow afternoon.

Warren had ordered a car to take them back to her place, which was completely unnecessary as far as Alina was concerned. She was perfectly happy walking the short distance, even in the cold weather. Christmas was nearly upon them, so everywhere was lit up with fairy lights, decorations, and tinsel-clad trees. It was a beautiful walk back, but clearly, he had other ideas.

She loved this time of year, but this Christmas she wasn't going home to Chicago to see her parents. Warren had booked them a chalet in the Berkshires for the holidays, and she didn't feel as if she could say no. She just wished he'd discussed it with her first. Her parents had been disappointed but understood that it was a long way to go, and that Warren also had a claim on her time now.

The driver dropped them off at her front door, and like he did every time they went to her place, Warren mentioned how he wished she'd rent somewhere different. She liked her little townhouse, though. It wasn't in the best neighborhood, but it was quiet, and her neighbors were friendly. She'd found it shortly after arriving in New York, and even though Stephen had said she could stay in the company apartment, she'd wanted a place of her own.

Warren wanted her to get a place uptown or buy a condo closer to Central Park where he lived. She didn't feel ready for any of it. Uptown was too fancy for her, and she still wasn't sure New York City was where she wanted to put down roots.

Fifteen

KIRAN, 1966

Kiran walked around the base like a zombie. They were gone. All of them. Henry, Susan, and every single one of those who'd boarded that plane were gone. Forever. He and Margaret were the only ones left of their original group. Of course, there were plenty of other staff who'd been here before they arrived, and many who'd come after, but they weren't part of what had made life bearable on the edge of this desolate piece of land.

They were surrounded by the vast open ocean on one side and jungle-clad mountains on the other. No nearby towns, barely any villages, and the enemy hiding in just about any direction. Before the attack, they'd felt invincible on the base with every fighter aircraft imaginable and a Marine Corps company stationed only a few miles away.

It no longer felt secure, and Kiran spent every waking moment expecting another attack. Margaret said little, but he knew she felt the same. They barely spoke at all about it. There was no need. Their feelings were mirror images of each other.

Kiran had lost all sense of direction and justification for his presence here. In the weeks since the plane was shot down, reports from back home of the treatment of returning soldiers had become the main topic of conversation.

He'd always known their presence in Vietnam was hotly contested, but he'd never thought the soldiers who were drafted against their will, and those who answered the call willingly, would be vilified and ostracized on their return. 'Baby-killers', they were called. People stared, said hateful things, and pushed them away and out of sight. All they had done was their duty.

To avoid the endless discussions, Kiran worked every hour he could — they were never short of patients — and stayed in his hut when exhaustion forced him to take a break.

That morning, after yet another night of performing surgeries on soldiers caught in skirmishes with the Viet Cong, he'd stumbled out of the field hospital, exhausted but still high on adrenaline, and feeling as if he were suffocating. He'd been unable to face the windowless walls of his quarters and made his way down to the beach instead.

No longer feeling safe on the hillside where he used to go to read, a small patch on the far end, surrounded by tall grass, had become his new sanctuary. He came here to be alone, to work on shoving his fears, desperation, and anxiety into the far recesses of his mind. Sometimes, he just curled into a ball and closed his eyes while his mind processed the blood, torn flesh, and shattered bones he witnessed daily.

The Viet Cong's attacks on nearby outposts and camps had increased in number and intensity since the downing of the aircraft, which meant many of the injured were sent to them when the smaller field units were either full or unable to cope with the severity of the wounds. He'd lost count of how many patients had crossed his operating table during the night.

When the crushing sensation on his chest eased, and he could breathe easier, he sat up and stared at the gray waters. A thick overcast had settled over them for the last few days, and heavy rain wasn't far away.

With a groan, Kiran pushed up onto his aching feet. In fact, every muscle in his body screamed for ten hours of sleep in a comfortable bed. Something that wasn't going to happen anytime soon. Rubbing his temples to ward off a pounding headache, Kiran steeled himself and headed back to the hospital section of the base.

Dragging his feet, he had to force himself to take step after step, pushing harder the closer he got to the hospital. The weight on his shoulders made him feel like the titan, Atlas, eternally holding up the celestial heavens.

Suddenly, an alarm blared, announcing the arrival of casualties, and four helicopters landed side by side behind the hospital building, with two more right behind. Adrenaline flooded his system, burning through his veins, and making his heart race.

"Dr. Mitchell! Doc! Doc! They need you!" a soldier shouted, waving frantically.

Kiran ran toward the building, urged by the desperation in the man's voice. Flinging the door open, he immediately spotted Margaret giving directions to orderlies and triaging patients on gurneys, that filled the entire space.

"What's going on?" he demanded as he pulled on a gown and gloves.

"An army camp a few miles away came under fire from heavy artillery last night, with many casualties," she replied, interrupting her explanation to give instructions to her nurses. "We're the nearest medical facility since the MASH unit moved farther west. I've sent the most urgent cases to the OR. Dr. Goldman and Dr. Perez are already scrubbing in."

"Right. I'd better go join them then. Will you be all right here?" he asked.

Margaret glanced at him. "Yes, I'm fine. I have two nurses in here, and two others looking after the patients still outside with the orderlies helping them."

Kiran blanched. There had to be at least thirty men on beds and gurneys in the triage area, and more waiting to be brought in. They didn't have enough staff or equipment to handle so many. With only three surgeons currently able to operate — one was in bed with a fever — it would be up to the five nurses to keep everyone alive until they could be treated.

"Get every available person in here to help with transferring the patients who can be moved onto the ward, fetching bandages, gauze, disinfectant, and anything else you need," he ordered. "You and your team need to concentrate on triaging the injured as much as you can, keeping them comfortable, and prepping them for surgery. I assume the OR nurses are ready?"

"Yes, of course," Margaret replied, her hands busy stacking bandages on a trolley. "I'd be in there myself, but as experienced as they are in an operating theater back home and having watched several injured soldiers arrive, they've seen nothing of this magnitude yet." Her shoulders dropped. "They're better off in there with you and the other docs."

Kiran nodded, giving her arm a comforting and encouraging squeeze. Then he made his way through the chaos of the large area and pushed open the doors to the surgical rooms to scrub in. He had a feeling he was in for a long day on top of his already long night. Popping open a cabinet above the sink, he found a bottle of Benzedrine and quickly swallowed one of the little white pills with a mouthful of water. It would help keep him functioning at the level needed for cutting into bodies and stitching them back together again. If he had to, he'd take another later on. It wasn't ideal, but saving the lives of these soldiers was more important right now than getting a few hours' sleep.

KIRAN LOST count of the hours he stood in that operating room with two other surgeons and five nurses — one each to assist them and two floating between the three tables to provide support. Three anesthesiologists also monitored the patients' vitals, making sure they were fast asleep and didn't feel a thing.

The temperature inside the metal shed climbed steadily, with the woefully inadequate ventilation system unable to keep up. As soon as they'd closed the wounds on one patient, he was rolled out and another one brought in. It was unrelenting, brutal, and soul destroying.

After what felt like an eternity, the pace slowed down somewhat, and he found himself waiting for the next wounded soldier to land on his table. Taking a deep breath of the hot, cloying air, the stench of blood, burned flesh, and iodine flooded his nose, burrowing its way into his lungs.

"Goldman. Perez. How are you holding up?" he called out to his colleagues.

Getting grumbles and gruff affirmatives in response, he asked the same of the nurses. The two not assigned to the surgeons nodded and smiled in response.

"Nurse Porter, will you go outside and find out who's next and how triage is getting on?" He jerked his head toward the door. "We need an approximate count of how many more patients we'll have on our tables. And could you please ask for more drinking water to be brought in?" Kiran directed the woman nearest him.

He watched as she scurried out, removing her mask, gloves, and gown in the scrub room before disappearing through the door to the main surgical areas.

While he waited, he assisted Dr. Perez with the amputation of an arm just below the elbow. The war was over for the young man on the operating table. He'd be going back to his family, but his future was looking uncertain. With the way they received Vietnam veterans in America, and the added complication of having lost a limb, this soldier had an uphill battle in front of him. Kiran just hoped he had enough strength, courage, and the love of a family to help him through.

"Dr. Mitchell, they're asking for you outside. We only have two more surgical patients left for Dr. Goldman and Dr. Perez to handle." An orderly pushed through the doors, mask and gown in place, ready to wheel out the young soldier Kiran had just finished working on.

The anesthetist had taken him off the sleeping drugs, so they could bring him to the ward to recover.

"Who's asking for me?" A deep crease formed on Kiran's brow.

He was needed here in the OR, not outside triaging the injured.

"Go, Mitchell. We're fine here. With only two cases left, there's no reason for you to stay. Perez and I can handle them." Dr. Goldman didn't look up from the leg wound caused by shrapnel he was cleaning out.

Kiran realized he was no longer needed and forced his leaden legs to propel him out of the operating theater.

A corporal stood outside the swing doors, waiting for him. "If you'll come with me, sir. The base commander wants to speak with you."

Without waiting for a reply, the corporal headed across the chaotic area outside the hospital unit, dodging vehicles and soldiers like an animal avoiding being trampled in a stampede of even bigger animals. Kiran kept up as best he could, but his legs felt like dead wood, and the last remnants of energy were quickly draining out of him. He needed a shower, three days' worth of sleep, and a decent meal, and not necessarily in that order.

Inside the commander's shed-like structure, several uniformed men with colorful ribbons on their chests stood around a table covered with what looked like topographical maps.

A squat, older man with a handlebar mustache turned to look at him when he approached. "Dr. Mitchell, you're here. Good." The man waved him closer. "We have a situation at a Marine camp that is getting worse by the minute."

Kiran frowned. He didn't think there were any Marines nearby except the ones at Pinner. He wasn't a soldier, nor an expert on warfare, so why they needed him he couldn't fathom, but then again, he was on his last reserves. His brain was on the verge of shutting down now that he was out of the hospital confines, and the Benzedrine was draining out of his bloodstream. It was as if his brain knew he no longer needed to maintain the same level of alertness as he did while around his patients and had given up on keeping any rational thoughts in his head.

"Camp Pinner? Is that where our casualties are coming from?" Kiran's frown deepened. "I didn't see any Marines insignia on their uniforms, but then I've been mostly elbows deep inside their bodies after the uniforms have been removed."

He'd never realized there were that many people at Pinner or how young they were.

"They're not from Pinner. They're all fine up there," the commander replied. "No, this is a different camp, which doesn't exist as far as anyone outside these walls is concerned." He tapped the map with a wooden baton. "All I can tell you is they need help, and they need it yesterday. I have men already on the way, but they can only lend a hand driving the enemy away. The guys out there need more than that, and the situation is getting desperate." The base commander stared hard at Kiran before averting his gaze and inhaling deeply, his fists clenching and unclenching by his sides, the baton close to snapping.

Whatever was going on clearly had the seasoned soldier agitated and frustrated.

"I see. And what do you need me for? Not sure I'd be much use in a firefight," Kiran muttered, shrugging apologetically.

The grizzled veteran smiled kindly despite the severity of the situation and shook his head.

"No, I won't put a rifle in your hands, doc, but they have more casualties than their medics can handle, so we need you to give them a hand. Treat the ones that can be treated, prepare the more seriously wounded for a helicopter ride down here, and keep the others alive long enough for the helo to return to pick them up." The commander leaned on his hands on the table. "So far, they're holding the Viet Cong off, but there's no telling for how long or if those commies will get reinforcements. Think you can handle it?" He fixed his gaze on Kiran, his slate-gray eyes hard and demanding.

Kiran nodded. If there were injured men out there who needed him, he would do his best to help. The obvious danger of the situation didn't even register in his mind.

"Of course, commander," he replied, mentally calculating how much time he needed to pack the essentials and be ready. "I need ten minutes to pack my gear, and I'll be ready to leave."

"Excellent. The corporal will give you a hand with whatever you need and take you to the helicopter when you're ready." The commander straightened and gave him a small smile. "I'll send a nurse with you as well, but please, be as quick as you can. I have men dying out there in that blasted jungle, and I don't want to lose any more than I have to. It's bad enough as it is."

Kiran spun on his heel and strode back to his hut as fast as his long legs would carry him. All tiredness had vanished, and he focused on packing a case with as many supplies as he could carry, hoping he didn't forget anything.

Not that it mattered much. They would fly in, drop him off, and after he'd assessed the wounded, they'd fly out again. He might have to wait for them to evacuate everyone before he could return, but as long as he had plenty of bandages, gauze, morphine, and a suturing kit, he should have enough supplies to keep the injured soldiers alive until they reached the hospital.

KIRAN WAS grateful for the headphones covering his ears and blocking the roar of the helicopter's engine. Margaret sat next to him on the hard bench, her mouth in a tight line, and her hands white-knuckling the edge of the seat. He didn't blame her. The door on either side was open, with a soldier manning a fixed machine gun on the right, and another with a rifle in his hand sitting on the floor with his legs hanging outside on the left. The man seemed perfectly comfortable despite his precarious position and smiled at Kiran when he caught him staring.

"Don't worry, doc! We'll have you and the lady on the ground before you know it!" the man shouted.

He looked to be in his early twenties, but it was hard to tell under the helmet and sunglasses he wore. Kiran smiled back hesitantly, feeling every dip and sway of the aircraft as it raced toward the camp of Marines deep in the hot and humid jungle below.

He couldn't help wondering what they'd been doing so far away from anywhere. The only thing of any importance was the demilitarized zone, so maybe they'd been trying to stop North Vietnamese soldiers from getting across and into the South to join up with the Viet Cong?

The Marines had run into trouble with the Viet Cong on the ground, but he wasn't sure if they'd had air support from the North Vietnam Army as well. Kiran hoped not, or at least, that any enemy aircraft had left the area by now.

"Thirty minutes to landing." The voice of the pilot crackled in his ears.

Shit. They must be right on the edge of the DMZ if they still had a half hour left in the air. His gut clenched at the thought of being so close to enemy lines. He was a doctor, not a soldier. With his limited modern fighting skills, he'd be of no use to the Marines in case of a gunfight. He knew how to fire a gun, or even a rifle, but actually hitting something was not guaranteed.

"Kiran? Are we going to be safe?" Margaret asked him, her voice trembling with nerves.

"Of course, we'll be safe." He squeezed her hand and gave her an encouraging smile. "They wouldn't send us out here if there were still a risk of attacks. We just need to patch up these guys enough so we can airlift them back to base," he explained, speaking into the microphone on the headset. "These helos can take six patients at a time, maybe seven, if we stay behind to be picked up later, so we'll be out of there in no time. I'll do my best to.keep you safe, I promise."

"You know, I never used to worry about flying in these helicopters, but after what happened to..." Her words trailed off, but Kiran knew what she meant.

They'd watched so many of their friends vanish in a huge fireball in the blink of an eye, and it had left a violent impression on their souls neither could ever forget.

Whether he came returned alive made no difference to him, but he wanted to make sure Margaret got back safely. She deserved to continue helping patients in the base hospital for a while longer before returning home to the States. He still didn't understand why she'd signed on for another tour, but it had been her saving grace. Otherwise, she'd be in tiny pieces on the bottom of the sea by now, together with everyone else on the downed flight.

Leaning against the bulkhead, he closed his eyes, trying to ignore the way his bones rattled from the helicopter's vibrations. Margaret still clung to his hand, and he was happy to give her that small comfort.

Kiran's eyes snapped open at a sharp crack from somewhere to their left. Gazing out the tiny, dust-covered window by his shoulder, he searched the impenetrable dark green carpet below them and as far to the sides as he could twist his neck, but he saw nothing. No one else seemed to have heard anything, and the two soldiers continuously scanned their surroundings with no signs of worry on their faces.

Relaxing back in his seat, he smiled reassuringly at Margaret, who'd tensed at his movements.

"Don't worry, there's nothing there. I was only imagining things. Our friends here will keep us safe."

Suddenly, the helicopter lurched and veered sharply to one side. From the cockpit, the pilot shouted instructions to his co-pilot, who responded by throwing switches and pressing buttons at blinding speed.

"Incoming! Evasive maneuvers! Grab onto something back there!" The barked command thundered in Kiran's ears.

Wrapping an arm around Margaret, he tightened their seatbelts, but there wasn't much more he could do. The sharp crack he'd heard earlier turned into the horrifyingly familiar staccato firing of a machine gun. It was followed by the whine of several aircraft, audible over the roar of the Huey's powerful engine and the whoop-whoop of the rotors.

Kiran felt as if he were back on the base that day when they lost their friends, only this time, they were even less protected. The two soldiers, previously so relaxed and affable, had quickly strapped themselves in, murderous expressions on their faces. The one with the rifle was half hanging out the open door, speaking into his headset. He must have switched channels because the man with the mounted machine gun replied before asking questions on his own. At least, that's what it seemed like to Kiran, since he could no longer hear what they were saying.

He couldn't hear the pilots either, he realized. Pressed tightly to his side, Margaret was shaking with terror. Kiran kept his breaths even, pushing back his own worries, to reassure and comfort her. He had to trust that the pilots and the two gunners would keep them safe, and he whispered as much to the woman clinging on to him for dear life.

The sound of machine guns came nearer as the noise of the planes grew louder. A strange thud from somewhere behind him sent the Huey on a new trajectory as the pilot yanked on the joystick and then wrenched it again in the opposite direction.

Kiran stared at the man at the controls. His only protection was a plexiglass bubble, and Kiran prayed it would be enough. More thuds sounded, and to his horror, he saw a spiderweb of cracks explode over the glass dome on the right-hand side. The co-pilot slumped over, his arms falling from the controls. From his position, Kiran could see a dark bloom spreading over the man's olive-green flight suit.

Unbuckling, he pulled the headphones off, throwing them on the seat behind him and staggered forward, bracing himself against the helicopter's twist and turns, until he could press his fingers to the airman's neck, confirming what he already knew. The pilot threw him a grim glance, nodding as if to say he already knew, and then returned his complete attention to keeping his aircraft flying.

Behind him, Margaret reached out her hand, silently begging him to return to his seat next to her. With the aircraft's violent twisting tossing him back and forth, he dropped heavily onto the bench and once again fastened his belt, cinching it tight. Then he put the headset back on and grasped Margaret's hand. He gave her a kiss on the head, and whispered into the microphone that everything would be all right, even while knowing chances of that being true were slim to none.

While the pilot fought to evade their attackers, the two gunners fired their weapons in a near-constant barrage, only stopping to reload a magazine or feed another belt of ammo into the chamber. Despite the dangerous situation they were in, Kiran couldn't help but admire the calm and determined demeanor of the two soldiers. Bullets whizzed over their heads and around them, narrowly missing their bodies on several occasions, yet they barely flinched and carried on shooting at the three enemy aircrafts.

One of them drew nearly alongside them while still keeping its distance, but Kiran could still make out the red roundel with a gold star in the center. He imagined he could see the whites of the pilot's eyes, but that was impossible, of course. The plane was much too far away. Still, it was as if he could sense the murderous intent in the attacker's mind.

A muted gasp from the other side caught his attention, and his head whipped around just as the gunner with the rifle fell out of the door opening, arms flailing, trying to find a grip in thin air. Still held by his safety straps, he hung doubled over, bouncing against the lip of the door, no longer consciously moving.

Despite Margaret's protests, Kiran unclipped his seatbelt again and crawled toward him, grabbing on for dear life to any handhold he could reach. Wrapping a piece of webbing used to hold down cargo around his hand, he reached for the soldier, his fingers closing around the back of the man's shirt, and began to haul him in.

Straining with all his might, inch by inch, he dragged the man inside the passenger bay until he could lay him down on the floor. His throat tightening, he saw his efforts had been in vain. The gaping hole in the side of the man's skull told its own undeniable story.

Kiran fell away, scooting back until he pressed against the side of the bench, next to Margaret's feet. Despite all his years as a doctor, both in civilian and military hospitals, the wars he'd participated in, the natural disasters he'd endured or succumbed to, and the cruelty of men against men, the sadness filling him squeezed his heart tightly. Each and every death was a waste of a precious life, and he mourned them all.

He was accustomed to living with fear and tragedy, but the woman by his side was not. She had seen plenty of deaths and ghastly injuries involving blood, bone, and even brain matter, but until this moment, her own life had never been at risk the way it was right now. Added to the loss of their only defense against the enemy and watching a man suffer a violent death right before her eyes, was the fear of dying from a bullet or the helicopter crashing to the ground.

Kiran knew Margaret came from a country hospital in small town in upstate New York where the biggest danger to life was getting frostbite in winter. Before coming to Vietnam, her world had been calm, quiet, and orderly, filled with the loving comfort of friends and family. She'd only signed up because she wanted to serve her country and help their soldiers come home alive .

Fighting against the lurching of his stomach, he pushed up on the bench and leaned forward with his head between his knees. Margaret shook uncontrollably by his side, her hands white-knuckling the edge of her seat, her eyes wide and unseeing.

The rapid gunfire from the remaining soldier, and that from the enemy planes, filled the surrounding air, and Kiran felt more than heard the bullets striking the thin, protective hull of the helo.

Suddenly, the helicopter started spinning, a high-pitched whine erupting from the engine as the tail rotor slowed its whirring gyrations. The bottom of Kiran's stomach fell out as the aircraft's nose pitched sharply downward. His world became a hellish cacophony of screaming engines, Margaret's crying, and the pilot's curses as he fruitlessly attempted to right his craft. Out of the corner of his eye, Kiran saw the soldier manning the mounted machine gun slump to his knees before drunkenly leaning forward, his safety strap preventing him from falling to the floor.

Kiran stared straight ahead, wrapped his arms around the terrified woman by his side and held his breath while his surroundings became an inferno of red, yellow, and orange. His ears filled with a thunderous roar, his equilibrium sent into a frenzy as everything spun, tilted, swirled, and cartwheeled around them. Closing his eyes, he waited for the blessed end.

He was ready.

Sixteen

ALINA, 2013

"**M**erry Christmas, Cupcake." Warren held out his glass of champagne, clinking it against hers.

"Merry Christmas. This is such a beautiful place, Warren." She waved a hand in the air, indicating the grand living room they were standing in. "But I thought it was a chalet, not a large house with staff on hand to wait on us."

He smirked. "I wanted to do something special for you."

"Thank you. I love it. It's too much, but it's very sweet." She kissed him on the cheek, taking a sip of the champagne.

"I have something for you. I know you'll like it." Warren looked smug.

He glanced toward the spectacular Christmas tree in the bay window. Alina arched a brow in confusion. She bit the inside of her cheek, a knot of anxiety suddenly growing in her throat, and she had to swallow past it.

"You've already given me a present. I don't need anything else," she forced out.

Warren's behavior set her on edge for some reason. Maybe it was being in this strange, enormous house with just the two of them and the staff for Christmas that felt weird. She watched in trepidation as he went over to the tree decorated with colorful lights, shiny baubles, and festive ornaments. At the top, a gold star, encrusted with sparkling gems glittered in the light, and on one of the points, a small item twinkled all by itself.

Reaching up, Warren pulled it off, hiding it in the palm of his hand. He took a deep breath, grasped her hand, and stared into her eyes.

Alina went cold.

Surely he wasn't about to do what she thought he was doing? No, there was no way he would do that. Would he?

With mounting dread, she watched as he sank to one knee, holding out a ring adorned with an enormous diamond.

"Alina, will you marry me?" he asked, a self-satisfied gleam in his eyes.

Alina stared at the man she'd been dating for a year, pulling her hand out of his. Suddenly, she felt as if she didn't know him at all. This was not what she wanted. He knew that. They'd talked about it. She'd opened up to him about Jonas, Theo, and Daisy, and how she wasn't sure she'd ever want to get married again.

Why was he doing this?

"Alina. Cupcake. Will you marry me?" Warren repeated the question.

Horror spread through her chest, and she felt nauseous. With one hand clasped over her mouth and the other pressed against her belly, she backed away.

"No, Warren. Don't do this, please. Don't— I'm— Why—" The words stacked in her throat, and desperation built inside her.

Anger ignited in Warren's eyes while he slowly got to his feet.

"You're rejecting me?" he hissed. "I should have known. I'm such a fucking idiot. You were just leading me on, weren't you?" Balling his fists by his sides, his eyes turned dark and stormy, his mouth twisting with fury.

Alina took another step back.

"Warren, I — I thought we talked about this?" she stammered. "You know how I feel, that I'm not ready."

Warren blew out a deep breath, relaxing his stance, and a condescending air replaced the anger. "You were just playing hard to get." His hand flew up in dismissal. "Just like you are now. Come on, stop playing games." He reached for her, but she backed away. His voice hardened. "This is the right thing for you to do, and you know it. I've invested a year in this relationship, and now I need it to move forward."

"No. I told you from the beginning how I felt, but clearly, you didn't listen," she snapped. "I'm not ready to get married again. I may never be ready." Her voice cracked, and she cleared her throat. "You said you were fine with it. What's changed?"

Alina felt blindsided but also irritated. She wasn't playing games, and for him to accuse her of that was both rude and insulting.

Warren stared hard at her.

"You're right, I did say that, but I thought you'd change your mind once you knew how serious I am about you and saw the ring. I spent a lot of cash on it, just to please you. Come on, Cupcake," he drawled, smiling, but it didn't reach his eyes. "You know you want to say yes." His voice was smooth, but it still jarred in her ears, sounding false.

She took a few steps back until the couch was between them, needing a solid barrier to separate her from Warren. "What's gotten into you? Does this have something to do with lunch with your parents tomorrow?"

Warren pressed his lips into a thin line.

"I was going to surprise you with this later, but I might as well tell you now." He straightened his shoulders, a triumphant smile on his face. "I've got a job at the Manhattan Center as head of their entire corporate events division" — he stretched his arms out wide — "so I'll be making enough money for you not to have to work. You can stay home with our children when they come along. Sooner rather than later, I'd prefer." One brow arched as he folded his arms over his chest. "I've put a deposit on a house in North Hills close to my parents, and they've already applied for us to become members of their country club. My mom will introduce you to all her friends" — one hand spun dismissively — "and get you on the right committees."

"Oh, my God, Warren." Alina sank on the couch, her head in her hands. "When I told you I didn't think I wanted to get married again or have more children, you just ignored it? Or did you think I actually meant the opposite?"

Disbelief coursed through her. She couldn't imagine living that kind of life. It sounded more like Warren wanted to turn her into his mom, chained to a vision of how a corporate wife should be. She'd loved her children, but she'd also wanted to keep her career, and between her and Jonas, they'd found a way that worked for both of them. He hadn't expected her to give up anything she wanted and had supported her in achieving her goals, the same way she'd supported him.

Warren leaned his arms over the back of a chair. "I assumed you'd want the same things I do. That's what a wife is supposed to do. She should help her husband further his career while she takes care of the home and the children, and organizes their social life." Warren's brows formed a deep V-shape as he stared at her. "At least, that's what my mom has always done and what my friends' wives do. And it's what I would expect of you." He threw his arms up. "Any woman would jump at the chance of living in North Hills and have automatic entry into the club."

Alina drew in a slow breath, trying to control her emotions, rubbing her temples to alleviate the headache that had started to burn there. "Maybe that's what the women you've known before wanted, but I was very clear on my goals and dreams. None of them included becoming a clone of your mom. I've only met your parents once, and they are lovely, but I'm not them. I never will be. If you can't accept that, then there's nothing more to say."

"What? You're crazy!" He shoved the chair away, making Alina flinch. "You can't do this to me. I've already told my parents I was proposing to you tonight. Tomorrow's lunch is to celebrate our engagement." Warren began pacing back and forth, his shoes thudding heavily on the hardwood floor. "They're taking us to the club afterward to meet their friends and get our membership approved. We can't let them down at the last minute. People will talk."

Anger burned in her stomach. What was Warren thinking? He'd mentioned none of this when they agreed to join his parents for lunch and obviously thought she'd go along with it just because he said so. That wasn't her. Being in a relationship with someone meant you made decisions together.

Alina got to her feet, too aggravated to sit still, and crossed to the window where the Christmas tree stood. She stared into the gray, late afternoon light, the front yard and driveway wrapped in softly sweeping snow drifts.

"You know what, Warren? I don't care what anyone thinks. They're not my parents or my friends, and you got us into this knowing full well how I felt." She spun to face him. "That's on you. I'm not marrying you now or any time in the future. Is that clear? The only one who's been playing games here is you." Her finger stabbed the air in his direction. "Putting a deposit on a house? Organizing an engagement party? Membership to a stupid country club I have never set foot in and have no intention of ever doing so? What were you thinking?" Incredulity suffused her every word.

Warren's eyes narrowed, a muscle twitching in his jaw. "As my girlfriend, you should want what I want." His nostrils flared, his fists clenched, and his voice lowered as he continued, "In my new job, I'll need to project a certain image, and a fiancée is a much better fit than just a girlfriend." His every word was delivered slowly and deliberately. "Having a wife or about to get married is what's expected in the social circles I'm part of. It's how I grew up, what my parents want for me, and what they expect I would want for myself. Not getting married — or at least being engaged — after a year of dating makes my parents look bad and people's attitudes toward them will change. My parents' standing in the community will drop, and I won't have it." He shook his head. "They've worked hard to get to where they are, and soon I will be at the same level. With you as my wife. Now, put this ring on and smile. We'll have more champagne and then enjoy a wonderful dinner together."

Alina stared at the man she thought she knew. How wrong she'd been. He was nothing how he'd appeared to be. His views on how a woman should behave was like something out of the sixties.

"You have got to be kidding. There is no chance in hell that I will put that ring on my finger," she hissed, her irritation quickly flaring into anger. "Or have dinner with you. I'm going home. To my house. You know, the one you wanted me to get rid of so we could buy a condo together? Thank God, I never agreed to that." Alina's chest heaved up and down as she tried to calm herself.

Warren rolled his eyes, stoking her ire further. "Don't be silly. You're just a little overwrought. I knew it would come as a bit of a shock, but

I'm convinced it's what you want deep down. All women do. You're just playing hard to get," he sneered, reaching for her hand. "Here, let me put it on."

Alina wrenched her arm free. "You arrogant, selfish, condescending asshole! I will not marry you! Do you hear me? It will never happen. Never." She squeezed her eyes shut for a moment, forcing herself to take a deep breath and grab hold of her simmering fury.

She couldn't lose control. Not now. Warren would only use it to his advantage, and God knows what he'd try on next.

"I'm not some subservient, inexperienced, wide-eyed little girl who will nod and do as you please. I make my own decisions and not marrying you is one of the best ones I will ever make." Alina spoke in a firm voice, resisting the temptation to shout, as she nailed him with a glowering stare.

Warren crossed his arms over his chest, a stubborn set to his mouth, and a defiant gleam in his muddy-brown eyes.

Not able to stand another minute in his company, Alina strode out of the room and up to the master bedroom. After calling a cab to pick her up, she began putting all her belongings into her small case, thankful she hadn't brought much, shoving it all in without worrying about any creases. She heard Warren come up the stairs behind her, shouting, and steeled herself.

"Alina, you can't do this! I won't allow it. You're my fiancée, and you do as I say. I know what's best for you — for us. Stop playing these games!" he bellowed. "You know I'm the best thing that ever happened to you. I don't care that you were married before. You should have gotten over that guy by now, and we'll soon have kids to replace the ones who died." He stopped abruptly.

Alina knew he was still there, though. She could hear him pacing in the hallway outside the bedroom.

"It'll be fine, better even. We'll have the perfect family," he muttered, sounding like he was talking more to himself than to her. "It'll be an improvement on your last one, you'll see,"

"Go away, Warren. There's nothing more for either one of us to say."

The door slammed back on its hinges as he barged into the

bedroom, breathing heavily, his eyes wild. "Just stop being stupid and put the ring on your finger," he barked. "My parents will be disappointed, and I don't like letting them down. Everyone knows they're going to announce our engagement tomorrow. It's just how it is. What will their friends think? And what about my friends?" His voice dropped to a muttering again, which Alina found unnerving.

She needed to get away from him as soon as possible. Throwing the last few pieces of clothing in the case, she grabbed her toiletries from the bathroom and tucked them in the best she could while listening out for the cab, hoping he'd honk loudly.

Warren paced back and forth, gesticulating wildly. "What are they going to think of me? That I'm not man enough to keep a woman? Not even someone who's already shown her lack of worth by losing the family she had. What did you do? Did you cause the accident to get rid of him? That's it, isn't it? Did he not have enough money or the right connections? Well, I do. I have plenty of money. My parents are rich, and we're connected with all the best people in the state. I'll get my trust fund soon, but I need to be married first." He stopped on the opposite side of the bed, fists propped on his waist. "Alina!" he growled. "Are you even listening to me? Listen to me!"

Silently screaming, Alina clamped her mouth shut, even though his comments sliced like a knife through her heart. Forget Jonas? Replace her precious babies? Who even thought that way, let alone said it out loud? How had she missed all this in Warren? He'd always been considerate and caring, if a little spoiled and selfish at times, but this was way beyond that.

She'd never cared about money more than to have enough to put food on the table and a roof above her family's head. They'd been a team, she and Jonas, and they'd worked hard for what they had. They weren't rich, except with love, which they'd had in abundance, but they'd had a comfortable life with everything they needed.

She blinked back the tears, swallowed the boiling rage, and focused on gathering the last of her belongings. Warren seemed to have given up, marching back down the stairs, grunting and muttering. She hoped he'd go sulk somewhere in the house and let her leave without causing any more fuss.

Taking one more look around to make sure she'd left nothing behind, she traipsed down the stairs, grateful to hear the honk of the cab's horn out front, passing Warren who stared daggers as she walked out. Just as she put her hand on the door handle, a menacing voice snarling in her ear caused her to flinch.

"You'll regret this. You'll soon come crawling back to me."

She wrenched the door open and hustled down the steps to the waiting cab, praying Warren wasn't following right behind, but he seemed reluctant to brave the snow that had started falling.

"You'll beg me to forgive you! But I won't take you back! You hear me? Not unless you're in time to go to lunch tomorrow! After that, it'll be too late. Do you understand? Before lunch tomorrow!" Warren shouted from the open doorway. "I expect to see you groveling at my door. I'll try to be generous, but you'll have to work hard for my forgiveness. It won't be easy. Before lunch. Remember that!"

Alina shook her head, passing her bag to the driver who put it in the trunk, eyeing her warily and casting glances at Warren, who spun on his heel and marched back inside, slamming the heavy door shut behind him.

With a sigh, she sank onto the leather seat in the back of the car and leaned her head back. Closing her eyes, she fought the angry tears threatening to spill.

How dare Warren do this to her? She'd been nothing but honest with him from the very beginning. She wasn't some kind of trophy wife to bring out when he needed his friends or business associates to be entertained. Her career was important to her, and neither Warren nor anyone else would stand in her way.

Staring out the window, the skies darkening by the minute, she mulled over everything she and Warren had talked about regarding long-term goals and relationship expectations. She came to the same conclusion no matter how she looked at it. She'd been very clear about how she felt and what she wanted from him — or rather, what she didn't want. Not once had he said anything about wanting to please his parents or the need for a 1950s style housewife.

The drive back took nearly four hours as the snow fell heavily, making the roads treacherous. Alina didn't care. She just wanted to get away from Warren and lock herself away in her house. Having expected to be away the rest of the week, she decided to spend the next few days watching movies, bingeing on popcorn and ice cream, and ordering in.

AFTER THE HOLIDAYS, Alina returned to work, knowing she'd have to face Warren eventually. He hadn't tried to contact her since that evening, and she was surprisingly okay with that. At least she'd found out now what his idea of a relationship was before it was too late. If he'd had his wish, they'd already be living on the Upper West Side in some apartment building with a doorman and snooty neighbors, planning their move to Long Island.

How could he have put a deposit on a house without talking to her? Buying a house was a huge decision, and she wanted a say in where she lived. Long Island was too much of a commute, and she enjoyed the fast pace of the city. Suburbia had lost its appeal after the accident in California, and she wasn't ready to go back to it. If she'd been a bitch, she would have wished he'd lose the deposit on the house, since she couldn't imagine him going ahead with it now.

The weather was cold with a fresh breeze, but the forecast had promised sunshine for the next few days. She wore a thick coat, a knitted hat, and gloves, and had wrapped her scarf around her neck and lower face to keep warm during her twenty-minute walk to Bryant Park, but she was glad to finally get inside the warm lobby. She reached her office without bumping into Warren and sank into her chair with a relieved sigh. If it took a week — or never — before she saw him again, she'd be perfectly happy.

After coming back from the Berkshires on her own, she'd boxed up the few belongings he'd left behind in her house and put them by the front door, texting him to let him know. He could come and collect it whenever he wanted. She hadn't kept much at his apartment, for which she was very thankful. If he decided to be difficult about letting her have it back, then she'd just leave it alone and replace the items later.

"Knock, knock." Stephen rapped lightly on her door.

She looked up and smiled. They'd become good friends since she started working for him and often socialized outside the office.

"Hi, Stephen. How was your vacation? You look disgustingly healthy."

Stephen and his husband, Carl, had gone to St. Lucia for the holidays to celebrate their wedding anniversary.

"It was wonderful, thanks. We had a great time drinking cocktails and soaking up the rays." A troubled expression crept over his handsome features. "But I need to talk to you for a minute. Can I come in?"

Alina frowned. Stephen had never before asked if he could come in to her office. After all, he owned the company and could go anywhere he liked. She waved him in and waited until he'd made himself comfortable in the chair opposite.

"So, Warren contacted me the other day and told me some things I found a little disturbing and upsetting. Now, don't get me wrong. I didn't take his word as gospel, but I felt I had to bring it up with you nonetheless." Stephen crossed and uncrossed his legs.

Alina had never seen him so fidgety and nervous.

"Go on. I have a feeling I won't like what Warren said to you."

Stephen rubbed his clean-shaven jaw. "Well, he kind of intimated that you've been looking for another job and spreading rumors about us — false rumors — so we'd get no more contracts or assignments here in the city or anywhere, for that matter. He also said you might try to sabotage his work, because he broke up with you over the holidays when he wouldn't buy a house with you. He mentioned something about you proposing as well." He held a hand up in a placating gesture when Alina opened her mouth. "As I said, I didn't take him at his word." Clearly unsettled, Stephen glanced at her before looking out the window to his right, his mouth in a tight line.

Alina stared at her friend, her stomach dropping to the floor. What was Warren thinking? He must have known he wouldn't get away with this. Especially since he was the one leaving to take a job with another events firm.

She felt sorry for Stephen and could tell he was uncomfortable relating Warren's preposterous and potentially damaging claims. He was clearly worried it was true and wondered what effects it would have on him and the business. Renewed outrage bubbled up inside her. She'd thought Warren wouldn't be able to make her angry again, but this was too much. He was being spiteful and vicious and behaving like a spoiled brat who was told he couldn't have every toy in the store.

"Stephen, I'm so sorry he has dragged you into this. None of it is true. In fact" — she swept a hand through her long hair — "it's Warren who's been offered a new job. And he proposed to me while we were in the Berkshires. I turned him down." Releasing a lungful of air, Alina told him everything that had happened on what should have been a relaxing vacation.

Stephen was clearly disturbed by what seemed like blatant lies by Warren and said he would confront him about it. To keep things fair, he wouldn't take Alina's story for the truth either until he'd had a chance to speak with Warren again. She was more than happy with that. She knew Warren would crack under a little pressure from Stephen.

He pushed up from the chair. "Look, leave this with me. I'll get it sorted today. In the meantime, I'd like you to look at this proposal we're bidding on. It's for a global tech symposium we're hoping they'll want to hold at our convention hall in Atlanta this fall." He headed for the door. "I was hoping you might want to visit the new offices there and take the lead on this if we win the contract."

Alina grinned. "Yes, I'd love to be involved. Is there anything you need me to do to put the contract together?"

Stephen tapped his hand against the doorjamb. "Not right now. I'm just looking at the proposal for the moment, and then we'll get into the details of the contract."

Excitement buzzed through her veins. This was exactly the kind of thing she needed to distract her from Warren and his antics.

After her friend and boss had gone back to his office, Alina mulled over what she'd been told. Warren was finished here, even if he wasn't leaving for the other job. If she knew Stephen right, he'd fire him instead of allowing him to resign once he found out the truth. Stephen hated deceit and lies and would come down like a ton of bricks on anyone who wasn't being honest with him. Especially if it threatened either his company or his marriage.

Alina shoved Warren's accusations out of her head and returned her focus to her work and the new proposal. Stephen would find out what really happened soon enough, so she had nothing to worry about, even if Warren's lies made her livid. She wouldn't let him impede her life after finally having found a little bit of happiness working with Stephen, and she would fight for it with everything she had if needed.

Seventeen

KIRAN, 1966

*S**ilence.*
   Kiran tried to open his eyes, but something seemed to have glued them shut. He would pry them open with his fingers if he could only feel his hands, arms, or any part of his body. Feeling as if he were floating in darkness, he reached out with all his senses for any sound, any movement, or the slightest touch, but there was nothing.

   Panic clawed at his throat as the total absence of anything at all sent spikes of fear to his chest. This wasn't how it was meant to be. He should have been sent to a new life, or he should have been returned to his original *state of grace*. This was neither, and he couldn't bear the thought of being here, wherever here was, forever. It was like a void. A silent, dark, empty nothing.

   Somewhere in the blackness, a brief flash of gold caught his attention. He whipped his head around, or he thought he did, but it had already vanished. Then another flash, but once again it was swallowed by the darkness.

   Kiran despaired. He wanted — no, *needed* — the light. The inky blackness threatened to overwhelm him, to invade his body and his mind. Somehow, he knew that if he allowed it to take control, he would be forever held its prisoner.

There.

Another flash of light. Like a flickering flame, it beckoned him. He moved closer to it. How he moved, he didn't know, and he didn't care. All he knew was that it was getting closer. It was also getting hotter. Sweat trickled down his face and back. At least, that's what he thought he could feel. He wasn't entirely sure of anything.

As he neared the hot, burning flame, an acrid stench invaded his nostrils, making him gag and cough. His eyes watered from a stinging sensation while the flame grew larger, spreading, surrounding him. No longer wanting to get closer, he tried to stop the advancing wall of red and gold plumes, but it drew him inexorably closer.

Too close.

Suddenly, his eyes flew open, and his gaze danced crazily around, trying to process what he was seeing, but there was no sense to any of it. Everything was spinning. Up was down and down was up. After several long moments of trying to calm his breath and gather his wits, his surroundings stopped moving long enough for him to look around.

Blinking to clear his vision, he saw loose items spread everywhere, even on top of him. He pressed a hand to the back of his head, feeling something sticky. Looking at his fingers, he saw they were coated with blood.

The helicopter!

We crashed!

As the realization dawned on him, crushing disappointment gripped his heart. He'd wanted it to be over. The need to be returned to his origins blazed through his soul, but yet again, He hadn't seen fit to bless Kiran with His serenity.

The disappointment stole his breath, and he fought to fill his lungs with air so as not to pass out again. Finally able to draw in a shuddering lungful, his chest expanded, and in an instant, his body erupted in agony. He howled. The cry bursting from his throat was filled with rage and grief. The sound of rattling chains echoed in his mind. The rusting metal links still holding him in their cold, unyielding grip.

Agony radiated to every inch of his body, making him shake and pant. Sharp pangs pounded his head, threatening to split his skull apart.

Despite the agony from moving even an inch, he wrapped his arms around his head to muffle the throbbing.

A moan from nearby made him flinch. Someone else was still alive! Lifting his head, he saw he was lying on the ground twenty feet away from the wrecked helo. He pushed up on his arms and knees, fighting the nausea in his throat and the excruciating pain flaring with every movement.

He couldn't stay where he was because someone needed his help, and no matter what, he was still a doctor. He helped people. It was who he was.

Crawling through the dirt and bits of wreckage, he headed toward the sound. It was louder now, turning into screams. A woman's screams.

Margaret.

Reaching the downed aircraft, the flames he'd seen while semi-unconscious made sense as the severed rear part of the helicopter — what was left of it, anyway — burned with intense heat. Flames licked the sides of the fuselage and would soon envelop it. The stench was back, singeing the inside of his nose, scratching his lungs, and forcing him to put his arm over his mouth and nose so he could breathe.

The forward part of the helo rested thirty feet away, and flames were taking hold where it had sheered off from the tail. He hauled himself into the passenger bay, looking for any sign of the nurse. She was no longer screaming, and Kiran didn't want to think what it might mean. No, she had to be alive. He'd promised he'd keep her safe, that they'd all go home. He needed to keep that promise.

The metal burned his hands and knees, and he realized the fire was creeping into the main cabin. He had to hurry. The jet fuel causing the overwhelming smell could go up in flames any second. In fact, he was surprised it hadn't already happened. Thankfully, the tanks were fitted aft of the cabin, in the part being eaten by fire over to his left. It wasn't far enough away, not by a long shot, but it gave him a tiny chance of finding what he was looking for. He prayed it didn't explode in the next few minutes. He needed every second he could get.

Staring around him, he saw one of the gunners crushed against a bulkhead by a supply chest. His lifeless eyes were already covered with an opaque film. The other gunner was nowhere to be found, his security strap torn off and hanging loosely in the open doorway.

The pilot was still in his seat with the co-pilot slumped beside him. Kiran swallowed hard. The plexiglass shield had caved in, the sturdy branch from a tree having penetrated the flimsy protective cover like a spear thrown with enormous force. It had gone right through the pilot's chest, effectively nailing him to his seat.

The nausea returned, clawing at his gut, but Kiran had no time for it. Finding Margaret was his only mission now after seeing the fate of the others. A whimper reached his ears, and he started toward it, grateful to leave the wrecked helo behind. Several yards away, he found the pretty nurse with the gentle smile. Kiran almost cried with relief.

Quickly checking her for injuries, he found several broken bones, a head injury, and most likely a punctured lung. From a large discoloration on her abdomen, he was pretty sure she was also bleeding internally. Despair gripped him. These were not the kind of injuries he could fix with a first aid kit. He didn't even know if his bag had survived the crash.

First, though, he had to find them shelter. The Viet Cong would be all over this site as soon as they saw the smoke from the burning wreckage. Of course, the North Vietnamese Air Force had probably already informed the VC of the shooting down of the aircraft.

After finishing his quick assessment of Margaret, he pushed off his knees to stand. A wave of dizziness assailed him, and he sank to a knee, gasping for breath, sharp pain erupting with every inhale. This was not the time to fall apart. He had a job to do, a woman to protect and to help heal, and he was damn well going to do it. With that thought in mind, he carefully got up, supporting himself against a tree until he got his bearings.

Looking around, he saw nothing but trees, low-growing scrub, and the sky peeking through the thick canopy overhead. The helicopter had come down in a small clearing, only feet away from some large, sharp-edged boulders. Kiran figured he had to be thankful for small mercies. Whether it was by the skill of the pilot or pure luck, he didn't know, and he didn't care.

He was pretty sure he had a severe concussion and several broken ribs as his vision was still slightly blurry, his side hurt, and he struggled to take more than shallow breaths. Aching contusions covered most of his body. His head was still bleeding from a blow to the back, and his left arm was sliced open from the top of his shoulder down to his elbow. That made him pause. The cut wasn't terribly deep, but it bled steadily. He ripped off the sleeve of his shirt to cover the wound and stop the bleeding, but it needed cleaning and suturing.

Drawing a careful breath, he saw the hopelessness of his situation. He had no idea if the pilot had gotten a mayday to the base, or if anyone knew they were missing. The camp they'd been headed for could lie in almost any direction, and he wasn't even sure which side of the DMZ they were on.

Those were things he would figure out later. First, he had to get himself and Margaret away from the crash site and into some form of shelter.

Bending down, he grimaced, fighting the blackness hovering on the edges of his vision, and tried to breathe through his pain as he lifted the slight form of the unconscious nurse. She whimpered weakly in his arms but didn't open her eyes. Kiran chose the path of least resistance as he trudged away from the clearing and into the heavily forested jungle.

Each step he took sent a knife slicing through his side, and he fought for every puff of air dragged into his lungs. It was hard going. Not only because he was carrying the woman in his arms, but because the trees grew close together, and if there was a gap between the trunks, heavy foliage covered it at root level. Kiran had to push his way through, vines tangling around his feet, and it only took minutes before he'd use whatever strength he'd had and was gasping for a drink of water.

AN HOUR LATER, he'd finally found a small thicket, shielded between large boulders, where he could lay Margaret down. He was exhausted but still had some work to do before he could rest. Inside the clump of scrub, he hollowed out a small area and made a pallet of dirt covered with soft leaves on one side. He settled Margaret on top and slumped to the ground, his breath coming in big, painful heaves.

After allowing himself a few minutes to rest, he forced himself to his feet. He needed to make his way back to the wreck and salvage as much of the supplies as he could. Finding his emergency medical kit was his first priority, then came food and water. Staggering out onto the faint track he'd made coming, he followed it back toward the small clearing, making sure Margaret couldn't be seen from outside of the bushes.

Staying as alert as he could, he followed the path back to the crash site, both horrified and grateful for the tracks he'd left behind. Anyone could follow his steps back to the thicket, but he could also retrace them to get back to the wreckage. It was both a blessing and a curse.

Once he'd scavenged what he could, he'd attempt to disguise his trail as much as possible. He resolved to make another, a decoy, leading away from the shelter, and then work his way back to Margaret while leaving as few signs of his footsteps as he could.

Before stepping into the clearing, he stopped, listened, and searched his surroundings. The forest had resumed its normal rhythm after the loud shriek of the doomed helicopter and the grinding of metal as it came down. Birds chirped and squeaked. The wind rustled the leaves in the treetops, and in the far distance, a primate let out a loud screech.

Sensing no danger, Kiran hurried across the clearing. The flames had nearly died down but were still flickering here and there, and he was surprised the tail part hadn't exploded. Maybe the fuel tank had been pierced by a round from the enemy aircraft and was empty. Although the fumes left behind in the tank alone should have detonated as soon as the fire reached it. He had no time to think about it, however, and scrambled through the scattered pieces surrounding the burning chunk of metal.

With an enormous sigh of relief, he spotted his medical bag underneath one of the helo's broken-off skids and dragged it out. A few bandages and a large pack of gauze were missing, but everything else was there.

Spending twenty minutes scouring the site, he pulled together as many supplies as he could carry, carefully avoiding the charred pieces of metal that were still burning hot. With his head thumping, his vision narrowing, and his ribs screaming in protest, he began the arduous trek back to the shelter where Margaret was waiting.

When he finally made it to the clump of thick bushes, having made a few wrong turns despite following his own trail, he collapsed on the ground outside and closed his eyes. Every inch of his body ached, burned, and stung, while his head sent bolts of lightning ricocheting off the insides, making him dry heave several times. His stomach was empty, and he was dehydrated, so there was nothing to bring up but some sour-tasting bile.

He rested on the damp earth and withering leaves, waiting until his heart had slowed enough for him to hear anything over its pounding rhythm. Willing the pain erupting all over his body to calm, he listened to the surrounding jungle. Birds chirped, insects buzzed around his head, and rustling noises came from a nearby tree. It all sounded normal and peaceful.

With a groan, Kiran staggered to his feet, the fiery agony stabbing his side and the jackhammer in his head flaring with renewed vigor. Carefully pushing the branches aside so as not to leave a trace, he bent low and snaked his body inside the thick bushes, pulling the heavy load of scavenged supplies with him.

Margaret hadn't moved since he left her earlier. He kneeled by her side to check her vitals. Her breathing was shallow, her pulse thready and barely discernible. He pulled his medical bag to his side and rummaged through for something to help her. A small vial of antibiotics and a syringe were the first items he needed.

Ripping open a pack of cotton wool, he poured a little antiseptic liquid on it and swabbed her arm before inserting the needle with the medicine. She didn't even flinch. Touching her forehead, her skin was dry and burning hot to the touch. If she had internal injuries, of which he was quite certain, the antibiotics wouldn't help her, but it was better than nothing. He had to use whatever he had to keep her alive until help arrived. He just hoped it would happen soon.

While searching the wreckage area, he'd left a scribbled message on a scrap piece of paper using some of the soot from burned parts of the fuselage that littered the area. Using as few words as possible, he'd given his would-be rescuers veiled directions to where he was hiding in the hopes they would understand and come looking for them — if they were even aware they'd crashed. He kept his fingers crossed the Viet Cong wouldn't find the message if they came across the downed helo, or if they did, that no one understood written English.

Once he'd done as much as he could for the injured woman, Kiran drank a few mouthfuls of water from a canteen he'd found. It had probably belonged to one of the pilots, or maybe the gunners. In any case, they no longer needed it, and Kiran did. He didn't have much, so until he found a stream or some other source of water, he'd have to conserve what he had. In one of the storage lockers on the helicopter, he'd also found emergency food rations, a couple of flares, and some water purifying tablets. It would have to be enough until they got out of this godforsaken jungle.

Suddenly overcome with fatigue, Kiran stretched out next to Margaret on a hastily assembled bed of leaves. Finding a position where his body hurt the least, he closed his eyes, exhaustion suffusing every cell, and was asleep within minutes.

KIRAN STAYED in the shelter for several days, tending to Margaret, who showed no signs of improving. In the hours he spent awake, his mind flipped unbidden through his memories like a slideshow. His earliest recollection of his time here on earth was toiling under a blistering sun, dragging enormous blocks of stone up a wooden ramp with only ropes to help him and those working beside him. Many died of a lack of food and water, others from injuries sustained falling off the vast structure.

Most of the many thousands of men working to construct the eventual resting place of Khufu, the Pharaoh, had been skilled craftsmen living in camps nearby, who'd been paid for their efforts, but Kiran and others like him hadn't been there willingly. The shackles fastened around their wrists and ankles at night had been a testimony to that. So were the scars on their backs from the stinging whips slicing open their skin. If they weren't careful, those wounds would become infected and fester. More than one man had succumbed to open sores spreading infections through their bodies. Even back then, Kiran had felt a need to help those who were suffering from various ailments.

Day after scorching day, they had pulled at those ropes, watching the stone structure rise higher and higher in the empty desert. He'd been told the final capstone would be of gold to herald Khufu's greatness. The outside of the gigantic blocks of stone, seamlessly and precisely fitted together, would be clad in white marble to make it shimmer and shine brightly under the burning sun.

Kiran never got to see the finished monument. The marble was being added from the base while they made the final adjustments at the top before adding the capstone when he fell — or was pushed. He wasn't sure which. He still remembered seeing the hewn stones spin past his eyes, his body bouncing off them as he plummeted.

He landed on the hard-packed sand with a dull thud and in a cloud of dust. He'd lain there, surprised he'd survived tumbling from such a great height, staring up at the blue sky. Slowly, he'd realized he was unable to move a muscle, not even his eyes, and his breath had been knocked out of his lungs and wasn't being replenished.

Beginning deep inside his core, an excruciating pain had spread through his every cell, setting them on fire until his entire body howled in agony. He'd screamed then. At least, that's what he thought the torturous shriek filling his ears was, even though he hadn't recognized it as his own. Before long, his vision faded. Blackness tinged the edges, slowly covering more and more of the cerulean heavens until everything was gone.

He was gone.

Somewhere in the deepest parts of his mind, he'd hoped it was forever.

When the last drops of water were gone from the canteen, Kiran knew he had to leave his makeshift sanctuary and look for more. The emergency food was also dwindling, so he'd have to search something to eat as well. Luckily, one of the cooks back at the base had become a good friend, and he'd taught Kiran a little about what kinds of fruits and berries grew nearby that were edible and which ones to avoid. If he could find a stream of fresh water, he might also be able to catch a fish or two.

After checking on the still unconscious Margaret, he scrambled out under the thorny branches and straightened, listening for… he wasn't even sure what. Voices? Aircraft engines? By now, he just wanted to be away from the hot and humid endless greenery. He wanted to be back by the ocean, sleeping in his tiny hut at night, standing for hours in the operating theater with his hands inside someone's body, feeling life returning to them — anything but being alone with a dying woman, who'd been so full of life and grace, undeserving of this fate, with no way of helping her.

He'd been bitterly disappointed waking up in the makeshift shelter, feeling faint and nauseous, but shouldn't have been surprised. It was clear he was no longer held in any favor, or even consideration, with Him, and his only choice was to endure.

Fighting the ever-present nausea and dizziness, Kiran put one foot in front of the other, following a path only he could see, and began his search for water first and foremost, but he tried to keep his eyes open for any food sources as well. He had a notion that seeking damper earth and richer foliage might lead him to some kind of spring or stream. It could be complete nonsense, but it was all he had.

He wasn't sure how long he'd been fighting his way through thick vines and around heavy tree trunks when a faint sound made him pause and listen. Praying he wasn't imagining things, he followed the sound and held his breath when it became louder with every step.

Breaking through a veritable wall of tangled and twisted underbrush, he nearly whooped with excitement when a small creek came into view. Half running the last few steps, ignoring the pain in his side, he dropped to his knees at the grass-covered edge and dipped his entire face into the cool water. Splashing it on his arms and neck, he relished the fresh feeling, almost giddy with happiness.

The quick-running water looked clean and clear, so he chanced filling his canteen and a plastic container he'd found in the helicopter.

When he got back to the shelter, he'd add a purifying tablet just to be sure.

Kiran sank back on the damp grass and drew his knees up to his chest. A tiny amount of joy filled his soul at having found fresh water, despite the precarious situation he was still in. Staring at the gently rushing creek, he once again returned to the questions he'd been asking himself for millennia. What was he doing here? Was there even a purpose to his many existences?

Before he Fell, he'd been the Overseer. His responsibility had been to watch over everything at once and ensure nothing too disastrous happened that could affect the future of the humans. They were precious to his kind and needed a guiding hand, even if they didn't know it or didn't think they received any kind of support.

In reality, they just didn't see the miracles he performed or the disasters — the world-altering ones as well as the extinction events — he engineered. He'd been everywhere, in both time and space, all at the same time, adjusting, nudging, snipping, flicking, and crushing. All with the sole purpose of shepherding the entire human race in the right direction, both past, present, and future.

Others were in charge of the more detailed events. The ones that affected a smaller number of people. They may still have far-reaching consequences, but not for the world as a whole. Of course, some of his more all-encompassing moments were stitched together by the smaller events. He hadn't acted entirely on his own. Most of what they did demanded assistance and cooperation from several areas of responsibility, but the overarching view was his.

Since he first appeared among men, he'd lost that perspective. Now, it was all smaller events, some infinitely more significant than others, but still not what he'd been used to. He missed it. Seeing how everything connected on such a huge scale with a limitless number of happenings and stitching it all together to create the vivid, ever-changing, and living tapestry of His priceless charges had filled him with awe and wonderment.

He didn't need to know what the individual events and moments were. That was for his brothers and sisters to take care of, and he'd never taken much interest in them. He knew there was always a knock-on effect of anything that happened. The humans called it the Butterfly Effect, he'd recently learned, but he'd never attempted to see the patterns or mosaics of them.

He enjoyed having his eye on the infinite canvas of Existence. What he did superseded all of his brothers and sisters' responsibilities. It was superior and of paramount importance to all.

The smaller, more insignificant events were of no consequence on the whole and were mostly there to keep groups of people or individuals happy or to alter their current course in some small way. He and his siblings all had their own responsibilities, and no one wanted to intrude on that of another. It was considered impolite and overstepping a boundary that shouldn't be crossed unless it was asked for or in an emergency. He'd never known it to happen.

They all focused on their tasks and only came together when necessary to change future paths. His brothers knew not to trouble him with inconsequential irritants. His domain was infinite, all-encompassing, and he'd demanded the respect this brought.

Eighteen

ALINA, 2014

Rubbing her forehead and sighing in frustration, Alina held the phone away from her ear to avoid burst eardrums from Warren's hollering. This had happened nearly every day since she threw his stuff out of her house. After calling to give him fair warning, she'd left the box on the sidewalk for him to pick up whenever he wanted. It was gone a couple of hours later, so unless he collected it, someone else had taken it. Either way, she didn't care.

His behavior had grown increasingly erratic since she refused to see him after he'd left the company. Stephen had confronted him about his allegations against Alina, but he'd maintained she was the villain and should be fired from the company.

Alina didn't know exactly what had happened after that, but later that day, Warren had packed his stuff and was escorted off the premises by a security guard. She hadn't seen it happen, but some of her friends in his department were only too happy to relay the incident down to the last detail. In truth, she didn't want to know what had transpired between Warren and Stephen. She was just glad she would no longer have to see her ex in the office every day.

She'd hoped that would have been the end of it, but ever since then,

Warren hadn't stopped trying to contact her. He'd sent countless texts, filled her inbox with voice messages, and sent a slew of emails to both her private and her work email addresses. She'd blocked him on both, and if he didn't stop calling, she'd block his number as well.

"Alina, did you hear me? I can't believe you're doing this to me! I gave you everything! You came to New York with nothing," Warren sneered, his voice betraying the New York drawl he usually tried to hide. "A West Coast, latte-sipping liberal who thinks she can fight it out in the big city. If I hadn't taken you under my wing" — he huffed loudly — "you wouldn't be where you are now. To think I offered you membership at the most exclusive country club in New York. I must have been out of my mind. You would never have fitted in there." A derisive laugh barked down the line. "The little country mouse all dressed up in frumpy clothes, trying to hide her hillbilly accent."

Alina sighed again. He was hurting, she understood that, but it was getting too much, and she needed to put a stop to it.

"Warren. Warren! Listen to me. I've had enough of your ranting and your accusations. This is the last time I will let you speak to me this way," she said. "From now on, you don't exist as far as I'm concerned. We no longer work for the same company, so there's no reason for us to talk, unless we happen to bump into each other at an event or something, in which case, we should try to be civil to each other or, better yet, stay out of each other's way." She kept her tone calm and firm, not wanting him to think she was anything but deadly serious. "I'm putting the phone down now, and then I'm blocking your number. Goodbye, Warren."

"You can't do this to me!" he screeched. "It's your fault I had to leave! You lied to Stephen and got him to fire me! You just wait. This isn't over. I will—"

Alina didn't hear the rest as she ended the call. After blocking his number, she put it on mute and tossed it on the cushion next to her, slumping against the backrest. His vitriolic rant spun through her mind on a loop. She couldn't understand what had gone so wrong. Sure, what he'd done to her in the Berkshires and the lies he'd told Stephen were pretty damn awful, but his being fired had nothing to do with her. That was all Stephen, and in any case, Warren had already gotten another job and was about to resign, so what difference did it make?

Shaking her head, she stretched out on the couch with a throw over her legs and reached for the remote control. After flicking through the channels, she settled on a nature program and watched disinterestedly until she could no longer keep her eyes open.

Switching off the TV, she pushed to a sitting position so she wouldn't fall asleep. Yawning and stretching her arms over her head, she trudged upstairs, switching lights off as she went, to get ready for bed.

In the bedroom, she flipped on the bedside light and pulled the drapes across the windows. This was her favorite room in the house. She'd painted it in moss green with wine-red accents and white trim. Recessed lighting in the ceiling gave it a modern feel, and she'd put a comfortable armchair by the floor-to-ceiling window where she could curl up and read, or sit and watch the world go by on the street below.

She padded into the bathroom, washed her face free from makeup, cleaned her teeth, and dragged a brush through her hair. Too tired for her usual skincare routine, she pulled a pair of pajamas from a drawer in the dresser and slipped them on before dragging the bedspread and scatter cushions off the bed. The sheets were cool and soft against her skin as she crawled under the comforter. Sleep tugged her into its embrace only seconds after her head hit the pillow.

THE FOLLOWING WEEK, Alina was so busy at work she barely had time to draw breath. She was finalizing the proposal for the tech symposium, organizing a few smaller events in the city, and working with the marketing team to raise their profile across the country. The company was quickly expanding. Besides Atlanta, they were opening new offices in Dallas and Minneapolis, with one more being considered in Sacramento. All the new sites were large event halls with space to extend if needed, and Stephen had his hands full recruiting staff to set up the new premises.

Alina had grown with the company since she started, and her

responsibilities had also increased. Stephen was passing more of his projects over to her as he focused on the expansion and setting up the new offices. She thrived on the responsibilities and worked her butt off to make sure she didn't let her boss and friend down.

Sitting behind the desk in her comfortable office, Alina stared out over the buildings opposite. New York was hectic, manic, and thrilling. She'd never thought she'd be happy living in such a fast-paced city, but she'd truly settled in and was loving every minute.

Jonas and the children were always in her thoughts, and she missed them every second of every day, but the pain was no longer as sharp and overwhelming, though she still had her moments when the grief hit unexpectedly, almost bringing her to her knees.

Despite feeling relieved she was no longer with Warren, his absence had left a small void in her chest, and she wasn't sure she ever wanted to fill it again. It seemed the universe was telling her she was better off on her own. Still, deep inside her heart was a tiny glimmer of hope and a feeling that somewhere out there, someone was waiting for her. Someone who could be by her side without feeling threatened by the memory of a dead man.

Warren had often thrown that in her face when he felt neglected. He didn't want to compete with a ghost, he'd said. It wasn't as if Alina could help still thinking of the family she'd lost. Jonas had been her first true love, and he would always be a part of her, as would Theo and Daisy.

Her phone jangling insistently on her desk startled her out of thoughts. Rolling her eyes when she saw the caller ID, she answered with as bright a voice as she could manage.

"Hi, Sophia. How are you?"

Her sister rarely called her unless she wanted something, but for their parents' sake, Alina kept it cordial whenever they spoke.

"Hello, dearest sister. I haven't heard from you since the wedding, so I thought I'd better make sure you were still alive. I had hoped you'd have called to find out how my honeymoon was, but I suppose you were too busy for that."

"I didn't think you cared, Sophia, but how was your honeymoon? I hope you and Frederic had a lovely time?"

"It was the most wonderful week I've had in my life. Everything was absolutely perfect. I'm sure you probably don't remember what it was like on your honeymoon. After all, it's been quite a few years, but Freddie and I had a magical time. It was a five-star luxury resort, and we had our own butler, couples massages, dinners on the beach, and every amenity you could imagine."

"Of course you did." Alina rolled her eyes again. "I'm glad you enjoyed it."

"I'm sure you are. Anyway, that's not why I called you. I wanted to be the first to give you the good news. I'm pregnant!"

Alina felt the world spin, and she had to swallow back the bile in her throat.

Pregnant.

Sophia is pregnant. She's going to have a baby.

My babies are gone. My husband is gone.

She's pregnant.

Oh, God.

They're all gone.

Forever.

With her heart thumping wildly, she drew in a shuddering breath, feeling as if the air had been shoved out of her chest, a tinge of black edging her vision. Gripping the edge of the desk, she prayed for help to find her bearings, the pain of the wood digging into her hand. Her eyes slammed shut, and she fought to get the words out to reply to her sister.

"That's... that's wonderful, Sophia. Congratulations to you both. I'm thrilled for you."

"I knew you would be." Sophia tittered, glee in her voice. "And now Mom and Dad will no longer have to mourn your kids. They'll have my baby to spoil and be proud grandparents. I'm only five weeks pregnant, so it's early days, but I can't wait to tell everyone. We're announcing it tomorrow to all our family and friends."

Each word hit Alina like a punch in the gut, and she wrapped an arm around her middle to prevent the pain from spreading. It was a futile effort. Agony raced through her nerve endings like wildfire, burning its way through her body and mind, leaving only ashes behind. She'd thought she'd started to come to terms with her loss, but she'd been wrong. Sophia's gleeful announcement was like a knife to her heart.

"Y-yes, I suppose so. Listen, Sophia. I have to go. My boss is calling me." She desperately needed to get off the phone before she had a complete breakdown.

"Oh, of course," Sophia drawled dismissively. "Well, that's all I wanted to tell you, anyway. I know how overjoyed you are for us, and I expect you will want to do lots of shopping for baby clothes, but please check with me before you buy anything, because I won't let my child be dressed in just anything, unlike some."

The barb stung despite Alina knowing her children had always been well dressed and never wanted for anything. She'd just refused to put them in expensive designer clothes that cost the earth and were either ruined after running around the backyard for a few hours, or grown out of after six months and needing replacing.

Hopefully, Sophia would realize that soon enough, and if what Alina sent her — if she sent her anything — wasn't good enough, then Sophia would just have to give it to Goodwill or throw it in the trash. She honestly didn't care.

Needing a few moments to herself, Alina went into the private bathroom in her office to splash some cold water on her face. Looking into the mirror above the washbasin, she barely recognized the woman reflected back at her. This morning, she'd looked healthy and happy. Now she resembled a ghost. Her face was chalky white, and dark shadows smeared the skin under her eyes.

After taking a few deep breaths, she straightened, gave her hair a quick brush, and returned to her desk. Forcing Sophia and her news out of her head, she spent the rest of the afternoon going over a long list of proposals and events schedules. By the time her workday ended, she had a blistering headache and headed straight home for a hot bath and a quiet evening on the couch.

"Alina, do you have a minute?" Stephen knocked lightly on the doorframe to get her attention.

She'd been buried in a mountain of seminar schedules and itineraries all morning and had barely had time for a bathroom break.

"Sure, boss. What's up?" She smiled, grateful for the interruption.

"I just had the coordinator from the pharmaceutical company call me. She was not a happy camper." Stephen's lips thinned. "It seems she received an email last night changing all the plans for tomorrow's seminar, including the venue, to a place we don't even use. Do you know anything about it?"

"What? No! Who was the email from? I haven't changed anything, and it's all set to start at ten tomorrow morning at the Wilmington." Alina went cold at the thought of one of their events having to be canceled because of something they did wrong. "I spoke to our liaison at the hotel yesterday afternoon, and they were just finishing the last-minute cabling for microphones and speakers. Everything else was done. I don't understand."

Reputation was key in this business, and Stephen relied on her to make sure every project ran as smoothly as possible.

"That's just it. It came from your email." Stephen's brow was furrowed, a pained look marring his normally carefree features.

He stepped into the room and perched on the edge of her desk, scratching his head.

Alina felt her jaw drop. It came from her email?

"That's not possible." She shook her head. "It must be a mistake. You know I would never do something like that without discussing it with you first. And it would have to be a dire emergency, like the hotel being on fire, for me to even attempt to move it at such a late hour. This is crazy!" She felt sick to the stomach seeing Stephen's worried face.

"I figured it had to be a mistake, but I needed to check with you first." His lips pursed. "I'll call her right back and let her know everything is ready for tomorrow."

Alina opened her email account and checked the outgoing messages.

"The last email I sent to Silvia was to tell her all her requests had been dealt with, and the room she wanted was reserved in her name.

There's nothing after that." She tapped the message on the list with her finger.

Stephen rose to stand behind her, looking at her Sent Items. Alina clicked on the deleted folder as well, but it was empty as well.

Staring at the computer screen, her brow creased. "I can't explain it, but I'll have security check our logs and get Silvia to forward the email to me."

Stephen patted her shoulder. "Sounds good. Thanks, Alina. Will you call her later to reassure her it's all in hand? I'll tell her someone on staff made a mistake, and the email was meant for a different event."

She gave him a reassuring smile. "Sure, I'll do that. She and I have worked well on this seminar, and I'd hate for the relationship to break down now. She's hinted that if it all goes well tomorrow, she'll recommend us for all their seminars and symposiums. It would be a great coup for us if we could get at least the majority of their business."

"That would be fantastic!" he exclaimed. "Especially with the new venues in Dallas and Minneapolis. We'll be able to stage events from all over the country with these sites. Pharmaceutical companies are big business and hold conferences all the time." Stephen grinned, excitement shining in his blue eyes.

Alina knew it would be an amazing opportunity for the company. As much as the business was growing and enjoying success after success, the two new convention centers were still a gamble, and a deal with a pharmaceutical company would go a long way to allay any fears of having overextended and dipping into the red.

After Stephen left, Alina immediately picked up the phone and called Silvia to reassure her the email had been a mistake, and the seminar would go ahead as planned. Silvia accepted the apology, and after finalizing some last-minute details, Alina hung up and leaned back in her chair. For the life of her, she couldn't understand who had sent the email and why. Who would try to sabotage the event and their reputation?

A thought popped into her head, and as she followed it through to the end, unease lodged in her stomach. She hoped she was wrong, but she needed confirmation. Dialing the computer services department, she went over in her head what she wanted to ask them to do and what information they might need.

After speaking to the department chief, she dropped her elbows on the top of the desk and rested her head in her hands. If her suspicions were correct, Stephen would be furious, but she wasn't sure there was much he'd be able to do about it other than ensure it couldn't happen again.

Stepping out of the cab, Alina paid the driver and opened her front door, kicking off her heels as soon as she was safely inside. Groaning, she wiggled her toes to get the blood flow going. She'd been on her feet the entire time since that morning, barely sitting down for five minutes. After a long week at work, she'd spent most of the day making sure the pharma seminar ran smoothly. She felt she owed it to both Silvia and Stephen to be on site in case of any issues on the day.

Thankfully, it had all gone without a hitch, and everyone had been pleased with the arrangements. Once the seminar had closed, she and Silvia had gone for a drink at the bar to decompress and relax for a few minutes. Neither had mentioned the email and discussed the possibilities of a long-term relationship between the two companies instead.

Alina hung her coat in the hall closet and continued into the kitchen. She pulled out a bottle of red wine from the rack fitted in the side of the marble-topped island and poured some into a stemless glass. Carrying it into the living room, she dropped on the couch, moaning in delight from the relief of taking the weight off her feet.

Tomorrow was Saturday, and she'd planned on sleeping late, have lunch at her favorite little Italian two blocks away, and maybe do some shopping in the afternoon. On Sunday, she would clean the house in the morning and then spend the rest of the day reading a book. It was the latest in a series by her favorite author, and she couldn't wait to dive into the pages. It'd been sitting on her coffee table for the past two weeks, and this weekend would be the first opportunity she'd have to get started on it.

After mindlessly scrolling through the channels on the TV, not finding anything that held her interest, she gave up and put on some music instead. She felt restless and uncomfortable, and not even the wine relaxed her. A feeling deep in her gut made her uneasy, as if it was telling her something was wrong, but that was stupid. She was safe inside her house. All her work projects were going as planned, and as far as she knew, her family back in Chicago was perfectly well and happy.

Alina jumped when her cell started buzzing insistently. A smile broke out on her face as she saw the caller ID, and she swiped across the screen to answer.

"Katie, it's so good to hear from you."

"Of course it is." Katie laughed. "You love me and miss me so much that you're coming back to California, right?"

It was the same thing Katie always told her when they spoke. She missed her best friend like crazy, but going back to the West Coast was something she still couldn't make herself do.

"Why don't you move the family out here instead?" she suggested, knowing the answer would be no.

Katie huffed. "Ugh, you know I would if it wasn't for the business, Bryce, the boys, school, our families, and oh yeah, the freezing weather up north."

Alina giggled. "The weather isn't that bad, you know. The summers are pretty hot and having actual seasons is great. They make you appreciate the warm weather more."

"Tell me what's going on with you?" Katie said. "I feel like we haven't spoken in ages."

Katie's voice sent a wave of longing through Alina. She missed her best friend and the easy, comfortable friendship they had. It was the kind of relationship where silence was as much appreciated as the chatter and giggles. She'd made friends in New York, but none as great as Katie. It would take time to forge that kind of connection, and she wasn't sure she'd be staying that long in the city.

After updating Katie on her work and social life, she told her about the incident with Silvia and the email.

"So you're saying someone sent this lady an email saying the event had to be moved at the last minute? And it was sent from your email account?" Katie sounded incredulous.

"Yes, but I don't know how it could have happened." She pulled her fingers through her long hair, snagging on some knots. "My sent mail and deleted mail had no message in them with that information, but I know it could have been deleted from the bin, so it doesn't really tell me that much. In any case, our computer department is looking into it."

Katie hummed. "That's really weird. I guess it's possible someone could have hacked your account or found out your password somehow."

"Hacked yes, but I never tell anyone my password, and it's not something anyone could guess either unless they've known me for a very long time," she muttered, her brain whirring, trying to come up with an answer.

"I bet I could guess." Katie giggled.

"Yes, but you know me better than my own parents" — she snorted — "so that's not very surprising. You know I tell you everything."

"Yes, and I tell you all my secrets too, except for all the naughty things Bryce does to me in the bedroom, of course."

"Eww, even that's too much. I'm gonna have to pour bleach in my ears now. TMI, girlfriend."

"Don't be ridiculous. It's nothing you've never done between the sheets, so no bleach is needed," Katie said. "And talking about bedroom activities" — her voice lowered — "have you replaced Warren yet? I don't mean the long-term dating thing, just the sex part. And if you have, why don't I know all the details?"

Alina rolled her eyes, even though Katie couldn't see her. "I know for a fact you are much more adventurous in the sex department than I have ever been, my friend. I should get the details from you. But no, I haven't dated anyone since I dumped Warren. It's only been a few weeks."

"Not even a one-night stand? A fumble in the copy room?" Katie whisper-shouted conspiratorially. "A quickie in the restroom at a nightclub? Nothing?"

Alina couldn't help but burst out laughing, and Katie soon joined in. The idea of her making out with someone at work or doing the dirty in a bathroom on a night out was preposterous, which was exactly why Katie said it. She'd always had a knack for making Alina laugh, and it was just what she needed.

They talked for a while longer until Katie's kids demanded her attention. Alina said a quick hello to her godchildren before saying goodbye.

Nineteen

KIRAN, 1966

Days passed, but Kiran barely noticed. He'd run out of what little food he'd managed to find, and with his injuries still not healed, it was hard to get water. Searching for edible berries and fruit was beyond him. Figuring he'd rest enough to heal a little, he spent most of his time lying on the mess of leaves and grass, drifting in and out of a daze. He was getting weaker, that much he knew, but he couldn't summon the wherewithal to get up and search for something to replenish his energy.

In his semi-unconscious state, impressions from his past lives drifted through his mind like a film running at half-speed. It was a cavalcade of things he'd seen and done, people he'd met, and the events that had flung him onto new paths.

As if from a great distance, he saw the Great Pyramid slowly rise on the horizon, heard the roar of the crowds baying for the gladiators' blood, watched the eruption of Krakatoa, and felt the bullets zing over his head in the last war he'd been in. Each one brought a distinct set of emotions.

Before long, his mind turned turbulent, unable to process the onslaught of images. Sinking deeper into unconsciousness, the memories wrapped around his mind and soul, forming new chains of unbreakable steel to add to those he already carried. Panic and despair vibrated along his spine, seeping into his bones, and suffusing every cell in his body. He fought against his bonds, struggling to force air into his lungs until he could do it no more. Giving into the overwhelming force, he simply gave up and allowed it to happen. After what felt like an eternity, the chaos finally receded, leaving only darkness behind.

Her skin was silky soft against the pads of his fingers as they traced a path across her downy cheek and down the slender column of her neck before trailing along the delicate collarbone. She trembled beneath him. She looked up at him, her face still in shadow, but there was no mistaking the desire radiating from her eyes. It penetrated his chest, spreading its heat to his hardened length. He wanted to fan those flames, make her wild with lust. The thought made him smile against her skin as he moved lower, his lips following the same pattern as his fingertips.

Unable to resist tasting her, he began exploring every inch of her velvety softness. From her face to her feet, no part of her body missed out on his worship. He was being selfish and wanted to fill all his senses with her sounds, smell, and taste. With his tongue, lips, and teeth, he used her body like a canvas to paint a masterpiece of want and passion. With every sweep of his mouth, some of his control tore away.

Her breathing sped up, and her heart beat a rapid staccato under his mouth. The moans spilling from her lips stoked the flames of his own desire, and his erection swelled to painful proportions. It throbbed against her hip, but he refused its cries for relief. Her needs came first. His were secondary.

Her body writhed, her hands fisting the sheets by her sides, as he continued his explorations. She rose to kiss him, her hands wrapping around his shoulders, making him burn with hunger and lust. Their mouths met in a dance of soft licks and bold strokes of tongues. A need to devour her zinged through his veins. He wanted to possess her, own her, claim her.

Her hardened nipples brushed against his chest as they kissed, reminding him of having deliberately not touched them yet. As he pulled away from their heated kisses, her whine of disappointment shot through his chest, making male pride and satisfaction swell in his heart. He did that to her. He made her tremble with passion and need. There was nothing more gratifying for him as a man than to see and feel the desire he ignited in her.

He lowered his head to feast on a rosy peak, filling his hand with the soft mound of flesh of the other breast. As he swirled his tongue around the pebbled bud, his teeth grazed the sensitive skin, eliciting mewls of pleasure from her mouth. The nipple swelled and hardened further from his demanding tongue, but she pressed closer for him to take more into his mouth. Her sweet taste flooded his senses, making his cock demand attention. He wanted to sink into her body, but not until his tastebuds were satisfied.

Having focused his attention on the darkened tip, he moved to afford the other one the same treatment while rolling the first one between his thumb and forefinger, tugging sharply. As he sucked harder, her nails dug deep into his back, sending shockwaves through his throbbing flesh, making a deep groan rumble from his chest. His muscles flexed and tightened under her hands, and he wanted more, needed *more, but he hadn't finished tasting her body.*

"Shh, I need to feast on you," *he demanded with a hiss.*

Once again, he sketched a path of kisses down her body, paying attention to the sensitive areas on the underside of her breasts and her belly button, and moved lower until he reached her smooth mound. Drawing a lazy pattern of circles and figures of eight on her delicate skin, he moved closer to the sensitive tangle of nerves at the top of her folds, never quite touching.

A suppressed wail burst from her mouth when his tongue found its way between her slick folds, licking a wide strip from the bottom up, but still barely dancing across her clit.

He relished her frustration with his close-but-not-close-enough touches. He wanted to stoke that lust until she was ready to explode from the slightest flick of his tongue or caress of a finger.

She was getting close, her breath catching in her throat on every exhale, and her fingers gripping his hair so hard it would hurt had he not been so turned on. He almost had her exactly where he wanted — trembling with passion and willing to let him do anything he desired.

Nipping the silky smooth crease of her hip, he blew gently across her heated flesh, almost making her fly off the bed, but with his hands wrapped around the tops of her thighs, he held her in a firm grip. Giving in to his own needs, he began lapping at her sensitive folds in earnest, her juices trickling out of her core in a steady stream.

For every swipe of his tongue, more flowed from her sex, and the bud at the top of her slit visibly throbbed. He licked nearer to it each time until he could resist no longer. Closing his lips around the swollen nub, he sucked hard and was rewarded with a high-pitched moan as she skyrocketed from the orgasm ripping through her. He slowed his licking and sucking, allowing her to gently fall back to earth, her breath coming in heavy pants.

Feeling her hands pulling at his shoulders, he rose on both arms above her, his heavy erection prodding her stomach. He slipped to her side, kissing her neck and the sensitive skin behind her ear, suddenly realizing he could never get enough of her taste.

The sudden touch of her hand around his swollen cock sent cascades of fiery lust from his chest to his sac, pulling a hiss of air through his gritted teeth, followed by a string of muttered cuss words. Lightning crackled behind his eyes, and his throat tightened. He fought hard to stave the orgasm threatening to consume him. He didn't want to come yet. Not until he was inside her.

This woman was a part of him, and yet a stranger. She belonged to him and he to her as if they were two halves of the same being. It was unlike anything he'd ever experienced, and it sent ripples through his soul.

She moved beside him, sliding down his body until her face was in line with his groin. With his throat constricted and no air in his lungs, he could only hold his breath figuratively as her mouth enveloped the most sensitive part of him in its soft heat. She sucked gently, moving her head up and down, and he knew the crown was steadily leaking pre-cum.

The sensation of her lips moving along his shaft, her tongue swirling the head, and the tip hitting the back of her throat each time she went deep, caused a stream of disconnected words to burst from his mouth. Before long, it became too intense, and he knew he'd detonate in her mouth if he didn't pull away. Another piece of his control ripped away. He knew he'd soon lose it altogether. The urge to brand her with his essence was getting stronger by the second.

He tugged her up beside him, and pushed up on his arm, holding himself above her. Her face remained in the shadows, and her rich brown hair splayed like a halo on the pillow. Without a doubt, she was the most beautiful woman he'd ever known, and as much as he needed to possess her, he also had to cherish her.

He pushed her knees apart, making room for himself between her legs and aimed his cock at the opening to her core. He searched her face, relieved at the slight nod she gave him. It was the confirmation he needed, and he surged forward, stroking hard and fast inside her. His heart stuttered at the intensity of the sensation, sparks of electricity zipping up and down his spine. Her long, lean legs wrapped around his waist, pulling him deeper into her core, the walls of her sheath pulsing around him.

As he surged in and out of her slick sex, each thrust was powerful enough to rock her body against the headboard. The last remnants of his control tore from his grip. All that existed was his body joined with hers, the slickness of her inner walls squeezing his cock, the throbbing, pulsing need to stroke as hard and as deep inside as he could.

He dominated her. Worshipped her. Controlled her. Adored her. Commanded her.

Her body writhed and undulated beneath him, her breath coming in shallow pants, and he knew she was close to falling apart again. He wanted it, needed it, and thirsted for it. His own eruption also neared with giant leaps. Heat surged in his balls, sending molten lava through his veins. He wanted them to reach ecstasy together, so he listened intently to the moans streaming from her mouth as they grew louder, mingling with the deep groans clawing their way from his chest.

Suddenly, her body tensed, her tight core convulsing and squeezing his cock so hard it was almost painful. She shattered before his eyes, the beautiful sight taking him with her over the abyss. A roar erupted from his throat, and he threw his head back, the tendons in his neck cording and tightening.

He pounded harder and faster into her until he was buried so deep no one could tell where one of them began and the other ended. From his rock-hard erection, his seed pumped in hot and thick bursts into the deepest recesses of her burning core. He wanted — no, demanded *— to leave his* *mark on her body so no other man could ever take his place. It was a primal urge, and one so strong it overwhelmed him.*

The fireworks setting off in his head caused red and white stars to burst in his vision, and he climbed higher and higher, his entire body filling with a passion so deep paradise was within his grasp. Reaching out with his mind and soul to enter his own private heaven, he murmured in the ear of the woman wrapped around him, "Take one small step."

He needed her with him.

In an instant, everything around him disappeared and darkness descended, almost obscuring the path to his blessed eternity. Only a small shard of light remained. With his hand outstretched, his fingers closed around it, and a warmth that—

KIRAN'S EYES BLINKED OPEN. An agonized NO ripped from his throat when he realized it had all been a dream. He was still in this hell-hole of a jungle, with a dying woman next to him, and no rescue in sight.

The woman in the dream was the same one he'd dreamed of before, and the one he'd seen in the graveyard at Juliet's funeral. How could that be? Who was she? It felt too real to be a specter from his fantasies, and all the time he'd spent on earth, he'd never dreamed of women before. He'd barely spent any time alone with a woman before Juliet, let alone had carnal desires for one.

His body stirred again, growing hard once more, remembering the dream. Exploring her body had felt so natural, so loving, so perfect. Somewhere deep inside him — in his soul, if he still had one — he felt she was a part of him. He carried a small piece of her within him, but something was still missing, and he wasn't sure he'd ever feel complete without it.

Whoever this woman was, she did something to him that was exciting, wondrous, and a little frightening, because he didn't believe he would ever find her. Or maybe he wouldn't be allowed to find her?

This could be another cruel joke from above to add to all the other ones. The biggest one of which was that they sent him back — every time — to suffer more hardship and losses. Never had he longed for his real life more than he did right now. He wanted to be back where he could see the events that shaped the long-term future of humanity.

It wasn't long term as in a few hundred years, or even millennia, but as in millions of years — sometimes even billions — and it had been that way for eons. It was *his* life's work. All the events he'd experienced since he Fell were so minute compared to what he'd held in his hands. They were insignificant in the grand scheme of things and could just as easily have been left out entirely.

Those of his kind who looked after the minor happenings insisted those were just as, if not more, important than what Kiran did, but he knew better. He created the future for humankind. A future so far ahead in time the people of today had no capacity for imagining even an infinitesimal fraction of it. Everything else was just filler to teach them about love, loss, joy, and sorrow. Things they needed to feel fulfilled, accomplished, and contented.

Kiran closed his eyes, pain and nausea warring for dominance of his body. He was tired and wanted it all to be over. He didn't care how it happened, but he wanted to it be now.

Crack!

The snap of a twig nearby made him scramble upright. Holding his breath, he listened intently for any other sounds. The murmur of voices drifted across the still, damp, early morning air. They were too quiet for him to make out the words, but it didn't sound like an English cadence and intonation.

The rustling of clothes and scrapes of boots on the ground came nearer, and it was soon obvious this was not a search party having come to rescue him and Margaret. This was the Viet Cong. They must have found the crash site and were looking for survivors.

Kiran held absolutely still, praying Margaret didn't start moaning. She'd been quiet for a long time, but occasionally, a low groan would slip past her lips. As the footsteps and mutterings receded, he let out a sigh, easing the tension in his shoulders. They were safe, for now.

Over the next couple of days, the enemy soldiers returned, scouring the area around his hideout. They must have found some signs of him near the shelter, because they seemed to search in an ever-decreasing circle around him. It was only a matter of time before they found his hiding place.

IT TOOK THEM FOUR DAYS. When they did find him, they hauled him out from the hideaway, dragging him through the thorny scrubs, and unceremoniously dumped him on the ground, his still aching ribs protesting wildly against the treatment. Margaret suffered the same fate, a sharp moan slicing the air as her unconscious body landed with a thud on the leaf-covered mud.

The South Vietnamese soldiers chattered excitedly, poking them with their rifles and laughing at their grunts of pain. A shouted reprimand from the leader quietened them down, and they stood quietly discussing for a few minutes. Kiran had no way of knowing what they were saying but felt strangely relieved they'd finally been found. Their situation was no longer fraught with uncertainty about whether they'd be rescued or captured.

Now, they were prisoners of war and could only hope they were treated reasonably, but chances of that were slim to none. The Viet Cong's reputation regarding the treatment of captured soldiers was something all US personnel were well aware of. On base, it had been talked about in hushed whispers and with a fierce determination not to end up in the VC's hands.

Chancing a glance at the small patrol of soldiers from his prone position on the ground earned him a swift kick to his side from a booted foot. The white-hot pain lancing through his side from his already damaged ribs sucked the air from his lungs and made black spots dance in front of his eyes. An agonized groan clawed its way from his throat despite him trying to hold it back.

Kiran held still for fear of further kicks, attempting to control his breathing and pushing the pain out of his mind. He had to hold it together for both his and Margaret's sakes.

After a lot of debating, the leader seemed to have come to a decision and yanked Kiran to his feet. They tied his hands behind his back while one soldier rummaged through the shelter, pulling out anything useful he found. The meager first aid supplies still in his bag were shoved into a sack and slung over the leader's back. The water was transferred into their own canteens and what was left poured out onto the ground.

Once they'd satisfied themselves that there was nothing more of value, they attached a long rope to Kiran's bindings, and the group moved toward the trail leading north. He began protesting, pulling against the ropes. He couldn't allow them to leave Margaret behind! Shouting and fighting against his bonds, he fell to his knees beside her, entreating her to wake up so they would take her along, but he got no reply. Of course, she was deeply unconscious, and she couldn't respond.

Once again, he was tugged to his feet and held securely.

"You can't leave her! You uncaring monsters!" Kiran all but sobbed. "How can you leave an unconscious woman all by herself in this jungle? It's cruel! You can't do this! I'll carry her. Please, let me carry her."

The thought of leaving the sweet and caring woman unprotected in the wilderness caused fury and devastation to surge through him. She'd been with him since they first landed in Vietnam over a year ago. With her warm smile, glittering eyes, and vivacious personality, she'd lifted him when things had been difficult, and made him laugh when he was down. They'd been a team — close friends — and having to turn away from her now felt like he was stabbing her in the back.

Wrestling out of the grip of the soldier behind him, he stepped toward the leader, the badly tied ropes falling to the ground. Suddenly, he was staring at the business end of several rifles, and he flung his hands up to show he was no threat.

"Please, I'll carry her. I'll take her wherever we're going. Just, please, don't make me abandon her here. I beg you. Don't do that to me. Show some compassion. Some humanity. I won't be any trouble if I can just carry her with me to wherever you want to go. Please!" he entreated.

The man's dark eyes switched between him and Margaret. His eyes went back and forth until they stayed on her. With his lips drawn into a grimace, revealing missing, stained, and rotting teeth, he pointed at Margaret and then at Kiran. Relief flooded Kiran's chest. He bent down, swept an arm under Margaret's back and the other under her knees, barely managing to stagger to his feet with his charge tucked against his chest.

He was weak from malnutrition, but he swore to himself he would carry her for as long and as far as he had to. It was the least he could do for a woman who, under different circumstances, could have been more than a friend. For a brief second, he closed his eyes and prayed for the strength to fulfill his promise — both to himself and to Margaret. He breathed easier not having to leave his friend behind. She was still alive, and he held a fragment of hope she'd recover.

With the prod from a rifle on his back, he stumbled forward, only to be halted again when the leader stepped to his side, a wicked gleam in his eyes. From out of nowhere, a pistol appeared in his hand and before Kiran could react, he aimed it point blank at Margaret's head.

A shot rang out, and Kiran staggered back from the impact. A warm wetness suddenly covered his face and neck. Horror rose like burning poison from his gut as he stared wild-eyed at the neat, dark hole that had appeared between her eyes, smoke lazily curling from the center.

"No!" The word wrenched from his throat as despair gripped his heart in a vise. The air in his lungs escaped with a whoosh, leaving a painful vacuum behind. "What have you done? Why?"

The only answer was a malicious snicker and a shouted command. The anger in his chest fought like a wild beast, clawing his insides to shreds, leaving him bleeding out. His heart slammed behind his ribs, his world tilting on its axis. In his mind, Margaret called out to him, begging him to protect her, to save her, to not abandon her.

His stomach heaved, and he bent double from the excruciating cramps slicing at his stomach. A wave of dizziness would have sent him to his knees had it not been for the man behind him grabbing his arm and yanking hard to keep him upright. Pain flared in his shoulders, but it was nothing compared to the anguish in his heart.

It wasn't he who had pulled the trigger, but it might as well have been. If he'd kept his mouth shut and somehow picked her up anyway, despite the ropes tying his hands together, maybe they would have left her alone, and she'd still be with them now. It was his rash actions, his display of emotions, and his disregard for the man in charge that had killed her. It was his fault, his responsibility, and his heavy burden to carry on his shoulders, instead of Margaret's light body in his arms.

A feral rage ignited in his core, and he threw his head back, as a scream burst from his lungs. The man holding him bore the brunt of his outburst, the back of Kiran's head hitting him in the face. With blood gushing from a broken nose, the soldier let go of Kiran's arms, and he wrenched free. Unable to retain his grip on her, Margaret's body fell back down to the squelchy soil with a heavy thud, the sound reverberating through his heart. Her arms splayed out from her sides, and her head turned to the heavens before tilting to face him. Kiran felt as if her eyes stared accusingly, reproachfully at him.

I probably deserve it.

His capturers poked her with their rifles, making her body roll from side to side. Their laughter boomed through the trees, silencing the natural inhabitants of the jungle.

An impassive mask fell over Kiran's face while he tugged all his feelings behind its frozen expression. These cruel and vindictive men would get nothing more from him. He closed the vault to his heart and soul and threw away the key. He still felt every tug, snap, and tremor of his emotions, but no longer would they be visible to his enemies. It was what he'd done so many times before, and would probably keep doing for millennia to come.

The soldiers bound his wrists again, tighter this time, the rope cutting off his circulation and rubbing his skin raw, but he didn't react, only stared straight ahead. As they picked up their sacks and water canteens, he waited while they deliberately jostled and shouldered past him. Finding an empty place in his mind, he filled it with sunshine, the glittering blue ocean, and a warm breeze caressing his cheeks like a long-lost love.

With sharp pokes and shoves, they herded him back down a narrow trail, heading north, chattering between themselves. Kiran steeled himself, grasped the sunny spot in his mind, and held on for dear life as he was shunted toward an uncertain future.

He managed a last look behind him before his shelter disappeared behind a bend. Margaret's lifeless body lay where they'd dropped her, staring at him with sadness in her cloudy eyes. Despair and disgust filled his soul as his captors forced him to take step after step away from his friend, leaving her to be ravaged by the elements and wild animals.

He no longer stood gazing across the abyss. Instead, he took just one small step over the edge.

Twenty

ALINA, 2014

After a relaxing weekend, Alina walked through the entrance at work on Monday morning feeling re-energized, ready to run the events they had planned, and eager to plan new ones. She'd had a few ideas over the last few days of how to market themselves in new areas of business and how to stand out against the competition. She'd talk them over with Stephen as soon as she had a chance.

Stepping out of the elevator, it surprised her to see him leaning against the wall, and the look on his face told her something was bothering him.

"Good morning. Are you waiting for me? How long have you been standing there?" She paused mid-stride. "What's wrong?"

"A while now, since I wasn't sure what time you were coming in, but I know you're usually here around this time. I didn't want to miss you."

"Okay, so what's going on?" Alina frowned, a lump forming in her stomach.

Stephen looked around, but no one else was in sight.

"Not here. Let's go into the old meeting room."

The old meeting room was an office they'd originally used when they needed more space to sit together and have team discussions, but as the company grew, it quickly became too small, and they built a bigger one in its stead. Now, they used it for one-on-one meetings, job interviews, and visitors who needed a space to work.

Alina had to hurry to keep up with Stephen's long legs as he strode to the end of the hallway and turned into the last room on the left before the main office areas. He went over to the window and looked out for a minute while Alina took her coat and gloves off and settled in a chair. Her stomach twisted uncomfortably. Turning around, her boss had a troubled look in his eyes, dimming their natural bright blue.

"You're worrying me now, Stephen." Her brow creased. "What's happened? Are you firing me? I swear I didn't send that email to Silvia." The lump in her belly grew to the size of a boulder.

"No, Alina. Absolutely not." Stephen shook his head. "You're invaluable to the company and to me. This has nothing to do with your performance. But it does have something to do with you." Stephen hesitated before continuing, "It's about Warren. Or rather, what he's done."

Alina felt her stomach sink to the floor. *Warren.* Would she ever get rid of him?

"Shit," she muttered. "What has he done now?"

"The computer people traced that email to Silvia. It came from your account" — he held up his hand to let him finish — "but the IP address was nowhere in our building. It came from his new office."

Alina felt like someone had punched her in the gut.

Warren tried to sabotage my work? Why? To get me fired? He must have known he'd never get away with it.

Her throat burned with guilt. "I'm sorry. I never thought he'd do something like this. I will talk to him and get him to stop."

"I wouldn't if I were you. That's not all he's done." Stephen's mouth drew into a thin line. "I found out that some of our quotes for seminars and events that I knew we would get since they were for people we'd worked with before had been rejected. The companies had gone with someone else." He sighed. "At first, I just figured it was one of those things, but I soon noticed a pattern, so I dug a little deeper. Each one of those contracts had been underbid by one company and one person. Warren. Of course, it could have been because he knows how we work and used that to cut us out" — he pulled out the chair opposite her and sank into it, bracing his forearms on the table — "but it was more than that. Some of our old clients refused to take my calls, and when I finally got hold of someone — and only because he owed me a favor — I found out Warren had been spreading rumors and lies about us and about you in particular. I put my friend straight, of course, and he promised to let others in the business know as well."

"No way," Alina groaned.

"My next question was how he knew what our quotes and proposals were. No one aside from you, me, and whoever from your department worked on each particular project had any knowledge of the details. So, once again, I spoke to our computer guys who thoroughly scrubbed our servers for any anomalies" — his hands swiped out — "and they found a keystroke logger on your laptop. Their next suggestion was to get someone in who could check our offices for any listening bugs. I thought it was crazy but after your laptop was compromised, I went ahead with it. I contacted a security company, and they did a sweep over the weekend of all our premises. They found four bugs. My office, yours, the boardroom, and your assistant's office." Stephen fell quiet.

A heavy silence fell over the room, stretching between them. Alina's head spun and nausea began churning in her gut.

Warren has been spying on us. He's listened to every word I've said in my office for goodness knows how long. How could he? I think I'm going to be sick.

"Oh, God. Stephen, I'm so sorry." Alina's head dropped. "This is all my fault. You'll have my resignation first thing in the morning, but I can pack up my desk now and leave immediately."

"No, stop," Stephen protested. "You're not going anywhere. This is not your fault. The only one to blame is Warren, and I've already taken steps to sort it out."

"But, I'm the one—"

"No. You did not cause this," he interrupted. "Since it happened at Warren's new company, and it can be construed as industrial espionage — I know, it's a little extreme, but he has to be stopped — I've had to inform his new boss. I'm expecting a call later today to say his contract with them has been terminated."

"I—I don't know what to say. I feel awful about all of this. I had no idea he would react this way."

"No one could have foreseen it, so don't blame yourself. We just have to deal with it as quickly as possible. And of course, no one else needs to know about it."

Alina nodded. She certainly wouldn't talk about it to anyone.

A FEW WEEKS after the trouble with Warren and his attempts at discrediting Alina, sabotaging the company, and spying on them in their offices, Alina was told he'd been fired from his new job for putting their reputation in jeopardy. The matter regarding the listening bugs had been referred to the police, who were actively investigating the allegations. Stephen was relieved Warren had done nothing worse than upsetting a client and losing them a couple of smaller jobs.

"Thanks for giving me a lift, Stephen. I really appreciate it," Alina said, turning in her seat to face Stephen.

"I'm not happy with you walking home on your own right now." His expression was troubled, his fingers drumming nervously on his knee. "I don't know why, but I have this bad feeling in my gut."

"You're so sweet, but there's nothing to worry about." She tried to look reassuring. "I've walked to and from the office every day for over two years now, and nothing has ever happened. Knock on wood." She let out a small laugh. "Saying that, I've probably jinxed it now."

Stephen rubbed his jaw. "I know you're perfectly capable and street smart, but I can't help worrying about you."

They were sitting in the backseat of the chauffeured town car Stephen used when he needed to get somewhere in the city and the subway was unsuitable. Lately, he'd used it more and more, since he often arrived early in the morning and left the office late at night. His workload was increasing by the day as the company prospered.

She squeezed his hand. "I love that, my friend, but nothing is going to happen to me. I have an alarm system in the house, and all the doors and windows are securely locked and bolted."

"I know, but this isn't the best neighborhood, and you're all on your own with few other residents around," he muttered. "It's mostly commercial properties on this street. Anything could happen."

"It's fine. I'm close to work, and it's quiet around here despite being so near to everything."

Stephen pulled his brows into a deep V. He still wasn't happy, but Alina had no intention of moving, despite the less than salubrious area. It wasn't as if criminal gangs were patrolling the street or a drug dealer was lurking around the corner — at least as far as she knew.

"I guess, but I still wish you lived somewhere safer," he grumbled. "You should come to the Upper East Side. The company has apartments there you could rent. You'd be closer to me and Carl as well." His face brightened. "You know he'd love it. I swear if he wasn't married to me, he would have proposed to you in a heartbeat. I don't know whether to be happy or jealous." Stephen laughed.

Alina grinned. Carl had quickly become one of her favorite people in New York, and no matter what happened in the future, she wanted to stay friends with both him and Stephen. They'd taken her under their wing when she first arrived, inviting her to dinner, introducing her to their friends, and making sure she wasn't on her own in a strange city.

After Alina promised she'd let him pick her up again on Monday morning, she said goodbye and walked into the house, waving briefly as the car drove away, red taillights disappearing around the corner.

Closing the door behind her, she flipped the switch for the hallway lights, but nothing happened. Frowning, she made her way to the kitchen with the dim glow from the street lamps lighting her way. Pressing the button for the kitchen lights produced nothing.

What is going on? Is the power out?

It could only be in her house in that case, as the building opposite had lights in every window.

Using her cell as a flashlight, she carefully made her way down the narrow staircase to the basement where the breaker was. She found the box, wiped off the cobwebs and flipped the lever, but nothing happened. She tried again with the same result. Sighing, she realized she'd have to call the power company and hope someone could come out right away.

Returning to the kitchen, she googled the number and dialed, keeping her fingers crossed. Standing in the dark, the shadows in the room seemed to come alive, every sound amplified. The recorded voice in her ear informed her they'd be answering her call shortly. She had a feeling she'd be waiting a while.

A quiet shuffling made her stiffen, but she relaxed again when she noticed the wind outside making the trees in the backyard sway, rustling their leafless branches. Padding into the living room, she figured she'd at least have some light from the street outside. Suddenly, the hairs on the back of her neck rose in alarm, and a cold breeze wrapped around her legs. She swung around, instinctively putting her arms up in defense, but it was too late. A sharp pain exploded in her head, and the world spun out of control. Her legs gave way, and the floor rose to meet her. The last thing she heard was a voice hissing in her ear.

"*Now you pay.*"

MUTED VOICES INTRUDED on the empty blackness in which she floated. Grumbling for them to go away, she hissed when fingers prodded her head and pulled her eyelids apart. A bright light shining in her eyes made her wince. She tried to push it away, but it came back in the other eye. Unable to see anything but black and white spots, she jerked her head away in protest. The sharp pain lancing through the center of her brain prevented her from doing anything more. A moan of agony pressed past her lips as nausea swirled in her gut. She sighed in relief when the fingers stopped their examination of her head and face, and she squeezed her eyes tightly shut.

"Alina, keep still. You've been hurt. The EMTs are here to check you out."

She recognized the voice but couldn't put a name to it.

What's happening? Why is my skull being split in two? Why can't I remember anything? Oh, God, I need help.

"Home invasion. One female, responsive but confused. Possible concussion. Several contusions, but nothing seems to be broken," someone said.

A stranger.

The response came in a garbled and tinny voice from far away. Alina couldn't make sense of it. It was like being trapped in a nightmare.

"Wha— what happened? Ugh, I'm gonna be sick." She tried to put a hand to her mouth, but her arms wouldn't cooperate.

Her entire body felt leaden, and she could have sworn she was on a ship fighting the rolling waves in a storm.

"Take it easy, honey. You were hit on the head."

Stephen. It's Stephen's voice. What is he doing in my house? Wait, EMTs? Home invasion? No, this can't be right. I must be dreaming.

Despite telling herself it was all just a dream, the excruciating pain in her head told her otherwise. Come to think of it, her whole body hurt.

"Stephen? I can't remember anything. Tell me what's going on. Please!" Her voice rose in pitch.

This couldn't be right. How could anyone break into her house without the alarms going off? She would have heard them if they'd been activated. She never slept that deeply.

"You don't remember anything?" he asked.

Worry cut through his words, and she cautiously opened her eyes to see his face, blinking against the bright light. His features were blurry at first but eventually came into focus. He looked pale, with dark shadows under his eyes.

"Stephen, the police have finished in here." A man's voice sounded from the hallway.

"Carl? What are you doing here?" Alina peered at the tall man in the doorway.

"I came with Stephen. He was worried about you, and so was I."

Alina was confused. Her head felt wooly, and the slightest movement sent new stabs of pain shooting through it.

"I still don't understand what's happened."

"You left your laptop bag in my car, so I tried calling you to let you know I'd bring it by in the morning. When you didn't answer your cell or the landline, I got worried," Stephen explained. "I tried a few more times, thinking you might have gone to take a shower or a bath, but two hours later, you still didn't pick up. So, I drove over here, and Carl came with me. I had a feeling something was wrong, and I couldn't settle for the night without knowing you were okay. When we got here..." He paused, his Adam's apple bobbing as he swallowed. "Your front door was open, and we found you unconscious on the floor. Your head was bleeding. You'd taken several blows to your face and a few kicks to your body, which is why your ribs are sore. A home invasion, the police say." Stephen drew a deep breath, and Carl put his hand on his shoulder, squeezing gently.

Alina stared at him. She couldn't even remember anything after saying goodbye to Stephen in the car. Desperately searching her mind for any recollection of the hours since she'd walked through the door, all she found were whispered words so full of venom she shuddered recalling them.

"What? Did you remember something?" Carl frowned as he searched her face.

"No. I don't know... maybe. I can hear these words being whispered over and over. It sounds evil..."

"What words?" Stephen cupped her face, his blue eyes darkened with concern.

"Something like 'you'll pay' or 'pay now'. But pay for what?" Tears spilled down her cheek.

A flash of anger swept across Stephen's face, and he turned to Carl, who nodded. Alina was too tired and in too much pain to decipher their silent communication. Every part of her hurt, and she dreaded to think what her face looked like. She struggled to sit up and after a nod from the EMT, Stephen and Carl both helped her into a chair.

The room swayed and dipped around her, and she fought hard to swallow back the nausea in her throat while her head threatened to self-detonate. Taking shallow breaths, she held perfectly still, willing her body to cooperate and settle down. When the imminent threat of emptying her stomach at her feet subsided, she carefully straightened.

She looked around her living room and, for the first time since she'd regained consciousness, noticed the mess and destruction. With fresh tears welling up, her eyes scanned the overturned furniture, smashed photo frames, and sliced-open cushions. Plants were dumped on the floor with the soil trodden into the carpet, and the curtains hung in tatters from broken rails.

A sob worked its way up from her chest, and she wrapped her arms around her. Closing her eyes to the chaos, she breathed in deeply through her nose, counted to five, then breathed out through her mouth, just like her therapist had taught her when she felt a panic attack coming.

A strong arm wrapped comfortingly around her shoulders, and she leaned her head against Carl's chest with Stephen on her other side, holding her hands. The dams broke, and she cried so hard her body shook. The stream of tears seemed endless, eventually reducing to a trickle before stopping altogether, but deep sobs still wracked her body for what felt like an eternity.

"Come on, sweetheart. After they've checked you out in the ER, we're taking you home with us. The guest room is ready and waiting with fresh bed linen and towels," Stephen said.

Alina had no energy left to protest, and she wouldn't be able to sleep in the house, anyway. It had been violated, and she no longer felt safe. She was tired down to her bones, in need of some powerful painkillers and a glass or two of a strong Bourbon.

Sitting in the backseat of Carl's Range Rover, Alina closed her eyes and tried to relax. It was nearly five AM, and the city streets were dark and quiet. Or at least quiet for New York. Cars were still cruising along the avenues, and a few people were either heading for an early shift or coming back from a late one. The old adage about it being the city that never sleeps was definitely true from what she'd seen.

She yawned widely, feeling exhausted physically and utterly drained mentally. To avoid thinking about the attack, her eyes scanned the activities on the streets they traveled while her mind bounced from one errant thought to another, never stopping long enough for the memories of her ordeal to solidify.

The EMTs had taken her in the ambulance to the nearest ER where she'd had x-rays and a CT scan done. Fortunately, she had no head injuries, but one of her ribs was cracked, so a nurse had wrapped a bandage around her torso for support. Painkillers and plenty of rest were the orders from the doctor who'd examined her.

Stephen and Carl had been with her the entire time, taking care of all the paperwork and filling her prescription for the pain medication. After four hours, she'd finally been released, and they were now on the way back to Carl and Stephen's house.

With her head against the backrest, she took a deep breath, trying to force her muscles to release the tension, when a sudden flood of sounds and images flooded her brain.

A fist. A growl.

Agony.

A boot. A scream.

Blood.

With a start, her eyes flew open, and she straightened, swallowing back the bile flooding her mouth. Glancing at her two friends up front, she was glad they hadn't noticed her sudden panic.

Unable to cope with more questions, she attempted to calm her breathing and appear normal. At least as normal as could be expected of her. As grateful as she was to both Carl and Stephen for coming to her rescue, and not leaving her side, she'd be glad to get back to their house and lie down in a dark room. She needed some time to herself to process what had happened and to cry. Alone.

His hand feathered across her cheek, down her neck, and skimmed across her collarbone. Trembling from the sensation, she looked up at him, but his face was in shadow, so she couldn't see clearly. All she could make out were his light-colored hair and blue eyes. As he moved lower, she felt him smile against her skin. Her breathing sped up as his lips and tongue began exploring every inch from her face to her feet. He left no part of her body untouched, and it wasn't long before her heart was racing, her pulse thundering in her ears.

She felt herself getting wetter with every press of his mouth against her heated flesh. Her hands fisted the sheets by her sides in an effort not to climax from the sheer pleasure he was giving her. Moans spilled from her lips, and she writhed beneath the ministrations of his hands.

She rose to kiss him, wrapping her hands around his shoulders, pressing him tighter against her breasts. Her nipples had hardened and were aching to be touched, but so far, he'd left them alone — much to her displeasure.

When his lips left hers, she whined with disappointment, but it soon turned to mewls of lust when they closed around one swollen bud. He nipped at it with his teeth, making it swell almost painfully, and still, she inched closer for him to take more into his mouth. Having concentrated his attention on the rosy peak, he moved over to the other while rolling the first one between his thumb and forefinger, twisting and tugging gently. As if directly connected, a corresponding flare of desire erupted in her dripping core, heat rising through her body. He sucked hard on her nipple, and she dug her nails into his back, making a deep groan rumble from his throat. She felt the strong muscles flex and tighten under her hands, and she wanted more — needed more.

"Shhh, let me feast on you."

The words were so quiet she wasn't entirely sure she'd heard them right, but the urge to allow him his pleasure was too strong to resist. It was more of a demand than a request. Once again, he trailed a path of kisses down her body, licking the underside of her breasts and circling her belly button until he reached her mound. He drew a slow pattern of circles and infinity symbols on her sensitive skin, moving closer to the sensitive bud at the top of her slit, but never touching it.

She nearly screamed as his tongue found its way between her folds, licking a wide strip from the bottom up, but only dancing across her clit. The sweet torture was driving her insane. Her breath caught in her throat on every exhale, and her fingers gripped his hair so hard she was sure it must hurt.

Nipping the crease of her hip, he blew gently across her heated skin. She almost flew off the bed, but with his hands wrapped around the tops of both thighs, he held her securely. He began lapping at her sensitive folds in earnest. She felt her juices trickling out in a steady stream, and no sooner had he licked them up than they flowed faster. With each stroke of his tongue, her swollen clit zinged with a burning fire, sending her pleasure receptors into a frenzy. When his lips finally closed around the swollen nub and sucked hard, bolts of lightning crackled through her body, and she was catapulted into the heavens with stars exploding all around her. Everything disappeared except for his mouth still lavishing his attention on her now oversensitive nub but gentler and slower until she came down from her flight into ecstasy.

Tugging hard at his shoulders, she pulled him up and over her, relishing his weight along her body. His hard shaft prodded her stomach, and she was more than eager to have it fill her. He slipped to her side, kissing her neck and the sensitive skin behind her ear. She wrapped a hand around the soft flesh with its core of steel, enjoying the sharp inhale and the ticking of muscles in his clenched jaw.

In some distant part of her brain, a voice was telling her to set herself free before she went any further. Shutting out the voice and ignoring the slight unease trying to settle in her chest, she pushed him to his back and slid down the bed until his cock nudged her face. She enveloped it in her warm mouth, sucking gently, pleasure zipping through her brain at hearing the unintelligible stream of words falling from his mouth. As she moved her head up and down, her lips slid along the heated skin, her tongue swirling around the head each time as the pre-cum leaked from the slit in the crown. Greedily, she licked every drop, swallowing the slightly salty fluid.

The sound of his voice sent tingles of heat to her stomach, but also a sense of something both familiar and unfamiliar at the same time. This wasn't Jonas, but neither was it a stranger. This man belonged to her, and she belonged to him. They were joined both in body and in spirit, as if they were two halves of a whole. She didn't understand it, and it sent a chill racing down her spine.

Before long, he tugged her away and up alongside him before rising on his arms and holding himself above her. Nudging her knees apart, he settled between her thighs, the tip of his cock poised at her soft entrance. She felt his gaze search her face and nodded.

It seemed it was all the invitation he needed, and he slid deep inside her, stealing her breath away. She wrapped her legs around his waist to pull him deeper, while her hands gripped his shoulders for something to hold on to. Surging in and out of her, each thrust so powerful her body sank deeper and deeper into the soft bedding, he dominated her, but in a reverent and worshipful way.

Feeling him claim her body so completely sent her on a crashing wave of desire, nothing existed but the two of them, and she wanted nothing more than to stay in his arms forever. He was all-consuming, his presence demanding complete submission while in the same breath handing her all control.

Jolts of electricity zapped through her from her core to her brain, heralding the impending detonation. Wanting to make the insane pleasure last, she tried to stave off the fireworks, but it was no use. Judging from the sounds emanating from his throat, he was nearing his peak, as well. She wanted them to come together, to reach the crest of their climax at the same time.

The moans streaming from her mouth became louder, mingling with his deep groans. His body tensed above her, and he threw his head back, a roar erupting from his chest as he stroked harder, faster, before burying himself so deep inside her core it felt as if they'd melded to become one. His seed pumped hot and thick inside her, the sensation so intense her orgasm ripped through her, sending flares of fireworks through her vision. Soaring toward infinity, she spiraled faster and faster until—

ALINA WOKE WITH A START, scrambling upright with her back against the headboard. Her chest felt tight, and her heart raced like she'd run a marathon, while cold sweat beaded her forehead. Her hands felt clammy at the same time as other parts of her were about to burst into flames.

It was a dream! The blond man didn't exist. She hadn't made love to another man. She hadn't cheated on Jonas. Her shoulders dropped, and she felt as if someone had punched her in the gut.

Jonas was gone. He was no longer around for her to cheat on him. Not that she would ever have done so, but this made her feel like she had.

It was stupid. You couldn't cheat on a dead person. So why did this make her feel that way? And why did it also make her feel as if it was meant to be?

She'd dreamed of the blond man before. Once, she'd watched him attend a funeral. His wife, maybe. And once, when they'd also made love—

No, we didn't make love, he just almost made me—

Shaking her head, she muttered to herself that it was a dream, not lovemaking, no matter how good it had felt. How could it be? This man was a complete stranger, so how could it possibly be love?

Alina huffed at her own stupidity. It was all in her head. They hadn't had sex. Not really. She hadn't orgasmed several times under his fingers... his tongue... his lips...

It was just a dream, not reality!

Still, she couldn't help but wonder why this man kept appearing in her subconsciousness, and why were the dreams so vivid, so visceral?

From somewhere far away in the deepest recesses of her mind, a voice drifted toward her.

Just take one little step.
I'll come for you.

She fumbled for the light on the nightstand, but it wasn't where it should be. In fact, the nightstand felt different. Where was she? A throbbing ache in her head jumbled her thoughts, making her feel sluggish. Suddenly, a blueish glow from the nightstand lit up the darkness around her, and she drew a sigh of relief. Her cell sat on the side, the screen activated with an incoming notification. It still didn't explain where she was and why she wasn't in her own bed.

Rubbing her temples, memories from the other evening trickled back. She was in Stephen and Carl's guest room and had been here since Friday night after the attack. It was now Wednesday — no, Thursday, since it was way past midnight. She hadn't been back to work yet and still couldn't face returning to her house.

Stephen had picked up more of her clothes and other necessities, but she'd yet to make it out of her lounge pajamas. All she wanted was to curl up in bed in a dark room. To be alone. To let the misery and self-pity consume her.

If only for a little while longer.

Twenty-One

KIRAN, 1966

Kiran paid no notice to where they were taking him. He stumbled blindly after his captors, the guilt of leaving Margaret behind slowly disappearing behind a veil in his mind where all his other trials and sufferings were hidden away. He'd survived everything else that had been thrown at him. He would survive this as well, and then succumb to injury, disease, or starvation like so many times before. Never had he died a peaceful, natural death.

It was slow going on the narrow jungle trails. After following a mostly northerly course, they arrived at a small camp with fifteen other soldiers. Their shelters were mainly tarps strung between trees, offering little to no protection from the rain or chilly nighttime temperatures.

The man in charge of the group shoved him toward a tall tree near the center of the little encampment. With his arms and legs tied to the trunk, Kiran could do nothing more than watch the goings-on around him. With no food for several days, and the only fluids coming from the raindrops trickling down the leaves above his head, it was only a matter of time before he began passing out for periods. In his already weakened state, the effort of keeping his weight off the bindings was too much, and he slumped forward. His shoulders wrenched back, and his spine arched painfully.

Another few days passed, and Kiran got weaker, but the soldiers knew how to keep him alive by giving him the bare minimum of food and water. Most of the time, he withdrew to that beautiful, calm place inside his mind to hide until he'd gathered a little energy to face them again.

Early one morning, after a brutally cold night, raised voices penetrated Kiran's sluggish brain. He blinked his eyes open, grateful for the murky pre-dawn light, to see another group of Viet Cong arrive with several prisoners in tow. They shoved the group of disheveled men into the middle of the camp and started debating amongst themselves.

After a lot of chattering back and forth, rapid hand gestures, and stabbing the air with pointed fingers, they seemed to come to some form of decision and began gathering all the belongings in the clearing, including the tarp coverings and straw mats they used to sleep on.

In less than an hour, they'd dismantled the entire camp, re-tied the ropes on the prisoners, and freed Kiran from the tree he'd been lashed to for so long. He fell to his knees in the squelchy mud, his body screaming in protest over being bent back into its natural shape, but he gritted his teeth, struggling not to let his enemies see how much he was hurting.

After they yanked him to his feet, he was slotted into the middle of the line of men and attached to their bindings like a flower in a daisy chain. A sharp tug told them to move forward, and soon, they were navigating the barely discernible paths through the undergrowth.

Hauled, dragged, shoved, and shunted, they spent the next day and a half stumbling toward the unknown. At least now, Kiran wasn't on his own.

By the end of the second day, they arrived at a much larger camp that seemed more organized and better equipped. After ordering them to sit down inside a pen made from bamboo poles, their captors gave them a decent-sized portion of rice and vegetables each and as much water as they wanted. Kiran drank carefully and slowly, refilling his cup several times. It tasted like the finest of wines and heavenly nectar, all rolled into one.

They stayed in the camp for a few hours, allowing them to get some much-needed rest. Curling up on the damp ground, they made themselves as comfortable as possible. The man next to him, a big, burly soldier with a tattoo of a dagger flanked by two golden wings on his shoulder, nodded in silent hello. Kiran furtively glanced around to see if any guards were near. All previous attempts at talking by any of them had quickly been stopped with a rifle butt to the stomach or the back.

"I'm Geoff. Australian Special Air Service. Nice to meet you, although I wish it were under better circumstances. They said this vacation would be full of action and adventure. They're not wrong." A crooked smile tugged at the man's mouth, and his brows waggled briefly. "But I think I'll stay home next time."

Kiran smiled back. He was glad for the attempt at levity in their precarious situation.

"I'm Kiran. US Army Medical Corps. All I wanted was a few days on the beach. Haven't seen the ocean in weeks," he deadpanned.

Geoff let out a bark of laughter, and then quickly tried to disguise it with fake coughing.

"How did they capture you?" Kiran whispered, keeping his head down so as not to attract the attention of their watchers.

"We were sent to find a small landing strip in the jungle from where the commies were staging their raids on our base. They'd already managed to drop munitions on our airfield and blow one of our vehicles to smithereens." Geoff glanced around before continuing, "It was sheer luck on their part, but we had to stop them from doing any more damage. We heard another group of them had already shot down one of your planes at a base farther up the coast. So, I left with my squad to search for their camp and destroy it." He paused for a moment, his mind elsewhere.

Kiran waited, understanding his companion's need to gather his thoughts.

"After hiking through this damn jungle for four days," Geoff resumed his story, "we finally came to a large clearing in a hidden valley between the two mountains to the east of Hue. We snuck in during the dark and placed bombs fitted with timers all over the place. We even attached one to a plane in the small hangar by the side of the landing strip. Then we hightailed it out of there but ran into one of their patrols on the way back. While my men left the area, I kept them busy... I haven't seen any of them since. I hope they made it back."

Kiran felt for the special forces man. He already knew no one was looking for him and didn't have to wonder whether Margaret had made it back to base. She was dead and wouldn't ever go back home.

Sour bile rose in his throat, and he swallowed it back while kicking any thoughts of the past few weeks down into the dark pit of his mind. It was where all the other things he didn't want to think about churned in a primordial soup, bubbling and reeking with a stench that coated the inside of his nose and mouth.

Before dawn, they were woken up with shouts and clanging of metal pans. Ordered to stand in a line once more, the VC soldiers roped them together again before moving out through the thick undergrowth. To their surprise, it wasn't long before they reached a dirt road and continued along the ribbon of hard-packed earth, the endless jungle surrounding them on both sides.

In a cloud of dust, they marched farther and farther north. Whether they were still in South Vietnam, Kiran didn't know, but after a few days of walking ten hours under a baking sun, he no longer cared.

From time to time, they'd leave the road and continue through the forest until they eventually tracked onto another rutted lane. Maybe it was the same one, Kiran had no way of knowing, and asking questions was a surefire way to get a knock on the head by something hard. Instead, he carefully watched his surroundings.

It hadn't taken him long to realize that one or two of the Viet Cong soldiers spoke some English and were listening to everything they said. He passed the message to the other prisoners to keep their mouths shut about anything concerning their home bases, personnel, or equipment.

Sand and grit found their way into his boots, eyes, and clothes, making everything chafe and scrape. Blisters formed on his feet, in his groin, and under his arms where the sand rubbed his skin raw. His eyes were stinging and weeping, and his scalp had sores from sunburn with grit caked in, stopping them from healing.

Food and water once again became scarce, at least for the prisoners, making them weak and lethargic, causing them to stumble and fall. They soon learned to pull each other up with barely losing a step, a symbiotic relationship forming between the twenty or so prisoners.

By Kiran's very rough estimation, it took them close to a month to reach their destination, but one night, after darkness had fallen, they finally saw the flickering light of torches amongst the trees. They emerged into what could loosely be described as a small village with wooden structures in rows on three sides of a larger open area, and several more huts spread out farther back on the edges. Most were made of wooden planks or bamboo poles lashed together, but a few were constructed with poured concrete.

The soldiers took the prisoners to a couple of shacks on one side of the encampment. After the ropes had been removed, they were ordered to strip out of their clothes and given a pair of loose cotton pants and a short-sleeved tunic to wear. Their boots were replaced with woven sandals, and each man was handed a straw mat to sleep on and a small food bowl. Clutching their meager supplies, they went into their new lodgings, ushered by a guard.

Kiran blinked in the darkness as the stench of unwashed bodies, human excrement, hopelessness, and fear assaulted him. The only light came from the torches outside, which barely reached across the threshold. As his eyes adjusted, his gut clenched. Every available inch of floor space was covered with men of various ages, all on their own sleeping mats.

The guard shouted something and poked the men nearest him. Wordlessly, they shuffled closer to the man next to them who in turn did the same, until they had created enough space for Kiran and his companions to put their mats down. The guard stomped out, securing the door behind him, leaving them in almost complete darkness once again.

Kiran was glad to see Geoff was still with him. The jovial Australian had been a constant source of lighthearted jokes and comfort despite their dire circumstances. Nothing seemed to dim his positive outlook, and when Kiran had asked him about it, he'd just said you either keep going or you drop to the ground and die. He chose to keep going.

Kiran was glad to lie down but was in too much pain from the blisters and bruises covering large parts of his body to sleep. Curling up on his least sore side, he retreated into his mind where the sunshine was.

Despite his aching body, he must have dozed off at some stage, because he was jerked awake by a guard, who dragged him outside, dropping him to the ground. The bright sunlight hurt his eyes, sending a stabbing pain through his skull. No matter how much he tried not to give his captors the satisfaction of knowing he was in pain, a muffled groan tore from his throat.

Snickers and laughter came from all sides, accompanied by some poking and prodding. He told himself it was fine. He could cope with their scorn, taunts, and even their kicks and knocks. The walk here had been bad, but it was over now. Whatever else happened, he would deal with it.

The ragtag bunch of soldiers surrounding him stood watching as he tried to at least sit up and not be sprawled on the ground like a throwaway rag. After several minutes, another soldier arrived, and it was clear he was in charge, since all the others shrank away, bowing and mumbling a greeting.

The man looked at Kiran and barked an order. Whoever he'd aimed it at clearly understood and grabbed Kiran under the arm, dragging him to his feet and over to a squat, concrete building with corrugated iron for a roof on the very edge of the compound.

Hesitating on the threshold, Kiran peered through the gloom to prepare himself for the worst. It was a bare room with only a wooden chair in the middle. Somehow, that made things worse, and the hairs on the back of his neck rose in apprehension.

A shove in his back pushed him to all fours on the rough stone floor. He stayed down for several seconds to catch his breath and gather some strength. Staring at the uneven ground, he noticed dark brown stains marring the gray surface. The smell inside the structure was even ghastlier than in the sleeping quarters, because mixed in with the body odors was the coppery tang of blood.

Kiran's stomach turned, and he had to swallow hard to force back the nausea. Yanked up by his hair, he was pushed into the seat and told not to move except for using the putrid waste bucket in the corner, but only once a day, or he'd be punished.

Kiran sat as immovable as he could, but inevitably, he'd move a leg or an arm, or even just twitch a finger, to relieve a cramp, or sometimes it was completely involuntary. He didn't know how they did it, but they were clearly watching for it because each time, he would be punished.

Maybe they didn't see anything and randomly beat him, anyway. He wasn't sure.

Days went by with the same pattern, hour after hour. Every so often, interrogators would enter the stuffy room and shout question after question at him. They were under the impression he was a member of the special forces and wanted information from him that he couldn't give.

These men were different from the others. They spoke passable English, and their uniforms looked newer and better cared for. Their hair was trimmed and mouths were mostly free from stained and broken teeth. Something told him not to let them know he was a doctor, so he kept his mouth shut and only answered with his name, rank, and serial number.

Strangely, it was a welcome relief when they came in, since he was allowed to move and could stretch out his sore and bruised muscles. When they left him alone again, he'd retreat into himself, and to avoid being consumed by the pain he was in, began recounting his story from the first moment he remembered after Falling until the day he left for Vietnam. He planned everything out and painted vivid pictures in his mind with sounds, sights, and smells, down to the tiniest detail.

After painstakingly outlining each existence in turn, he began telling the story as if he were writing a book. If he forgot anything, he'd go back, erase what he'd plotted, and restart the chapter or paragraph. He had a lot of material to use from the building of the pyramid to battling the Western Xia Dynasty by Genghis Khan's side and facing the Black Death on a ship on the Mediterranean Sea.

Once a day, he'd get a small cup of water and a bowl of watery, green soup. Sometimes, a piece of stale bread would be added to his meager ration. Mostly, he was too weak and in too much pain to be able to eat or drink anything.

To keep track of the passing days, he scraped a small mark in the dirt under his feet. This is how he knew they kept him there twenty-four hours a day, for ten days straight. He didn't sleep, just existed in some kind of vacuum between the sessions with his inquisitors, a distant part of his brain keeping his body as still as possible.

On the eleventh day, Kiran was jolted out of his stupor by the door crashing open and someone shouting orders to the guards. Two men ran in, grabbed him under the arms, and dragged him outside. He howled from the pain of being jostled about after keeping still for so long. His tendons went taut like guitar strings, and every muscle contracted beyond normal.

They left him writhing on the ground, tears streaming down his face, his lungs caught in a vise, and his heart slamming against the insides of his ribcage. After an interminably long time, his body finally began to relax, and he could once again breathe without a knife stabbing his lungs with every exhale.

Lying still on the damp ground, he listened for the guards so he could be ready for another beating, but they seemed to be waiting for someone. Kiran was happy where he was. Breathing fresh air for the first time in a week and a half felt heavenly, and the earth beneath him was like duck feathers after the wooden chair and concrete floor of the shed.

A loud shout had his guards scrambling to form a line. Another shout, and they pulled him to his feet, marching him away toward a different part of the encampment. Kiran had expected them to take him back to the sleeping hut, but instead, they threw him in a different, much smaller concrete box. His head bounced off the cement, pain exploding behind his eyes, and a wave of nausea washed through his gut.

A heavy metal door slammed shut behind him with a deafening clang, the sound reverberating through his bones. He was alone in a pitch-black, airless, and stifling hot box.

Curled into a ball, he began to prepare himself for more torture. He was no stranger to it. Nonetheless, before coming to Vietnam, he'd hoped he was done with this kind of suffering. Evidently, He had a different opinion.

I got through it before. I'll get through it again.

With his head spinning, he told himself the words over and over before a cool, comforting darkness enveloped his mind, giving him a welcome relief from the renewed agony that had been blasting through his body like flames licking a log on a fire.

When he finally woke again, the temperature had risen to unbearable levels, and the air was suffocating.

Then his nightmare truly began.

Twenty-Two

ALINA, 2014

Dropping her feet to the floor, she padded silently across the plush carpet into the adjoining bathroom to wash her face and give her teeth a quick brush. Once she'd freshened up, she wrapped her robe around her, cinching the sash carefully around her waist. Her ribs were still sore, and the skin tender and bruised, but better than it had been a couple of days ago.

She'd been lucky, as whoever the intruder was had broken no bones. The contusions and abrasions were bad enough, even though they were more blue and yellow than black and purple now. Since they covered large parts of her face, she didn't want to go back to work just yet. She'd only be bombarded with questions she didn't want to answer.

Alina looked out the window at the busy street several stories below her. A pale winter sun filtered through the thin clouds, bathing the frozen ground of the little park opposite in warm hues. She'd been staying with Stephen and Carl for almost two weeks now and still couldn't face going back to her house. Carl had gone back there several times to clear it and make it secure again, but she doubted she would ever feel as safe as she had before the attack.

The police had finished their investigation and taken her statement, but she'd heard nothing since. She could only assume it had been someone looking for valuables to sell to fund his next fix. Her overactive imagination had probably created the threat she thought she'd heard, fueled by fear and adrenaline, so the attack would make some sort of sense in her mind.

Alina's shoulders dropped. Nothing could make the assault on her home and body make any kind of sense. The intruder had stolen only a few items, and most of them were of insignificant value. It was more the destruction of her furniture and belongings that worried her. It seemed vengeful, nasty, and personal, but why would anyone want to wreak havoc on her home? The only one she could think of was— No, Warren might have tried to sabotage her professionally, but he'd never been violent.

She shook her head, feeling guilty for even considering him, then shoved her feet into her slippers and traipsed downstairs. She needed coffee, and lots of it, before she sat down to work out what she was going to do about the mess her life had become again.

As she stepped into the brightly lit, cozy kitchen, she realized how hungry she was when her nose filled with the aromas of fried eggs, bacon, sausages, and grilled tomatoes. Expecting Stephen, it surprised her to see Carl standing at the stove. He looked ridiculously attractive in a t-shirt and low-rise sweatpants, and Alina couldn't help wondering how many women had been disappointed to find Carl was gay and happily married.

For sure, there had to be a lot of both men and women drowning their sorrows over never having the chance to be with men like Carl and Stephen. They were gorgeous, funny, caring, and protective of anyone they loved, and they would go out of their way to help those who asked for it. She considered herself incredibly lucky to have Stephen as both her boss and close friend. Carl was the cherry on top of that sundae.

"Morning, beautiful. How did you sleep?" Carl smiled at her.

Alina hopped up on a stool by the island and propped her elbows on the counter.

"Not too bad. I woke up a few times and dreamed a lot, but I can't remember any of it. They weren't nightmares." She added, "I think." They hadn't felt like nightmares, but they hadn't been pleasant dreams either.

Carl busied himself with the eggs in the pan while keeping an eye on the bacon in another and the tomatoes under the grill.

"Help yourself to some coffee. It's freshly made." He pointed at the French press next to mugs and spoons, with creamer, sugar, and flavored syrups on the side. She poured the hot, black goodness into a cup, added some of the creamer and a shot of vanilla, and stirred. The rotating motion was familiar and calming, easing the twisting in her stomach.

A fancy, all-bells-and-whistles coffee machine sat in a corner of the marble counter, but Carl preferred grinding the beans himself and using the press. Stephen liked popping a pod in the machine, slipping a cup under the spout, pressing a button, and standing back to wait for the contraption to do its thing.

Alina had a machine herself, but the rich, dark aroma of the freshly ground beans with just a touch of creamer and vanilla added had her seriously contemplating getting a grinder and a press when she went back home. It would be great for the weekends when she could linger over her coffee and the morning papers.

Her stomach clenched again at the thought. She wasn't sure she could ever go back there. Maybe she'd be better off breaking the lease and finding somewhere different? As much as she loved the little townhouse, it no longer felt like her home.

"Stephen will be back soon. He had to go into the office to pick up a few files to work on over the weekend."

Alina grimaced. She felt guilty for bailing on him for the past two weeks. She should have been brave enough to go into the office with her head held high and ignore the inevitable water cooler gossip.

"Nuh-uh. No, you don't." Carl arched a brow and pinned her with a stern look. "You've done exactly the right thing by staying here after the attack."

She squirmed under his piercing stare, on one hand knowing she'd been in no state to get any work done, and on the other, feeling as if she were letting Stephen down when he'd literally dropped everything to help her.

"You can't know what I was thinking. I was just..." She let her words trail off, knowing there was no point in arguing with the man.

Carl barked out a laugh at the pink flush she could feel creeping up her cheeks. "Yeah, sure. You weren't thinking you'd let Stephen down by not being at work this week? And that you're inconveniencing us by staying here?"

The man was perceptive as well as direct.

"Okay, I was, but only because I feel like such a fraud being waited on hand and foot when I'm perfectly capable of doing things myself." She wiped a hand across her brow, consternation niggling in her chest. "I have so many projects that need my attention at work, and I can't expect others to pick up the slack."

Carl slid a plate of food in front of her and prepared one for himself. "You are not a fraud. You were just assaulted in your own home and badly hurt. It's going to take some time to heal from those injuries. Both the physical and the mental ones. Give yourself a break and rest before you think about going back to work." He sat on the stool next to her and started eating. "Stephen says everything is in hand in the office, and he's got your staff taking care of whatever needs taking care of. In the meantime, I'm the lucky man who gets to spoil you" — he twirled his fork in her direction — "and cater to your every need. Stephen loves it when I fuss over him, but I'm usually out the door early in the morning, and he's often home late, which doesn't leave me much opportunity to treat him the way I want to. Having you here fills my nurturing needs. It's a win-win situation." A lopsided smile pulled at his mouth, and he winked at her.

Alina couldn't help the giggle bursting over her lips. He looked so adorable and cheeky, and she knew he meant every word. She'd happily stay here forever if it would make Carl's caring heart beat faster. It was a dream, but a nice one. Thinking of her house, her heart sank again. Something had to be done about the place, and she needed to sit down and seriously think about what she wanted to do.

The front door opening and closing pulled their attention to the hallway, and Carl's face lit up when Stephen walked in. Alina's heart warmed at seeing the two of them together, so happy and in love. One day, she might have that again with a bit of luck and a lot of soul searching.

"How are you feeling, Lina?"

Unprompted, Stephen had started using her old nickname. She'd never corrected him, since it made her feel part of a family.

"I'm much better now with Carl's fabulous cooking filling my stomach. If he keeps making meals like this past week, you'll never get rid of me," she joked.

Stephen dropped his keys on the hall table and hung his coat in the closet before returning to the kitchen. Taking her hands in his, he scrutinized the bruises on her face before giving her an encouraging smile.

"You know you can stay here for as long as you like. We love having you, and you're no bother. Okay?"

"I tried telling her that, but she won't listen," Carl chimed in.

"Yes, okay. I hear you," she replied, her hands up in mock surrender. "You've both been amazing, but I have to resume my life eventually, and I want to go back to work."

"Take your time. There's no need to rush things. See how you feel Monday morning." Stephen straightened and rounded the island to give his husband a kiss and a hug before taking the mug of coffee Carl had prepared for him.

He settled on the stool next to Alina and smiled gratefully when Carl slid a plate heaped full of food in front of him. A comfortable silence fell over the kitchen as they ate their breakfasts, taking sips of coffee between mouthfuls.

ALINA AND STEPHEN spent some time in the afternoon going over numbers for several companies wanting quotes on a selection of seminars, conferences, and corporate days out. Once they were happy with the figures, Stephen would send them back to their liaisons, so the companies could decide whether they wanted to use them.

Alina knew they were competitive and had a great reputation for going above and beyond with any function they ran. She just hoped Warren's interference wasn't still lingering in the corridors of the New York business community. It was a huge world, but still small enough for failures and disappointments to stick like glue. Even false rumors and bad-mouthing were enough to give people pause for thought and make them go with safer options.

Pursing her lips, she shoved Warren's betrayal and childish antics from her mind. It did her no good to let him take up any more of her energy than he had already. He was a finished chapter and would soon find some nice girl from his parents' country club to grace his arm instead. Someone who would fit in, and whose family was part of the same social circle as his was. He needed a woman who was content with staying at home, raising a family, and spending her spare time on club committees and organizing charity galas.

That wasn't her. She wanted to forge her own career, and Jonas had supported her in everything she'd wanted to do. She'd loved her job, even if it sometimes meant spending hours chasing down caterers, florists, photographers, and wedding cake creators from morning until night. He'd never complained, just taken the kids off her hands, or called his parents to come and babysit for a few hours.

God, she still missed him and their babies so much it was like a knife to the heart at every instance she thought of them, which was many times every single day. As the months and years passed, the pain was easier to bear, but it never went away, and she doubted it ever would. She could only hope that one day, the love accompanying the pain would dull its edges and soften the blow. That day wasn't today, and it wouldn't be tomorrow either, but maybe in the future she would wake up and realize it had finally happened.

Alina inhaled deeply. Thinking of Jonas always sent her emotions reeling, but she didn't want to cry in front of Carl and Stephen. Not that they would mind in the slightest. Instead, they'd offer comfort and a shoulder — or two — to cry on, but they'd already had to deal with so much from her in the past two weeks. Enough was enough. She could and would stand on her own two feet again. The attack on her house — she refused to call it an attack on herself, she was just collateral damage — was a temporary setback, and come Monday morning, she'd be back out there fighting for everything she wanted.

THE THREE OF them had settled on the couch with a bowl of popcorn and were watching a movie when a knock sounded on the door. Stephen went to open, and Alina heard his voice mingling with those of two other men. Her brow creased when the voices lowered, taking on a more intense tone, and she looked at Carl who was trying not to show he was listening as well, but he just shrugged and returned his gaze to the big-screen TV on the wall in front of them.

They both turned to look when Stephen came back with two strange men in tow. Dressed in suits with badges on their belts, their expressions were serious, and a chill went down Alina's spine when they all swung their eyes toward her. Stephen looked stricken, and Carl jumped from the seat, putting his arm around him. Alina reached for the remote control and paused the film, rising from the couch to face the men.

"Alina, these detectives need to have a word with you about the attack." Stephen spoke in a subdued tone, grasping her hands and peering into her eyes, his gaze warm but with a hint of worry.

She nodded, a pit opening in her stomach. She wanted the police to find her attacker, but she also didn't want to think about it anymore.

"Mrs. Montgomery," the taller of the two said. "We're sorry to intrude on your Saturday afternoon. Can I ask how you're feeling?"

"I'm fine, thanks, but I'd like to hear what you've got to tell me." A tremor in her voice made her clench her fists.

She hated sounding weak.

"I'm Detective Baker," he said, "and this is Detective Kozlov. We've been investigating your case and have some questions for you, if you feel up to it?"

Alina nodded. "Yes, of course."

Detective Kozlov opened the folder he was carrying and brought out a photo for her to look at.

"Do you recognize this man?" he asked.

She stared at the grainy photo. It was a still from some CCTV footage and showed a man getting into a parked car. His face was turned toward the camera and illuminated by a street lamp. A feeling of dread lodged in her stomach like a boulder.

Warren.

"Yes, that's my ex-boyfriend. Why? He's not involved in this. He can't be." Even as she said it, she knew in her heart Warren was responsible.

She'd had a nagging suspicion it was him ever since it happened, but had always dismissed it, not wanting to believe someone she'd cared for was capable of hurting her. She chewed on her cheek, trying to suppress the shudder working its way through her body.

Kozlov looked at his notebook. "He was seen leaving your house at around the time of the attack. Was he there to visit you? Did you speak with him?"

Alina couldn't take her eyes away from the photo of the man she'd been dating for over a year. She didn't want to believe he was in any way involved in this mess, but why would he have been at her house that night?

It sounded as if her voice was coming from far away when she replied, "No, he wasn't there to visit me, and I didn't see him. We broke up several weeks ago." She swallowed past the giant lump that had suddenly traveled to her throat.

"Right. I see," Kozlov muttered. "Is it possible he'd be visiting anyone else in the street, or even in the neighborhood?"

"No, he doesn't know anyone else there as far as I know." She rubbed her cheeks with both hands. "He — that is, we — didn't exactly part on good terms, but I can't believe he'd want to attack me over it."

"Alina, don't forget what happened at the office," Stephen interjected. "He wasn't happy when he was terminated at his new job, either. He could be blaming it all on you if he's angry enough."

Alina turned away from Stephen and the detectives. She slumped on the sofa, burying her head in her hands.

"I can't believe this." She swiped at a tear that insisted on trickling down her cheek. "I know he was upset when I ended it with him, but not enough for him to attack me and destroy my house. I just..." Her voice trailed off.

Stephen and Carl sank on either side of her, giving her their quiet support. Boxed in between the two men, she felt safe and protected.

She looked up at the two detectives who stood quietly watching her. "So, what happens now?"

"He'll be brought in for questioning," Detective Baker replied. "And depending on his answers, he'll either be arrested or, if we can't hold him, be set free while we investigate further."

Alina nodded, uncertain that her voice would hold.

"Is that all, detectives?" Stephen asked.

The two men looked at each other and nodded.

"We might need to ask you some follow-up questions. I assume that won't be a problem?" Detective Baker studied her face, and she had to stop herself from shrinking under his scrutiny.

She'd done nothing wrong, so why was she feeling so exposed?

After the detectives had left, Alina scurried into her bedroom — well, it was the guest bedroom Stephen and Carl graciously let her stay in — and strode to the windows looking out on the street below. The sun had disappeared behind the tall buildings, and people were heading home after a day of shopping or doing other Saturday things in the city.

She watched as families wandered back from Central Park, after a visit to the zoo maybe, the children clutching cuddly animals they'd been given as mementos of their day. She couldn't see it from her high vantage point, but she enjoyed imagining them having had a wonderful day out together. The thoughts filled her with sadness and longing, but it was better than having to consider her ex-boyfriend being responsible for the violent assault on her and her home.

As soon as she said his name in her head, the allegations by the detectives came rushing back to the forefront of her mind. Not that they'd really gone away in the first place. Their working theory was that Warren had been so incensed over losing his job and his reputation he'd wanted revenge. Apparently, rumors of his demise had spread among his family's friends and acquaintances, and his parents were being shunned as well. Losing their social standing was probably worse than losing their fortune, and they would do anything to protect themselves.

A gentle knock on the door pulled her from her thoughts.

"Alina? Sweetie? Dinner is ready, so please come and join us." Carl spoke softly, but there was no mistaking the command in his voice.

He'd insisted on her eating three meals a day since she got here, saying she needed to put some meat on her bones. Ever since she'd broken up with Warren and he'd started calling and texting her endlessly, she'd had little appetite and had lost a few pounds on her already thin frame. It seemed Carl and Stephen had made it their mission to fatten her up.

"I'll be right there. Just need to freshen up."

Carl's footsteps disappeared down the hallway, and Alina plodded into the bathroom, washing her hands and face to remove as much of the tears as she could. There was no hiding her puffy and red-rimmed eyes, however, but it wouldn't be the first time in the past two weeks they'd seen her cry, so she decided not to worry about it.

Rubbing her hands on her jeans, Alina settled in the comfortable armchair. The room had a calming decor of earth tones and soft fabrics. A tidy desk occupied a corner, and a couch sat under the bright window with a coffee table and another plush chair next to the one she'd chosen.

"Can you tell me a little about yourself, Alina?" the psychologist asked.

She was in her late thirties, with sandy hair, hazel eyes, and a smile that created dimples on her cheeks. Leaning back in the chair, she crossed her legs and rested a notepad on top of the knee, a pen held loosely in one hand.

Alina looked out the window, the skies gray and foreboding with the promise of rain, while she gathered her thoughts.

"Well, I'm from California," she began, "but I've been here in New York for two-and-half years now. My parents and my sister are in Chicago."

"Why did you leave California?" the therapist asked.

Alina stifled a sob and drew a deep breath.

"Because I needed a change. My life had... taken an unexpected turn, and I needed a new challenge."

"How do you find New York?"

"It's been mostly great. I have a job I love, a great boss who's also a close friend, and a fun social life. At least when I have time for socializing. My job keeps me quite busy with irregular hours."

The woman regarded her for a moment. "Do you want to tell me why you've come to see me today?"

Her heart picked up the pace, thudding in her chest as her leg bounced up and down. Unable to sit still, she jumped to her feet and stood by the window, pretending to look out on the quiet street outside, while her mind swirled with images of the night of the attack.

It was Carl who'd suggested she see a therapist after she'd woken up several nights in a row screaming in panic and fear. After the detectives' visit, she'd remembered more details of the assault, and the viciousness of it clawed at her chest. Warren was still the prime suspect and had retained one of the city's top lawyers to represent him.

Thinking of her nightmares sent nausea churning in her stomach. The strange thing was that the nights she didn't have nightmares, she dreamed of the blond man instead. Sometimes, they made love. Sweet, passionate, and amazing love. Just thinking about it had her heart squeezing and warmth flooding her chest, chasing away the specters of the bad dreams.

Jonas was still in her heart, but it almost felt as if he'd given her permission to love someone else, which was ridiculous. The blond man was only a figment of her imagination — an illusion her mind had created to help her deal with her worries — and yet, he felt so real. His skin under her fingertips was smooth, firm, and warm. When he kissed her, her insides tingled, and his taste lingered in her mouth long after the dream had ended.

The sadness she'd sensed in him when she saw him at the funeral was still there, mixed with anger, hopelessness, and resolve. It was crazy, but he felt like a real person, not an illusion, and it was only made crazier by the fact he and the other mourners had worn clothes like something out of the sixties.

"Alina? Are you all right?" The therapist's voice pulled her out of her thoughts.

She stayed with her back turned. "Yes, I'm fine. Sorry, just zoned out a little."

The therapist nodded. "That's okay. I understand you have a lot on your mind."

Taking a long, slow breath, Alina said, "The reason I came is that I'm having nightmares."

The woman cocked her head to the side and gazed at her, her eyes kind and warm. "What kind of nightmares?"

"Bad ones. Like, really bad. I wake up screaming and hyperventilating." She turned, leaning her backside against the windowsill and bracing her hands on either side of her hips.

She dropped her gaze to the floor and inhaled slowly, filling her lungs, before letting it out again. The action calmed her mind somewhat. Tilting her chin up, she swung her gaze to the woman.

"A few weeks ago, I was attacked in my own home. Luckily, a friend found me a couple of hours later, badly beaten, with a concussion, bruised ribs, and colorful contusions all over my body." She smiled humorlessly.

It was the only way she could stop from crying while remembering the pain she'd been in.

"Was it a home invasion or someone you knew?" The therapist's tone was soothing, making her feel more relaxed, but she couldn't remember her name.

Wait, Maxine, that's it. Her name is Maxine.

Alina felt better for remembering it.

"The police suspect my ex-boyfriend. He was seen in the area right after the attack." She scoffed. "I've got great taste in men, haven't I?"

"Why do you say that?" Maxine asked. "Do you think it was your fault he attacked you? If it were him?"

She looked down at the floor. This was a question she'd expected and had prepared for.

"No, I don't think I'm to blame for him assaulting me, but I was part of the reason he's struggling right now." She looked up at the ceiling as if she could find some answers there. "I didn't make him do this, or any of the other stuff, but I'm not sure I handled breaking up with him very well. I could have been a little more sympathetic and listened to him more, I guess."

"Were you nasty to him? Cheated on him? Gave him no reason why you wanted to break up?"

Alina's mouth twisted. "No, he wanted things from me I couldn't give him, and I told him so. I would never cheat on someone I was dating. But he wanted to get married, have children, and expected me to stop working to look after him and join his parents' country club..." Her words trailed off. "It's not me. I don't belong there, and I have no wish to stop working." She went back to her chair and sat down.

"Did he ever hurt you when you were together?" Maxine asked, studying Alina's face.

"No, he didn't. He was a little explosive when he was angry, but never took it out on me physically. I would not have stayed with him if he had hit me. Or at least, I don't think so."

Maxine studied her, leaving her feeling exposed and vulnerable. Then she looked away, tapping the pen against her lips as if in deep thought. Alina was glad for the short break. She needed a few moments to calm the emotional storm that had started brewing in her chest.

Maxine refocused on her and said, "I know this is a little out of the ordinary, but can I tell you something about myself?"

Alina nodded, her curiosity piqued, and leaned back in the chair, shifting to get comfortable, and Maxine began talking.

"So, it can be very easy to fall into a pattern of acceptance. An abuser's behavior often grows over time, making it hard to spot when it's gone too far," she explained. "And then it's even harder to break away and stand on your own two feet. I was lucky. I had my mom nearby for support." Maxine finished after twenty minutes of telling her story.

Alina sat in stunned silence. What Maxine had gone through was horrific, and she could see the similarities between Warren and Maxine's ex-husband and understood why she'd told her what had happened.

A wrinkle traveled across Alina's forehead. "Did your husband try to get you to come back?"

"He did. Several times, in fact." Maxine's chin dipped. "The last time could have turned out very differently if it hadn't been for a kind man coming to my rescue. He was staying in my mom's guest house, where I was living when Grant forced his way in. He threatened me, saying if I didn't go home with him, he'd beat me." She paused for a moment, the memory clearly difficult to handle. "I was about to agree when my guardian angel came back from running errands, grabbed

Grant by the scruff of his neck, and threw him out on the street, saying he'd heard everything and would call the police if he ever came back again. Grant never did. Our lawyers handled our divorce, and I never saw him again."

Alina leaned forward, touched by the emotional story. "You were very lucky. Who was the man? Did you see him again?"

"Yes, I did. My mom ran a small bed-and-breakfast, and he was our handyman. I must admit, I had a huge crush on him and hoped for more, but he wasn't interested." Maxine smiled. "Instead, he introduced me to a friend of his and six months later, we started dating. Two years after that, we were married, and we're still happy together. We were living in St. Augustine then, and we moved here five years ago." She chuckled. "The reason I'm telling you this is because of the pattern of behavior as you've already realized, but also that people do things when they're emotional. And the stronger that is, the stronger their actions. You are not responsible for how others feel, and neither are you responsible for what they do."

"Yes, I understand. It might take me a little while to wrap my head around it, but you've definitely helped me see things clearer," Alina mumbled, her head filling with a tangle of impressions, but also a sense of clarity. "I think I always knew, deep inside, that I didn't make Warren attack me, but I wasn't thinking straight."

"That has probably a lot to do with whatever made you leave California in the first place."

"How did you know?" Alina's brow creased in confusion.

"It's what I do. I read people. You showed me so much more with your body language, micro expressions, and the words you didn't say than you did with the things you've just told me. But you don't need to tell me that story now." Maxine straightened, putting her notebook away. "I'd like you to come back next week, though, so we can see if our chat has had any effect on your nightmares. It's not something that will happen overnight, but you might feel a little calmer, and the dreams will hopefully be less intense."

"Okay, yes. I will come back next week," Alina agreed. "It'll do me good to talk more about it. Thank you. You've been so lovely and helpful."

She meant it. Talking about what had happened with Warren and her feelings surrounding it with a stranger and a professional who knew how to make her see things in a different light had had a positive effect and given her a new angle to work from.

Alina left Maxine's office feeling a little lighter. She was just around the corner from the office, so she decided to go back there and see if Stephen was still around. It was only five-thirty in the afternoon, and he rarely left before six. While she strolled along the sidewalk, she went over what Maxine had told her. Her explanation about acceptance of someone's behavior over time made so much sense. She'd definitely done that with Warren, but as is often the case, it wasn't until now when someone else pointed it out that she could see it.

Hearing Maxine mention St. Augustine had brought back some sweet but also painful memories. She and Jonas had spent a vacation in St. Augustine before the children were born. Her parents had met them there for a few days, and they'd had an amazing time exploring the old quarters and strolling along the beach. She couldn't help wonder if the Bed and Breakfast they'd stayed in was the same one Maxine and her Mom had owned. Back when she and Jonas visited, it was an older couple who ran it, so maybe they'd sold it to Maxine's mom.

Before long, she was back at the office, and as she'd suspected, Stephen was still in his office getting ready to go home for the evening. She was glad she'd caught him. Although she no longer jumped at shadows, she was still not confident enough to take the subway home on her own. Stephen took a car back to the Upper West Side most nights, and since she was still staying with him and Carl, she'd happily wait until he was done for the evening so they could go home together.

Twenty-Three

KIRAN, 1967

He'd always believed he knew what being alone meant. Ever since he Fell, he'd been on his own, seldom forging meaningful relationships, and rarely enjoying the companionship of close friends. The nearest he'd come were the colleagues at the hospital in Los Angeles and marrying Juliet. He'd known them well enough to call them friends, and he'd truly cared for his wife even if it hadn't been the overwhelming, passionate, and burning love he'd heard others talk about.

That kind of alone had been a gentle whisper compared to what he was experiencing as a 'guest' of the Viet Cong. Solitary confinement was worse than Hell. He knew a little of what being in Hell entailed, and this was worse. Much worse.

For the past five months, he hadn't spoken to, or even seen, another American, nor heard a language other than Vietnamese or the broken English they used to communicate with him. Even that was only when they came to get him out of the concrete bunker he'd been locked inside for *enhanced interrogation*, as they liked to call it. The rest of the time, he was utterly alone.

The bunker was dark with only a foot-long slit at the top of one wall for air and light, and another slot at the bottom of the door where his food tray was shoved through on the days they remembered to feed him. It was freezing cold at night and sweltering hot during the day. He didn't know which was worse, but with no way of protecting himself from either heat or cold, all he could do was suffer through it.

"Tell us what we want to know!" the guard with the broken front tooth hissed, following with a backhander that made Kiran's teeth rattle.

He tried to speak, but his lips and tongue were so swollen it all came out muffled.

"What they plan? Where attack come from?" The man paced in a circle around the chair he was slumped on.

"I — I... on't... ow," Kiran forced out, blood pooling in his mouth and trickling down his chin.

He'd heard enough of their mangled pronunciations to know what he was being asked.

Smack!

Another blow to his jaw, this one so hard he saw stars. If he hadn't been tied to the chair, he would have gone flying across the floor.

"Tell us! Many men? Many planes? When attacking?" Broken Tooth shouted in his face, saliva spraying from his mouth.

"N — n — not — not... a c — c — mand ... ficer."

Only the officers high up in command would be privy to that kind of information, and he wasn't even a real soldier.

Kiran had been given the rank of captain in the army since his position as a surgeon required it. He had no military training whatsoever, and he'd given up rattling off his name, rank, and serial number, because it only made them more determined to break him.

He'd still not mentioned being a doctor, either, although he wasn't entirely sure why. Something made him hesitate, a voice at the back of his mind telling him to give them as little information about himself as possible. He could only imagine what they'd do to him if they knew he was a surgeon and not a high-ranking member of the officer corps. Any information he may have had always came after the fact, rendering it useless.

It often wasn't until an attack or a raid had taken place and the injured ended up on his operating table that he knew anything at all had happened. He couldn't tell them what he didn't know, but there was no convincing Broken Tooth.

Once his interrogators got fed up with beating him senseless, they came up with other techniques to try forcing information out of him — information he didn't have, but he no longer bothered saying it. After being knocked unconscious during one exceptionally brutal session, once his senses returned, he discovered he was blindfolded and trussed up like a pretzel. Thick leg irons shackled his ankles, his wrists were tied behind his back, with a rope binding his elbows just above the joints.

It didn't bother him as much as it would most men. He was used to chains and shackles, even though these days, they were physical ones rather than mental.

The guards tightened the bindings by putting their feet against his arms and pulling on the ropes until they wouldn't tighten any further. Then his ankles were tied to his wrists and a ten-foot pole was jammed between his back and elbows.

After a few hours, the ropes began to cut off the blood flow, first causing searing pain, then making his arms go numb. Then they left him lying on his stomach on the damp concrete floor for hours.

Each time Broken Tooth and the other guard — Kiran called him Frank, because he reminded him of a grumpy janitor back at the hospital in LA — returned, they used their fists to make sure he knew who was in charge.

They guffawed at his cries of pain, sneered at his pleas for mercy, and lobbed question after question at him each time they pulled him off the ground. It went on for hours, days even. Kiran could no longer tell, losing all track of time as his world became a living nightmare.

BETWEEN THE PUNISHMENTS and interrogations were the endless hours of solitude. To keep his mind active — despite the ferocious headaches — Kiran continued to create book after book of his different and varied lives. To begin with, it had been one epic spanning his whole existence. However, once he'd recounted everything up to World War Two and the years immediately after, he went back to the beginning, creating a separate novel for each of his lifetimes. He added as much detail and description as he could, and if he'd forgotten something, he'd wipe it clean and start over, being even more specific and precise.

It was a way to keep himself distracted when he was surrounded by silence and darkness for at least eighteen hours a day. Pain was a constant companion, and the mental strain was even more agonizing than the physical one. A dark fog would creep over his consciousness, attempting to suck away his last remaining powers of reasoning, and he had to do whatever he could to stop himself from slipping away through the beckoning black hole the agony created.

No matter how much he resisted the efforts of the VC to crush him, his body would be the first to give out. He couldn't stop himself from convulsing, puking, screaming until his voice was gone, and passing out from the horrors they inflicted on him. He might survive the beatings, but if he allowed them to crush his willpower, his reasoning, and his desire to live, nothing would keep him from dying. He was grateful to find he could detach himself from it all and observe it from a distance, as if it were happening to someone else. It was a way of preventing his mind from splintering.

However, that created an even bigger issue of staying in touch with reality enough to keep alive, because the effect of detaching himself was an insidious drug, infiltrating his mind and dulling the danger signals it tried to send out.

He fought hard, refusing to give in to the savagery, until one day, when it all stopped.

Broken Tooth and Frank left him alone, and the only sign of human life around him was when the food tray was shoved under the door. He was completely alone.

FALLEN UNCHAINED

THE SILENCE SCREAMED in his head, and Kiran groaned from the searing pain accompanying it. Pulling his knees to his chest, he wrapped his arms around his head to stop the darkness from sucking his mind out of his brain and setting it alight. His mind was all he had left. His body, although partially healed, felt as if it belonged to someone else. Parts had knitted back together... differently.

He'd been alone for an eternity. All his books were written, re-written, cataloged, indexed, referenced, annotated, and cited. So many lives. So many deaths. Was he dead now? Had he passed and not been thrown into a new timeline? A new life?

Maybe this was his new life. So far, with every new existence, he'd opened his eyes to normal surroundings, but maybe this time would be different? Maybe this time, he'd start in a nightmare and work his way out, or stay there, depending on what infernal ideas lay behind this particular life.

Kiran tried to push away the encroaching darkness in his head and focus on any sounds or smells in his surroundings, but everything was as before. He sighed or sobbed. He wasn't sure which, when all he could hear was more silence. It was a strange thing. He'd never known you could hear it, but silence had a sound of its own. A terrifying and soul-crushing sound.

The bunker was pitch black since they'd blocked the small opening at the top of the wall, and the one below the door was only uncovered when the tray was pushed in. It was done eons ago, or maybe only a few years. He'd not seen or heard a human voice since. His entire existence consisted of darkness and silence. Closing his eyes, for whatever good that did to him, he shoved his way through his mind to that one place where he could be happy, but this time, it was as black and empty as everywhere else.

He screamed.
His lungs burned.
His head throbbed.
His body convulsed.

He gave up.

It happened over and over. He searched his mind for that sunny, tranquil, happy place, finding nothing but darkness — an oozing, slimy soup of fear, rage, pain, and anguish. When he tried to think back to happier times, to when Juliet had been the light in his life, when he'd had friends and a purpose to his existence, no matter how short-lived, he found to his sorrow he could barely recall any details. Her face was a blur, her voice a distant whisper in the wind, and the years as if they'd barely existed at all or was something he'd read in a long-ago past.

A SHARP LANCE of light speared his eyes, setting off a chain of explosions in his skull. The pain was excruciating. He gasped from the intensity, a moan rising from his throat. Covering his eyes with his arms, he curled away from the blaze, expecting to feel the heat of fire singeing his bare limbs, but nothing happened. Unfamiliar sounds and smells overwhelmed his senses, making his head spin and nausea rise from his gut.

"Get up. Time for questions," a voice barked in his ear in broken English.

Kiran stiffened. He recognized that voice. It was one that had filled him with hate and rage once upon a time. Now, he wasn't sure it was even real.

"This place stinks. Put him on the chair and throw water over him. Clean him up. I don't want to be near such a vile, dirty, reeking piece of trash," the voice grunted.

Kiran was reeling. He couldn't be entirely sure this wasn't some new kind of nightmare. Maybe his mind had decided this was a better vision than the empty darkness he'd existed in for so long.

Still struggling to open his eyes after so long in complete darkness, he heard two pairs of boots approaching, hands gripping his arms and feet. They carried him over to a metal chair they must have brought in with them and strapped him down.

Is this real? What is happening? The voices. I remember them from before. When I was not alone. When I was surrounded by people. The voices brought pain. They brought misery. Will they bring that again?

Managing to pry his eyelids open a fraction, he watched as blurry shapes moved around him in light that had dimmed since they first came in. As his vision cleared slightly, he realized the brighter rectangle in the far corner was the open steel door where they'd first brought him in. His senses gradually settled, and new smells registered in his nose. The scents of fresh air, trees, moss, and damp earth fought to replace the stench in his prison. He was alive, but how much was left of his sanity?

The sensations were overwhelming, but slowly, he began to take in more of his immediate surroundings — things he'd either gotten used to or his mind had chosen to ignore. Not that he'd been able to see anything, anyway. The putrid waste in the corner, the flies buzzing around it, the mosquitoes attacking his skin, adding to the bites already covering every inch of his bare flesh. The stinging sores on his hands and feet from scraping against the concrete, the repugnant odor of a body not washed for much too long.

He blinked again and again, his eyes stinging and burning, but he could see more of his prison. Everywhere he looked, there were rusty stains on the floor and walls, dead insects littering the ground, and mold growing on the ceiling. Small, vertical lines were etched into the concrete below the narrow opening on the wall as if someone had tried to mark the passing of days. Large sets of marks had a longer, horizontal line separating them from each other. There were too many sets to signify weeks, and enough to count months close to a year.

His heart ached knowing there had been men here before him, and he couldn't help but wonder what had happened to them. Were they still alive, or had they succumbed to the cruel treatment of solitary confinement? Had they slowly gone insane from the lack of human interaction?

A bucket of ice-cold water dumped over his head viciously yanked him from his daze. He gasped from the shock and blinked furiously while another bucketful sluiced down his torso. His body screamed in pain while at the same time, his mind relished the sensation of dirt being washed off his skin. The conflicting sensations were so visceral he was starting to believe he was, in fact, alive.

The names of his tormenters slid back into his head. He was slowly remembering more and more from before his eternal, dark solitude.

The man Kiran had named Broken Tooth snickered as he shook his head, trying to catch his breath.

"Now, time for questions," he grunted.

The janitor-lookalike, Frank, whispered something in Broken Tooth's ear, and Kiran's gut clenched as the man's eyes lit up with malicious glee. The guard disappeared out the door again but returned after a short while with a couple of bowls and a small table, which he set down far enough away from Kiran so he couldn't see what was in them, but he could smell it. He'd had nothing more than watery soup or pieces of stale bread since they threw him in here, and his stomach growled at the smells wafting toward him.

Frank nodded toward the bowls. "You want?"

Kiran stared at him through thin slits in his puffy eyes. Hunger made him want to say yes, but his brain was telling him to be cautious, that this could still be a hallucination brought on by his solitary existence. Frank pushed the bowl toward him, but his hands were barely functional and permanently swollen after being stomped on too many times by heavy boots.

Frank moved the bowls a little nearer. Kiran glanced down. Just then, Frank knocked the bowl off the table, the meager contents spilling and soaking into the dirt floor. Kiran squeezed his eyes shut, his lips pressing together in a thin line as his empty belly wailed in protest.

The guttural bursts of laughter from his tormentors echoed in his ears, but he steeled himself not to care. Let them get their kicks out of humiliating him. It only made him more determined not to give in. Resisting their assaults on his body and mind was the only revenge he'd get, and he'd try to hold out as long as he still drew breaths.

Kiran shook his head. The room spun and fluctuated like something at a fun-fair. He wasn't sure he could take much more abuse, but he wasn't ready to give up just yet. It had already been hours since the door to his prison was unlocked. He could tell from the changing of the light outside. So far, they'd limited themselves to the odd well-placed kick or punch and plenty of insults and haranguing, most of which he couldn't even get the gist of, but it wasn't as if he cared, anyway. The knocks to his head had made him dizzy and nauseous, and instead of it just pounding, it was now being split apart with a sledgehammer. His ribs ached and burned, and he was sure some of them were cracked or broken again.

He eyed the three men talking out of his earshot. After ten minutes of heated discussions, they seemed to come to some decision, and Broken Tooth waved away the other two. They scurried out the door and were gone for a while before returning to the bunker.

Broken Tooth stood back, arms folded across his chest and his feet wide apart. The attempt at looking intimidating and powerful wasn't lost on Kiran, no matter how confused and tormented his brain was right now. It was a wasted effort, anyway. He'd long since stopped caring about anything but staying alive and refusing to answer any questions.

Frank and another man with only one eye stepped closer, carrying the small table between them. One Eye left for a few minutes and returned with another bucket filled with water.

He tensed as Frank walked up behind him and yanked his head back by his hair, but then he let go and joined One Eye by the little table. Broken Tooth grunted a command, and the two men grinned at each other. Pushing the table closer to Kiran, they introduced him to a bowl of water, some grimy rags and a wooden stick.

They smiled maliciously as they placed a piece of cloth over his face. When water dampened the rag, he suddenly felt like he was drowning. Renewed panic crashed through his mind, and he struggled against the hold the guards had on his arms. He thrashed violently, but a vise-like grip on his chin prevented him from tearing his head away as more water trickled down his face and into his mouth and nose. As he passed out, thinking he was finally dying, he thanked Him for relieving him from his agony and misery.

Kiran tumbled down an abyss, wrapped in a black nothing that was comforting in its removal of all his senses.

Sometime later, when consciousness rapped its knuckles on the door to his mind, he awoke to a fire burning throughout his entire body. Screams tore from his throat, the only action he was capable of. Instinctively knowing they had injured him beyond anything he'd already experienced, he didn't even attempt to move from his prone position on the rough floor. His heart slammed inside his chest at a dizzying speed.

Staying like that for what was probably hours, with no strength to stand, or even sit, he tried desperately to regain his strength and some semblance of control over his limbs. When the soldiers finally came back, he could only just roll onto his back. Despite his sorry state, he wouldn't let them think he was beaten, so he forced himself to move, propping himself up against the wall, desperately trying to gather his thoughts and prepare for what was coming next.

To his surprise, his captors pulled him up by the arms and took him outside of the dungeon-like bunker he'd been in for so long. Mercifully, it was after sundown and nearly dark, which spared his eyes the pain after not having been exposed to full daylight for so long.

His injuries were so severe that he was unable to stand, his pain receptors shut down, leaving him numb, and he no longer cared what they did to him. They dragged him across the quiet compound and dumped him inside one of the sleeping huts.

The man he found himself next to peered at him, and without a word, moved off his straw mat, nudging the person beside him out of the way, and gestured for Kiran to stretch out on the woven ground cover. It felt like the softest bed beneath his broken body, and he closed his eyes, a deep, shuddering sigh escaping his chest. He slowly relaxed, muscle by muscle, nerve ending by nerve ending, until he fell into a heavy sleep.

Twenty-Four

ALINA, 2014

Alina relaxed in her seat of the Boeing 747, exhausted from the past week, and checked her phone one last time before she put it in flight mode. She'd hoped to have a few days of peace and calm and some time to think while back home in Chicago, but it had been anything but relaxing. Mulling over the past few days, she shook her head at the craziness of it all. She'd wanted to get away after the revelation that Warren was most likely behind the assault on her, and she'd booked a flight to O'Hare on the Monday morning.

She felt bad about leaving Stephen in the lurch after already having had two weeks off, but he'd been a sweetheart as always and told her to go. He'd send her some stuff she could work on remotely but said he'd be fine without her for another few days.

On her way to La Guardia to catch her flight to Chicago, her mom had called in a panic, saying Sophia had been taken to the hospital with cramps and bleeding. Alina's heart had sunk. No matter how she felt about her sister, she didn't wish this on her and kept her fingers crossed that everything would be all right.

"Oh, Alina. I can't bear it. What if she loses the baby? Haven't we lost enough children already?" her mom had cried. "And where's Frederic? We can't get ahold of him." The words had filled the phone in a panicked stream. "He's supposed to be in Peoria for a deposition, but Sophia hasn't heard from him since yesterday. I'll get your dad to pick you up from the airport. Just message me your flight details."

"Mom, don't worry. I'll get a cab straight to the hospital when I land," Alina had reassured her. "Stay with Sophia, and I'll find you when I get there."

Alina put her phone away, having had no further updates on her sister, and looked out the small window, deep lines creasing her forehead. A cabin attendant walked past, making sure the overhead lockers were securely latched and everyone was buckled in. The plane pushed back and taxied toward the runway. Before long, they were climbing into the skies, headed west.

She switched on the screen in front of her and found a local news channel to watch. A breaking news icon flashed in the corner, and she clicked on it, hoping it wasn't a pile-up on the freeway from the airport to the city center.

It jumped to some CCTV footage, and it took Alina a few seconds to register what she was seeing. They'd blurred the sensitive parts, but it was obvious what had been going on. The headlines underneath screamed about the son of a prominent Chicago family being caught having sex in a back alley with a woman who wasn't his wife.

Alina stared in shock. As the video rolled, the couple finished, straightened their clothes, and walked back inside a nightclub. The man cast a glance around him before he disappeared through the door, his face clearly visible in the light from the bare bulb above the entry.

Frederic.

The news presenter came back on, but Alina only caught some of the details. She was too horrified to take it all in, but it seemed Frederic hadn't gone to Peoria for a deposition. Instead, he was in Atlantic City on a dirty weekend with his mistress. She had yet to be identified, but it wouldn't take the media long to work out who she was.

Feeling sick to her stomach, she looked at her watch. She had another hour until she landed, and all she could do was wait and hope neither Sophia nor her parents were watching the news. Willing the flight to go faster, her leg bounced nervously up and down, and she had to force herself to take slow, deep breaths. Sophia's possible miscarriage was bad enough, but to find out that her husband was cheating on her was pouring salt on the wounds.

Her sister may have been shoving her wedded bliss and her pregnancy down Alina's throat, but she didn't deserve this, and what kind of person would Alina be if she didn't feel sorry for her own flesh and blood?

As soon as the plane had landed and come to a stop at the gate, Alina rushed off, grateful she'd only brought a carry-on, and got in the first available taxi, telling the driver to get her to the hospital as quickly as he could. The man threw her a concerned glance in the rearview mirror, but Alina assured him it wasn't she who was ill but a family member. He nodded and moved out into the early afternoon traffic. Thankfully, the freeway wasn't too clogged and before long, she'd paid for her ride and jumped out by the entrance to Chicago's biggest hospital.

Hurrying inside, she found the directions to Sophia's ward and quickly crossed the wide lobby to the elevators. A few minutes later, she stood outside the door to a private room. She could hear low voices conversing inside, but they didn't sound upset, so there was still hope she'd arrived in time. If possible, she wanted to break the news to Sophia herself, even if it would probably damage whatever was left of their relationship. Her sister would most definitely shoot the messenger, especially if it was Alina.

She took a deep breath and put her hand on the door handle, but before she could push it open, a high-pitched wail erupted from inside, and the voices changed from calm to worried and frustrated.

"No! This can't be true! He wouldn't do this to me. It's a mistake. It's fake. No, no, no. I can't— This isn't— Where is he? I need to speak with him. Now!" Sophia's voice took on a note of hysteria, and Alina knew she had to step in.

"Alina, there you are. I'm so glad you're here!" her mom exclaimed.

She allowed a tiny smile on her lips in hello. "Hi, mom. I got here as soon as I could."

Her mom enveloped her in a big hug, whispering in her ear. "She lost the baby. She's absolutely devastated, and now Frederic... I don't know what to do."

Alina's heart sank. "Oh no. That's awful. Poor Sophia."

She glanced over her mom's shoulder at her sister, who was curled up in a ball.

"Look, I can take over for a little while. Why don't you and Dad go down to the cafeteria and get something to eat? I'm sure you could do with a break." She gave her dad a quick kiss.

He sat quietly in a corner, looking shocked. Her mom was about to protest, but her dad took her hand and led her out of the room. Once her parents had left, Alina turned to her sister.

"Sophia," she murmured, "I'm so sorry about this. I wish I could do something."

Sophia had fallen silent, her head turned away, but her body shook with held-back tears. The TV on the wall still played the video while the presenters discussed the ins and outs of the shocking revelation.

Frederic's family was well known in Chicago and a prominent member of the city's social elite, so this was juicy gossip and would have the newshounds baying for blood.

Alina couldn't bear to watch any more of the gleeful and gloating reporters. They loved nothing more than a good scandal.

"Why are you here? Did you come to feel sorry for me? Go ahead. I don't care," Sophia snarled, her voice hoarse.

Alina said nothing. Her sister was lashing out, and she understood why. It was all she'd wanted to do after she lost her family. To make everyone else feel as miserable as she did.

"I am sorry, Sophia," she said truthfully. "This was never something I wanted for you. I only ever wanted you to be happy, and I was looking forward to becoming an auntie. If there was anything I could do to make it go away, I would." She kept her voice low.

Sophia glared at her and opened her mouth as if to say something but clamped her lips together instead.

A flash of emotion flared in her otherwise dark and listless eyes, and Alina thought she detected a spark of... something. Gratitude? She wasn't sure, but she'd hold on to it and wait for more. Sophia was hurting, and Alina would do anything to help her recover. Her sister had just lost her baby, and her relationship with Frederic was over, Alina was sure of it. Sophia didn't give many second chances, and this was unforgivable, adding insult to an already devastating injury.

Behind her, the door flew open, and she swung her head to see who it was. Anger rose in her gut when Frederic rushed in with a panicked expression plastered on his face.

"Sophia! Darling, I came as soon as I heard. I was stuck in depositions all day yesterday and slept like the dead last night. When my secretary called, I drove straight here. I'm so sorry." Frederic fell to his knees by the bed, reaching for Sophia's hand, but she snatched it away, a steely glint in her eyes.

"Don't touch me! You're a liar and a cheater!" she shrieked.

"Sophia?" Frederic put his hand over his heart. "What are you talking about? I've never lied to you, and I wouldn't cheat. Not ever!" Despite his words, a hesitant note crept into his voice.

Alina grabbed the TV remote and clicked the power button. The video had just started playing again, and the voiceover recounted all the gory details.

Frederic slowly rose from the floor and turned, his mouth agape, a horrified expression on his face. However, it didn't take long before a blank mask fell over his features instead, and a calculating look gleamed in his eyes.

"That video is fake." He stabbed a finger at the TV. "It's not me. I was in Milwaukee. You can ask my secretary."

"You were in Milwaukee? Even though you were supposed to be taking depositions in Peoria?" Alina pinned him with a glare, and Frederic squirmed.

"I was supposed to be in Peoria, but it— it— it got changed last minute," he stammered.

"Really? And you didn't think that was something you should have told your pregnant wife?" Her brow lifted quizzically. "And are you honestly going to deny that it's you in that video? It's so obvious. You're still wearing the same clothes, for God's sake. Don't be so spineless. It doesn't suit you." Alina couldn't keep the distaste from dripping from her words.

Frederic stared at her for a long few seconds before straightening, a haughty look replacing the earlier blankness.

"So what if it was me?" He shrugged. "She's a good fuck and a better partner for me than Sophia will ever be. Her family may not be of old money, but they have plenty of it. And political connections. I want to be a senator one day, and she can help me get there."

Fury washed over Alina, and she had to forcibly stop herself from punching the arrogant bastard in the face. "So why the hell did you marry my sister and get her pregnant?"

He cast her a condescending look. "She was a bit of fun, and I guess I lost my head a little over in France, but my parents helped me see sense when I returned." Putting his hands in his pockets, he rocked back and forth on his feet. "Unfortunately, it took until after the honeymoon for me to realize it, and by the time I'd decided what to do, she'd gotten herself pregnant." Frederic sneered at Sophia, who just stared at him, eyes burning with rage.

Frederic clearly enjoyed torturing his wife, because he continued, "The funny thing is, Audrey is also pregnant. A few weeks further along than you, my darling."

Sophia flinched and curled into herself, as though his statement was a physical blow.

"How dare you?" Alina hissed, her anger making her entire body vibrate. "You're a callous, cheating, gutless, narcissistic asshole, and when I'm through with you, you'll wish you'd never met my sister." She stepped closer to Frederic, invading his personal space, and nailed him with a stare so loaded with barely controlled fury he took a step back.

Grabbing his arm, she dragged him out of the room, not wanting Sophia to be subjected to his nastiness for another second. She pushed him onto a chair, and when he made to stand, she gave him another death stare, forcing him to think better of his actions.

"You're going to tell me everything" — she stabbed her finger at his chest — "and if I think for a moment you're holding back on me, I'll get some of my friends from New York to pay you a visit."

Frederic swallowed and, in a much weaker voice than previously, gave Alina the whole sordid story. By the end, she felt sick to her stomach and hoped she wouldn't have to tell her sister a single word of it, but she knew that was impossible. Sophia would find it all out eventually.

The woman Frederic had been seeing was his ex-girlfriend from college, and he'd started up with her only a week after he'd returned from France with Sophia.

Audrey getting pregnant wasn't something he'd planned, but once it was a fait accompli, he'd figured he'd find out which one of them was carrying his son. His parents had made it very clear they expected him to produce an heir and didn't much care if it was out of wedlock or not. If Audrey was expecting a boy, then so much the better. They could marry quickly and quietly before the baby was born.

He shifted on the chair, crossing his legs. "Sophia losing the baby was probably the best thing that could have happened." His hand swept out. "It just shows how defective she is, and I won't have to feel awkward about divorcing her," he drawled.

Something inside Alina snapped. Her hand flew out, smacking Frederic hard on the cheek. His head flipped sideways, and he nearly toppled off the chair but managed to right himself.

"You bitch! You're gonna pay for that! I'll sue you for assault."

"Oh yeah," she snarled. "It'll be your word against mine. Look around. There's no one here."

Movement in the corner of her eye made Alina's head swivel, and she gasped when she saw Sophia standing in the doorway to her room, clearly having heard at least Frederic's last statement. The look of deep grief, horror, sorrow, and humiliation on her sister's face broke Alina's heart.

"Don't think you're going to get away with this scot-free, you dickhead," she hissed. "I won't let you."

Frederic got to his feet, palming his reddened cheek but still smirking. "And what do you think you can do to me? Getting a divorce will be easy. And Sophia won't get a penny out of me, I'll make sure of that. If she tries, I'll bury her under so much litigation she'll end up destitute at the end of it. She hasn't got the money or the lawyers to fight me."

Alina stared at him, then crossed her arms and straightened. "Maybe she doesn't have the money, but I do. And I have many friends who are lawyers. Legal sharks. The New York kind. They will chew you up and spit you out before you can even call for your daddy to help you out. Does the name Stadler, Schenk, and Rosler mean anything to you?" she asked. "It should. It's one of the biggest law firms on the East Coast, and I just so happen to be very good friends with Mr. Rosler himself. In fact, I had dinner with him and his wife only last month. I know he'd be only too happy to help if I asked him. I'm sure he knows plenty of like-minded lawyers who practice family law here in Chicago."

By now, Frederic had gone white.

"Why would you help Sophia?" He jumped to his feet. "You two hate each other. She can't stand you. She's told me that many times. And you've always had it in for her. She's told me that as well."

"You stupid, sorry excuse for a man." Alina backed him up against a wall.

He was at least four inches taller than her, but she didn't care. As far as she was concerned, he was a worm and deserved nothing but scorn from her.

Standing close enough for her to see the red veins crisscrossing the whites of his eyes, the hot anger burning inside her turned to an icy indifference, and a strange calm fell over her. He wasn't worthy of the truth, but she couldn't let him go without putting him straight.

Frederic nervously shuffled backward, clearly uncomfortable with being confronted this way.

"Sophia is my sister," she said. "I will do anything to protect her. I don't care what she thinks of me, or believes I have done. I will always be there for her. If anyone hurts her, they have to deal with me, and I have been through too much crap in my life to go easy on an entitled, nasty, delusional man-whore like you." She took a step closer, once again invading his personal space. "You don't even deserve to be called a man. A real man would honor the commitment he's made and treat his partner with the respect and dignity she deserves. I'm going to make sure everyone in this town knows what a disgusting piece of shit you really are. I will destroy you." Punctuating her last words with a poke in his chest, Alina finished what she needed to say, spun on her heel, and marched back into Sophia's room, closing the door behind her.

Later that afternoon, Alina was in need of a break and made her way down to the hospital cafeteria. Scanning the food items available and smelling the stale coffee, her nose wrinkled in disgust. She went back the way she came, strode into the main hospital lobby and looked around. Spotting a small shop, she made her way over.

A couple of refrigerators, one with cellophane wrapped sandwiches and one with drinks, filled one wall, and the other held racks of newspapers, magazines, and paperbacks. In the center were more shelves with snacks, chocolates, candy, and fresh fruit, together with a section of small gifts and greeting cards. After picking up a bottle of water and an apple, she found a small seating area with a few sofas and chairs. She settled on a seat, grateful for a few moments alone and away from the ward.

She nodded and smiled at the middle-aged couple sitting quietly together in a corner. They smiled back and said hello. Pulling out her phone, she saw messages from Stephen and Carl hoping she was doing okay. Quickly typing her replies, she put away her cell and fished out her e-reader from her purse. The thriller she was reading would help pass the time until her mom got back.

Alina had promised her mom she'd stay until she returned and could have waited in Sophia's room, but her sister was too fragile to stand Alina being around too much. Her old grievances all centered on Alina and the impression that she, in Sophia's eyes, had been handed everything on a plate. The tragic accident that took her family from her was only a blip, as far as Sophia was concerned. It was easier for Sophia to focus on that than confront her own misery.

"Excuse me. Could you tell me where the cafeteria is?"

Alina looked at the woman who'd been sitting opposite her.

"Yes, of course, but I wouldn't recommend it. There's a small shop in the lobby where I got the water and the apple. It seemed a much safer option," she replied. "You'll find it near the hospital's main entrance. There's coffee, if you can call it that, from a vending machine down the hall here to your left."

The pretty redhead looked at her husband, who nodded and disappeared out the door. Gesturing to the chair next to Alina, she sat down after getting a nod and a smile in acquiescence.

"Have you been here long?" she asked Alina.

"No, not too long. I'm just waiting for my mom to come back. She needed a rest and a shower after having been here since yesterday morning. It's my sister who's been admitted."

"I'm sorry," the woman said. "I hope she's okay. My mother-in-law was brought in this morning with heart palpitations, and the doctors are examining her now. The waiting room was so busy we decided to come down here for a few minutes."

"How's your husband taking it? It must be hard for him to see his mom in the hospital. Are you close to your mother-in-law?" Somehow, Alina felt comfortable asking the questions, as if she'd known the woman for years.

"We weren't close until about fifteen years ago," the woman explained, "but now we see each other every week. My name is Sarah, by the way, and my husband is Richard."

"I'm Alina, and my sister is Sophia. It must be so wonderful for you to have your mother-in-law as part of your family again. Do you have children?" Alina was glad for the conversation, as it would keep her mind off Sophia and her troubles for a while.

Sarah broke out in a smile. "Yes, a son and a daughter. They're in their mid-twenties now. One is married, and the other engaged. It's partly because of them that we reconciled with my mom-in-law."

"It must have been good for them to have their grandmother in their lives. And I'm sure she was thrilled."

"She was ecstatic." Sarah paused for a moment. "It was so stupid, really. When I met my husband in Providence, where I'd moved for work, I was terribly insecure about myself after growing up with parents who were overachievers and two younger brothers who were even more so. I was good at school, but not as academic as they were." She grimaced. "Becoming a school teacher was all I'd ever wanted since I was about ten years old, but my brothers wanted to be lawyers or doctors. My parents were both lawyers for big firms in DC. Of course, when my oldest brother became a doctor and is now a surgeon, and my other brother followed in my parents' footsteps, they would always see my choice of career as not good enough. That's what I thought, at least." She looked at Alina, a wry smile on her face.

"Did they really see it that way?" Alina asked.

"No, not at all," Sarah replied. "It was all in my head, but I didn't realize that until years later. When I met Richard, who happened to be a lawyer, those insecurities raised their ugly heads again, and I thought his mom looked down on me." She shook her head. "She'd been a very successful district court judge and had been overjoyed when her only son became an attorney as well. Richard's dad had passed away suddenly only six months before we met, and I think Ellen hadn't even begun to get over it when I came on the scene." Sarah's lips pursed. "I think I mistook her emotionally fragile state for disdain and distrust. From there, it just spiraled, and when our children were born, I wouldn't have anything to do with her." She glanced at Alina again, her hands twisting in her lap. "Richard tried to mediate, but I wouldn't listen, and we ended up not seeing her for many years. He would visit her every week while we still lived close, but then we moved to Jacksonville because of his work. I'm ashamed to say it was a long time before we saw her again, and it took an accident to bring us back together."

Alina's brows knitted. "Really? An accident? How awful for you."

Memories of her own car crash came rushing back, and she had to push them back inside their box at the depths of her mind. It was bad enough sitting in a hospital. She didn't need to experience that horrific time of her life through them again.

"It wasn't us. It was Ellen," Sarah explained, sadness washing over her face. "She was driving back to Providence from a few days in Hartford, visiting a friend, when she lost control of the car and swerved into a ditch. It was raining heavily, and she was on a deserted country road when it happened. The weather had been fine when she left, and she was trying to get home before a storm blew in, but it moved faster than expected." She paused for a moment. "She must have gotten knocked out pretty hard because when she woke up, she swore she saw what looked like an angel in front of the car. She said he was all lit up with a halo and sparkling wings spread out behind him. She passed out again, and when she came to a few minutes later, she realized it wasn't an angel at all. It was a passerby who'd spotted the car and came to help."

"Wow. That must have been some vision," Alina murmured, not wanting to interrupt the flow of the story.

Sarah nodded, continuing, "She'd shunted around so the hood was pointing toward the highway, and when he stood in the beam from the headlights, she thought God had sent an angel to help her. Maybe he did, because this man was most surely her guardian angel that night." A weak smile crossed Sarah's lips, but her gaze was fixed on something only she could see. "Anyway, the accident and seeing her in the hospital afterward helped me realize how short life is, and shutting Richard's mom out of our lives didn't just hurt her but Richard and our children as well. And it hurt me — more than I'd understood." Her lips curled in one corner. "We went to see her again not long after and talked things through. She thought I had seen her as an interfering old woman, and I'd thought I wasn't good enough for her son. How wrong we both were... and it's sad how much time together we'd lost because we were both too scared to speak up."

"What an amazing story. What happened to her guardian angel?"

Sarah's voice became wistful. "I don't know. He came to visit her at the hospital, but she was only there for one night before they released her, and he never gave her his contact details. I wish I could have met him and thanked him properly for letting us have another chance to be a family. Our children needed their grandmother in their lives, and so did Richard and I."

"I'm glad he found her when he did, and that you reconciled with your mom-in-law," Alina said. "Family is so important, and we need to keep them close."

"You're right, which is why we asked her to come with us when we moved from Jacksonville to Chicago. She lives a couple of houses down from us, and we spend a lot of time together. The kids see her all the time as well."

"That's wonderful."

"So, do you have any family? Apart from your mom and sister, that is," Sarah asked.

Alina had expected the question, and was relieved when Richard came back, saying his mom was waiting for him and Sarah to take her home, so she didn't have to explain about losing Jonas and her children.

She left the seating area and returned to wait for her mom outside Sophia's room. She mulled over Sarah's story while she sat by a window overlooking a small courtyard. Hearing Sarah mention Providence had reminded her of a summer she'd spent there while she was at college. Her roommate, Zoey, came from there, and she invited Alina to spend a summer with her at her parents' house. She'd had the best time sailing on the river, exploring the nearby towns, and hanging out with Zoey's friends at parties or lounging around a pool.

ALINA STAYED in Chicago for a week to help her sister and her parents. Frederic tried to reconcile with Sophia, despite his mistress' pregnancy, and when she refused, attempted to coax her into keeping her mouth shut. When she'd have none of it, however, he resorted to blaming the entire thing on her. Sophia had thrown him out, but not until after she'd promised to tell anyone who asked what had happened, and how he was screwing his mistress while she was in the hospital miscarrying their baby.

Next, it was his parents who tried to pressure her into staying quiet, but again, Sophia refused to even entertain the thought. They'd offered bribes in the form of money, property, and luxury holidays, but all she'd done was laugh in their faces.

As soon as Sophia got out of the hospital, she threw herself into filing for a divorce. Alina tried to slow her down, but it was her sister's way of coping. She needed something else to focus on than losing her baby. Alina let her be. The grieving would come soon enough. She just hoped Sophia would allow her or their mom or dad to help her through it.

"Alina, I need a favor," Sophia announced behind her.

Alina turned and looked at her sister, who stood with a straight back and her hands clasped behind her. It was only the pallor of her skin and the dark hollows of her eyes that betrayed the emotional turmoil she was going through.

"Of course, I'll do anything I can to help."

"You told Freddie you know lawyers in New York. Good ones. Any divorce attorneys among them? Someone who'd know one here in Chicago?" she asked. "I need someone who can rip him apart and give me everything I deserve."

"You didn't sign a prenup, did you?"

"No, Freddie never asked me, even though I know his father tried to force him to have one drawn up. So, now I'm going to take him to the cleaners."

Alina studied her sister, but she could see the determination and stubbornness overshadow her despair.

"All right," she replied. "Yes, I do know a good divorce attorney. I'll call him. I don't think he's licensed in Illinois, though, but I'm sure he'll know someone here he can recommend."

Sophia's voice took on a razor sharp edge. "I need a real shark. Isn't that what you said? That you know some real New York sharks? I want someone like that."

Alina watched her sister stride out of the living room, her heels clicking against the hardwood floor and a dark cloud over her head, like a swarm of angry bees. She sighed. It was going to be a long time before Sophia recovered from the pain, sorrow, and humiliation she'd suffered.

THE EVENING before Alina was leaving to go back to New York, she found Sophia sitting on her own in the living room. The lights were off except for a small lamp in the corner, but she could still see the streaks of tears on her sister's face.

"Sophia, I'm so sorry you're going through this. I can't imagine how you're feeling," Alina said gently.

Sophia barely acknowledged her presence. Alina turned to leave but stopped when she heard her quiet whisper.

"I'm sure you know exactly how I feel, but it must have been many times worse for you."

Alina's shoulders slumped. "I don't think there's a scale for how much you can feel when you lose a child. Even if it wasn't born yet," she murmured. "You have every right to feel as sad and devastated as you want. You lost your baby and your husband at the same time. Frederic may not be dead, but your relationship is, and that's a kind of death in itself. Allow yourself to feel everything your heart tells you to feel."

"I was so happy." Sophia's voice was so low Alina could barely hear. "Everything was going great. I love my job. I thought I had a husband who adored me, and we were starting a family." A deep sob wracked her body. "Now, I have nothing except for the job, and I don't even know if I want to stay there after all this."

Alina raised her gaze to the ceiling, sighing. "Don't make any decisions on that yet. Take one step at a time and see how you feel when you're not so overwhelmed."

Sophia rose and stood by the windows overlooking the back lawn and the trees dotting the shoreline. The sun had set, but it wasn't quite dark yet, and the black swath of Lake Michigan was still visible.

"I just wanted what you had." A shoulder lifted and dropped again. "A husband, a family — everything. Now it's all gone."

"I don't have any of that, though, do I? I lost it all in a split second," Alina said, a bitter note in her voice.

"But you weren't betrayed, humiliated, made a laughingstock of, and shunned by those you thought were your friends." Sophia spun, her eyes burning with anger.

"No, you're right. That didn't happen to me. But I'm here for you if you want to talk. You're my sister, and I love you despite our differences."

The anger drained from her sister as quickly as it had flared up. Sophia's shoulders dropped, and she turned toward the windows again.

"Thank you," she whispered.

Alina turned to leave, a spark of hope in her chest that maybe something good could come out of this. If there was a chance of her and Sophia becoming closer again, she would take it, but until she saw more of this kinder, softer side of her sister, she wouldn't get her hopes up too high.

"I'm just as good as you. You'll see. One day, I'll have it all, and you'll be the one to envy me."

The whispered words were clearly not meant for Alina's ears, but she did hear them. She shook her head, disappointed at the backward step right after she'd thought they'd made progress, but not wanting to let Sophia know she'd overheard, she padded away as quietly as she could manage.

She didn't understand why Sophia had this idea in her head that Alina thought she was somehow better than her. She had nothing for her sister to be envious of and would always want her to be happy, successful, and content with her life. God knew Alina wasn't exactly having a wonderful time right now, and it was certainly nothing of which to be envious.

While she'd been away, Stephen had called and told her Warren had been taken into custody after the police had found his fingerprints in a smear of her blood on the kitchen counter. He'd denied everything, of course, and as soon as the judge set bail, his father had paid it and taken Warren to their home on Long Island. No trial date had been announced, but it was likely to happen soon as his father would exert his influence and press for a swift handling of the matter.

As much as it shocked Alina to hear it confirmed that it was Warren who'd assaulted her, she'd had time to come to terms with the idea. She was both saddened and outraged by what he'd done to her, and she refused to feel sorry for him. He'd committed a vicious and nasty attack and needed to pay for it.

Twenty-Five

KIRAN, 1972

The cheerful sound of a bird chattering in a tree nearby stood in stark contrast to the early morning sounds of the camp. Groaning, muttering, and snoring by close to fifty grown men of various ages in a tiny wooden shack created a harsh background chorus, punctuated by the shouts of their jailers. The hut was so cramped there was no floor space to walk on when everyone was shut inside. The ventilation — if you could call it that, since it consisted of the gaps between the bamboo poles — was great, however, except for when it rained.

The roof was sparsely covered by large leaves and palm fronds woven together so long ago the twine was worn and frayed and, in some places, missing altogether. It did nothing to keep them dry during the frequent, heavy rain showers. Their sleeping mats were always damp and moldy, because they never had a chance to dry in the humid air. Kiran barely noticed. He was so used to it by now.

Tightly bound poles sunk into the ground, which didn't budge even with every single one of them pushing against them, made up the four sides. They knew because they'd tried many times on each of the four walls.

The prisoners were a mixed bunch of men from several countries, including America, Australia, New Zealand, and Thailand. All of them were soldiers except him. Shortly after Kiran had first arrived, another doctor and a corpsman had been brought into camp. He never met them since he was thrown in the bunker almost immediately after they got there. Not long before he'd been released from his too-long solitary confinement, the doctor died from dysentery, and the corpsman was killed in front of everyone when he tried to escape. It was meant as a deterrent, but for most of the prisoners, it made no difference at all. They had long since given up any hope of escaping.

Kiran wasn't sure how long he'd been held by the Viet Cong, but if he had to guess, he'd say it was probably close to four or maybe even five years now. It was impossible to gauge it accurately, since there were only two seasons — the drier season and the wet season — but he tried to keep track of them the best he could.

His time in solitary confinement still haunted him in his dreams. Once he'd recovered from the worst of his injuries and was able to stay awake for more than a few moments at a time, he'd found Geoff keeping vigil by his side. The usually so affable Australian looked drawn and heavy-hearted. He'd lost hope after not being able to find out what had happened to Kiran. It was as if he'd had vanished into thin air. Even though Geoff was overjoyed to see Kiran alive, he was distraught over his friend's physical condition. All skin and bones, were his words.

By Geoff's estimate, Kiran had been in the concrete bunker for at least eight months, probably more. Kiran had been shocked to hear it. No wonder he'd felt as if he'd gone insane when they finally brought him out of there. He knew he'd been in there for at least five months, while they were still talking to him and before the narrow slit that let in light was boarded up, because he'd been able to see the moon through it.

If Geoff was right, he'd spent another three or four months completely isolated. Not hearing, seeing, or even sensing another soul for that length of time would have broken the mind of most people. Why Kiran still had his sanity intact was anybody's guess, and it was being tested every day helplessly having to watch good men suffer.

During his time in the camp, he'd seen many men arrive, and even more die from disease, festering wounds, and malnourishment. Unable to do anything to help with no tools, medicines, or even bandages, he had been forced to stand by and watch his fellow prisoners perish, many of which had become his friends.

For most of his time here, he'd kept his skills as a surgeon under wraps — something several of the prisoners who were already here when he arrived had strongly advised him to do as the VC would demand he treated every injury, cut, and scrape on their men, and for every one of them he couldn't save, the repercussions would be severe. At no time would they allow him to treat any of his fellow prisoners. They'd seen it happen with every medically trained prisoner previously.

Kiran heeded the advice and did what he could for his friends without being detected.

STANDING at the bottom of a new hole dug for the latrine, Kiran wiped the sweat from his brow. The midday heat was unrelenting, exacerbated by the high humidity. His mouth was dry, and he desperately needed something to drink, but he still had several hours of work before he could put the shovel down. He could only hope they sent someone else to relieve him, so he could get at least a mouthful of water.

"You! Keep digging! No be lazy!"

The shout from above prompted Kiran to resume the backbreaking work with large blisters on his hands. They never had the chance to heal and form calluses before new blisters appeared from the rough handles of the tools he was forced to use day in and day out.

Kiran toiled under the burning sun, his muscles cramping and aching from being bent into positions they were never meant to be in. The alternative was giving up, but he was far from ready to let these cruel and vicious scumbags see him capitulate. He couldn't let them win, no matter how much they tried to break him.

To distract himself from the burning pain, heat, and intense thirst, he allowed images of his brown-haired woman to float through his mind. As always, her face was obscured, but her gray eyes shined with warmth, kindness, and love. A soft smile played on her full lips, and he watched while they moved to form words.

Just take one small step.

"You! Finish! Up here, now!" the same voice shouted, breaking through his soothing thoughts of a woman he'd never met, but one who always evoked love and desire in his heart.

It was crazy to have such feelings for a figment of his imagination, but he didn't care. She kept alive his hope of one day being released or moved on from this torturous existence. He'd been through a lot of pain and hardship in his different lives, but this was the worst one so far. His life in Ancient Egypt had also been backbreaking work under a burning sun, but as much as they were slaves there, their owners had treated them as human beings who needed decent food, water, and at least a few hours of rest every night.

The pain, the loss of lives, the hardship, and the humiliation, it was all packed together into a few horrifying years — enough for the lifetimes of several men. Somehow, the woman in his dreams made everything worth it. He'd long since stopped feeling guilty about betraying Juliet. She was gone and had been for many years. If she were watching over him, she'd be happy for him to have something to stop him from giving up. She'd been his rock and comfort throughout their marriage, and he still missed her terribly, but she was never coming back.

Maybe his dream woman existed somewhere out there? It was the thought that she might be real and waiting for him that nourished his soul to resist the malice and lack of human decency among his captors.

Kiran scrambled up the rope ladder thrown over the side, with his shovel in a firm grip in one hand. Once, he'd made the mistake of not holding on tight enough, dropping it into the trench he'd been digging. He'd jumped down to retrieve it, but when he turned to climb back up, the rope ladder had been removed. It was too deep to clamber up without it, and he ended up spending the entire night in the muddy trench.

The heavens had opened that night, and by the time the sun's rays lightened the skies above him, he was frozen to the bone, shivering so hard his teeth rattled, and starving. Not long after daybreak, the guard had shouted at him to begin his day's chores, and he'd had no option other than to start digging again. That evening, when the rope finally dropped into the hole, he'd gripped his shovel as if it were the most precious diamond.

LATER THAT NIGHT, Geoff had once again proved a great friend when he gave Kiran half of his meal, as well as a piece of bread he'd squirreled away from his lunch. Kiran knew what a sacrifice it was, because the portions they were given were barely enough to survive on as it was. It wasn't the first time the guards decided to feed only some of them. They enjoyed the power they had over their prisoners.

"Thanks, my friend," Kiran said, accepting the scraps of food.

"No worries, mate. You'd do the same for me. We need to stick together. If we do, we'll get out of this hellhole soon enough." Geoff chewed slowly on his bit of stale bread. "I heard from a newbie that there are talks of a prisoner exchange. With a bit of luck, we might be out of here sooner than we think."

Kiran could hear the hope in his friend's voice, but somehow, he didn't think freedom was coming anytime soon — not for him, anyway.

"Did you ask what year it is? What month?" Kiran mopped the last of the thin broth with his bread crust, taking small sips from his cup of water between mouthfuls.

"It's December 1972. Can you believe that? We've been here for nearly five years. These commie bastards have robbed me of half a decade." A dark look stole over his face. "I wonder if my wife knows I'm alive, or if I'm listed as killed-in-action by now. Maybe I'm on an MIA list rather than presumed dead. My kids will have grown big, and I've missed out on their childhoods," Geoff mused. "If I ever get out of here, will they even recognize me? I wouldn't blame Delia if she's found someone else. I wouldn't be happy about it, but I couldn't fault her either. It wasn't my choice to come here. It was the military bosses who sent me," he lamented. "Who's waiting for you back home, Kiran?"

Kiran swallowed his last piece of bread and stared into nothing before he replied.

"No one. There's no one waiting for me. My wife died four months before I signed up. Cancer. And I have no family to miss me. A few friends, maybe, but they've probably forgotten all about me by now."

"Damn, man. You signed up? Voluntarily? I'm sorry about your wife." Geoff put a hand on his shoulder and squeezed it in gentle sympathy. "That's a terrible thing to go through. Is that why you came here?"

Kiran nodded, the tangle of emotions in his throat too tight to force any words past.

THE NEXT DAY, they assigned Kiran to lashing bamboo poles together to form the walls of a new building. It was less backbreaking than digging, but just as hard on his hands. The twine securing the poles cut into the skin, and since it had to be pulled tight to be as sturdy as the VC wanted it, the tough strands of fiber sliced through the blisters, shearing away the skin. To alleviate the stinging pain, he tore a couple of strips off his shirt and wound them around his bleeding hands. Soon, all the men in his work group had done the same. Talking as little as possible, they gritted their teeth and got on with the work. Thankfully, the sun was hidden behind a bank of clouds, so the temperature was just about bearable. For once, their captors had left them alone, probably assuming they were too weak to attempt to escape into the deep jungle.

A loud commotion nearby interrupted the relative quiet, and everyone stopped what they were doing to see what was going on. Kiran frowned when a group of men came crashing through the undergrowth toward him, carrying someone between them. They'd been working farther away, cutting down bamboo trees to build the hut Kiran was working on. It was where Geoff had been assigned for the day.

As they rushed past, he heard them shouting at each other.

"Press down hard!"

"He's bleeding too much!"

"Find something to wrap it with!"

"Damn, it's too deep. I can't stop it. Put him down!"

Kiran dropped the ball of twine he was holding and rushed toward the men frantically working on their comrade lying prone on the ground. Skidding to a halt in their midst, he gasped as he realized it was his friend they were working on.

"Let me help," he cried. "I'm a surgeon. What happened?"

"One of the scumbag guards shoved him from behind just as he swung the axe to cut the wood. The fucker just laughed as the damn thing cut through his thigh," one of the men grunted.

Kiran went ice cold as he saw the extent of the injury. A six-inch gash in the Aussie's leg grinned at him like a bloody mouth. The glint of white bone showed every time the man trying to stem the bleeding shifted his hands.

"You. Get me some shirts or rags. Anything you can get your hands on that I can use as bandages. Quickly!" Kiran whisper-shouted to the man standing next to him.

He didn't need to be asked twice and raced off to find the requested items. A few of their captors stood a short distance away, watching them, but not trying to interfere or stop them in any way. It was odd, Kiran thought, but he didn't have time to reflect over it.

"Geoff, can you hear me?" Kiran rubbed his knuckles against his friend's chest to stimulate the heart.

"Yeah... I'm here. I feel crook, though. Not sure... just leave me be. Don't let them... know... a doc..." Geoff sounded weaker by the second.

Kiran wasn't surprised. The blood was pumping out of the leg despite the pressure he was putting on it. The wound was just too big, too deep, for mere hands to hold it together. He needed something to make a tourniquet and then an operating theater, sutures, antibiotics — all the things he didn't have access to.

"We need to get him into the hut. I can't do anything out here in the open," Kiran stated.

They lifted Geoff and carried him as quickly and as gently as they could to their sleeping quarters, where they were met by the man Kiran had sent to find wrappings. He'd clearly ripped an entire shirt into long strips and bundled them into a ball.

Kiran gestured to a place along one of the bamboo walls. "Over here. Lay him down on this mat."

Placing Geoff on a sleeping mat nearest one of the openings that served as a window, Kiran put the bundle of rags within easy reach and slowly removed his hands, instructing the other man who still had his hands clamped down on the gash to keep them there until he'd readied a pressure bandage.

"Will this help?" a voice by his elbow asked.

Kiran looked up and saw a hand holding a thin needle. Surprise and disbelief coursed through him. How had that not been confiscated by the VC? *Never mind*, he told himself. Now he just needed some thread. Looking down at the scraps of fabric in his hands, he realized he had plenty of cotton thread for sutures — if they would hold, that is.

Feverishly, he began yanking at the thin threads until he had a handful, which he placed on top of the cleanest-looking of the rags. Holding one of them up to the man with the needle, he told him to thread it through.

Then he set to work.

Twenty minutes later, the open wound had been closed, and Kiran sat back on his heels, deep tremors running through him from the tension and the strain of stitching his friend's leg without any anesthesia. The other men had had their hands full, holding Geoff down and preventing him from screaming. How none of their prison guards had come to investigate was beyond him, but he was too tired to think about it or even care.

Geoff had lost a lot of blood and wouldn't be able to move for days, if not weeks to come. It wouldn't go over well with their captors, but if Kiran had to work for both of them, he would.

1973

EVER SINCE KIRAN had saved Geoff's life by stitching his leg together, he'd been working as a doctor for their captors. It was inevitable they'd find out what he'd done, and it hadn't taken an hour before they'd dragged him in front of the commander. Trying to hide his skills had been pointless, and they'd immediately taken him to what served as the medical ward and told him to start working. Now, he spent every day taking care of Viet Cong soldiers who often arrived in the dead of night and left or were taken away as soon as they were able to move.

He narrowed his eyes and concentrated hard as he carefully moved the arm of a newly arrived Viet Cong soldier until he felt the bones slot together correctly. Wrapping a firm dressing around the broken limb to hold it in place, he kept a close eye on the young man on the table. His tanned skin had turned a sickly gray pallor, sweat beading his forehead. Kiran had given him a mild sedative to keep him calm, but it was wearing off, and the man would soon be fully awake.

He was the last of Kiran's patients for the day. He'd been working nonstop since breakfast when a patrol came back in much worse shape than they'd left. From what he understood of their chatter, they'd been in a skirmish with a small outpost of the Vietnamese Army and borne the brunt of it.

On tired and aching legs, he shuffled toward the supply cabinet to grab another bandage to fashion a sling for his patient. After wrapping it around the arm and tying a knot behind his neck, he helped the soldier sit up and instructed him to keep the arm still for as long as possible, and then sent him on his way — hopefully to get some rest.

After clearing up, Kiran returned to the sleeping hut but hesitated before entering. He knew what was waiting inside, and his stomach churned at the thought. Things had gone from bad to worse in the last month or so. Dysentery was spreading like wildfire through the camp among captors and captives alike. Only a few of them were still unaffected.

Geoff's leg wasn't healing properly because of the unsanitary conditions, and due to his weakened state, he'd been one of the first to fall ill. Kiran had tried everything he could think of to help his friend, but without large doses of antibiotics, there wasn't much he could do. All he'd managed was to sneak small amounts of penicillin and antiseptic wash. The cut in Geoff's leg was an angry red wound, and he was only just holding an infection at bay.

Ever since he'd been forced to take charge of the medical treatments, the guards had given him bigger and better portions of food, plenty of clean water, and several changes of clothes. He'd attempted to share with fellow prisoners but each time, he'd been stopped by the guards, and anyone he'd helped was savagely beaten to discourage him from trying again.

The other prisoners had become distrustful of him and shunned any talk or offers of help. Kiran couldn't really blame them, but suddenly being treated as a pariah struck deep, and he lost a little more of his faith in them all being rescued one day.

The most recent arrival of new captives had brought more news of peace talks and prisoner-of-war exchanges. A renewed sense of hope had spread among the men, but Kiran had a nagging feeling something would go wrong, and they'd be forgotten in the jungle or not be part of the exchange. He couldn't explain it and didn't want to dash anyone's hopes, so he kept quiet. Not that the others would talk to him, anyway, except for Geoff.

His Australian friend never stopped smiling despite the frail state he was in and berated anyone who would listen over their treatment of Kiran. It made him smile and appreciate the man even more.

Kiran took a deep breath and stepped inside the hut. The stench of vomit and human excrement was overwhelming, and he put his hand over his mouth and nose until he'd acclimated. Finding his way among the sick and listless men, he found Geoff over by the wall where he'd moved him when he first became ill. The air was fresher there, and he only had one other person next to him.

"Hey, buddy. How're you doing?" he whispered, putting his hand on Geoff's arm, trying not to wince at the skeletal limb under his fingers.

"I'm as good as new, mate. Another day, and I'll be up and around as normal." Geoff smiled weakly.

They both knew the truth.

"I've got some water for you."

Kiran helped Geoff drink from a canteen he'd found in the supply cupboard. He'd managed to mix the antibiotic powder he'd stolen in the drink and prayed it would help Geoff's immune system fight both an infection and the parasites ravaging his body.

Kiran encouraged his friend to take a few more sips. He was severely dehydrated on top of everything else. When he'd had as much as he could stomach, Geoff laid down again and closed his eyes, immediately drifting off into a fitful sleep.

Kiran settled next to him. Despite the bone-deep weariness, sleep wouldn't come, and he thought of what his life had become since he left Los Angeles. He could cope with the maltreatment, the starvation and dehydration, the knocks, shoves, and hard labor, but watching his friends — whether they still thought of him the same way — slowly fade away, unable to keep any food or water down, and not be allowed to help, was the cruelest thing anyone could have done to him.

They made him take a dose of antibiotics every morning so he would stay disease free and be able to treat their soldiers, but when he'd asked for some of the medicine for the worst affected prisoners, they'd laughed and pointed their guns at him, shouting for him to get to work.

The next morning, he woke up to find Geoff dead beside him. Losing his only friend made Kiran decide he'd had enough. Whispering a prayer for the jovial Australian, he got up, carried him outside and carefully placed him in the already dug mass grave, next to the other prisoners who'd also succumbed to the ravages of the disease.

Grief and sorrow tore at his heart, and he wanted to scream, shout, and rage at the heavens, at the one responsible for allowing these atrocities to take place. He found no answers, only that deafening silence he'd long since become accustomed to.

After spreading dirt over the body, he hung Geoff's dog tags — the only personal possessions they'd been allowed to keep — around his neck and walked away, shoving every shred of emotion he had left down a deep, dark abyss inside his mind.

Arriving at the medical hut, he went through the motions of taking his antibiotics, but he was no longer under the watchful eye of the guard, who just assumed he was taking them as normal, and stowed the powder inside a folded piece of paper. If he was infected with the parasites, so be it.

The camp was quiet around him. Almost everyone, guard and prisoner alike, had come down with dysentery, including Kiran, and was confined to their sleeping quarters. With no one able to watch the prisoners, and them too weak to move, no one guarded the hut. Kiran dragged himself outside — refusing to spend his last moments confined inside a dirty, stinking shed — collapsed on a patch of grass, and turned his head to the inky sky. For once, it was a clear night and millions of stars glittered on the vast, vaulted canopy.

His stomach churned and roiled, but there was nothing left inside. He was so dehydrated his body couldn't even produce bile. Dry heaves wracked him periodically, but he was too weak to even turn his head to the side.

Drifting off in a feverish unconsciousness, he dreamed of a beautiful woman with long hair the color of chocolate, and eyes as gray as a rain cloud in spring. With her delectable form tucked close to his, he luxuriated in the feel of her curves, her scent, and her warmth. In dreams of their lovemaking, he'd gotten to know her every dip, every rise, every swell, and he knew it better than his own.

The connection between them was inexplicable but tangible, nonetheless. The way she responded to his caresses was something he'd never experienced before and in his dream, his own body reacted in turn with a need so fierce he felt helpless to resist. Not that he wanted to. His desire for his dream woman was overwhelming, astounding, and utterly breathtaking.

He'd never been able to make out her face clearly, only her captivating eyes and luscious mouth. It was something he'd always be sorry for, but it was too late for regrets. Now was the time to take a breath, clear his mind, and wait. Wait for the end.

"I'm sorry, my lovely. I wish we could have met in life, but it's not to be. This is the end of me, I'm sure. I believe I have paid my penance. My sin was to not have seen this coming, for not seeing the cruelty men can inflict on others. Next time, I will ensure things are different. I don't know how, but I will," he whispered, still in his dreamlike state, hoping she could somehow hear him. "You have been a comfort to me, a glimmer of light in the dark, an awakening when I thought my heart had turned to stone. I now know it is possible to love two women at the same time, equally and differently, and I thank you." He fell silent, fighting against his rising fever to keep his thoughts coherent. "I thank you for walking beside me, before me, and behind me, for lifting me, and for setting my body on fire, and for allowing me to experience such exquisite and magnificent passion. You have become entwined in my soul, and I will always keep you in my heart. I'm sorry for leaving you like this, but I have to go. I'm being called back, I hope, but I will watch over you and rejoice when you find another love. A love that is worthy and deserving of you."

Kiran opened his eyes, the scattered diamonds above twinkling and shimmering. Feeling heavy, he fought for another breath, his heart slowing in his chest until it beat its last rhythm. From far away, a voice full of sorrow and regret drifted on a breeze of fading hopes and dreams.

Just take one small step.

Twenty-Six

ALINA, 2014

On her return from Chicago, Alina had gone right back to work, needing the distraction and wanting to return to normal. Sophia was doing better, and if she wasn't entirely pleasant to Alina, at least she wasn't a bitch like before. The miscarriage and Frederic's betrayal had made her reexamine her own actions and feelings, and she'd been easier to get along with than previously. Okay, so they weren't exactly the best of friends, but they also weren't in a one-sided war where Alina refused to engage, and Sophia did nothing but use any ammunition she could find to lob at her. They'd reached a status quo, and Alina was happy with that.

The first few weeks had been busy, but she'd enjoyed being back in the office and working with Stephen and her other co-workers again.

One afternoon, her phone had rung, and it had surprised her to see Warren's mom's name on the display. She'd debated whether to decline the call but decided she might as well take the bull by the horns and find out what she wanted.

Warren had been arrested and was pleading not guilty, which meant Alina would have to testify. "Alina, I'm glad you picked up. We need to talk." The woman's voice grated on her ears.

Alina stifled a sigh. "Hello, Marlene. What do you want to talk about?"

"Warren, of course," Marlene said matter-of-factly. "He's so unhappy since you two broke up, and I was hoping you would reconsider?"

Alina squeezed the bridge of her nose. "I don't think so. Warren isn't just unhappy, he's unstable."

Marlene huffed. "Don't be silly. I'm sure you can explain to the court that it wasn't he who attacked you. Once you've done that, and they have released him, I will pay for the two of you to go away somewhere for a few weeks. How does a nice, long, all-expenses-paid vacation in Aruba sound?"

"Listen, Marlene. Warren pleaded guilty, so there's no chance of him being released any time soon."

"But this is ridiculous. Warren would never break into someone's house, and he's never been violent in his life," Marlene screeched. "I know my boy, and he's just not capable of doing anything of the sort. He only pleaded guilty for your sake. As his fiancée, I'd have thought you'd be a little more interested in making sure he's set free. He's completely innocent, after all."

"Please, listen —" Alina started.

"I wasn't going to tell you this until after the wedding, but I have put down a deposit on a house for the two of you," Marlene interjected, as if Alina hadn't said anything. "I know Warren had already done it on a different house, and I wish he'd spoken to me first, but this property is twice the size and only two doors down from us." Her voice became shrill. "You two would be so happy there, and we could see you every day. I know Warren doesn't like to be too far away from me, and I could come over to cook his meals and do his laundry if you were too busy with your little party planning business. It would make my boy so happy."

Stunned, Alina was silent for several moments, not knowing what to say. She couldn't believe the audacity of the woman. Delusional was the word that came to mind. Was she really trying to buy her son's freedom by offering Alina expensive vacations and a house in an exclusive part of Long Island? Besides, the woman had staff taking care of laundry and cleaning for her. Alina wasn't sure Marlene had ever seen a washing machine or a mop, let alone used one.

"As I was going to say before you interrupted me," she began, "Warren did break into my house, and he did assault me, and now he's going to jail for it. There's nothing I can do about it, and I sure as hell wouldn't lie to the courts even if he retracted his guilty plea. That's called perjury, which is a criminal offense. I think we'd better finish this conversation and forget it ever happened. Goodbye, Marlene." Alina hung up before the other woman had a chance to say anything else.

Afterward, the conversation with Warren's mom had swirled in her head, and no matter how she'd twisted and turned the woman's comments, or from which angle she'd looked at them, she kept coming back to the same thing. Marlene had tried to bribe her to get Warren out of jail.

From then on, things went from bad to worse. Warren's parents gave up on the idea of bribing her and instead started making threats of suing her for libel and defamation of character, lying to the courts, and making false statements. It was preposterous, but when Stephen informed her that he'd heard on the grapevine that Winston and Marlene had become persona non grata in their social circles, it became somewhat more understandable.

They were being ostracized by those they'd considered friends, barred from the country club, disinvited to social events, and asked to step aside from various committees, all until the 'situation with Warren' was cleared up. It had to have hit them both hard since they thrived on being part of the elite, and their entire lives revolved around the country club and the organizations of which they were members.

ALINA FELT as though she were living on airplanes. It had only been a few weeks since she returned from Chicago, and here she was getting on another flight. This time it wasn't just for a quick visit. She was moving to Georgia. The thought both excited and saddened her.

She'd loved her time in New York. It had been the change she'd needed to get her life back on track, but the trouble with Warren had marred her new-found happiness, so when Stephen had offered her the director's position in Atlanta, she'd jumped on it.

Hearing the announcement call to board, Alina gathered her bags and made her way to the ticket check and onto the plane. After finding her seat, she stowed her bag under the seat in front as usual and had her cell and e-reader handy. The middle and window seats were still empty, but she had a feeling they wouldn't be for too long. The flight was busy, and she expected every seat to have been sold.

As the plane filled up, she was pleased to find a mother and daughter taking the seats next to her. The little girl was around five years old, holding a well-loved cuddly toy in her arms, and once seated, she pressed her nose to the window, fascinated with the hive of activity on the tarmac.

Leaning back, Alina took a deep breath, pushing away all thoughts of the current tangle her life was in and tried to focus on what lay ahead.

"Hi. My name is Ellie. What's yours?" a small voice next to her asked.

Alina opened her eyes and peered to her right. To her surprise, they were already up in the air, and the seatbelt signs had been switched off. She'd completely zoned out during takeoff.

"I'm sorry, take no notice of her. She's a little chatterbox and very excited." The mother smiled apologetically.

"Please, don't worry. I don't mind in the slightest," Alina said and switched her attention to the little girl. "My name is Alina. How old are you?"

Big blue eyes gazed up at her. "I'm five, nearly six. I'm going to Atlanta. Where are you going?"

"I'm going there, too. It's my new home."

"Mommy and I are meeting my daddy, and he's taking me to the zoo! And to an acwium." Ellie wiggled over her mom's lap, asking to switch seats, which the mom agreed to after a questioning glance at Alina.

The mom mouthed 'aquarium' to Alina. Clearly, Ellie hadn't quite learned how to pronounce the word yet, but Alina understood, nonetheless.

She had no problem having the inquisitive child next to her. It would be a delightful distraction and hopefully calm her apprehension.

"Why are you gonna live there? Don't you like your old house?" The little girl peered at her, frowning.

"I do like my old house," Alina explained. "But I have a new job and that's in Atlanta."

"I like my house too, but we're gonna stay in a hotel. My daddy went to see a friend who was sick, but now he's better, so daddy can come home again. Mommy and I went to see my grandma and grandpa in New York, and now we're gonna go see daddy and then we're going home to Houston again. But first, we're going to see the monkeys at the zoo. And the fishes. I love fishes. And spaceships. This is my favorite toy." The words flowed like a waterfall from the little girl's lips.

She held out her cuddly toy so Alina could see. It was somewhat threadbare and tattered, but still recognizable as a NASA space shuttle.

"Oh, I love your space shuttle. I wanted to be an astronaut when I was your age." She grinned, examining the toy.

"My mommy works with space stuff," Ellie replied. "She's going to Mars soon."

"She is?" Alina raised her gaze to the mom, who smiled.

"Not quite," the woman replied. "I'm working on a project that will be included on a Mars mission in a few years."

"Wow! That's incredible. It must be really exciting to work on something like that," Alina gushed.

The woman smiled. "Yes, it is, but it's a long way off, and you never know what's going to happen. My father worked for NASA in the control room many years ago, and I guess I inherited my love of space from him."

Alina gaped. "That's amazing. He must be so proud of you."

The cabin crew bringing refreshments interrupted their conversation, and Ellie climbed back into her seat, pressing her nose against the window. Alina accepted the tray of food and ordered some white wine to go with it. Flying always made her hungry. While they ate, Ellie talked quietly to her mom about where they were going, what they'd be doing, and how much she looked forward to seeing her dad, and Alina turned her thoughts to what the next few months might hold for her.

The flight to Atlanta was smooth and passed quickly. Alina chatted with Ellie, who was curious and clever. She probably got a lot of that from her mom, Evie, who was clearly a very smart and educated woman. There seemed to be no end to Ellie's questions, but they were intelligent and thoughtful, and Alina found her curiosity and inquisitive mind entertaining.

Evie's job working on experiments to send into space seemed fascinating, and Alina wanted to know what it was like to work with such an incredible goal as a Mars exploration.

"This will be the first spacecraft to actually land on Mars, right?"

Evie shook her head. "No, NASA landed a craft on Mars back in 1976, and then the Pathfinder in 1997. The data that was sent back is incredible, and with that, the next mission and any experiments can be improved on."

Alina thought for a moment. "It's still a very male-dominated environment, isn't it? Has it been hard for you to make your way and become as successful as you are?"

Evie adjusted Ellie's head on her lap. The little girl had fallen asleep clutching her stuffed toy, the excitement of traveling taking its toll.

Pursing her lips and furrowing her brow, Evie considered Alina's question. "I'm not sure I'm that successful yet, but it hasn't been too hard for me. I'm lucky to be working in a lab with several other women and with men who respect and value us as equals. But it hasn't always been like that. Throughout high school and college, I had to fight to be included, but with my parents' support, I forged through it."

"Your dad must have been a great role model for working in the field."

"Yes, he was," Evie said. "Even though I went into a slightly different sector from him, the fact that he worked at NASA always made me believe I could one day work with something space-related as well."

Between them, Ellie snoozed peacefully.

"To be honest," Evie picked up her story again, "a huge part of my self-belief came from a friend of my parents. When they met him, I must have been around Ellie's age. I remember little of how it happened, only that he rescued my toy shuttle — the one Ellie has now — when it got caught by the wind on the beach. I think he lived near us in Corpus Christi for a few years, but when we moved to Houston to be closer to my dad's work, we lost touch." She fell silent for a few seconds before continuing, "What I remember most about him was his golden hair, and that he always seemed to have this light around him. You couldn't see it looking directly at him, only if you glanced out of the corner of your eye. He was incredibly kind, compassionate, and encouraging. It's strange, but my parents barely remember he even existed. I don't know how he made such an impression on me, but for them, he's only a vague memory."

Evie's description of the man reminded Alina of the one in her dreams. She assumed it was a common theme to dream about — a golden-haired man — although none would be glowing, she was sure.

"On the last day I saw him," Evie continued, "he told me to follow my dreams, and that I could be anything I wanted if I just worked hard enough. He said to make him proud, and he would always look out for my name in anything to do with space missions." Her eyes took on a faraway look before focusing again. "Of course, back then, I wanted to be an astronaut, so I didn't exactly achieve my childhood goal. But I know this is what I'm supposed to be doing. I'm happy, and I hope he's out there somewhere feeling proud of me. My parents lost touch with him soon after we moved, so they don't know what happened to him." A sad smile pulled at Evie's lips as she looked at Alina.

"That's such a moving story. Have you ever tried to find him?" Alina murmured.

"Yes, several times." Evie nodded . "But there's no mention of him anywhere. It's such a long time ago, he might even have passed away by now. Although he'd only be in his sixties, so I hope he's still around somewhere."

Alina flashed her a smile. "I hope you get to meet him again, so you can tell him what his words meant and how he encouraged you to be what you are today."

"Enough about me. What do you do, Alina, and have you lived in New York long?" Evie asked.

"Well, I'm an event organizer, and I'm transferring to Atlanta to take a new position within the company," she replied.

She told Evie a little about having lived in California since childhood and how her parents moved to the Midwest just before she started college. Without mentioning the traumatic loss of her family, she explained about needing a fresh start, which precipitated the move to New York, and the reasons she was now on her way to Atlanta.

Before long, they were descending into Hartsfield-Jackson Airport, and everyone got busy gathering their belongings. Alina only had her small carry-on and purse, but she made sure she stowed her cell and reader safely inside a pocket and zipped it closed, not wanting to lose anything.

After saying goodbye to Evie and Ellie, she stepped off the plane and followed the overhead signs to collect her baggage. Once she had her two suitcases, she headed out to the arrivals hall to find a cab. It was time to start yet another chapter in her life.

"How do you find Atlanta now you've been there a while, sweetie?" Stephen wondered.

Alina smiled at him, his face filling the screen of her tablet. "I've been rushed off my feet since I got here and really had to hit the ground running, but I'm loving it."

"That's great, but I can't help wish you hated it so you'd come back to New York. Carl is miserable without you, and I hate it when my husband is upset," he grumbled.

"I'm sure you can think of something to cheer him up, but tell him I miss you both, and I'll fly back as soon as I can to see you." She snickered. "Besides, he should blame you. You're the one who sent me out here. I can't believe it's been six months already."

He groaned. "Don't remind me, and whatever you do, don't tell Carl, or he'll become unbearable. But I guess it'll have to do, and I actually have something in mind that'll make him very happy." Stephen's chuckle made Alina grimace.

"Ugh, too much information." Her hands flew up in mock horror. "I really don't need to know the details of how you keep each other happy. Not in that way, at least."

Stephen smirked. "What do you mean? I was talking about taking him to the opera with a fancy dinner beforehand. You have a dirty mind, Mrs. Montgomery."

Alina rolled her eyes but couldn't help laugh at the easy banter.

"Changing the subject completely. Warren's parents haven't caused you any difficulties, have they?" she asked.

"They've tried to blacklist us in the business community, but too many people know what Warren did to you, so it's not working. No one is listening to them. They've not been welcomed back into their social circle yet, either, and last I heard" — Stephen's voice lowered conspiratorially — "his dad had been kicked off the board of three large firms in the city and had lost all his golf buddies as well. But it's not just because of Warren. It seems his attack on you gave some influential industry people the impetus they needed to suggest to the IRS to look a little closer at his father's business affairs, and it seems as if not everything is as it should be. There are rumors of tax evasion, insider trading, and the like. I'm just glad you've escaped even more trouble with that family."

"You're serious? Wow. I didn't expect that. I thought they'd be back hobnobbing with their friends at the country club by now, having put the whole 'unfortunate business' in the past." Alina made air quotes, making Stephen chuckle.

"The higher you climb, the harder you fall," he said.

"You're right. I'm just sorry Warren snapped like that. He was good to me when we first met, and I had nothing to complain about until the very end. Okay, so he could be a little self-indulgent and condescending but nothing I couldn't whip out of him pretty quickly." She shrugged, an impish grin on her face. "I hope he gets the help he needs and recovers. I won't be around to see it, but I don't wish him ill in any way."

"You're a kind person, Alina. And much too good for the likes of Warren Heller." Stephen fell silent for a couple of seconds. "So, have you had any more nightmares? I don't like the thought of you waking up all on your own in a panic."

She nodded. "I still get them occasionally. Maybe once every two weeks, but I can handle them. The weird thing is that I dream of a bridge nearly every night."

"A bridge? What kind of bridge?"

"It's really high, with a fast-running river far below. I feel as if I should know where it is, and I have the strangest urge to go there. But I have no idea where it is or what I should do there if I did find it..." She trailed off, her lip between her teeth. "Never mind, it's just my mind playing tricks on me. Forget I said anything."

"Maybe it is, and maybe it isn't." Stephen cocked his head in thought. "It could be your subconscious trying to tell you something. It doesn't have to have anything to do with an actual bridge and be a representation of something totally different instead. You should look up dream interpretation. Actually, a buddy of mine was into that kind of stuff a while ago. I'll call him later."

"Seriously, Stephen? All your buddies are into either the esoteric, the occult, or astrology and stargazing. Where do you find them all?" Alina giggled.

She'd missed this. The fun, easy conversations around the most varied topics. Stephen was extremely intelligent and could have become a quantum physicist, a rocket engineer, or a neurosurgeon, and would have kicked ass at any of it. His IQ was off the charts, and the NSA, FBI, CIA, and Homeland had all been after him to join them as an analyst after college. He saw patterns and connections where others saw only grains of sand on a beach.

However, he'd refused them all and started the events company instead. It was almost as if he'd decided to do something that none of the alphabet agencies would have any interest in whatsoever. In a way, it was understandable. He would have had to keep secrets from Carl, and if it was something they both valued above all else in their relationship, it was being totally honest with each other. Working for a federal security agency, he would have had to sign an iron-clad non-disclosure agreement, and much of his life would have been out of bounds for Carl.

Alina and Stephen chatted for a little while longer, but when she glanced at her watch, she realized she would be late for her next appointment if she didn't cut things short.

"Look, I have to run. I have another conference this evening to supervise. It's the one for the Georgia Pharma Board."

"No problem. You go and do your thing. Let's set up another video call next week to go through any quotes we need to send to clients."

"Sure, sounds good. Love you and hugs to Carl."

"Love you too, sweetie." Stephen clicked the button to disconnect, and his face disappeared, once again leaving Alina to her thoughts while she hurried to her appointment.

Twenty-Seven

KIRAN, 1989

Kiran's eyes fluttered but didn't open. He wanted to stay where he was — in the blank nothingness he'd floated in for an eternity. When they came to usher him back into the fold, he wanted to be as rested as possible with his mind clear from all he'd suffered. He got it now. The lesson he'd learned when Juliet passed away was still fresh in his mind, but it was nothing compared to the experiences he'd gained during his time in Vietnam.

A human life was like a grain of sand on all the beaches of the universe. It was gone so fast it didn't even register in his world. Yet, it held so much energy and promise, and his tweaks of the tapestry had shortened countless lives, losing all of that in one lazy stroke. No one would ever know what those men and women would have accomplished had he not felt the need to change their destinies.

It was all too clear how the human events he'd believed were insignificant and inconsequential were, in fact, life changing and of great importance to every person going through them. They may be necessary for the fabric of the universe, but never again would he insert any event into their lives without careful thought. He would ensure all of his siblings were fully aware as well. Just as soon as he returned to his normal existence, of course.

Kiran waited patiently, quietly, but nothing happened. No one came for him. Instead, a soft breeze caressed his neck, ruffling his hair, and the sun's rays heated his skin. Gradually, the sound of a pounding surf and the cry of a gull entered his mind.

The despair rose like a wave in his chest. It couldn't be true. Maybe it was the after effects of his treatment as a prisoner of war. He prayed that was all it was.

No. Please, not again. Let me come home. I can't take it anymore. I've seen the horrors, felt the pain, grieved for my loss. What else do you want from me?

Despite his fears, Kiran tried to open his eyes. He couldn't bear it if he was still in Vietnam. What he'd been through in that camp was worse than anything he'd ever experienced in all his human lifetimes, and he couldn't do it again. The pain, the humiliation, the anguish still crashed through his chest like the grinding of a millstone. Bile rose in his throat at the thought of having to endure more of the Viet Cong's cruel and inhumane methods.

Once again, the ambient sounds filtered through his mind. Squeezing his hands into fists, he noticed soft sand running through his fingers. If that was indeed the ocean he could hear, he was no longer in the jungle camp, which was a relief in itself. He was clearly on a beach, lying flat on his stomach. The question was where? In what country? What year? Or was he in some pain-induced dream, never having left the camp?

The only way to find out was to open his eyes and look around. Slowly, he forced them open. Everything was blurry, but after blinking several times, his surroundings came into focus. He didn't move, just peered around him as much as he could without turning his head. If he was still a prisoner, he didn't want to attract the attention of his captors.

Seeing only part of an empty beach and glimpses of a glittering ocean, he slowly pushed up on his arms, dropping back on his butt so he could take in more of where he was. He'd not been lying in the open, he realized, but in a small hollow among tall reeds and bristly grass. In front and to his sides, a wide swath of sand stretched as far as he could see.

If he was still in Vietnam, he was no longer a prisoner, that much was certain. He could still feel the weight and hear the rattle of his chains, though, even if they were of his own making and not by someone who considered him an enemy. He rose carefully and took a few steps, expecting to feel weak, nauseated, and in agony, but instead, he felt strong and healthy.

A wave of relief washed through him at the same time as a crushing grief exploded in his chest. He fell to the sand, pulling his knees to his chest, unable to contain the deep sob working its way up from his chest.

He'd been thrown back.

Once again, he'd have to learn a new place, time, and life — once again as a man. Yes, he'd checked. He still had a male body and still felt like a man. It was something that had stayed consistent throughout the millennia.

Tears spilled down his cheeks as the horrors of his last life rolled through him unbidden. If he'd known, he would have nudged that particular war off the board, or at least changed it somehow.

Next time, I'll be more meticulous and will fully consider the consequences in the trenches — literally — much more carefully. If there ever is a next time.

Still sobbing, he curled into a ball, allowing his emotions to obliterate any rational thought. He needed a release, and this was as good as any while he was still alone and no one could see his pitiful breakdown. He should be stronger than this after all these millennia, but he couldn't bring himself to care. This time, the events leading up to his death had been horrific. The worst he'd ever suffered. Worse even than drowning below decks on the Lusitania in the frigid waters of the Celtic Sea in 1915. That had been terrifying but didn't even come close to Vietnam. Neither did being burned alive on the slopes of Krakatoa.

KIRAN STAYED in the grassy hollow until the sun had traversed the sky, dipped below the horizon, and shined on the far side of the earth, before bringing its life-giving light back to the beach. It took him almost as long to get over his disappointment at having been thrown into yet another life, but once he'd resigned himself to the fact, he pushed his emotional baggage to the back of his mind. He'd done this many times before. He would do it again. Inhaling deeply, slowly, he let the salty sea air fill his lungs before exhaling again. The slurry in his mind had cleared, and he felt more balanced and levelheaded.

His recent experiences had receded and became a part of all the other memories stored in a distant part of his brain. He never forgot any of it, and once he started a new life, the previous one usually became more like a film reel in his head. This time, however, he had a feeling the horrors and trauma he'd experienced would leave a deep scar in his mind. It was too raw, too cruel, and too painful to fade completely.

He shuddered at the thought of the concrete bunker he'd spent so long in without seeing another soul. Names and faces of the people he'd known and lost in a country so far away flitted through his mind.

Susan. Henry. Margaret. Geoff.

His throat closed at the thought of how Margaret and Geoff had been left behind in that jungle. *Were their families notified?* he wondered. Did they ever find out how they died or were they just told they were missing in action and presumed dead? Resolving to find out, he pushed those thoughts aside for now and surveyed his surroundings with a clearer mind.

The sun had climbed high in the sky, burning his face and bare arms. For the first time since he awoke, he noticed he was wearing a pair of tan pants and a short-sleeved, moss-green shirt. Right for the climate, he guessed, even if he didn't know where in the world he was. All he could see was a deserted beach that seemed to stretch to either side as far as the eye could see.

A child's wail reached his ears on the breeze, and his head whipped in that direction. A young girl and a woman dashed out from behind one of the dunes, something small tumbling across the sand in front of them, bouncing and spinning as the wind tugged and pushed at it.

"My shuttle! My shuttle! Did you catch it, Mommy? Did you? Where's my shuttle? No! It's going in the water!" Her words carried on the wind despite the distance, and Kiran strode toward them.

Lunging forward, Kiran caught the object, clasping it in one hand. On closer examination, he saw it was a cuddly toy — a space shuttle like the Columbia or Challenger, the recognition sliding into his head without effort. He watched, his brows drawing together in consternation as the little girl and her mom came rushing toward him.

He felt apprehensive, not sure how he looked after waking up on the sand. However, he needed to know what year it was and what part of the world he'd ended up in, and here was his chance.

Wait, the little girl speaks American English, and her toy is a Space Shuttle. Chances are, I'm back in the US again.

He wasn't sure how he felt about that, but it could be worse, he guessed.

The child came to a skidding halt in front of him, and when he held out the stuffed toy, she hesitated for a second before she took it from his hands.

"Thanks, mister, for saving my shuttle." The little girl beamed at him, crushing the toy to her chest.

"You're welcome, young lady." Kiran couldn't help but grin at her.

Her innocence shined from her bright eyes, tears still clinging to her lashes.

Her hair was a dark blonde, and her eyes were gray with flecks of blue. Her mom put a protective hand on her daughter's shoulder, giving him a small smile.

"Yes, thank you so much," she said. "We thought it might get swept out to sea, and Evie would have been devastated. She's only four."

"No problem. I'm glad I could help. I'm Kiran, by the way."

"Nice to meet you. I'm Andrea, and Evie here is my daughter."

Dropping to one knee, Kiran took Evie's outstretched hand and shook it, mimicking her serious expression.

"So, tell me, Evie," he said. "Why is this shuttle so important to you? And which shuttle is it?"

Somehow, Kiran knew all about the space program and its shuttles. He even knew about Neil Armstrong landing on the moon while he was stuck in Vietnam. If that didn't put some perspective on that war, nothing would.

"This is the Challenger. It blew up. And people died. It was so sad," Evie stated. "I didn't see it, but my dad told me what happened. He works for NASA. In H — Hu — What's it called again, Mommy?" Evie tilted her face up to her mom for help.

"Daddy works in Houston, sweetheart," Andrea explained patiently.

"That's it. *Huston*. Did I say it right, Mommy? Daddy said I should practice."

Evie's mom bopped her gently on the nose. "Yes, you did, but practice makes perfect." She turned to Kiran. "She hasn't quite learned how to pronounce it yet."

Kiran smiled. "It's not an easy name for a little girl to say. I think she's doing great."

Andrea took her daughter's free hand, the other one was tightly gripping her cherished toy.

"Anyway, I'm sorry for disturbing your morning on the beach. We should head back." She raised her chin in the direction they'd come.

"No problem," Kiran said. "I was leaving, anyway."

Hesitating, Andrea peered at him. "Are you here for a visit, or do you live in the area?"

It occurred to him he probably looked a little out of place on the beach the way he was dressed in a shirt and pants.

"Uhm, I live downtown." As always, the number and street of wherever he was staying popped into his head, and he suddenly felt some keys jangle in his pocket.

"Oh, I see. Well, we live a little farther out, but Evie wanted to come to the beach this morning. We thought we'd get here before it got too busy."

Evie tugged at her mom's sleeve, wanting attention.

"Mommy, can he come for breakfast with us? To say thank you for saving my shuttle?"

Andrea hunched down in front of her daughter. "Sweetie, I'm sure Kiran is busy and has somewhere to be this morning," she replied.

Evie gazed up at Kiran with big brown eyes. "Please, Mr. Kiran. Can you come for breakfast? We're having waffles and pancakes at Lottie's."

"Well, I'm..." Kiran wasn't sure what to say.

He didn't know where he was going or how he was going to get there. An image of an older, but well looked-after motorbike, materialized in his head, and another set of keys weighed down his other pocket.

Huh. So I ride a motorbike now. Good to know. At least I have some transport, even if I don't have a clue where I'm going. Come to think of it, I still don't know what year this is.

Andrea straightened. "You're very welcome to join us, if you'd like, but don't feel obligated just because Evie asked."

Kiran studied Andrea's face for a moment. Spending an hour with Andrea and Evie might just give him the information he needed to familiarize himself with his new surroundings. He had a new life to get used to, and he might as well start right away.

"You know what, if you're okay with it, I'd love to join you," he said. "I only came here this morning to get some fresh air. I can look at the ocean for hours, but I must admit, I'm absolutely famished. As long as you're sure your husband wouldn't mind me tagging along?" Kiran knitted his brows.

The last thing he wanted was for Andrea to be in an awkward position having a meal with a man who wasn't her husband. He knew all too well how quickly tongues could start wagging and wouldn't allow that to happen because of him.

"No, it's fine." She waved away his concern. "Doug won't mind, and he'd be upset if I didn't thank you properly for saving Evie's favorite toy. Even if he bought her another one, it wouldn't be the same, and she'd be inconsolable for weeks."

"Well, if you're sure. My bike is parked..." He looked around to get a clue as to where it was parked and felt drawn to a spot behind the grassy dunes. "Just over there."

He pointed vaguely behind him.

"You ride a bike? I saw one on the nearby lot where I parked," Andrea said. "Is that yours? It was black with a white stripe, I think."

"Yep, that's the one," Kiran replied, crossing his fingers that it was the right one, or he'd look really suspicious.

WITH LITTLE EVIE hanging on to her mom's hand, chattering brightly about every little thing that caught her eye, they made their way across the sandy dunes to a parking lot alongside a quiet road. Spotting a road sign, Kiran smiled to himself when he saw the name Corpus Christi and realized he was in Texas at the very bottom of the Lone Star State. That solved his first problem of finding out where he'd been spat back. Now, he had to work out what year it was and anything big that was going on in America and the world.

Kiran sighed with relief when the key in his pocket slid into the ignition of the only bike in the lot, and it rumbled to life. Surreptitiously examining the cars parked nearby, the unfamiliar style told him he'd jumped at least ten years ahead. It was 1965 when he left for Vietnam, and the cars back then had looked very different from the ones he saw here. Andrea's car was smaller than he was used to, with a sloping design on the rear, giving it a more streamlined shape.

He waved to Andrea to drive ahead, and he would follow. After strapping Evie into what looked like a child's seat, she jumped behind the wheel, gave him a thumbs up, and pulled out of the parking lot onto the narrow blacktop.

It wasn't hard to follow the gray car on the motorbike, not even when the traffic became heavier the closer they got to the city. When they reached the waterfront, Andrea flashed her hazard warning lights before pulling up to the curb outside a small diner. Kiran slotted his bike in behind it, hanging the helmet on the handlebars before dismounting.

He watched as Evie was unbuckled and lifted onto the sidewalk. To his surprise, she skipped to his side and slipped a tiny hand into his, peering up at him with wide-eyed wonder.

"How do you make that thing go?" she asked, pointing at the motorbike.

Kiran chuckled.

"It works just like a car with an engine. It's got a gas tank right here" — he pointed to the teardrop bulge in front of the seat — "and I have a brake on this handle to slow down, and with the other handle, I make it go faster. The trickiest thing is to balance on two wheels, but it gets easy with a lot of practice."

"Can I ride it?"

Kiran ruffled her hair, smiling. "Not until you're a lot bigger. But when you're a grownup, you can have a go. Although I think you'd be more comfortable in a car."

Andrea joined them after having locked the car and dropped the keys into her purse.

"The diner is just here." She pointed to a storefront with a bright red awning and tables and chairs outside.

At the counter inside, they placed their order before finding a booth by the window. Kiran was suddenly starving and wondered how long it had been since he ate something. Food for the prisoners in the camp had always been scarce, and the dysentery caused by parasites had plagued his last few weeks there. No matter what he'd had to eat or drink, it all came back out one way or another without stopping to do him any good.

His stomach twisted at the thought. The memories, even from behind the wall in his mind, were still raw. The stench of the camp clung to the inside of his nose, the screams and wails from the other prisoners echoing in his ears, while Geoff's last few words — still so full of optimism — had etched themselves to the inside of his skull.

"I'm good, mate," Geoff muttered in his Australian twang. *"We'll all be away from here soon, and then we'll have a cold one to celebrate."* For the last few minutes, Geoff had perked up, but Kiran knew it was probably his body's last-ditch effort before succumbing to the disease overwhelming it.

"Sounds like a plan, my friend. Where do you want to meet?" Kiran asked, trying to sound much more chipper than he felt.

With effort, Geoff cocked his head slightly. "Where are you going back to?"

Kiran thought for a moment. There was no telling where he'd end up if he had to start all over again, but where would he go if he lived through this? He picked the first city that came into his head.

"Atlanta," he said. "That's where I'll be."

He'd never been to Atlanta, but it didn't really matter. Geoff wasn't leaving this jungle, and most likely, neither was he.

"That's good, mate. Atlanta." Geoff nodded slowly. "I'll remember that. I'll look you up through the Veteran's Association when I get there, so don't forget to register your address with them."

Kiran squeezed his arm. "I won't, buddy. If I'm not there, I'll make sure they know where I am and how you can contact me. Get some rest now, my friend."

Geoff closed his eyes, his voice weakening. "We'll make it home, Kiran. You'll see. We'll make it home."

"Mr. Kiran? Are you okay?"

Evie's voice shook him back to the present.

He blinked several times. "Yes, I'm fine. I just got lost in my thoughts for a moment. How are your pancakes?"

Her little hands flew up in the air, her fingers waggling, showing smeared chocolate and blueberry stains. "They're yummy. I love lots of blueberries and chocolate chips on them, but not syrup. It's too sticky."

"I agree. Syrup is sticky, but I love it on my waffles." Kiran winked at Evie and stuffed an enormous piece of waffle, dripping with maple syrup, in his mouth.

Evie giggled as a drop of syrup escaped from his lips, and he had to quickly lick it off before it ran down his chin.

Andrea watched their interaction with a smile on her face. Their conversation had been slow to start, but it wasn't long before she was telling him all about herself, Evie, her husband, and his work at NASA.

While Andrea took Evie to the bathroom to wash her hands and face, sticky from the chocolate chips, Kiran snagged an abandoned newspaper from a nearby table. He quickly found the date, November 15, 1989. He'd left California for Vietnam twenty-four years ago. It wasn't as big a jump as he'd done in the past — the biggest one had been after he fell from the Great Pyramid in Egypt and woke up in Ancient Greece nearly two millennia later.

The change had been jarring and disorienting, and he'd kept himself hidden as much as possible until he'd learned more about life in the society he was about to join. Before long, he'd integrated and, having found himself in Sparta, joined the army as a foot soldier. Life had been tolerable, partly because as soldiers the people admired them, and they were treated well by the ruling King Archelaus, and partly because they'd not been involved in any wars for almost a decade.

A few years after he arrived, the big talk among the soldiers and all free Greek men was a new religious festival, which was to be held near Olympia in honor of Zeus. Kiran and many of his fellow soldiers wanted to take part and traveled from Sparta to the games to measure their speed and fitness against men from all over the country. His name back then had been a little different — Koroibos — to allow for the Ancient Greek culture he lived in.

To his surprise, he won the very first stadium race and was hailed by his brothers-in-arms as a hero and proof of Sparta's superiority, while he attributed the win to his training in the army. He never took part in the games again, not wanting to draw too much attention to himself, and thirty-three years later, he died in the Messenian War, fighting for King Alcamenes.

2001

KIRAN STAYED in Corpus Christi for nearly two years, becoming close friends with Andrea, her husband Doug, and little Evie. He'd found a job in a bar near where he lived and enjoyed the busy nights, with regular customers during low season and tourists swarming the waterfront in the summer. It made a change from the stress of being a doctor. He'd gone on a few dates, but never took it any further than that since he didn't want a repeat of what happened with Juliet.

His dreams of the brown-haired beauty with the soft gray eyes were a regular occurrence, and little by little, he felt he got to know her even though they barely spoke except for words of endearment and enjoyment during their lovemaking. They didn't always have sex, however. Sometimes, they lay entwined, gazing at each other and communicating without words.

Her face remained obscured, or he forgot her features as soon as he woke up, but she was the most enchanting woman he'd ever met — or dreamed of since he'd never actually met her. He still wasn't sure what that encounter at Juliet's funeral had been, or if that had been conjured by his grief-stricken mind as well.

When Andrea and Doug broke the news that they were moving to Houston to make it easier for Doug with his work, Kiran knew it was time to move on. He had no direction or specific reason to leave, but something prodded him to go and find his next adventure.

The night before the family was leaving, Kiran went over for a farewell dinner. They talked for hours, lingering after the meal over a couple of bottles of wine, reminiscing, laughing, and shedding a tear or two. They sat on boxes, eating takeout on paper plates with plastic knives and forks.

Before he rode off on his bike, Evie came flying down the path, her long chestnut hair billowing behind her, and threw herself in his arms.

"Uncle Kiran, I don't want you to go. I want you to move to Houston with us. Please, please, please?" Her pleas were accompanied by a flood of tears.

He hunched down on one knee before her, stroking her cheek with his knuckles. "I'm sorry, sweetie, but I can't. You have an exciting new life waiting for you, and I have to get on with mine. We can keep in touch, though. I have your new address, and as soon as I know where I'll be, I'll write you a letter."

"But when will I see you again?" she murmured.

"I don't know, honey. But you need to promise me something."

"What?" Evie looked up at him with tear-stained cheeks, her bottom lip quivering, and Kiran's heart broke at the sight.

"Follow your dreams. You can be anything if you just work hard enough. Make me proud, Evie," he said. "I'll always look out for your name in anything to do with space missions, so when you become an astronaut, I'll know you kept your promise."

Her head tilted to the side, lips in a pout. "But what if I don't become an astronaut?"

"Then you become the best at whatever you decide to do. It's not the goal that counts, but the journey you take to get there and the work and effort you put into it to be the best you can be. Will you do that for me?"

"Okay, I will." She nodded. "But you have to write me letters, and birthday cards, and Christmas cards. Promise?"

"That's a lot of writing, but I promise to do my best, pumpkin." His heart clenched at making a promise he knew he was highly unlikely to keep, but Evie would forget about him one day, and he would always look out for her name mentioned anywhere.

"I got you this, so you don't forget me." Evie gave him the drawing she'd been working on while he and her parents talked. "It's me, Mommy, Daddy, and you. But I made you look like an angel since you saved my shuttle. Mommy said you were my guardian angel on the beach. Look, you're glowing. Because you always look like you're all lit up. Mommy says I'm imagining it, but I'm not. You do glow."

Kiran was taken aback. He knew there was a light surrounding him. It came with who he was, but he didn't think anyone could see it. Clearly, he was wrong.

"Thanks, Evie. I will treasure it always." He choked up, and tears pricked behind his eyes.

"And I want you to have this. Daddy bought it when he was away for work. You can fill it with water, so you always have it with you if you get thirsty."

Doug and Andrea came down the driveway and stood behind Evie.

"I was doing some equipment testing in Colorado," Doug explained, "and Evie had asked me to get something from there. That was the only thing available. Sorry, but she insisted on giving it to you. It's never been used, I promise."

"It's a great gift. Thanks, Doug. I'm grateful for all you've done for me these last couple of years. You've both been amazing friends, and I wish you all the luck in Houston." He shook Doug's hand before giving Andrea a big hug.

"It was fate, meeting you and Evie on the beach," he whispered in her ear.

Andrea nodded mutely, tears spilling down her cheeks, and she hugged him tighter.

"I'm sorry. We should have given you a better goodbye present, but I've been so busy with packing the house and everything," she croaked, clearing her throat.

He pulled back slightly so he could see her face, gripping her shoulders. "Are you kidding? This drawing and water bottle are the best presents ever."

He gazed down at the little girl holding tightly to his jacket.

"Evie, whenever I use this bottle, I'll think of you. And I'm going to frame this picture and hang it on the wall in every house I ever live in."

Kiran straddled his bike, the engine starting with a growl. With a nod and a wave, he sped back toward his place downtown. He glanced in the mirror, and once again, his heart clenched seeing Evie crying while being consoled by her dad, and Andrea waving until he turned a corner, and they disappeared from his view. He would miss them.

Twenty-Eight

ALINA, 2016

Another year had passed, and Alina loved Atlanta more and more, but there was a restlessness in her chest that wouldn't leave her alone. It was as if she needed to get away, or maybe go toward something, but she couldn't work out what it was or what caused her jittery feet. She enjoyed her job, the city, and the new friends she'd made. The only thing missing was Stephen and Carl. If they lived here as well, or at least a little closer, it would be perfect. As it was, they alternated between her flying to New York and them coming down south.

They were the ones bringing her the news Warren had been sent to prison despite his lawyer trying to get him into a psychiatric hospital instead. She'd left right after her testimony without waiting for the end of the trial and had asked Stephen to let her know the outcome. The judge had ordered him to undergo therapy while in jail, but nothing more. Alina was pleased. Had they sent him to a hospital, he might have been out after a year. This way, he'd get the treatment he needed and still pay for his crimes.

Strolling through the park, she soaked up the sun rays, enjoying the warm air and blue skies. It was a pleasant change from New York, with its blustery winds and plummeting temperatures. Thanksgiving was around the corner, and she was spending it with Stephen and Carl in the Berkshires where they owned a house. Fortunately, it was nowhere near where Warren had taken her that fateful Christmas.

That was all in her past now, and she should be looking forward to the next step in her life. If only she could get rid of this nagging feeling that she had to be somewhere else. Her blond dream-lover continued to visit her in the still hours of the night, but the dreams had changed. They were still full of passion and desire, but also a sense of urgency. More and more, she dreamed of the high bridge with the raging river below and white feathers falling from the skies.

It constantly set her on edge, and she often found herself searching on the internet for anything to do with bridges. Was it a warning? A sign of upcoming difficulties? She'd definitely had to overcome more than her fair share of difficulties and hardships. She didn't want any more to deal with.

A wave of sadness swept through her chest, remembering the last Thanksgiving she'd had with her little family. They'd had a turkey with all the trimmings, hot apple cider, pumpkin spiced coffee, and apple pie. Katie, Bryce and their two boys had joined them for the weekend. It'd been full of love, laughter, friendship, and togetherness. Would she ever have that again?

Her heart squeezed at the thought of being alone for the rest of her life. She was still young, and she wanted to have a family. She wanted a husband to love and who'd love her back, children to raise and dote on. She hadn't dated again since Warren, so maybe she should put herself out there?

Her steps slowed on the path while she considered the consequences of getting back onto the dating scene. She'd been out of it for so long that things had changed, the rules were different, and she wasn't sure she was ready for all of that. Dating apps and websites were the norm, and she felt out of touch and inadequate. Why couldn't she meet a decent guy the normal way? Whatever that was. She'd met Jonas in a bar in college, and he'd asked her out the next day, having begged one of her friends for her phone number. They'd been inseparable since that night.

Suddenly, the afternoon didn't seem so warm and relaxing, and she picked up the pace to get back home as quickly as she could. She couldn't explain it, but the feeling of needing to find something — someone — increased in her chest, settling like a rock and constricting her lungs. It was a little like a panic attack, yet different.

She entered her apartment, closing the door behind her with a resounding thump and leaned her back against it to catch her breath. The urge to get home had gotten stronger the closer she got, and if she'd been in tennis shoes, she would have run the last few blocks. On the way to her bedroom, she stripped off, feeling hot and sweaty after her dash from the park.

Dumping her clothes in the hamper, she padded across the sumptuous carpet and into the travertine-tiled bathroom — one of the best features of the place — and turned on the shower for the water to heat. After adjusting the settings and angles on the many heads and sprays, she stepped under the flow, letting the heat seep into her bones and loosen her muscles.

"Place your hands above your head and widen your legs a little."

The voice wrapped around her like silk, and she obeyed without question. The tile was cool against her skin, but the water kept her warm as it sluiced down her back. She flinched but then relaxed when soft fingers began massaging her shoulders, the scent of her body wash filling the air. The slippery suds eased the friction on her sensitive skin, turning the massage sensual and seductive. She quivered as a tingle began in her core, sending jolts of electricity racing down her spine.

"Just relax, love. Let me take care of you. I want to pleasure you, worship your body," he whispered.

"I want that. I want you. Please, touch me... everywhere." She sounded breathless and needy even to her own ears.

He growled low in his throat. *"Oh, trust me, I will. You are my treasure, and I will make you feel it."*

Up and down her limbs, his hands slipped from her neck to her toes and back again. Gently kneading her calves, thighs, and up over the globes of her backside, he touched every inch of her skin. She felt as if she were on fire, flames building in her center and quickly spreading outward.

"More, I need more," she panted, her pulse rocketing, her heart beating faster in her chest.

He chuckled. "Patience, my love. Your reward will be so much sweeter that way."

When his fingers trailed lightly up the center of her spine, her sex flooded with her juices. Lust coursed through her, and she knew she wanted him deep inside her. Her breath hitched while his hands splayed wide around her ribcage, his long fingers brushing against the underside of her breasts. He cupped both of them in his hands, squeezing gently, and a deep moan escaped her mouth.

His breath grew heavier, and he pulled her tight to his front, his cock nestling between her asscheeks. He was rock-hard, throbbing, and burning against her skin. She couldn't help wiggle her hips to tease him a little, and she smiled when a deep growl rumbled in his chest.

Peppering her neck and shoulders with kisses, he nipped the sensitive skin before swirling his tongue over the sting to soothe it. To get better access, he swept her long dark hair aside, winding it around his fist, tugging to tilt her head to the side. With her slender neck exposed, he sucked hard on the skin behind her ear. It would bruise, she knew, but she wanted it. With her hair down, no one would see it. It was his way of marking her as his, and she loved it.

Now, when she'd found him, there would be no letting go. He would be her home, her heart, her soul. They would become one and would never again have to suffer the grief of losing their other half. He would be it for her, and she would move heaven and earth to be that for him. He was all she'd ever need.

"Can you feel what you do to me? I need to be inside you so badly," he murmured. "But first I'll send you sky high. I'm so hard it hurts, but it's a good pain, and when I'm finally where I belong, it will be heavenly."

"Oh, God. Please, touch me. I need you to touch me." Her voice was raspy and heavy with desire.

Her nipples had puckered and tightened under his touch. As he plucked, twirled, and tugged at the rosy peaks, his ministrations sent shards of heat to her clit as if there were a direct connection between them. She couldn't help the moans and wails dripping from her mouth as he pushed her higher and higher. To get a little relief, she squeezed her thighs together, but he grunted in her ear to keep her legs apart.

"*Your bud is mine, and I want to be the only one to touch it. Your orgasm is for me to give you, and I'll let you fly when you're ready.*"

"*Y-yes. Yes, please. Just don't keep teasing me. I'm so close. So close.*" The words were more like a keening whine, but he understood them all the same.

"*Don't worry, I know exactly what you need.*"

One hand snaked down her taut belly, over her mound, a finger slipping through her soaking wet folds. Gently, he started circling her swollen nub, making her scream from pleasure. From behind, his thick and long cock slid between her cheeks, attacking her pussy from a delicious angle without entering her.

On each of his strokes, she pushed back against his hips, eliciting a stream of grunts and growls from him as the swollen crown of his length nudged her entrance. She spread her legs wider, wanting him to surge inside her, but he held back.

His whispers filled her head as if he were a part of her consciousness. "Not yet, my love. First, you're going to get swept away by that sweet wave of pleasure, and I'm going to enjoy watching you explode in my hands. Let go, gorgeous. Let go and just feel."

With his fingers rubbing, tweaking, pinching, she spiraled higher and higher. Her body tensed, and he must have known she was about to erupt as his hips pushed harder and faster, his cock sliding back and forth through her folds. The heated drops of pre-cum from the head burst against her clit, and she shattered, riding the crest of a wave so high and dizzying she feared she'd never come down.

"*Oh, oh, oh, ooooh!*" *she screamed as the pleasure overtook her senses, stars bursting in her vision, her body convulsing from the grip of her earth-shattering climax.*

As the orgasm waned, her legs turned limp, and he wrapped his arms around her to hold her up.

"*Sweetheart, you are incredibly beautiful when you let yourself go and give in to your body's reactions. There's nothing I enjoy more than to feel you fly apart and tumble over that edge. You give me so much pleasure. You are mine...*"

ALINA JERKED out of her dream, blinking furiously. With her breath ragged and her legs trembling, she realized she was still in the shower — alone. What the hell just happened? Did she have a sex dream while she was still awake? This was crazy. Normal people didn't have these kinds of visions while standing in a shower, did they? It wasn't as if she'd been thinking of him. Not in that way, at least.

Like a distant song of a breeze in the reeds of a riverbank, she heard the familiar words.

Just take one little step.

After turning off the shower, Alina grabbed one of the thick towels on the vanity shelf and wrapped it around her body, and then another around her hair. From the dresser, she pulled out a pair of leggings and an oversized sweatshirt to wear. Her movements were slow, and she took her time getting dressed. She was still reeling from the dream, or whatever it was. Her mind spun with the aftermath of the intense feelings and sensations it had evoked.

It was Saturday, and she wouldn't normally go into the office, but they had a small, exclusive event running later that day, and she wanted to be on hand to make sure everything ran smoothly. It was being held in the hotel next door to the convention center, so she figured she could sit in the bar with a cup of coffee while the clients were busy.

One of her event coordinators was in charge, so she didn't want to step on her toes or make her nervous, but these clients were important, and if anything went wrong, she could intercede and help immediately. If everything went well, which was what she expected, she could leave once the meeting was over and go home for a good night's sleep.

She still had a few hours before she needed to leave, so she dried her hair, put on some makeup, and read the paper while lounging on the couch for a few hours.

Before she left for the hotel, she'd change into something more appropriate and put her hair up in a neat bun at the nape of her neck. It was so long and thick it still felt damp even after using the hairdryer. Having it up would just be easier and seem more professional.

When she arrived at the hotel, she left her car with the valet and went in search of the staff member in charge of the meeting. She found her setting up the room with everything the clients had asked for, and after a quick chat to make sure she had all she needed, Alina settled in the bar, but instead of a coffee, she asked for sparkling water with lime. She didn't want alcohol since she'd be driving home later and wouldn't make a great impression on the clients if anything happened that required her help.

She found a table in a corner and texted the coordinator where she was, before digging out her laptop to finish reports she'd been working on the day before.

"Excuse me, is this seat taken?" A woman's voice interrupted her focus.

Alina looked up to find a young woman standing by the empty chair opposite hers. She looked around and realized the bar had filled while her attention was on her work. All other seats were taken, and the volume in the bar had increased tenfold.

"No, please, help yourself." She smiled and gestured to the chair.

The woman gave a relieved smile. "Thank you. I didn't want to sit at the bar with all those men, and this was the only seat available."

Alina glanced over to the bar where a large group of middle-aged men stood drinking and talking. Their laughter was raucous, and the female bartender had her hands full making drinks, clearing glasses, and taking payments, while also having to put up with their lewd comments and jeering. Alina hated when that happened and got up from her chair.

"Stay as long as you like," she said to her new companion. "I'm just going to have a word with someone."

She stepped up to the bar and squeezed into the middle of the group of men in suits.

With her voice raised, she said, "Excuse me, gentlemen. You will get your drinks a lot faster if you leave the staff alone to do their job. After all, that's why you're in a bar, right? To have a drink?" She pinned each one of the men with a hard stare and knew she'd hit a nerve when they shifted on their feet.

Only one of them stood his ground.

"How about it, babe?" He waggled his brows and leered at the young bartender. "Wanna join us for some fun? You look like you could do with some attention and a bit of harmless fun. Whaddya say?"

"If I was your sister, or that bartender your daughter, would you want a man of your age to be hitting on them?" Alina took a step closer to him, arching a brow.

The guy clamped his mouth shut, staring at Alina, his friends nudging him, and he had enough sense to back down and look sheepish. He held his hands up in a placating gesture.

"Sorry, miss. We were only having a little fun. We meant nothing by it."

Alina studied him for a moment and then nodded before returning to her seat. The young woman had watched the incident and quietly clapped her hands when she sat back down.

"That was amazing," she said. "I'd be too scared to do something like that."

Alina grimaced. "It was nothing. I'm used to dealing with men who get a little overconfident after a few drinks and turn into lecherous douchebags to impress their friends. You just need to pop their overinflated egos with a pin, and they soon see the error of their ways."

"Still, I admire your gumption." The woman smiled. "I'm Chloe, by the way."

Alina looked at her as she spoke. She was in her mid-twenties with a bright smile and chocolate brown eyes. Her English had a twang to it that was definitely not North American, nor British, but similar.

"I'm Alina. It's lovely to meet you. Are you staying here in the hotel?"

"Yes, the American VA is holding an event here this weekend for veterans from the Vietnam War," Chloe explained. "My grandfather died over there, but he wrote so many letters to my grandmother that I feel like I know him. At least he did" — a sorrowful look flitted across her face — "before he was captured and held in a POW camp until his death."

"I'm so sorry." Alina leaned closer, giving Chloe's hand a gentle squeeze. "Your grandmother must have been devastated to hear that."

"She was, but my aunt and uncle were toddlers, and my dad was on the way, so she needed to focus on bringing them up."

"What brings you here, then?" Alina wondered.

Chloe settled back in her chair, tugging at an errant strand of hair. "The only POW who survived the camp my grandpa was in came to visit my grandma when he'd recovered. He told her all about the camp, although I'm sure he spared her the awful details." She grimaced. "And he also talked about an American man, a doctor, who helped everyone else survive the horrors the best he could."

Alina listened quietly.

"It seems this doctor had been close friends with Grandpa and when he hurt his leg, this man risked his own life to help him. My grandma couldn't remember if the soldier who came to talk to her told her the man's full name, but she never forgot what he'd said." Chloe paused, taking a sip from the coffee she'd ordered. "He wasn't among the prisoners who were freed, but they also never found his body. They listed him as MIA since they couldn't confirm he'd been killed. The soldier mentioned the doctor had told my grandpa he'd be in Atlanta after the war was over, and if grandpa ever made it over here, to look him up. He said he'd make sure the VA had all his contact details."

Alina tilted her head to the side, studying the young woman. "And now you've come to find this man?"

"Yes, or at least find out what happened to him, if I can. I was coming here from Australia anyway, so I decided to take a few extra days to see what I could find out. My grandma doesn't have much time left." Sadness filled her eyes. "I'd love to be able to thank him for helping my grandfather. The way this soldier spoke about this guy, he must have helped a lot of prisoners in that camp. All I've got to go on is the name Mitch. The soldier didn't know if it was his first name, a nickname, or maybe his last name was Mitchell."

"That's not much to go on." Alina's brow creased.

"No, it's not, but it's all I've got." Chloe shrugged. "I know where they were held, so maybe that will help. I don't think there could have been too many doctors with the name Mitch or similar held in that one camp. At least I hope not. In any case, I have an appointment with a VA coordinator tomorrow who has promised to help me. The soldier told my grandma he was their guardian angel and many more would have died in that jungle camp if he hadn't been there."

"What an amazing story. I hope you find the answers you're looking for. If not, at least you tried," Alina said. "I'm sure your grandmother will be thrilled to know you did that for her."

Alina and Chloe talked a while longer about Australia, her home in Melbourne, and her recent travels that brought her to America. The time passed quickly, and then the coordinator, Tiannah, came back to inform Alina that the meeting had concluded, and the clients had left happy with the organization of it. Alina thanked her and sent her home to enjoy what was left of the weekend.

She said goodbye to Chloe, wished her luck with her mission, and collected her car from the valet service. The drive back to her apartment was quiet, with little traffic on the streets, her mind mulling over Chloe's story. As soon as she was home, feeling tired and out of sorts, she got ready for bed and slipped under the covers. She was fast asleep within minutes. Vivid dreams slid into her mind a few hours later, filling her head with bridges, fast-flowing water, and angel wings.

Twenty-Nine

KIRAN, 1991

Leaving Corpus Christi behind, Kiran headed east because something inside tugged at him to go in that direction. He didn't know why, and he didn't care. Spending too much time wondering and worrying was pointless. With the miles disappearing under the wheels of the bike, added to the countless others he'd already traveled, he tried to keep his thoughts under control.

In the beginning, he'd always wondered if each new life was a chance for him to redeem himself for his wrongdoings, but since he didn't know what they were, he couldn't work out if he was doing the right thing or not. Too many times, he'd wished for guidance, a hint, a clue, but nothing. Having wandered blind for so long, he had no reason to think this life would be any different. At least, everything had stayed the same so far in that respect.

Leaving Evie and her family behind had been sad, but he knew he had to move on. His heart, his mind, or just plain itchy feet told him so. Could that be it? Was his urge to move on simply a case of a traveler's soul? Maybe there was no purpose to his wandering other than to satisfy his curiosity, or to stop him from getting bored. Maybe one day, he'd get his answers, but it didn't look as if that would happen anytime soon. In the meantime, he'd keep moving.

Choosing smaller roads, Kiran bypassed Houston where Evie, Andrea, and Doug had moved, and forged onward, only stopping for short breaks. With a small camping tent strapped to the bike, and a duffel bag containing his meager possessions, he found plenty of places to rest at night, and stopped in diners along the way for food.

He never rested for long. The restlessness drove him hard toward the unknown, and only subsided when he was on the road. Town after city after town ended up in his dusty rearview mirror as he crossed from state to state. The vibrations of the engine merged with his bones, and the sound of the wind was like a rushing river in his ears while the bike ate up the miles.

IT WAS STILL DARK when he crossed the St. John's River. He was in Florida, that much he knew, but only because a sign told him the name of the river and that he was entering the Sunshine State. After several days of fusing himself to the saddle for hours on end, he finally felt the driving need seep out of his muscles.

Exactly where he was going was still a mystery to him, but he had a feeling he was nearing his next destination. It would be the first time he was conscious when he moved to a new place. Maybe this wasn't another shift?

Never before had he gone from one place to another without it being a shunt forward, except for the journey to Vietnam. So what was happening? He didn't dare hope he'd be spared the time jump, so he fixed his gaze forward on the end of the long bridge. He couldn't see it in the dark, but he sensed the earth and trees on the other side.

The gray light of dawn was lightening the shadows, and before long, the sun would fill the skies with pinks and gold like its own private painting. He loved this time of day. It made him think of his sister. She was the one who created the beginning of each day and always tried her best to make them as beautiful as possible. Their brother Uriel, however, was in control of the weather, and his capricious nature made it difficult for Eos to give everyone a glorious dawn every day.

Rolling slowly onto the bridge, Kiran could feel the might of the water beneath his feet despite its lazy flow as it meandered north. He couldn't explain it, but there was something about bridges and rivers that sent little electric shocks to his chest, as if he needed to pay attention to them. For sure, he'd dreamed about them often enough, but this one was nothing like the raging river and the wide span and gut-clenching height of the bridge in his dreams.

As he neared the end of the long causeway, a knot formed in his stomach, winding tighter with every revolution of the tires on the blacktop. Finally, he rolled onto dry land. Just as both tires left the bridge, a violent tremor shook Kiran's body from its core, making his head spin. The bike swerved wildly, and he fought to keep it upright. With the back wheel sliding out from under him, the machine tilted hard to the side, forcing him to shift his weight on the saddle to compensate. Twisting the front wheel in the opposite direction, he turned it too much and nearly laid it on its side, but at the last second, he dragged the bike upright. Slamming hard on the brakes, he came to a screeching halt, the motorcycle skidding onto the gravel verge.

2001

SWITCHING OFF THE ENGINE, he pried his fingers from the handles, one by one, where they'd gripped tightly enough for his knuckles to lock inside his gloves. Dismounting, he shoved down the kickstand and settled the motorcycle on it. His heart slammed inside his chest, his pulse roaring in his ears, and his chest moving up and down in sharp heaves.

What the hell was that? I nearly wrecked the bike and myself!

Kiran flipped up the visor on his helmet and looked around. The river behind him looked the same, and so did the road ahead, but something had changed. Taking a few calming breaths, he scanned his surroundings. He was still on a county road, and it was still pre-dawn, so what was it that made things feel different? Pulling the helmet off, he closed his eyes and breathed in the cool air, which held a tang of salt and the ocean.

His eyes flipped open and studied the winding blacktop and the trees on either side. Something was off, he could feel it. His gaze swept from side to side, surveying the area nearest to him, and as far into the distance as he could make out. Turning on his heels in a circle, he opened all his senses to figure out what bothered him.

The trees.

The leaves had changed color, and some of them had dropped to the ground. It was fall.

When he left Corpus Christi three days ago, it had been the middle of the summer, but in the blink of an eye, the season had changed. Was it still the same year?

Rubbing his chest with his knuckles, he breathed slowly in through his nose and out through his mouth. He felt strange. It was as if his insides had been mixed up and were out of place. Or something. He couldn't quite put his finger on it.

Leaning on the bike, he knitted his brows and pinched the bridge of his nose, gathering his thoughts to think everything through. Once he'd regained his senses, he knew the only way to find out what had happened was to carry on driving until he got to his destination — wherever that was. It certainly seemed like he was getting close, and the nearest town was either Jacksonville or St. Augustine.

As the latter name swept through his thoughts, a warmth spread in his chest, and an image of the dark-haired woman danced through his mind. It was her. The woman he'd come to... love? No, that couldn't be right. How could you love someone you'd never met? But maybe this was why he felt drawn to St. Augustine. Was it possible she was there?

He growled out his frustration. She was a figment of his imagination. A very real, tactile, and overwhelmingly sensuous one, but still something his mind had conjured. She wasn't in St. Augustine, Jacksonville, or anywhere.

Kiran shook his head at his stupid thoughts. Of course, she wasn't real. He'd only ever seen her in his dreams. *Not only seen her*, his inner voice prodded. He'd touched her, kissed her, pleasured her, but still only in a dreamscape. Except for that one time at Juliet's funeral. Yet, that couldn't have been her. He must have been mistaken.

Pushing it all out of his mind, he shoved the helmet back down on his head and mounted the bike. With a roar and gravel spitting from underneath the back tire, he pulled back onto the blacktop and sped along the deserted road. On the horizon, the first rays of the sun spread a warm glow low in the sky.

A FEW HOURS LATER, he'd found a small Bed and Breakfast to stay at and had checked out his new home town, if it could be called that since he never knew how long he'd be staying. From a newspaper in the tiny reception lobby of the B&B, he'd found it was now 2001 and November, which explained the drop in temperature when he first felt the shift. Not only was it a new decade, but the beginning of a new millennium as well. So much time had passed, and he had nothing to show for it. It was a depressing thought, so he quickly shoved it aside.

The more he thought about the incident on the bridge, the stranger it was that he'd shifted while still awake. He'd always been asleep, or at least dozing — or dead. Never had he been on the move like this morning, and he didn't feel like doing it again. He could have crashed the bike and got killed. Not that it would have made much difference. He would only have been brought back, anyway.

That night, he went to bed early, exhausted after the long hours of driving and the time jump. On this occasion, it had been ten years, and so much had changed. Computers seemed to be everywhere, and people walked around with telephones in their hands. They were completely portable and so small you could be forgiven for putting it down and losing it. He still hadn't wrapped his head around that one.

Kiran tried to empty his mind of all the things he'd discovered in only a few short hours. He needed sleep more than anything, and it could all wait until the morning. Despite his best efforts, he tossed and turned for a few hours, his mind going back to the shift and how different it had been this time. All his other shifts had been peaceful, and he'd just woken up in a new time and place. Why was this one so different? If only he had someone to ask.

His low, derisive laugh echoed in the otherwise silent room. He'd never had anyone to ask. All his prayers and pleas for answers or explanations had always fallen on deaf ears. He was on his own as always. With that thought spiraling through his mind, he finally fell into a restless sleep.

2002

"Put both hands above your head, and spread your legs," he growled quietly in her ear.

Without questioning, she did as he asked. He made sure the warm water cascaded down her body to keep her comfortable. He began massaging her shoulders and smiled when, at first, she flinched from his touch. Using her body wash to make his hands glide easier over her body, he worked his way across her back, loosening every knot in her tense muscles. With gentle fingers, he seduced every sensitive part of her skin, enjoying the sensual moans and whimpers slipping from her lips as she trembled from his touch.

"Just relax. Let me take care of you. I will pleasure you, worship you," he whispered.

"I want that. I want you. Please, touch me... everywhere."

"Oh, trust me, I will. You are mine, and I will make you feel it."

His hands glided up and down her limbs, from her neck to her toes and back again. Kneading gently on her calves, her thighs, and up over the globes of her ass, he touched every inch of her skin.

His cock rose, swelling and throbbing as it strained toward her, and his hips bucked of their own accord.

"More, I need more," she panted.

"Patience, my love. You'll get your reward." It would be so much better to make her wait, but damn if he didn't want to sink deep inside her without waiting a second longer.

He filled his hands with her slick skin, sweeping up and down her body from her legs to her neck, squeezing her ass cheeks, the soapy suds easing the friction. Her breath hitched as his hands splayed wide around her ribcage, his fingers teasing the underside of her breasts. He cupped both of them in his hands, squeezing gently, and a deep moan escaped her mouth.

With his breath growing heavier, he pulled her tight to his front, his cock nestling between her butt cheeks. He was rock-hard and throbbing, and her skin burned against the sensitive crown, pre-cum leaking from the slit. She wiggled her hips, and a growl rumbled in his chest. In reply, he peppered her neck and shoulders with kisses, nipping the soft skin before licking away the sting.

Sweeping her long, luscious, dark hair to the side, he wrapped it around his fist and tugged gently to tilt her head for easier access. With her slender neck exposed, he sucked hard on her skin, just behind and below her ear, leaving a red mark. It would bruise, he knew, but with her hair down, no one would see it.

It was his way of marking her as his. Now that he'd found her, there could be no letting go. She would be his home, his heart, his soul. They would become one and would never again have to suffer the grief of losing their other half. She would be it for him, and he would move heaven and earth to be that for her. She was all he'd ever need.

"Can you feel what you do to me? I need to be inside you so badly, but first, I'll make you fly. I'm so hard it's painful, but it feels good."

"Oh, God. Please, touch me. I need you to touch me." Her voice was raspy and breathless.

Her nipples had puckered and tightened under his touch. Plucking, twirling, and tugging at the rosy peaks, he watched while her eyes grew heavy with desire, and she squirmed, squeezing her thighs together as if to get relief from the lust he knew was coursing through her.

"Keep your legs apart. Your clit is mine, and only I can touch it. Your orgasm belongs to me, and I'll let you come when I think you're ready."

"O—o—okay. Just don't keep torturing me. I'm so close. So close." The words were more like a keening whine, but he understood them all the same.

"Don't worry, I know exactly what you need."

One hand snaked down her taut belly, over her mound, a finger slip-

ping through her soaking wet folds. Gently, he circled her swollen nub, making her scream from pleasure. His thick and long cock slid between her cheeks, attacking her pussy from a delicious angle without entering her.

On each of his strokes, she pushed back against his hips, pulling a stream of grunts and growls from him each time the swollen crown of his length nudged her entrance. She spread her legs wider, silently urging him to plunge inside her, but he held back.

"Not yet, my love. First, I'm going to make you come so hard the only thing you'll remember is me. Let go. Feel what I do to you. Come on my hand."

With his fingers rubbing, tweaking, pinching, he felt her spiraling higher and higher. Her body tensed, and he knew she was about to erupt as his hips pushed harder and faster, his cock sliding back and forth through her folds. The heated drops of pre-cum from the head burst against her clit, and she shattered, shaking in his arms as she came.

"Oh, oh, oh, ooooh!" she screamed as the orgasm swept through her body, making her tremble and convulse.

When it waned, her legs turned limp, and he wrapped his arms around her to hold her up.

"You are so beautiful when you come," he murmured. "I love feeling you explode and tumble over that edge. Your pleasure is my pleasure. You are mine..."

WITH A START, Kiran's eyes snapped open. A fine sheen of sweat covered his body, and his chest moved in great heaves. He pushed upright, leaning against the headboard, looking around him. It was still early, but the sun sent slivers of light around the edges of the floral curtains covering the windows, and sounds from outside filtered through the glass.

Exasperated, he realized he'd had another dream of the woman and not just any dream, but a sexual one. His cock was still hard, but he was grateful he hadn't ejaculated in his sleep like a horny teenager. How would he have explained the messy sheets to the hotel owner?

He'd been in St. Augustine for over six months now, and what should have been a brief stay until he found a place to rent had turned into something much longer. Caroline, the lady who owned the B&B, and her daughter, Maxine, had asked him to stay as their handyman after he'd helped them with a few things in the building.

Some leaky faucets, a loose floorboard, and wonky cupboard doors had been easy to fix, but they'd insisted on paying him on top of offering free room and board. Neither would take no for an answer, and he would have been stupid to turn down such a great offer. In return, he did a lot more around the old property than they knew about, because he didn't want to feel as if he were taking advantage of their generosity.

Located on a quiet side street in the heart of the Colonial Quarter, a stone's throw from the waterfront, they had a steady stream of tourists arriving throughout the year to enjoy the rich history of the town. He'd been lucky, or maybe it was all pre-arranged, the day he knocked on the door. They'd just had a cancelation of guests who were supposed to arrive that day, and the room hadn't yet been snapped up by anyone else. Kiran had paid upfront for a week but never left.

Swinging his feet to the floor, he trudged to the attached bathroom to empty his bladder and take a shower. As he stood under the warm stream of water, his dream raced back into his mind with unrelenting force. Feeling himself grow hard again, he couldn't resist wrapping his hand around his shaft and pumping it up and down. He stood with one hand braced against the wall while the dream played like a film reel in his head, and he felt the familiar tightening in his balls. Before long, he shot his load against the tiles with a shout, his knees buckling underneath him.

After cleaning himself off and shampooing his hair, Kiran finished his shower and dried off with a towel. Walking back into the bedroom, he found a pair of boxers, a T-shirt, and a pair of shorts to wear. He quickly made the bed and pulled the curtains away from the window.

The sun was shining, and the tourists were out in hordes despite the shops and attractions only just having opened. He could hear the hum of voices and cars from the nearby streets. The main tourist strip was on the other side of the building. The entrance to the inn was below his window in the quieter side street, and if he leaned forward at just the right angle, he could glimpse the ocean between the two buildings in front of him.

Grabbing his wallet and keys, he descended the stairs, calling out to Maxine, who was in the kitchen, that he'd be back in a little while, and stepped out on the sidewalk. With the historical property in need of constant repairs, he'd become a regular at the local hardware store and headed there now to pick up some materials for mending a couple of broken handles and a dripping shower in one of the rooms. He also wanted to replace some shelves in the kitchen and fix the gate out front where it listed like a drunken sailor.

He'd parked his bike around the side underneath a tin roof, next to where Caroline's car usually sat. It was her morning off, so she had a yoga class first thing and then went to a café with some of the other ladies for a cup of coffee and a chat. Maxine was in charge of the inn, and because they were fully booked, with no arrivals or departures scheduled, she was in the office, doing the paperwork.

ONCE HE'D PICKED up everything he needed, Kiran drove slowly back to the inn. The hardware store he used was on the other side of town, and he enjoyed the fresh air and sunshine before getting stuck into the chores he had planned for the day.

Negotiating his way past tour groups, families, and couples on romantic getaways, he finally turned onto the street leading to the inn. A car parked right outside sparked a flash of surprise in his chest. All guests were asked to put their cars in a parking lot adjacent to the inn to avoid blocking the road, but this one sat squarely in the middle of the lane like a cork in a bottle.

Kiran squeezed the bike past the obstruction and pulled into his usual spot. Caroline was still out and wasn't expected to return before lunchtime. Removing his purchases from the storage compartment, he ambled up the little path that ran alongside the building but stopped on the porch with his hand on the door handle. A loud male voice sounded somewhere inside the house, and a woman's cry rang out.

Reacting on instinct, Kiran shoved the door open and raced into the hallway. The reception area was empty, but voices filtered from behind the closed door to the kitchen.

"Do as I say, bitch!" the man shouted.

"No, Grant. Please, don't do this!"

"You're my wife, and I can do what I want. Now pack your shit and let's go."

Kiran stopped outside the door, his heart hammering in his chest. He knew Maxine had been married, and it hadn't been the most loving of relationships. She'd said little about it, but he'd read between the lines. If he had to guess, the husband had come back to take what he felt belonged to him, but Kiran had no intention of letting him bully and abuse Maxine again.

Slamming the door open, he strode into the kitchen, taking Grant by surprise. He was kneeling next to Maxine who cowered on the floor, tears streaming down her face as she twisted in his grip in a vain attempt to free herself.

"Who the fuck are you? Get out before I throw you out," Grant growled at Kiran.

"Let her go. If you leave quietly, I won't call the police."

Grant glared at Kiran, a cruel smirk pulling up one corner of his lips.

"Your new boyfriend, is it?" he snarled at Maxine.

Kiran took a step closer. "I said, let her go."

"Or what? You gonna make me? I'd like to see you try."

Without warning, Kiran lunged forward and pried Grant's hand away from Maxine's arm, twisting the hand as he bent the fingers far beyond their natural position. Grant howled, his body bending with his arm to relieve the pressure, and before he could react to what was happening, Kiran had him on the floor, with his arm wrenched behind his back, and Kiran's knees between his shoulder blades. His howls turned into grunts from the pain, and he started pleading for Kiran to stop between threats against both him and Maxine.

"I'm gonna fuck you up! You hear me?" Grant shouted. "Just you wait. And her too. That bitch took off in the middle of the night with no warning and for no reason! She's a useless, good-for-nothing whore."

The vitriol spewed from Grant's mouth, and Kiran wished he could plug his ears so he wouldn't have to listen.

Maxine had crawled into a corner, one cheek blossoming red with a hand print clearly visible on the pale skin. Her throat was covered in purple marks, and her lip was split on one side. Contusions and discoloration were forming on her arms, and the way she wrapped them around her middle made Kiran think she may have some bruised, if not cracked, ribs, as well.

Anger surged through his chest. This was not the way to treat anyone, least of all an innocent woman.

"Maxine, sweetheart? Are you all right? Can you move?" he asked, carefully studying her face.

Maxine nodded almost imperceptibly.

"Okay, good. I need you to call 9-1-1. Can you manage that?"

He got another nod.

"Now, please, love. I'd like them to come and get this piece of trash out of here."

Quietly sobbing, Maxine scrambled on hands and knees across the floor before using the wall to pull herself upright. A phone sat in a cradle on a small desk in the corner. She snatched it up and pressed the buttons with fingers trembling so violently Kiran could see it from where he was kneeling several feet away.

When she'd finished the call, she placed the phone back in the cradle and slumped in the chair. Kiran smiled encouragingly and prepared to wait. He eased the pressure on Grant's back where his knee was digging in to allow him to breathe easier. Despite being subdued and lying face down on the floor, Grant's mouth had not stopped its diatribe of accusations, cussing, and threats. Kiran tuned it out as he waited. Keeping an eye on Maxine, he looked around the kitchen, noting any little thing that needed attention as a way of distracting himself.

Before long, the wail of police sirens split the air, and seconds later, the thud of heavy boots shook the house. The doorway filled with uniformed officers, each with a hard expression on their face. A domestic disturbance was always at the top of their list of least favorite jobs to be called for, but at least at this one, the perpetrator was under control, and no one had sustained any major injuries.

Once the officers had finally finished asking questions and taken Grant with them in handcuffs, Kiran made Maxine a cup of tea and sat her down on the couch in the inn's living room. Minutes later, Caroline rushed through the door after Maxine had called her to let her know what had happened.

"Maxine, are you all right?" Caroline dropped to her knees by Maxine's side, brushing her hair out of the way and wincing at the bruises and split lip.

"Yes, mom. I'm fine. A little banged up, but nothing that won't heal in a day or two," Maxine murmured, her tongue popping out, carefully testing her sore lip.

"Thank you, Kiran." Caroline glanced up at him, tears forming in her eyes. "I don't know what would have happened had you not been here. That man, and I hesitate to call him that, is a menace." Caroline rose to pace the room, highly agitated, and Kiran quickly fetched a cup of tea for her as well. "Their divorce just came through, so maybe that's what triggered him, but this time, I hope they put him away for a long while. He doesn't deserve to be free to assault women."

"Mom, please. The cops have him now. I'm fine, and he can't come after me again."

"I really hope so. You've suffered enough with that lying, cheating —"

"All right! Mom, we get it. Please, calm down," Maxine interrupted her mother.

Caroline took a deep breath and sank into the seat next to Maxine.

"Oh, honey. I'm just so sorry you had to go through all this after everything that's already happened. But you're right, this time he must be in for some kind of punishment. He's gotten away with far too much for a long time."

That evening, Caroline insisted on cooking a big dinner for Kiran to thank him for stopping Grant from really hurting Maxine — or worse, forcing her to go with him. Kiran told her it wasn't necessary, but she insisted, and he didn't want to seem ungrateful.

A FEW MONTHS LATER, Kiran felt the all-too-familiar feeling of restlessness and impatience. Most nights, he dreamed of bridges and rivers. One dream in particular appeared more often than others. The bridge was high, at least eight hundred feet above the churning white waters below. It disappeared into a heavy forest far away on the other side. He never crossed the bridge, but a few times, he'd dreamed he'd been standing on the edge, waiting for something — or someone.

They all left him unsettled, adding to the uneasiness already lodged in his stomach. He knew it meant that he needed to be on his way soon. Whether he left voluntarily or was shoved through time again, he had yet to find out. It was probably best he didn't stay in St. Augustine much longer, anyway.

After the incident with Grant, who was now in the county jail awaiting sentence for not only assaulting Maxine but also the woman he'd cheated on her with, Maxine had developed a crush on Kiran, and no matter what he did to discourage it, her feelings didn't change. She was a sweet woman, but he didn't want to get involved with anyone again. Juliet's death had been painful, and he couldn't bear losing another person he was that close to. He'd already lost too many he cared about.

Instead, he discreetly arranged for Maxine to meet Brady, the young man who owned the hardware store across town. When they went out on their first date, Kiran knew he could leave and not worry about breaking her heart. He packed his bags that night, left a note on the nightstand, and said a quick goodbye to Caroline. She smiled and hugged him tightly.

"Thank you for everything, Kiran. She'll be happy now, I'm sure. Brady is a good man, and he'll look after her."

Kiran nodded and walked out, closing the door behind him. Strapping down the duffle on the back of his bike, he started the engine and drove away without looking back. Picking a route out of town at that felt like the right one, he followed the highway, not caring where it would take him. He was so tired of this life, this continuous jumping forward in time. He wanted to settle down somewhere, make some friends, get a real job.

Humans lived extraordinary lives compared to what he'd first thought. Before he Fell, he'd always assumed their lives were too fleeting to really matter, but to them, they were precious and worth filling with happiness and love. They worked hard, took care of their families, and loved them as much as they were capable of.

From his lofty position up high, he'd never considered their existence before, other than as a means to enrich the great tapestry of creation with finer nuances of colors and shades. It hadn't been part of his responsibilities, but if he was ever allowed back, he'd pay closer attention to how his siblings decided the fate of humanity.

Thirty

ALINA, 2017

Atlanta life had quickly grown on Alina. The pace was slower, more genteel and relaxed. A New York minute was now a foreign concept, something she'd left behind in Manhattan. It had taken a while to get used to the different way of life, but now she enjoyed it.

Strolling down the sidewalk, she relished the cooler temperatures October brought. The summer had been sweltering hot, but fall meant more comfortable weather and fewer tourists. Business at the event center was as hectic as always, though, and Alina barely had a moment to herself between conferences, seminars, and trade shows.

Today, she had a rare day off and was getting the grocery shopping done. She'd found a great apartment within walking distance of the center, and the neighborhood had a great selection of bars, restaurants, boutiques, and artisan delis.

Alina's favorite was a little mom-and-pop grocery store a few minutes' walk from her apartment. They knew her well by now and had treated her like family, ordering in her favorites and even items they just thought she'd enjoy. They constantly surprised her with goodies they'd stocked on their shelves, and the joy on their faces when showing it off had her in tears every time.

"Alina, my sweet girl. Where have you been? I haven't seen you for over a week!" The store owner, George, exclaimed.

"I've just been busy, George. Work has been crazy, and I was in New York last weekend."

"Are you looking after yourself? You look pale. Come, I have fresh pasta and gnocchi for you," George's wife, Paulina, scolded but with a smile on her face, scurrying down the aisle toward them.

Alina laughed. They were always trying to fatten her up, and back in New York, Carl was doing the same thing. Her weekend with him and Stephen had been filled with eating, more eating, and lots of laughter. They'd gone to a few museums, two gallery openings, and a classical music concert, and they made her feel relaxed, appreciated, and loved.

It wasn't that she wanted a relationship, but it partially filled a void in her heart. It was a yearning to be needed by somebody. Having that special someone saying they were happy to see her, enjoyed her company, and missed her when they were apart made life so much better.

"Here, Miss Alina. We got these in for you. Scrumptious chocolate with pistachio nuts. Perfect after a delicious pasta dinner." George held out a cellophane-wrapped box.

Alina laughed. George already knew her weakness of allowing herself a little bit of chocolate every weekend. If she didn't ration it, she'd gorge on huge bars of the sweet stuff and then feel guilty afterward.

"Thanks, George." She accepted the proffered chocolate box. "I'll have to let out my waistband if I eat all this."

"Nonsense. You're too thin. Look at my Paulina. She's the perfect size."

Alina smiled. Paulina was short, pear-shaped, and several pounds too heavy to be healthy, but it suited her, and she was always smiling, happy with her life and her family.

"He's so sweet, my George." Paulina beamed. "And he feeds me well. You need someone like him." She gave Alina a pointed look. "You're always on your own. It's not right for a young girl like you to be alone. I will find you a nice boy. My friends all have sons. One of them will be perfect for you."

"Thanks, Paulina, but I'm happy the way things are. I don't need a man in my life. Work keeps me busy enough, and I have my friends," Alina stated and worried slightly about the kind of men Paulina would try to set her up with.

She had a feeling they'd be the kind to expect a woman to stay at home, looking after the children, and having dinner ready on the table as soon as he walked in. That was great if she were the type of person who enjoyed her life revolving around her home, but she wanted to work, have a career, and know she was fulfilling all parts of her life and her dreams.

Paulina *tsked* but left her to it, disappearing into the storeroom. George was busy stacking a shelf, so Alina meandered down the aisles to find what she needed. Picking up vegetables and potatoes, she spotted strawberries and blueberries in the chiller and added them to her basket.

"Excuse me, dear. Could you please help me?"

Alina twirled to find the owner of the voice. A woman in her eighties peered at her, an apologetic look on her face.

"Of course. What do you need?" Alina asked.

The lady pointed to a shelf. "I wanted to find Junior Mints, but I can't see them anywhere. George usually stocks them for me, but I can't find him to ask."

Alina glanced to where she'd last talked to the store owner, but he'd finished his restocking and was nowhere to be seen. Turning back to the woman, she smiled, scanning the shelves with confectionery.

"They're for my husband," the woman said, her voice trembling slightly. "He's always loved them, and I buy them for him every week. I wouldn't want to disappoint him."

"Well, let's see if we can find them." Alina walked a few steps up and down the aisle to check each item on the shelves, but it wasn't until she bent down to look on the bottom one that she found the white and green box. Only a few remained in the display carton, but one was all they needed. "Here we go. One packet of Junior Mints, as requested." She held it up, triumphantly, then handed it to the woman.

"Oh, thank you. It's very kind of you to help." The lady clutched the little carton tightly in her hand, her eyes shining with gratitude.

"These days, I'm finding it more and more difficult to bend down. I'd have never seen them on the low shelf."

It was clear the chocolate-covered treats meant something special to her and her husband. Alina could tell there was a story there.

"I'll ask George to move them higher for you."

She smiled as the woman took her shopping to the checkout, where Paulina was waiting. Happy that she could help, Alina ambled farther into the little store to find other items on her list. She could have gone to one of the big supermarkets but preferred the familiarity of a smaller one with people like George and Paulina, where she could find foods and delicacies she'd not get in a chain store.

After paying and having exchanged a few more words with her friends, she waved goodbye and walked outside into the sunshine. Turning to head back to her apartment, she noticed the elderly woman farther down the sidewalk talking on her cell with a resigned look on her face. Alina couldn't help pausing her step to listen. It was impolite to eavesdrop, but if she needed assistance, she'd be happy to offer it.

"I understand, dear. No, I'll wait. There's a bench right next to me, so I'll sit here until you come for me. Please, it's not a problem. You can't help the traffic. Yes, I'll be absolutely fine. I'm only outside the grocery store, and George and Paulina will take care of me if it takes too long. Good, I'll see you soon." She put her phone in her purse and shuffled over to a bench under a tree.

Alina debated what to do. Should she offer her a ride to wherever she needed to go? Or would that put her in an awkward position since her husband, or whoever was picking her up, was already on the way?

Lowering herself to the bench, the woman pulled the box of mints from her bag, looking at it with a wistful smile on her face, before tucking it away again. Then she settled the shopping bag on the bench next to her and cradled her purse in her lap in a secure hold.

Seeing how the woman held it close as if she were worried someone would snatch it made up Alina's mind for her, and she walked over.

"Excuse me. Is someone giving you a lift home?" she asked, not wanting to let on that she'd overheard the conversation.

The elderly woman looked up, a hand shielding her eyes from the bright sunlight, the other tightening its hold on her bag, and then smiled when she recognized Alina.

"Yes, my nephew is on his way, but he's stuck in traffic." She sighed. "So, I thought I'd just sit here and wait until he comes. He'll be about thirty minutes, he said."

Alina felt bad for leaving her on her own. Half an hour could feel like a long time when waiting for someone.

She looked around, an idea popping into her head. "Would you like to join me for a cup of tea or coffee in the café over there?"

The lady waved her hand. "Oh, you don't have to go especially for me. I can just wait here."

"I was going there anyway, so you might as well join me. I'd love the company."

Once Alina had stowed her shopping in the trunk of her car, they entered the little cafe with its blue-and-white-striped awning. As soon as they pushed the door open, the smell of home-baked cakes and pastries mixed with the aromatic scent of freshly ground coffee beans enveloped them.

Alina ordered a sweet tea and a cappuccino together with a pastry each, and they found seats by the window.

"I'm so sorry. I haven't introduced myself," the woman said, holding out her frail and veined hand. "I'm Clara Miller. You're being very kind to a total stranger. Not many people would take the time these days, you know. Everyone is in such a rush, and people barely have time for each other, let alone anyone else."

Alina took her hand in a careful grip and gave it a small shake, worried about holding it too tightly, but Clara's grip was surprisingly strong. "I'm Alina Montgomery, and it's my pleasure. We almost know each other. We both know George and Paulina. That's enough for me."

Clara smiled, her eyes glittering with mirth. "That's very true. Maybe we'll meet again in the grocery aisles."

When Clara asked, Alina told her about her job, her family in Chicago, and how she'd moved from New York a year and a half earlier. She didn't mention California or anything about Jonas and their children, even though Clara said she'd lived there until the sixties when she and her husband, Edward, moved to Atlanta for work. She still didn't feel comfortable talking about them to strangers, always worrying she'd burst into tears.

"Tell me about your husband, Clara. What was his job?"

Clara placed her hand over her heart, a dreamy look sweeping across her face. "Oh, my Edward is a very clever man. He worked for a company that made medical equipment and always tried to come up with improvements on the design and even inventing some of his own," she said. "When he first started, he developed a wonderful working relationship with some doctors at a hospital in Los Angeles. There was one doctor, I forget his name. Marshall or Mechler?" Her brow furrowed. "My memory isn't what it was, but I remember Ed having long discussions with him. He was a surgeon there and very forward-thinking, often asking Ed for changes or different versions of the tools he used daily in the operating room. From those adjustments, Ed would come up with even more variations and improvements."

"That's amazing. Ed must be a brilliant man." Alina was fascinated by Clara's story.

"Well, he was." Clara's face fell slightly. "Now, dementia is breaking down his mind, and he's in a care home nearby. But we've had a long and wonderful life together. It was his work and his ingenuity that took us from Los Angeles to Atlanta." She nodded, but more to herself it seemed, while she recalled old memories before pulling herself back again. "The company only had a small department for developing new equipment when Ed started there," Clara explained, "but as the business grew, and they opened more branches across the country, they also set up a brand new research facility here in Atlanta." Her hand swept out to indicate their surroundings.

Alina listened intently. Something about Clara's life story felt personal to her, as if they were connected somehow.

Clara continued, "Ed was asked to move across and become the director, and of course, he couldn't say no. His only stipulation was that he could stay involved with the research aspect."

"What kind of things was he involved in developing?" Alina asked, wanting to know more.

Clara took a sip of her tea, the glass shaking slightly in her hand. Whether it was from emotions or old age, Alina couldn't tell.

"They manufactured anything from scalpels, scissors, and clamps to much more advanced equipment such as heart monitors and x-ray machines," she explained. "But the one thing Ed was most proud of, the crowning achievement of his career, was a device, I forget what it's called, that revolutionized keyhole surgery." Clara leaned forward, her face lighting up with pride. "It was a tiny change to an already developed attachment, but the way Ed changed the shape and construction of an integral part of the equipment was genius. At least, that's what he called it when he first thought of it." Clara smiled at the memory.

Alina stilled, and a shiver ran down her spine. Vivid memories of a frightening and worrying time surged to the forefront of her mind. Keyhole surgery was something she was quite familiar with.

When Theo was born, he'd been diagnosed with 'patent ductus arteriosus', a condition where a small blood vessel connecting the two main arteries, which come off the heart to feed the lungs and the body with blood, doesn't close on its own after birth. She and Jonas were relieved when they were told Theo didn't need open heart surgery, and immensely grateful to the specialist team who looked after him, but any kind of medical intervention on your child is frightening.

They'd both cried a lot those first few days, and with all her hormones out of whack after the birth anyway, she was almost surprised Jonas hadn't locked her away in a padded cell. One minute she'd been upbeat and positive, only to fall apart the next, crying, wailing, and blaming herself for somehow causing the heart condition.

Jonas had been her rock, as he'd always been, and never lost his patience with her. He just held her when she cried and smiled when she was buoyant. She went from one extreme to the other at the drop of a hat, but Jonas never wavered.

If he wasn't cuddling her, he was changing diapers, helping her nurse Theo, or giving him a bottle of expressed breast milk, all while staying in touch with his office and keeping their friends and family informed. He even made sure they both ate, showered, and put on clean clothes every day. It was all Alina could do to be there for their son. Taking care of herself came at the bottom of the list.

Those first six months were still a blur, and she'd be forever grateful to Jonas for carrying her through it all without a single complaint. He'd smiled, kissed away her tears, and held her tight, giving her all his warmth, strength, and love.

Theo had only been a few weeks old when the procedure was performed, but it was successful, and her precious baby quickly recovered. Even so, she'd been a nervous wreck for months after, expecting something to go wrong, and they'd lose their beautiful boy.

Clara's soft voice pulled her back to the present.

"His dementia has stolen his mind and forced me to put him into care, but I still remember everything. Once a week, I bring him Junior Mints," she said wistfully. "He bought them for our first date. It was 1948 and things like chocolate were still expensive after the war, but he'd wanted to treat me and keep his breath minty fresh in case he was lucky enough to be allowed to kiss me."

"And was he? Lucky, I mean?" Alina grinned and quirked a brow, intrigued by Clara's story.

"Of course, he was lucky. He was so sweet, polite, and attentive, and very romantic. I'd have been a fool to deny him an innocent kiss." She winked. "But we nearly didn't have that first date. After Ed had bought the mints, he dropped his pocketbook when leaving the store, which had my address in it. Without it, he wouldn't have been able to find his way to my house, and who knows if we'd have ever met again? Luckily, another customer saw him drop it and chased after him. In fact, it was the lovely doctor from the hospital who found it, but they didn't know each other then. It was how they first met."

"Oh, my gosh. That was incredibly lucky," Alina exclaimed. "And what a coincidence it was the same doctor he'd meet later on. He must have had someone watching over him that day."

"That's what we both said the day we got married." The smile on Clara's face was heartwarming, making Alina's own heart clench and wish for that kind of joy in her life again.

"So, how is Ed doing?" she asked. "You said he's got dementia. How bad is it? If you don't mind me asking."

The smile faded from Clara's lips. "He's got some days that are better than others, but he no longer recognizes me. I still sit with him every day, though, but on his bad days, I just watch him from the other side of the room."

"It must be so hard for you to visit, not knowing if it's going to be a good or a bad day. If he doesn't recognize you, why do you go every day?" Alina wondered, feeling upset on Clara's behalf.

She didn't know what was worse, losing the love of your life to a tragic accident before you'd had time to grow old with each other, or spending your whole life with someone only to watch them fade away and forget who you are.

Clara smiled sorrowfully. Her eyes misted over, and she dabbed at them with a little white handkerchief.

"He may not know who I am anymore, but I still know him. He's my husband, my best friend, my everything, and I will be with him until one of us takes our last breath," she stated with conviction. "After that, I will wait for him to either join me or for me to find him wherever he is. We will be together again."

"What a wonderful story, Clara." Alina placed her hand over Clara's. "Thank you for telling it to me. Meeting you has really made my day."

"Oh no, dear. Without you, I would have been sitting on my own outside on that bench. It's not often I meet someone who's willing to take time out of their day to help an old lady. You are a kind and generous woman."

Alina rummaged through her purse, in search of her business card holder, pulling out the green metal bottle and setting it on the table to see better inside the bag. She often used the battered old bottle for taking coffee with her, saving on takeout cups and cardboard.

"I do hope we meet again. In fact, here's my card." She held it out. "It has my private number on it, so if you ever need anything, or want some company and a cup of coffee, please call me."

Clara thanked her again and tucked the card away in her purse. "Well, I can see my nephew's car, so I'd better be going." She rose and gathered her shopping bags.

With her purse slung over her shoulder, she put her frail-looking hand on Alina's cheek and patted it gently.

Her eyes took on a thousand-mile stare, and her voice sounded distant. "Don't worry, when it's your time, you'll find love again. It won't be long now, I promise. He'll find you if you just take one small step."

Then she turned on her heel and walked out the door to where her nephew was waiting. Alina stared after her.

What did she mean? Who was she supposed to find? She wasn't looking for someone new to fall in love with.

Jonas had only been gone... A deep V formed on her brow as she tried to think how much time had passed since Jonas was ripped away from her. Her heart clenched when she realized how many years had gone by. Seven years without her best friend by her side. Seven years without her precious babies. So much time lost. Would she ever feel that happy again?

A sudden restlessness took up residence in her gut, twisting and coiling, making her feel nauseous. She swallowed it down and inhaled sharply, shoving her emotions and recollections of that horrible time away. It did her no good to dwell on it.

She paid for their drinks and cakes before leaving the coffee shop. As she ambled toward her car, Clara's last words echoed in her mind, and she gasped, a chill skittering down her spine.

He'll find you.

Just take one small step.

She'd heard those last words before. In her dreams, spoken by the blond-haired man.

Thirty-One

KIRAN, 2002

Once again, Kiran was headed north. He wasn't sure why, but the pull in his chest seemed stronger from that direction. He'd been sad to leave St. Augustine. The quaint little town had somehow felt familiar, and in places, he'd sensed faint impressions of deep love and pure joy, as if someone's life had left behind a residue or an imprint in the town's fabric. He only felt it in certain areas but always wanted to linger there and absorb the sensations.

It was no surprise the town was infused with an entire spectrum of emotions, since it was home to seventeen thousand souls and further inflated with the millions of tourists visiting each year. Despite this, Kiran felt as if the impressions he sensed were more than those of people living, working, or visiting the area. They felt... personal.

HOUR AFTER HOUR, day after day, he pushed the bike hard, chasing the need to reach some unknown place or event, passing city after city — Jacksonville, Charlotte, Washington DC, New York — while his mind flicked through the catalog of existences he'd lived through. Some had been filled with great trauma and hardship, others with fantastic adventures and brutal battles.

He'd had the great honor of leading the First Crusade in the Holy Land, sanctioned by Pope Urban II. Kiran would be forever immensely grateful he hadn't been there *eleven hundred* years earlier. That's when His earthbound son had so cruelly met his fate. He wasn't sure he could have borne witness to that atrocity without attempting to prevent it, no matter how selfless and benevolent the sacrifice had been.

After the crusade, he'd woken up in a tent outside Lingzhou where Genghis Khan had laid siege to the city. From there, over the next half a year, Khan's army had seized several provinces in quick succession until they marched on Yinchuan, the capital of Western Xia.

Kiran had been Genghis' most trusted commander, assisting him while defeating his enemies and also overseeing the division of the Mongol Khan's empire between his sons and making his third-born, Ögedei, his successor. After six months of several military operations on many flanks, Yinchuan fell, but Genghis, already weakened by an infection in an arrow wound, died by Kiran's side from another, well-placed arrow to his throat.

It was while Kiran had seen to his fallen leader, dragging him off the battlefield, and placing him on the bed in his tent, that he'd noticed the arrow sticking out of his own side and suddenly found it hard to breathe.

As Kiran lay dying, one last memory flashed through his mind of the Khan's triumphant pronunciation after seeing five bright stars in a straight line in the midnight sky. The Khan had claimed it was a sign from the gods that he was rightful in his quest and would be victorious. Kiran knew better. It had filled his heart with hope and joy at the time, because he was certain it was a sign from his siblings. It had always been a family joke between them in the upper echelon. They were the Pentarchy — the five rulers. Only one of them would have thought to send him that kind of message. Someone was still watching over him. It was the only sign he'd had since he was cast out.

Slumped on the floor, barely aware of the many healers rushing to the Khan's side, and hearing the Emperor's death announced, he'd closed his eyes and succumbed to his injuries.

WITH TWELVE HUNDRED miles already behind him, Kiran fought the exhaustion of the long hours in the saddle but refused to slow down. The driving force inside him was getting stronger, and the thought of delaying, even for a brief rest, felt unbearable.

Darkness had fallen. The narrow beam of the bike's headlights cut through the shadows of the road ahead, leaving the sides shrouded in inky blackness. Tall trees flanked the lonely road, standing watch like swaying sentinels over the few travelers that dared disturb the ominous silence.

A heavy weight pressed on his shoulders, and the longer he drove, the more crushing it became. Rationally, he knew he should stop for the night, but he hadn't seen a single sign of any town or village for hours. Nor had he seen any signposts for the larger freeways or interstate roads, which was unusual. He hadn't reflected much over it at first, but the farther he traveled, the more apparent it became. It wasn't normal.

Without warning, an explosion of fireworks went off in his head, accompanied by an agonizing headache. He cried out, hunching over the handlebars as the pain caused a surge of nausea to climb from his stomach into his throat. A paralyzing weakness spread through his limbs, and he lost control of the bike.

The large machine spun one hundred and eighty degrees, skidding on loose gravel, and he frantically clung on until the wheels slipped from beneath him. As the ground rose to meet him with alarming speed, he squeezed his eyes shut, and prepared for the impact. The grinding of metal, screeching of tires fighting for grip, and muted thuds of his body hitting asphalt rent the still night air.

Then silence fell again, abruptly, and with no consideration for the still shape that was Kiran lying twenty feet from the motorbike of which he'd so recently been in command. A single wheeze of air rose in a tiny vapor cloud from his mouth, made visible by the chilly night air, and then dissipated.

FALLEN UNCHAINED

2004

A HEAVY RAIN had started while he trudged forward, putting one foot in front of the other. Juliet's words from so long ago slid through his mind.

Just take one small step.

It was all Kiran was capable of at that moment. His entire body ached, not just from exhaustion, but from what felt like one giant bruise covering him from top to toe. His head pounded with each jarring movement, and his exhaustion knew no bounds. He'd left the mangled bike somewhere behind him, the engine refusing to start and one tire ripped to shreds. Where he was going, and what he was doing were questions he had no answers to and was too tired to even bother asking himself.

All he knew was that his feet were dragging along a darkened road, and a heavy tiredness had seeped into his bones. The weather was getting worse by the minute as the strong winds brought more rain, slowing him down even more. He couldn't see farther than his hand in front of him, the foggy air swirling and undulating as he pressed on.

As he stumbled around a bend, a weak glow lit up the darkness in the distance. Kiran paused, frowning, while the cogs in his brain attempted to make sense of what he was seeing. No streetlights lined the sides, and he didn't notice any buildings nearby either.

He moved forward again, nearing the strange glow with each step. As he got closer, his breath hitched when he realized it was a car, halfway in the ditch, with dim headlights pointing across the blacktop at an angle. Fearing someone was severely injured after a crash, he willed his feet to move faster despite his protesting legs.

Finally reaching the vehicle, he stood in the weak headlights, rainwater streaming in tiny rivulets into eyes and down his face. He pushed the wet strands of his hair away to see better and squinted, trying to peer through the windshield. A dark shape was slumped against the backrest on the driver's side, but the passenger seat was empty, and he couldn't see anyone in the rear either.

With his heart thudding in his chest, he tapped gently against the side window and frowned when what appeared to be an older woman didn't respond to the sound.

"Are you all right?" he shouted through the glass, but the wind made it impossible to hear anything.

As he pulled at the door handle, relief flooded through him when the door easily opened, squeaking a little as he shoved it open wide. The woman blinked at him.

"Ma'am, are you all right? Are you hurt?" he asked.

"N-n-no. I'm I'm fine. I think. Just a little dizzy."

Kiran visually examined her as much as he could, but he saw no obvious bruising or bleeding. He felt her hand on his and dropped his gaze to her face.

"You look like an angel," she whispered, peering at him with pale blue eyes.

Kiran smiled. He'd been told that before. Those were almost the exact same words Evie had said when she gave him her drawing before he left Corpus Christi. The glow surrounding him wasn't visible on Earth, so he didn't know what she had seen, but children had vivid imaginations and made stuff up all the time. This lady, however, had most likely just taken a knock to the head when her car swerved off the road.

"I'm glad I could help, but I'm no angel. Just a passerby who got here in time."

"No, in the light... you had a halo... and white, shimmering wings. Like an angel." Her voice was weak but held conviction.

"It was only a trick of the headlights and the rain, but I'm glad I got here when I did. Now, we just need to get you some help." Kiran squeezed her hand reassuringly, and the woman leaned her head against the neck rest, a small sigh slipping from her lips.

Kiran straightened and looked around. It was completely dark except for the vehicle lights, and he wasn't sure how long they'd last before the battery was depleted. As he stood there considering his options, a faint rumble in the distance caught his attention. He strained to hear over the growl of the wind, but when a bright glow shined through the trees where the road curved out of sight, he knew another vehicle was headed their way.

He pulled a flashlight from his duffel to flag down the approaching car. While the light became brighter, he could hear the change in the whine of an engine as the driver downshifted before the bend, and then Kiran saw it. A big truck came barreling toward him, a row of lights on top of the cab and more along the bottom edge, adding to the huge headlights that lit up the dark ribbon of the asphalt.

Kiran stood in the middle of the road, swinging his flashlight from side to side. Despite its powerful beam, it felt pitiful in the advancing brightness of the huge rig. Holding his breath, he waved the light up and down and left to right to attract the attention of the driver. Relief flooded his chest when the heavy truck slowed down, coming to a stop thirty feet from where the car lay in the ditch.

"I need help. Can you call the emergency services?" Kiran called out to the driver, and when he rolled his window down, he explained what had happened.

"Sure thing. I'll get them on the radio," the heavyset man replied, reaching for his CB radio.

Kiran rushed back to the lady in the car who was still conscious but seemed dazed.

"Help is on the way, ma'am. Are you in any pain?"

"No, no pain, but I'm cold," she mumbled.

Kiran looked through the car and found a coat on the backseat, which he draped over her. She thanked him with a smile and seemed to relax a little.

"I got the message through, and emergency services are on their way. Nearest town is only seven miles away, so it shouldn't take too long," the truck driver informed him, jogging over from his vehicle.

"Thank you. She's awake and talking and doesn't seem too injured."

Why does it feel as if I should know more?

Kiran's head ached, and his mind felt oddly blank, as if a wall had been erected with all his memories behind it. One thing was clear, however. He had shifted again.

THE SUN SHINED from a break in the clouds, and most of the puddles from the previous night's weather had already dried up. If it wasn't for a fallen tree, several broken boughs and limbs littering the ground and overturned trash cans with their contents spread far and wide, no one would ever have known a storm had just swept through the area.

The truck driver had given him a ride into Providence, the nearest town, after the ambulance had left with the woman from the car, and he'd found a motel to stay in for the night. A wall calendar had told him it was 2004, so he'd only jumped two years since leaving Florida.

He'd still been in a bit of a daze and unsure of what was going on. His memories seemed jumbled, and he'd struggled to make sense of them. All he'd been certain of was that he'd been in some kind of accident himself, judging by the scrapes and bruises covering his skin. Somehow, he knew it would all come back to him once he'd had some rest, though.

Getting off the bus near the hospital, Kiran shrugged off his heavy jacket, grateful for the light shirt he wore underneath, and made his way to the main entrance. Already feeling hot, he was glad to get inside the cool air-conditioned comfort of the small hospital. The reception desk was busy, so he waited for a moment and thought about what he was going to say.

The ambulance had taken Ellen, the lady he'd rescued, to the ER and as far as he knew, she'd been admitted overnight for observation and was still here. He wanted to check in on her to make sure she wasn't badly hurt and had family nearby to take care of her.

He knew the hospital wouldn't let him see her or tell him anything about her condition unless he was family, so he hoped saying he was her nephew would be enough to give him access. As much as he kept his fingers crossed that they'd notified her relatives, he also didn't want them to have arrived yet. It was still early and visiting hours just started, so with a bit of luck, he'd be in and out in a few minutes.

The receptionist had finished dealing with visitors and phone calls for the moment and smiled when he approached.

"How may I help you?"

"Good morning. My aunt, Ellen Thomas, was brought in here last night after she had a car accident," he said with confidence injected in his voice. "Can you tell me where she is?"

"You're her nephew, you say?"

"Yes, on my mother's side. My mom passed a while ago or she'd be here with me." Kiran tried to look as honest and trustworthy as possible and smiled at the young man behind the desk.

His fingers clattered over the keyboard as he entered the woman's name into his system.

"Yes, here she is," he said. "The EMTs brought her in to the ER, and she was admitted for observation. She's in Ward Four, which is on the top floor. Take the elevator over there and ask for her room at the nurse's station."

Kiran thanked him and crossed the lobby to the elevators. He stepped out on the fourth floor. The muted hum of voices and rubber soles on vinyl floors, machines whirring and beeping in the distance, and phones ringing filled the air, and he took a moment to adjust after having been away from hospitals for such a long time.

After checking into the motel, he'd spent most of the hours before dawn committing his time in St. Augustine to memory. The shift had been violent and traumatizing, not giving him any time to readjust or even recognize what was happening. It took hours before he'd pieced everything together, and once he did, the avalanche of all his other lives hit him so hard he'd almost passed out.

Looking around the small nurse's station and the hallways leading away from it, he noted the differences in the ward since he was a surgeon in Los Angeles in the fifties. It had been thirty-five years since he practiced in a hospital, but less than thirty since he'd performed any kind of medical procedure at all. The last one had been stitching Geoff's leg with a sewing needle and cotton thread torn from a shirt. The memories made Kiran's stomach clench. It had all been in vain as his friend died from the infected wound when he was denied antibiotics.

The typical smells of a hospital assaulted his nose and, combined with the sounds, brought him back to his last days in the Vietnamese prison camp. Taking a deep breath, he shoved the memories away. If he gave them too much time and space, they'd only bring him down a deep, dark hole. It wasn't helped by the fact he'd found out while staying in Texas that the authorities had freed all POWs only a week after he'd succumbed to sickness, dehydration, and malnutrition alongside most of his fellow captives. One week — seven measly days — had stood between him and freedom.

"Are you here to visit a patient?"

The voice startled him out of his thoughts.

"Yes, I am," he told the woman behind the desk. "Mrs. Ellen Thomas. They brought her in last night after a car accident, and the receptionist downstairs told me she was here."

The older nurse knitted her brows, staring at him. She was obviously the gatekeeper and took her job of keeping her patients safe from unauthorized visitors seriously.

"And you are?"

"I'm her nephew. My name is Kiran Mitchell."

The tag on her white uniform said her name was Gloria, which Kiran found amusing. Somehow, he'd always associated the name with an ethereal, petite, and slender being. Not this formidable lady in her late forties. She wasn't big by any means, but just didn't fit the image he had in his head. It must have something to do with the name and what it meant to him.

"Mr. and Mrs. Thomas are on their way, so you might need to leave when they arrive. We only allow two visitors at a time. I assume you're well acquainted with her son and daughter-in-law?"

"Of course. I haven't seen" — he wracked his brain for any first names and grasped the first two that came to his mind — "Richard and Sarah for a long time, though."

The nurse looked at her notes and nodded, seemingly satisfied with his answer, and then pointed down the corridor.

"Right. In that case, Mrs. Thomas is in room eight. Down the hall, turn left, and it's the second door on your right."

Kiran gave her his most charming smile — or at least hoped it was charming — and strode down the hallway, following her directions.

He stopped outside the open door with the number eight on it and knocked softly on the jamb. Ellen was sitting in a chair by the window, and apart from a slight bruise on her cheek, she appeared to be none the worse for wear.

"It's you! Oh, I'm so glad you came!" she exclaimed. "I wanted to thank you, but no one knew who you were."

"I couldn't leave without making sure you were being taken care of properly." Kiran stepped into the room. "How are you feeling?"

"I'm just fine, thank you. I can't tell you how grateful I am that you came down that road and saw me." She waved to another chair for Kiran to sit. "The weather was terrible. I left Hartford too late and tried to make it home before the storm hit, but I must have been going slower than I thought. Or the storm came at me faster. Anyway, I will forever be in your debt." She grasped Kiran's hand, squeezing it gently as tears formed in her eyes.

"It was my pleasure to be your guardian angel," he murmured. "I'm just glad nothing worse happened. What did the doctors say?"

Ellen smiled in relief. "A few bruises, but nothing worse than that. They kept me in overnight to check for concussion, but I seem to have escaped that as well. They just want to check my cheek since I must have banged it against the steering wheel."

They spoke a little while longer until a nurse came to take her for an x-ray to make sure the swelling on her face was going down and there were no fractures. If everything looked good, Ellen hoped they'd release her that afternoon.

Kiran took the opportunity to say goodbye when Ellen was wheeled away, and she thanked him again, saying she would forever think of him as her son, and she would tell her son and daughter-in-law all about him when they arrived. She'd told Kiran she was nervous about seeing them because they'd been estranged for a few years. She missed her grandchildren terribly but had felt unwelcome and didn't want to interfere in her son's life.

Ellen had given him a short version of her fraught relationship with her daughter-in-law, and it saddened him that she felt she couldn't be a part of their lives. Hopefully, them coming to the hospital to take her home and look after her for a few days would lead to a reconciliation. He had a good feeling about it and wished her all the luck in the world.

The last he saw of Ellen was her waving and smiling warmly, her pale blue eyes sparkling with life as the elevator doors closed, taking her to wherever the Radiology Department was located.

As Kiran left the hospital behind, Ellen's declaration that she now considered him a son warmed his heart. He'd never been someone's son before. Unless you counted before he Fell, which didn't really count as they were all 'sons' there. It was a strange notion, and it filled him with joy and gratitude.

A wide smile broke out on his face, but it quickly faded when he realized he once again had no plan, no direction, no means of transport. He'd taken the bus here, but a small part of him had hoped he would have been provided with a new bike, or even a car, by the time he left the hospital. He patted his pockets, but there was no jingle of keys of any kind.

A heavy lump settled in his gut. He wasn't supposed to stay in Providence, that much was obvious, or he'd have been given some kind of sign or feeling. At least, he assumed he'd have some notion of what to do or where to go like he'd had every time previously.

He shoved his hands in his pockets and ambled out of the building. The skies had clouded over while he was inside, and a chilly nip in the air tried to penetrate his clothes. Without a clear idea of where he was going, he headed away from the hospital, following a busy road.

As he spotted a roadside diner up ahead, his stomach growled, reminding him he hadn't eaten in much too long. Checking his pockets again, he huffed in relief when he felt the solid weight of his wallet. At least he had something going for him.

The smell of burgers, fries, and coffee assaulted his nostrils as soon as he stepped inside the busy diner. A young man waved at Kiran to take a seat while he brought him a menu and a pot of coffee. Without even looking at the menu card, Kiran ordered a house-special burger and a large portion of fries.

While he waited, he made his way to the bathroom, washed his face and hands, and tried to comb his hair with his fingers. The duffel bag with all his belongings had vanished together with the bike. All he had left was the bottle, which he'd found sticking out of the pocket of his jacket. He could only hope his bag would turn up again somewhere along the way.

A couple of hours later, with his belly full and the bottle from Evie filled with hot coffee, he hitched a ride with a friendly trucker who was headed to Pittsburgh. It sounded as good a place as any, and the yanking sensation in his chest seemed to agree with him. If only he could work out what was going on and where he needed to go.

He'd felt it leaving Texas, and it was stronger when he left St. Augustine. He'd had the same urge before that when he decided to stay for another tour in Vietnam, and even when he signed up in the first place. Maybe it had always been there, and he'd just never noticed? Even the time jump had been far more jarring and disorienting than when reaching Florida.

The question as to why kept spinning through his mind, but he still had no answers or even a theory. It was incredibly frustrating not to have any means of finding out the reasons behind the overwhelming shifts, or any way of knowing beforehand so he could prepare himself.

He recalled all the times he'd taken a different path or direction in one of his lives or made a choice of his next steps. Over the millennia, he'd made too many decisions to remember them all, but that need or drive to move on had certainly been present at many of them, he recognized, and it had influenced his judgment.

He cradled the metal bottle in his hands, feeling a warmth spread through his body. It wasn't long before the thrum of the engine, the swaying of the cab, and sheer exhaustion took over, and he fell fast asleep.

Thirty-Two

ALINA, 2017

Startled, Alina scrambled upright, scooting back until she was pressed against the headboard. Her heart slammed in her chest. Her skin was covered in sweat, her lungs starving for air. Fear billowed in her core like a menacing specter.

Pulling her knees to her chest, she wrapped her arms around them and rested her forehead on top. Remnants of a dream still swirled through her head, making everything tilt and spin. Forcing herself to slow her breathing, she regained her bearings and could breathe normally again.

She threw off the covers and padded into the bathroom to splash some cold water on her face. With the light off, she couldn't see her reflection in the mirror, but she knew what she would see. Hollow cheeks, dark shadows under her eyes, deep creases around her mouth — the same as she'd looked for the last few weeks.

It was all because of the dreams. Or nightmares. They'd been getting more frequent over the last couple of months, and now she had them every night in so many shapes and forms she'd lost count. What bound them together was the high bridge, the cascading water, and the wings. Always the iridescent, ethereal wings. Every detail was painfully clear, and unlike normal dreams, these didn't fade once she woke up. She remembered everything about them.

The wings were snowy white with a faint shimmer. The bridge stood at a dizzying height, and the river's turbulent waters were icy cold against her skin. It was as if she was physically there each time and only returned when she woke up. Impossible, of course, but it didn't stop the unsettled feeling in her chest every morning.

She always arrived there alone, but at some stage in the dreams, someone else turned up, standing silently by her side, always obscured until a faint glow colored the mists surrounding them. It was the blond-haired man from the cemetery and her *other* dreams.

His face was in constant shadow, so she still didn't know what he looked like — except for his eyes. Those piercing blue eyes, like a cloudless sky on a summer's day, penetrated her heart and her soul. She felt a deep love emanating from him, but it couldn't possibly be for her. He couldn't love someone he'd never met. Could he? *Could she?*

All she'd ever seen clearly of this dream-man was his hair and eyes, but he'd awoken feelings in her she'd thought she would never have again. Feelings of love, desire, lust, passion, and admiration. Or was it adoration? She had enjoyed his body against hers in a very intimate way, reveled in his fingers giving her pleasure and pleasuring him in return. It had all felt so undeniable, so tangible, as if they'd really been together, but on a different plane or reality.

Alina shook her head at the turn of her thoughts. It was ridiculous. No one would fall in love with an illusion, an apparition the mind conjured. The idea was stupid, and she needed to put it all out of her mind so she could get some rest. And yet... something stirred in her heart whenever she thought of his gaze on her.

She dried her face and returned to her bed, pulling the comforter over her. The window blinds were up, and she stared at the inky blackness outside. It was still a few hours before dawn, and she curled up on her side, willing sleep to come, but every time she closed her eyes, the bridge, the rushing water, and the feathered wings were all there, creating a swirling mass of images and sounds. It made it impossible for her to get any rest, so after another hour, she got up and made herself a cup of coffee, sinking onto the couch in the living room.

Pulling her legs underneath her, she opened her tablet and scrolled to the news app. The world was full of enough sports events, natural disasters, and political grandstanding to keep her mind busy for a little while.

The peace in her mind lasted only as long as her coffee, and then the restlessness surged through her core again. She couldn't sit still and felt as if she had to go somewhere. *Be somewhere.* If only she knew the destination.

With her mind like a maelstrom of images, thoughts, and dizzying emotions, she dropped her head back on the cushions and closed her eyes.

She realized she'd come to a crossroads of sorts in her life. The gnawing feeling that she was meant to be somewhere other than here in Atlanta wouldn't leave her alone.

He was there, as always, in her head and now also in her heart. She didn't know when it happened, but somehow, she'd developed feelings for a man she'd never met. Or maybe she had met him? Could this be Jonas in another form? A reincarnation of her dead husband? If so, would he have his memories, his mannerisms, his voice? All of that had been different in her dreams, but would she recognize them in this blond-haired, blue-eyed man if he was real and she met him?

She desperately wanted her husband back. Was this a way for it to happen? Was it even possible? Alina had never been religious or even spiritual before, but she needed her best friend, her love, her other half back. Needed him like she needed air to breathe.

The realization hit her like a punch in the stomach. She'd never gotten over losing Jonas. All this time, she'd been going through the motions, packing everything in neat little boxes, just like a grief counselor had told her, but he'd meant for the boxes to be opened, one by one, when she was ready to deal with what was inside them. She thought she'd done that, but what if she didn't have to bring them out? If Jonas came back — even if in a different shape — she'd never have to worry about those boxes again.

A decision slowly formed in her mind. She opened her browser and booked a flight to New York. Later that afternoon, her bag was packed, and she jumped in a taxi to take her to the airport. She felt cold and jittery, uncertain she was doing the right thing, but needing to do it, nonetheless. At least it was a Friday night, and she wasn't required in the office until Monday morning. By then, she hoped to have everything settled and in place.

"Alina, are you sure about this?" Stephen frowned, concern showing in his brown eyes.

"No, I'm not, but I've got to find out what this urge, yearning, whatever the hell it is, is coming from. It's driving me crazy, and it wasn't until I decided to come here that it... I don't know... settled down, somehow."

"Does this have anything to do with your husband or your sister?" Carl stood behind Stephen with his hands on his shoulders.

Alina flopped back against the cushions of the squishy couch, squeezing her eyes shut and blowing out a big huff.

"Honestly? I don't know. It feels as if it's something to do with Jonas, but I can't for the life of me figure out what it could be." She rubbed her forehead. "He's been gone for so long, and I still miss him so much. And my babies. My heart cries every time I think of them." Her eyes brimmed with unshed tears. "They'd be so big now, but I'll never see them graduate, get married, or have children of their own, and it hurts. It hurts more than I could ever describe or have imagined."

"What do you need us to do, sweetie? You know we'll do whatever we can." Stephen sat next to her, taking her hands in his and rubbing the tops of her palms with his thumbs.

A sob worked its way from her chest, and nothing would stop it.

"I don't know that either. I need to take time off work, but I can't say when or even if I'll be back." She hung her head. "So, it's probably best if I resign effective immediately. I'm so sorry. I never wanted to do this to you."

"Oh, sweetie. Don't worry. Why don't we say you're taking a leave of absence and then see where we go from there?" Stephen said.

Alina nodded, grateful for the support and reassurance. She

rummaged in her bag to find her water bottle. Her throat was parched from holding the tears back. Whenever she held it, a warmth spread through her chest, and her anxiety settled a little. It had become like a security blanket ever since the young man had given it to her in Yellowstone. Back then, she'd still been so raw, so full of grief, and his kindness had given her hope for the future.

"Alina, where did you get that bottle?" Carl asked, his forehead creasing.

"This one?" She held it out. "Someone gave it to me ages ago. It's become my lucky charm. Why?"

Carl stared at it. "I haven't seen that logo for such a long time, that's all."

Alina looked at the faded picture and writing, turning the bottle over in her hands. "You recognize it? I never knew where it came from." Her gaze switched to Carl's face. "A young man gave it to me when my coffee cup broke outside a small diner in Yellowstone. I've kept it with me wherever I've gone since then."

"I was only a kid when my dad took me to this place in Colorado," Carl murmured. "I can't remember exactly where, but we were on a camping trip, just him and me. We slept under the stars when the weather allowed, spotted a lot of wildlife, and fished in the rivers." His voice held a note of wistfulness. "The only civilized place we went to was this little town where we stocked up on supplies. It was called Angels Rest. At the time, I thought it was a stupid name, but I still wanted this ball cap they had in the little grocery store, and my dad got it for me." He chuckled. "I wore it every day for years after that. In fact, I think I still have it in a drawer somewhere." Carl smiled at the memories.

"Angels Rest? That's a beautiful name," Alina said.

"I remember there was something there that people came from far away to look at. Maybe a building? Or a dam?" Carl's eyes took on a faraway look. "I can't remember now, but there was definitely something at least mildly famous there."

Alina stared at the bottle, her fingers caressing the faint writing. Now when she knew the name, she could picture it, even if the logo was almost worn away. As she sat looking at it, a spark lit in her chest, spreading like a river of lava through her veins, burning hotter with each second. She shifted in her seat, growing more and more uncomfortable. Suddenly, she knew exactly what she had to do and where to go. The only question remaining was why?

"That's it," she exclaimed. "That's where I have to go. To Angels Rest. I can't explain it, but I need to get there as quickly as possible." Jumping to her feet, she began to pace back and forth. "It's like I have to do something or... no, I have to meet someone. I think. I don't know. God, I'm so confused. Am I going crazy?" She looked up at Stephen and Carl with tears brimming in her eyes.

They looked back at her with identical expressions of concern and sympathy on their faces.

"No, sweetie. You're not crazy." Stephen wrapped his arms around her in a warm embrace. "I can't explain what this is you're going through" — he pulled back slightly to look in her eyes — "but it can't hurt to go to Colorado and find out. It's not a million miles away, and one of us can go with you, if you want."

"Thanks, Stephen. You're the best. You both are. But I think I need to do this on my own. It's probably a wild goose chase, but I don't think I'll be able to settle if I don't do it." Alina strode to the window, looking at the familiar street scene.

After leaving Atlanta, she'd come straight to New York to speak with her closest friends — after Katie, of course, but she didn't want to worry her with this. Katie had her own family to think about, and she'd only want to meet Alina in Colorado to be there for her — wild goose chase or not.

An hour later, Carl had booked her flights to Denver with a short layover in St. Louis. Denver was the nearest airport to the tiny town of Angels Rest, population three-thousand-one-hundred-ninety-three, and he'd also rented a four-by-four truck for her to drive the rest of the way.

Meanwhile, Stephen had secured a room in the only hotel the town provided. It wasn't fancy, but she didn't care. She'd sleep under the stars if she had to. As long as she got there and rid herself of this crackling energy under her skin.

"Okay, I think everything is set. But don't forget, sweets, that you can change your mind anytime you want." Carl lifted a brow, pinning her with a look. "You don't have to fly off to the middle of nowhere to find something you-don't-know-what, with no one to help or support you."

"I know, Carl, and I love you both for everything you've done for me," she said, "but Colorado is hardly the other side of the world, and I'm not hiking or camping. I'll be staying in a hotel, in a town — even if it is tiny — and I'll have a car to get me out of there if need be." She cupped his cheek. "I'll be fine. This is something I have to do. I can't explain it. I have no idea what I'll find when I get there, but I need answers. Maybe this place can give them to me. Or someone there can tell me what on earth I'm supposed to be doing. At the very least, I hope I can get rid of this unease and restlessness that's plagued me for so long. It's getting worse, and I can't just ignore it."

"When you put it that way... but I wish you'd let one of us go with you," Carl grumbled, admitting defeat, jumping to his feet.

Alina uncurled from her tucked-up position on the sofa to give him a big hug. He held her tightly, and then Stephen stepped up from behind and sandwiched her between them.

"We love you, Alina, and we'd hate for anything to happen to you." Stephen murmured in her ear.

Alina nodded, tears spilling down her cheek. She felt so lucky she had these two caring and protective men as her friends.

LATER THAT EVENING, after a home-cooked meal and a bottle of wine, Alina was once again curled up on the couch, with Stephen and Carl snuggled on the sofa on the other side of the coffee table.

She watched them as they spoke quietly with each other, a look of excitement and joy in their eyes. Something was up with them, and she'd been too caught up in her own troubles to notice until now.

"Boys, what's going on?" she demanded, a brow raised quizzically.

They looked at each other, identical grins tugging at their lips. In silent communication, they seemed to agree on something and nodded.

"Well, since you're asking..." Stephen began.

"There's something we've been keeping from you, from everyone, in fact," Carl continued, glancing again at his husband, who was nearly bouncing out of his seat in excitement.

"Tell me. The suspense is killing me here." Alina dropped her feet to the floor and leaned forward, forearms braced on her knees.

"The thing is..." Carl put his arm around Stephen and tugged him close.

"We're going to be parents!" Stephen exclaimed.

Alina's jaw dropped.

"You are? Oh, my God! That's so exciting!" she squealed. "Wow, I'm so happy for you. How? When? Tell me everything." A warm glow of joy made her heart swell.

If anyone deserved to be parents, it was these two. They had the biggest hearts, and any child would be lucky to have them love and care for them. They were born to be fathers and would do a great job bringing up a child, regardless of any prejudice or bigotry they may encounter.

"We've got a surrogate mom helping us. This time it's Carl's swimmers who have done the deed, and, hopefully, next time it'll be mine." Stephen grinned. "Our son is due in five months' time. Can you believe it? We're going to have a son. A little boy." His voice was filled with wonder. "We can't tell you how excited and overjoyed we are. You're the first person we've told, because we wanted to be sure the pregnancy would hold through the first trimester. We're telling our parents and then the rest of our families next week."

Alina felt proud and honored to be the first to know their wonderful secret, and she hoped she'd be able to watch their son grow up.

THEY SPENT THE WEEKEND TALKING, laughing, and enjoying each other's company, not knowing how long before they'd see each other again. On Monday morning, Carl and Stephen drove her to the airport. Up until she walked through security, they tried to convince her to abandon her quest, or at least postpone her travels until she'd had time to think about it more, do some research on where she was going and what she might find there. Alina refused. She knew she had to go.

The restlessness, or jitters, was only getting worse. The only time it had calmed even a little was when she'd decided to go to Colorado. Since then, the feelings had grown stronger. Maybe she'd find nothing when she got there. It could be a complete waste of time and be nothing more than trees and wilderness, but at least she would have tried.

"I'll call you as soon as I land and when I get to the inn. I promise." She wrapped her arms around Stephen's neck. "Thank you again for everything. I don't know what I would have done without you."

Stephen held her tight. "We love you, you know that, and I will need you back at the Atlanta office. Your assistant can take over for now, but she hasn't got your experience. Take as much time as you need, though, and make sure whatever you decide is the right thing for you. And let us know every step of the way where you are and what's going on, or we'll come looking for you." He gently gripped her shoulder and held her so he could look into her eyes. "Our son is going to need his godmother when he's born." He arched a brow, as if challenging her to stay, but she was determined to go.

"You want me to be his godmother?" Her heart skipped a beat. "Are you sure? I'm not exactly the most stable influence these days. I won't be upset if you change your mind."

Stephen glanced at Carl, who nodded and smiled. "Carl and I have talked about it, and we can't think of anyone more suitable for the role. We know you'd love our son as your own and will be a great influence on him."

Alina was touched by their confidence and trust in her. It boosted her spirits and gave her a reason, a foothold, to come back to New York and not get lost in the wilderness — in either Colorado or her mind. With a last kiss on their cheeks, she turned on her heel, straightened her shoulders, and strode through the automatic doors to security.

Thirty-Three

KIRAN, 2005

"This is Pittsburgh Intermodal. Departure will be in thirty minutes. Stretch your legs, folks, use the restrooms, and stock up on food and drinks if you're with me all the way to St. Louis. This is Pittsburgh," the driver announced.

Kiran blinked awake at the screechy rasp from the voice over the public address system. Around him, passengers were getting up, some with carry-ons, and some just wanting to take advantage of the brief stop by using the facilities and snack shop at the bus station. Rubbing his eyes, he stood and followed everyone else off the bus.

I've shifted. Again. But this one was peaceful, like they used to be. Damn it, I wish I could work out what's happening with the jumps. At least then, I could do something about it, or even just brace myself against the discomfort and confusion.

The last thing he remembered was falling asleep in the truck headed for Pittsburgh. The shifts were becoming more and more frequent, and it didn't look as if it had been much of a time hop, either. Inside the small waiting room, a discarded newspaper lay on a bench, and Kiran snatched it to check the date and year. August 1, 2005, the top of the front page claimed. He folded the paper and tucked it into his jacket pocket to read once he was back on the bus, not even questioning the certainty he was staying on until the last stop.

After buying a few bottles of water, snacks, and sandwiches, he stepped outside the station to get some fresh air. Waking up in the seat on the bus had made him feel cramped and hemmed in, and he craved space around him. The weather was surprisingly hot and sultry, and when he looked at the newspaper, the headlines talked about the extreme temperatures the area had been experiencing all summer. He wondered if it was one of his brothers' doing or more of a natural occurrence. The Earth was akin to a living organism that reacted to his siblings' actions — sometimes with unintended consequences.

With his metal flask refilled with water from one of the bottles he'd purchased, he contemplated the latest turn of his existence. He didn't care that he'd shifted again. All these lives he was passing through were becoming meaningless. What did he gain from them? Only misery and sorrow as far as he was concerned.

Sitting down on the edge of the sidewalk with his back to the small shop, he chewed on a sandwich and studied the people scurrying back and forth across the wide parking lot. Were they rushing to work, home, or running errands? Those with bags or suitcases were clearly going somewhere or had just returned from a trip. Did they have loved ones waiting for them? His gut clenched at the thought. He wanted that, too. Someone who was happy to see him, someone whose love for him showed in their eyes and their smile when they saw him.

It was late morning, and the sun blazed from a clear sky with only a few cottony clouds drifting past. He tuned out the traffic noise and turned his face to the vast expanse above. Could his brothers see him? Did they even remember him and try to find him?

Absentmindedly, he rubbed his knuckles over the left side of his chest where an ache sprang up. The need to move toward something unknown niggled at his heart, mixing with the longing for his home and his family and a yearning for his wandering of earth to be over.

It was where he'd felt his power the most. The swiping, nudging, eliminating, appending, and combining of existence-level events, and the nipping, tugging, and altering of a human's life, had been inconsequential to him. If it enhanced the fabric of the universe, then the suffering of humans was negligible in comparison.

At least, that's what he'd always believed. Now, he wasn't so sure he'd be willing to subject anyone to the horrors he'd endured. Not that his thoughts on the matter made any difference to anyone. He was down here. An eternity away from his home. To be honest, he wasn't even sure he belonged there anymore.

The image of a woman with silky hair the color of melted chocolate drifted through his mind, her soft skin and enticing scent tickling his senses. A deep impression of love and longing swept through his soul. She awoke emotions in him the likes of which he'd thought himself incapable. It was futile madness. No one could have feelings for someone they'd never met — a dream conjured by his lonely existence and desperate need for something more than simply stumbling from life to life.

Yet, he couldn't stop himself from hoping, wishing, dreaming, praying. Against his will and better judgment, words appeared in his mind, forming sentences.

I'll come for you.
I'll find you.
Just take one small step.
I love —

"Passengers to St. Louis, please board for imminent departure."

The announcement rasping from speakers mounted on the building behind him stopped him from finishing that last sentence. Kiran rubbed his cheeks and then shoved his fingers through his hair, making it stand on end. He was going insane. How else could he explain it?

He rose from the sidewalk and made his way back to the large bus that would take him to St. Louis. Why he was going there, he had no hope of knowing. He'd long since stopped asking why and just tried to accept what was.

As he crossed the wide expanse, where several buses were idling and fumes filled the air, the intensity of the sun forced him to shield his eyes from the glare, as sweat trickled down his back. The air was suffocating, and he hurried his steps to get inside the cool air-conditioned bus.

Once he reached the open door, he waited patiently for other passengers to board first. Once he got on, he sank into the same seat he'd woken up on. He watched as people stuffed their carry-ons on the overhead shelves and found their own seats.

He smiled when he cast a glance at the shelf above his head. His old duffel was still with him. It had disappeared after the motorcycle crash but suddenly turned up by his feet in the truck to Pittsburgh. He'd left it stowed away when he got off to stretch his legs and buy the sandwiches.

He couldn't remember when the first incarnation of the duffel had appeared and what it had looked like. It would have been something suitable for whatever era he'd lived in and had changed appearances many times since then. The current version had lasted ever since He sent him to London during World War II. He didn't always have it right after a shift, but sooner or later, it would turn up when he least expected it, or maybe when he most needed it. He wasn't sure.

As he waited for the bus to pull out from the station, an elderly woman boarded with a young boy of around twelve years, dragging his feet behind him. Overwhelming sadness, confusion, and fear surrounded the boy like an icy shroud, and Kiran drew in a sharp breath. Something had happened to him recently. Something that had altered the course of his life forever.

The woman smiled at Kiran as she took the seat in front of him. The boy slouched down without looking at anyone. He seemed mentally closed off from everything that was happening around him, as if he worked on autopilot. His despondency made Kiran's gut clench.

The bus pulled away from its spot, and the driver joined the traffic on the busy streets, heading for the interstate leading west toward St. Louis. Kiran made himself comfortable, resting an elbow on the edge of the window and his chin in his hand, watching the scenery unfold outside. He felt his eyes closing and his mind drifting, the thrum of the bus, and the muted hum of voices fading into the background.

"Grandma? Are you okay? Grandma!" The urgency in the boy's voice woke Kiran from his half-slumber.

He straightened and craned his neck to see what was happening. The setting sun had cast the interior of the bus in a dim light. The overhead lights were still not on, but the reading light above the elderly woman shined down, so he could see her clearly.

Her face was ashen, and she seemed dazed. The boy tugged on her arm, panic bleeding through his quiet voice.

"What's going on? Can I help?" Kiran stood up in the aisle and examined the woman.

Her skin was dry and her eyes unfocused. He rubbed her hands to get her circulation going, speaking gently to get her to focus. The boy watched from his seat, the fear and worry darkening his eyes as he chewed nervously on a nail. Luckily, it seemed the other passengers were unaware of what was going on. The last thing they needed was an audience.

"Ma'am? Can you hear me? Come on. Listen to my voice. Look at me, please." He smiled when, finally, her gaze swung toward him. "There you are. You had us a little worried there for a while."

"I—I—I'm—" The woman struggled to get the words out.

"Don't try to speak. Just have some water." Kiran grabbed his trusted old water bottle from his seat and held it to her lips.

She took a few sips of the water, and then a few more. He kept encouraging her to drink until half the bottle was gone.

The logo on the bottle was worn, but he could still see the name of where it was from and the shape of the bridge and its suspension cables. Evie had said the steel cables had looked like wings, which was why she'd liked it so much.

Kiran stared at the bottle. In his mind, pieces of a jigsaw puzzle spun and twirled, slowly clicking into place. Suddenly, the picture became clear to him. How had he not seen it before?

"Is she okay? What's wrong with her? Is she going to die? Grandma? Don't leave me. Please, mister. I can't lose her, too." The boy fired the questions and pleas in rapid succession.

"What's your name?" Kiran lifted his head to look at the boy, who was curled in on himself with his arms wrapped around his middle.

"Tyler. My name's Tyler, sir."

"Okay, Tyler. Your grandma is going to be fine." Kiran smiled reassuringly at Tyler. "She just got a little too hot and needed some water. Can you reach up to the airflow vents above your head and make sure they're fully open? And twist them in this direction. That's it. Well done."

A FEW HOURS LATER, the elderly lady, Kathleen, had fully recovered and was telling Kiran her life's story. She'd switched seats and was sitting next to Kiran to give her grandson some extra space to lie down and sleep since they were still a good five hours away from St. Louis.

"It was horrible. I'll never get over seeing the pictures on the news, and knowing my family was right in the middle of it was terrifying. My heart was racing for weeks, and I couldn't breathe until Tyler was back with me. The poor boy." She shook her head, placing her hand over her heart. "He's been through so much. His mom was my only child, and now he's the only family I have left. I'm worried about him." She cleared her throat, her voice breaking with emotion. "He's been getting himself into a bit of trouble with some of the older boys in the neighborhood."

Kiran's heart cracked as he listened to how Tyler and his family had been caught up in the Christmas tsunami while on vacation in Thailand. His parents and younger sister were swept away in the turbulent waters, and their bodies weren't found until a week later.

Rescue services had taken Tyler to a hospital far from the resort they were staying in. He was too traumatized to communicate and had no identification on him since he had only been wearing a pair of swim shorts. Because of that, the authorities had taken an additional three weeks to locate his grandmother. She'd already been in the country, desperate to find her family, and had returned home with only Tyler, but grateful for that one small mercy.

The bodies of his parents and sister were repatriated with the help of the US government and buried in St. Louis near her home. Tyler had only briefly returned with her to Pittsburgh to say goodbye to his friends and finalize a few legal matters with his parents' attorney. They were going back to St. Louis, where he was about to start a new school and a new life. He'd refused to get on a plane, so they'd chosen to take the bus all the way to Pennsylvania and back.

A deep ache settled in Kiran's chest at the thought of the trauma poor Tyler had suffered. No wonder he'd been so frantic when his grandma had become dehydrated earlier. He'd lost his entire family in a tragic disaster and was naturally worried sick he'd lose her as well.

Whenever Kiran was finally allowed to return to where he belonged, he'd try to make sure events like this didn't take place — or at least minimize their impact on people.

Why would He have created humankind if all he wanted was to inflict pain and suffering on them? It made little sense. There had to be other ways to ensure the fabric of the universe didn't tear or rip without putting them through this kind of horror.

Tyler slept peacefully for another hour while Kiran kept Kathleen company. Their conversation turned to more pleasant topics, and it wasn't long before Kiran knew all about Kathleen's life in Missouri.

Once Tyler woke up, he switched seats with his grandmother to let her rest and settled next to Kiran. He was quiet for a long time, but when Kiran offered him a candy bar, he accepted with a soft thank you. After some gentle coaxing, Kiran got the boy to open up, and before long, he was chatting animatedly about his favorite sports and the latest video games for his PlayStation 2.

Kiran had no idea what he was talking about. He didn't follow any sports. He didn't see the point since he could be thrown forward in time without warning at any moment, but he was happy to listen to the young boy describing all the top goals in the ice hockey matches he watched and the touchdowns in football.

Kiran looked up in surprise when the bus driver announced they were only half an hour away from St. Louis. Beside him, Tyler quieted and hunched in on himself.

Kiran nudged him with a shoulder. "Hey, buddy. What's up?"

Tyler shrugged and kept his gaze fixed on his lap.

"Come on. Talk to me. Maybe I can help."

"I don't know... I just... I miss them. I miss them so much." Tyler's voice was strangled as he blinked away tears.

"I know you do, but they're watching you from above, you know." That was one thing Kiran was absolutely certain of.

He knew how things worked up there and was sure Tyler's parents and sister would watch him all the time. Time worked differently there, but there was no limit to how often they could keep a watchful eye on their son and brother. They would see him grow up, go to college, date someone, and hopefully marry one day. They'd be there to watch him have his own children and grandchildren. Then one day, far in the future, they'd all be reunited again.

"What if they don't like what I grow up to be? What if they wanted me to do something different? What if they're disappointed in me? What do I do then?" The plea in Tyler's words put a crack in Kiran's soul.

This young boy had already seen too much of life's dark side, and now he was worried about disappointing his deceased parents. Kiran brought out his water bottle and offered it to Tyler, who accepted it with a grateful nod. Kiran had already refilled it from his stash in the duffel, and the bottle kept the water cool with its double walls.

"Listen to me, Tyler. If you live life on your own terms, grasp every opportunity that comes your way, and work hard at school and at whatever job you find yourself in, there is absolutely no chance you could ever disappoint your parents."

"Are you sure? I just wish they were here with me. And my sister. I don't want to do this without them," Tyler murmured, holding the bottle out for Kiran to take, but he shook his head.

"Keep it. You might want more water before you get back home." Kiran paused for a moment, weighing his next words. "I'm sure they wish just as much that they could be with you now as well. Since that is impossible, you have some choices to make. Only you can decide how your life is going to turn out. You can spend your time in school slacking, getting bad grades and not learning as much as you can, but how would your parents feel about it?" He glanced at the boy, who seemed to be listening intently. "What would they want for you after already having lost so much? My advice is you go out and make them proud the best way you know how. Make a wonderful life for yourself doing things you enjoy and let that fill you with self-respect and pleasure. I can't tell you what those things are" — he placed his hand on Tyler's shoulder — "only you can do that. If you make yourself proud of your achievements, your parents will be too, I promise you."

Tyler straightened in his seat, his eyes fixed firmly on the bottle, slowly turning it in his hands as if studying every detail. Then he nodded and swung his gaze to look at Kiran.

"I can do that. I'll make them so proud their hearts will burst wherever they are." A small smile curled the corners of his mouth.

Kiran smiled, gently squeezing Tyler's shoulder in encouragement.

When they reached St. Louis, Kiran helped Kathleen and Tyler to catch a cab to take them the last bit to a suburb just outside the city. They both thanked him very much, and he waved goodbye until the taxi disappeared around a corner. Then he picked up his duffel bag and wandered down the street with no idea of where he was supposed to go.

When he came across a late night diner, he decided to go in and work out what he would do next. Despite having been sitting down for far too long, he had no desire to walk the streets of a strange city in the dark of night.

2011

When he stepped across the threshold, he felt as if he slammed into a wall. A crippling headache exploded in his head, and a wave of dizziness assailed his equilibrium. If he hadn't been holding onto the heavy metal and glass door, he'd have fallen to the ground in a heap.

As it was, he stumbled heavily before regaining his balance. No one in the diner seemed to have noticed, sparing his blushes for looking clumsy. He quickly found a seat in a booth, swallowing back the nausea his movements had caused.

What was that? Another shift? Am I still in the same year? Am I in St. Louis, or have I just gone somewhere else? Damn it, I'm so tired of this. I don't think I can take much more. Why are they becoming painful? Hopefully, it means I'm nearing the end of my penance for whatever I'm being punished for.

His head pounding, he ordered a black coffee and eggs, bacon, and fries. The nausea was subsiding, and he needed some real food inside him after the meager sandwiches on the bus from Pittsburgh.

The searing need to be on the move toward only He knew where was still burning under his skin, but he ignored it as best he could for now. When the server arrived with his coffee, he smiled but didn't engage in a conversation. He couldn't summon the energy.

All he wanted was to sit in peace and contemplate the heavy tome of events he'd been subjected to over the past four and a half thousand years. Of course, he'd not lived through each and every year since working on Khufu's pyramid, but enough to know he was done. If only he could work out what to do to get back to where he belonged with his brothers and sisters   his family.

However, the thought of returning didn't sit quite so well with him after all this time. He felt abandoned, rejected, punished for deeds he didn't know he'd committed. It was a great injustice, one of which Kiran had never believed He was capable. What else had he been wrong about? Was his real life in fact a lie? Had his work on the great tapestry been a false pastime? Maybe what he'd believed was acting in the best interests of humankind and destiny was, in reality, only a mirage. Something to keep him and his siblings busy, like children playing house.

The thoughts tumbled through his head, making it pound even worse. He needed to stop thinking about things he had no control over. Taking a large gulp of the scalding hot coffee, he leaned back and closed his eyes, fighting an almost paralyzing wave of tiredness.

Like a soft murmur, a woman's image danced through his mind. Visions of a pair of velvety soft, gray eyes, rich chocolate-colored locks, and golden skin teased his senses. In his head, he reached for her outstretched hand, grasping it as a tendril of light wrapped around his heart. In the same instant, pain flared from his shoulder blades, scorching heat spreading through his body, and he gritted his teeth to hold back a roar of agony.

Her voice entered his head, a gentle whisper filled with love and compassion. Holding tighter to her hand, he was desperate not to lose her again. He couldn't bear the loneliness, the desolation.

Just take one small step.
I'm waiting for you.

Soon, you will never be alone again.
Come to me.
Hurry, please.
I love—

"Excuse me, can I sit here?"

Kiran almost jumped at the voice by his shoulder. He looked up, surprised to still be in the small restaurant with no one looking at him as if he were crazy. Maybe he hadn't shouted out loud or flailed his arms about him. Either that or everyone was used to crazies sitting by themselves in a diner in the middle of the night.

"Uh. Yes, of course. Sure, help yourself." He blinked rapidly, still partially caught in his dream, or vision, or whatever the hell it had been.

The teenage girl slid into the seat opposite him, a cup of tea in her hands and a small backpack hanging off one shoulder. The cup looked as if someone had discarded it since it had lipstick around the rim, and her lips were bare. She tucked herself as far into the corner as she could, her eyes wary of him and the other customers occupying nearly every other seat in here.

Trying not to be too obvious, he studied her pale, dirty face with eyes like large hollows and skinny shoulders. She looked like she needed a decent meal and a full night's sleep in a safe place. Without thinking about it, bits of information filtered into his mind about her. A runaway after an argument with her dad, she'd found herself with nowhere to go and too scared — or maybe too embarrassed — to contact her parents or any other family members. She hadn't eaten anything all day, and her hunger made his own stomach rumble uncomfortably.

Kiran smiled to himself. This, at least, was something he could help with. When the server passed by, Kiran quietly asked him for a full breakfast for the teenager and to put it on his tab. The young man nodded and disappeared through the swinging doors to the kitchen. Glancing at the girl, Kiran realized she was completely lost in her own thoughts and hadn't noticed the exchange between him and the waiter.

When the food arrived, the girl looked up, with fear in her dark eyes, protesting that she'd not ordered anything.

"It's okay. I ordered it for myself, but I'm not hungry anymore. The coffee has filled me up, and I'm supposed to meet a friend for brunch later." Kiran gestured for her to dig in. "Please eat, so it doesn't go to waste."

After several seconds' hesitation, she picked up the silverware wrapped in a napkin and began eating. Soon, she was shoveling the food down as quickly as she could, her hunger casting all good table manners out the window. Kiran suppressed laughter and hid his smile behind a hand. She'd obviously been brought up to eat properly with a knife and fork and not to fill her mouth with too large a bite, but here she was with probably the first hot meal she'd had in days, and those manners dropped to the bottom of the list of importance.

Furtively studying her while she ate, Kiran tried to figure out his next move. She needed to be reunited with her family, that much was clear, but how could he convince her of that without sending her running? The bust-up with her dad was still very fresh in her mind.

First things first, however. He had to get her to trust him enough to have a conversation. Then he'd steer the subject toward family and the love of a parent. He could do this. At least, he thought he could. Someone clearly believed him capable of it, or he wouldn't have been sent the snippets of the girl's background and her reason for leaving home.

"I'm sorry to bother you while you eat, but can I ask if you're from around here? I've just arrived from Pittsburgh, and I'm not sure where the best place is to find a motel," he began, thinking it was an innocent place to start.

The teenager looked at him from under thick bangs. Her forehead creased as if she were trying to assess his motives. Then she slowly nodded and swallowed the mouthful of food she'd been chewing.

"There's a decent place just down the road from here. At least, it looked that way when I walked past it. I'm not from the city, so I can't be sure." She was well spoken, with a soft voice, and Kiran thought she'd probably had a good education so far.

He'd hate for her to become part of the city's homeless population — or worse — and miss out on being a normal teenager with friends, dates, and a high school prom. All kids deserved to have those experiences, and most of all, feel safe and loved.

Slowly and carefully, Kiran drew her into a conversation about noncontroversial topics. When she started asking him questions, he almost punched the air in triumph. He was gaining her trust. He told her a little of his most recent life, embellishing it with a few white lies here and there to make the pieces fit. When an opening presented itself, he recounted the story of Tyler and his grandmother. Losing his parents had been an immense blow to the young boy, and he'd expressed his sorrow at never again being able to tell them how much he loved them. Kiran explained how he'd told Tyler that he was sure they already knew and would always watch over him.

"You see," Kiran concluded. "Parents will never stop loving their children no matter what happens and will forgive them for any silly mistakes they may have made. The most important thing in life is the love we have for our family, and knowing there is next to nothing a child can do that would upset their parents so much they turn their backs on them," he said, keeping his voice low. "I told Tyler to go live his life the best he could, to make himself proud, and that it would make his parents proud. That's what being a mom or a dad is all about. You raise your child to have the strength and confidence to conquer the world, and whatever they end up doing, as long as they are proud of their achievements, you will be as well." He straightened and leaned against the padded backrest. "You may not always like what your child gets up to, but you never stop loving them and will always welcome them back with open arms. I think Tyler understood what I was trying to say, and maybe one day" — he took a sip of his lukewarm coffee — "I'll see his name in the papers having accomplished something wonderful."

Shannon, as Kiran had found out her name was, studied him carefully while he told Tyler's story, her lips pursed, a deep V forming between her eyes. He could almost see the cogs whirring in her head and prayed he'd sown a seed deep enough to take root.

While Shannon finished the last few bites of her breakfast, he rose and went to the counter to pay his bill, taking the opportunity for a quiet word with the older woman who owned the diner. She glanced over at Shannon as he spoke, a motherly expression on her face, and nodded, agreeing to his request.

While speaking with the lady, Kiran noticed the small-screen TV behind her. A news channel was on mute, but it displayed the time and date at the top of the screen. He knew he'd jumped, of course, but this confirmed it. Seeing the year, he sighed. He'd been shoved forward another six years. It was 2011, but still August and the height of summer.

A crackling under his skin made him wince, and he instinctively knew he had to be on his way. How or where to, he still had no idea, but he hoped he'd soon get his answer. He walked back to the table where Shannon had finished eating. He dropped a sheaf of dollar bills on the table and looked Shannon in the eye, keeping his voice low.

"That's for you. Use it wisely." Then he patted her hand before pivoting and walking out of the diner, nodding to the lady behind the counter on his way.

She nodded back in acquiescence, and before he walked off down the street, he watched as she approached Shannon with a cell phone in her hand. The teenager gazed apprehensively at the grandmotherly woman, but nodded, accepting the phone. The last thing Kiran saw was Shannon's face lighting up, tears spilling down her cheeks in great big rivulets, as she spoke eagerly to someone on the other end. Kiran smiled to himself, a warm, fuzzy feeling spreading through his chest.

He continued down the street, the burning under his skin becoming unbearable, forcing the breath from his lungs. Stumbling down a side alley, he was grateful that it was empty of any witnesses. Forced to his knees, he fought for air as the world began spinning, faster and faster.

His hands clawed at the dirty cobblestones while he struggled for control and with a guttural grunt, gave up and allowed himself to be swept away in the avalanche, feeling as if rocks and boulders bombarded his body while he bounced and somersaulted into the black abyss awaiting him.

Thirty-Four

ALINA, 2017

Alina stared out the windshield of the car, barely believing she'd made it. After two flights with a long layover in between, she'd reached Denver Airport. From there, she'd picked up the four-by-four truck Carl had rented for her, and after a night's stay in a hotel on the city outskirts, she set out on the last leg of her journey.

Traveling the winding roads with tall spires of pines flanking each side and stunning views of craggy mountains both behind and in front of her, she couldn't wait to reach her destination. Excitement and apprehension rose ever higher inside her the closer she got. She was strung tight as a drum, her heart thudding behind her ribs, and the booming roar in her ears from her pulse rivaled that of any jet plane.

When she spotted a sign showing she had less than ten miles to go, she let out a small whoop, which quickly turned into a groan when she came around a sharp bend and was confronted with barriers blocking the road and state troopers flagging her down. A big sign announced the road was closed. At the trooper's direction, she lowered her window.

"You'll have to turn around, ma'am. There's been a landslide up ahead, and the road isn't safe," the man said, leaning down to speak with her.

"Oh no. How long will it take to clear?"

"Won't be done for a few days, I'm afraid." The policeman straightened, waving at a car behind her to pull in as well.

His colleague went to speak to the driver while he returned his attention to Alina. Anxiety clawed at her gut. She didn't know the area and wasn't sure there was another road into the town. Her GPS could probably tell her, but what if there wasn't any other access?

"I'm sorry, but I'm not from around here. I'm just visiting the area, and I need to get to Angels Rest. Is there another way to get there?"

"There is, ma'am. You'll have to turn around, drive back the way you came for about ten miles, then swing a right, follow the signs for Eagle Springs, head west about another fifteen miles, and then take the turning for Gabriels Peak. From there, you'll see signs for Spirit Falls and then Angels Rest. It's about an extra forty miles, but it can't be helped, I'm afraid." His expression was sympathetic.

"Thanks, officer." She sighed. "As long as I get there tonight, I'll be fine."

"Well..." He took off his hat and scratched his head. "It'll add nearly two hours to your journey the way the roads are, so take it easy, ma'am."

"I will, thank you." Alina put the car into drive and made a U-turn to head back the way she came.

Retracing her route, she pounded the steering wheel and cursed the universe for making things difficult for her. Then she took a deep breath and calmed herself before she had an accident. She could do this. It was just a bit of a detour, but she'd get there, eventually — assuming there wasn't another landslide, burst dam, tornado, avalanche, or volcanic eruption, of course.

Taking the much longer route gave Alina plenty of time to think. Too much time. Her restlessness ratcheted higher with every mile going south and then west, and she drove until her hands were gripping the steering wheel so hard her knuckles whitened. When she finally saw the signs for her destination, she felt ready to explode. Her body was vibrating with the tension, and her shirt clung to her clammy skin.

Driving into the picturesque town of Angels Rest, some of the tension seeped out of her body and she could release her grip on the wheel. Slowing down while she found her way to the little inn where she'd be staying, she could somehow see how the town had gotten its name. It was surrounded by lush, dense forest with a river running past on one side and the steep side of a mountain on the other.

AFTER CHECKING into the rustic-looking Bed and Breakfast, she headed out on foot to explore the small town and its surroundings. As she meandered down the short Main Street, she walked past a cute café, but she needed more than coffee and pastries. Fortunately, a little farther up the street, a cheerful awning outside a diner beckoned and she entered, finding a space to sit by the window. A teenage girl came out from behind the counter to offer her coffee and pass her a menu.

Alina was starving, and since it was nearly lunch time, she decided to eat before going back to the B&B. Once she'd placed her order, she gazed around the bright restaurant. With the breakfast rush long over, and the midday guests yet to arrive, only a few other customers were in here.

In the far corner, near the jukebox, a small group of high-school-aged kids were drinking milkshakes, eating burgers, and joking around. They seemed to be having a good time, and Alina envied them their carefree lives.

She'd been like that once. So full of hope and dreams, and with an insatiable zest for life. With Jonas, she'd found her place, and when the children came along, she'd been so content, so happy, and not wanting anything more than to see Theo and Daisy grow up, and for her and Jonas to grow old together.

A drunk driver and being in the wrong place at the wrong time had snatched it all away. Painful memories of waking up in the hospital sliced through her mind. She almost cried out from the sudden stab of agony but stifled it at the last second. Throwing a nervous glance around her, she was relieved when no one seemed to have noticed her losing what little control she had of her volatile emotions.

Whereas before, she could have pushed them all into that safe place at the back of her mind, that strong safe, she now struggled to contain them enough not to alert anyone to the fact she was losing her grip on her sanity. At least, that's what it felt like to her.

After wolfing down her food and coffee, she paid her bill, left a small tip on the table, and returned to the safety of her room at the inn. She almost barked a short, mirthless laugh at the thought. A room at the inn. Two thousand years ago, there'd been no room at the inn for a young woman about to give birth.

She shook her head. Where had that thought come from? Maybe she had slid farther into madness than she'd thought. Or was it those who didn't know they were going crazy, the ones who truly were? And those who wondered if they were insane were perfectly rational, but feeling unbalanced? Who knew? It hurt to think about, and she had far more pressing concerns than that.

Gazing out the open window of her cozy room, she breathed in the fresh air, rich in oxygen and free from the pollution of the city she was so used to. For a moment, her head spun, and she huffed a short laugh. The clean air must be playing havoc with her senses. It was probably what caused her almost morbid introspection.

Scanning the view outside the front of the hotel, a structure above the treetops in the distance caught her eye, and she gasped in wonder and exhilaration. That was why she had come here.

Curved, slender arches rose in the air, as if about to take flight, creating an illusion of strength and grace. With her heart hammering in her chest, Alina knew she was in the right place. This was the place she'd been inexplicably drawn to. The logo on the water bottle was based on what she was seeing. Wetting her dry lips, she wondered what her next step would be.

She still didn't know why she was here, but the feeling of waiting for someone had grown exponentially since driving into town. With a gasp, a vision slammed into her head. It was of her, reaching out her hand and *him* grasping it. Unbidden, words formed on her lips, floating into the air.

Just take one small step.
I'm waiting for you.
Soon, you will never be alone again.
Come to me.

Hurry, please.
I love—

She quickly swallowed the last of that sentence. How could she possibly be feeling this way about another man? Jonas was the only man she'd ever truly loved, and she still missed him terribly even after all these years — him and their babies. And yet, the blond-haired man with the vivid, blue eyes evoked feelings in her she couldn't deny. No, it had to be Jonas in some reincarnated form. There was no other rational explanation.

Deep down in her soul, the knowledge she'd refused to accept began spiraling its way to the surface and into her consciousness. She was here for a reason, and the blue-eyed man was an integral part of that reason.

AFTER A LONG PHONE conversation with Stephen and Carl to let them know she'd arrived safely, and them yet again trying to persuade her to give up on her quest and come home, she lay down on the bed for a nap. She was exhausted. Her body ached after hours on a plane and even more hours in the car, but sleep wouldn't come. In the end, she gave up and picked up her e-reader instead, but after having read the same page several times and still not understanding a word, she gave up on that as well.

The restlessness simmered through her veins like an electrical current, and she knew she wouldn't get any rest until she'd been to the bridge — this mythical, mysterious, often-dreamed-about construction that she was finally so close to. She could touch it if she only dared to walk out of her room and go down the road.

As she stood in the middle of the floor, yet again questioning her sanity, a small, white feather floated through the air. Alina stared at it as if it were trying to convey a message. Warmth spread through her chest and her heart, and she knew what she had to do.

With a mental cuff to the chin, she pulled on her runners and a thin jacket. Making sure her cell was fully charged, she slipped it into a pocket and left her room, locking the door behind her. It felt final somehow. As if she'd never come back again. Which was crazy, of course. All her belongings were still here, and she'd need to check out before leaving, no matter where she went.

The reception area was warm and welcoming, with wooden floors and beams in the high ceiling. The adjoining great room was flooded with afternoon sunshine. Several couches with squishy cushions and armchairs occupied one side, with the breakfast area on the other. It looked like a comfortable space for reading or playing board games on a rainy day.

The owner of the inn, a good-looking man in his late thirties with a warm smile and unusually colored eyes, looked up when she approached.

"Heading out, Mrs. Montgomery?" he asked.

"Yes, I am. I'm only taking a short walk for some fresh air. And please, call me Alina."

The man, Kit if she recalled correctly, smiled and nodded. "Alina, then. Enjoy your walk."

"I will," she replied. "Have a good night."

She put a smile on her face and gave him a quick wave. After a deep breath, she left the inn and trekked down the sun-dappled road toward the bridge.

It was only a twenty-minute walk, but it was strangely dark on either side, with no cars or houses nearby. Her heart pounded in her chest, and her pulse fluttered under her skin like the wings of a hummingbird. Was she making a mistake? Was this all just a crazy dream and wishful thinking after losing her family? Alina didn't know, but she had to find out.

The closer she got, the more intense the feeling became that she was meant to meet someone here, a first step toward a new future. She couldn't explain it but owed it to herself to find out. If she didn't, she'd have to live with the thought that she'd missed out on something life-changing.

This was her chance to live again. If nothing came of it, if no one was there to meet her, she'd go back to Atlanta, or maybe New York, and pick up where she left off. Maybe one day she'd even meet someone to spend the rest of her life with. It might not be a scorching love, but she'd already had that, so she would make do.

A chilly wind grazed her skin, and she suddenly noticed the sun had disappeared behind a heavy layer of dark clouds. The atmosphere had changed, and she wouldn't have been surprised to hear thunder in the distance. However, she wouldn't be deterred and carried on her path. As she walked around a bend in the road, the black ribbon stretched out into the distance, and a muted roar rose from a chasm far below.

The bridge.

She was here. She'd finally reached it. Trepidation gnawed in her chest as she hesitantly neared the tall metal structures. She didn't stop until she was standing right before the steel beams rising on either side with their heavy suspension cables arcing down to the ground and reaching out toward the far side.

Unnerved by the strange gloom that had descended, she switched on a flashlight she'd found in the room, aiming the beam upward and staring at the vision it created. Shimmering in the light, the cables formed an elegant shape that soared toward the sky. They were like the wings of an angel, and on the other end of the bridge, its twin stood facing her. She could barely see it in the dark, but she knew it was there.

The two stood like sentinels watching over the people crossing the wide expanse over the rushing river below. Alina's jaw dropped, and she stared with awe and wonderment, her neck craned. This is what she'd been seeing in her dreams — the wings of an angel — but why?

Too weirded out to continue onto the bridge, she made her way a small outcropping on the rocks overlooking the river and sat down. She sank into deep thought, her surroundings all but disappearing. Her life since the accident floated through her mind, the people she'd met, the things she'd experienced, the places she'd been, and the friendships she'd made.

The memories of her family flowed through it all like a silvery path, supporting her, comforting her, even if she'd never realized. They were gone, but their love still remained in her heart, and she would always keep them close.

By the time she came out of her reverie, the sun had set and the darkness of evening had fallen. She rose gingerly from her perch, wary of misstepping and tumbling over the edge, and made her way back to the road and the reason she was here.

Her legs shook as she stepped onto the bridge and started walking, determined not to stop until she reached the center. The roar of the water below sent a sickening feeling through her stomach, and she held on tight to the railings running along the stone parapet. Closing her eyes, she searched for a connection, an apparition, a message — anything to explain why she was here and who she was meant to meet.

When nothing materialized, she began pacing back and forth, stopping every so often to stare into the darkness. She wasn't sure how long she stood there, but several hours seemed to have passed when she finally gave up and sank to the ground. Disappointment and despair rushed through her soul, and tears rolled down her cheeks.

She'd been so sure this was where she was meant to go. Had it all been for nothing? Was it all in her head, and she was slowly going insane? With her knees drawn to her chest, heart-wrenching sobs surged from her chest, and she cried. She cried like she hadn't done since her family died. Everything had been taken from her, even this. Now she had nothing left to give.

Alina felt like screaming out her pain. What had she done wrong? She'd come here, followed the signs, put her life on hold for this. Now what? Deep tremors worked their way through her body, her hands shook, and her lungs worked overtime trying to force air in and out. An overwhelming anguish surrounded her like an icy blanket.

Curled into herself, she rocked back and forth, slipping into a daze. The hours ticked slowly by. Twice, she thought she heard something or someone, but when she looked, no one was there. Something had disturbed the constant crackling and popping of electricity under her skin, though. It surged and ebbed as if drawn to a presence, but she was utterly alone on that bridge. Not even a car passed by.

She ignored the cold and damp seeping into her bones. She didn't care anymore. What was the point in pushing herself forward when it all came crashing around her ears each time? She'd lost her family. Jason thought she was a frigid tease and had assaulted her, and she'd thrown caution to the wind for an inexplicable feeling. Now, here she was, in the middle of nowhere, with nothing to show for her efforts. She'd given it all she had. Even so, it wasn't enough. Her energy, her willpower, her resolve — it was all depleted, reduced to nothing but an empty shell.

This was it.

This was the end of the road for her.

When a gray shimmer began to lighten the sky, Alina stood. Then, after a moment's indecision, carefully climbed onto the parapet and stepped over the metal railings on top. She balanced herself with the central steel support to her left, grabbing onto it with stiff hands. Her heart sped up as she stole a glance at what was below her feet, but she jerked her head up again when a wave of vertigo threatened to unbalance her.

Swallowing hard, she forced her feet nearer the vertical tower. The parapet continued on the outside like a small ledge. Inch by inch, she shuffled around to the outside until she stood with her back pressed against the wide steel girder. Close to hyperventilating, she closed her eyes and focused on her breathing.

In through the nose, count to five, out through the mouth, count to five... After what felt like an eternity, she finally got her lungs to cooperate, although her heart was still threatening to burst out of her chest.

She slowly opened her eyes, keeping her gaze fixed on the horizon where the first rays of the sun were now daubing the sky in pale pastels. It was breathtaking. She stared at it as the minutes ticked by, taking in the miracle that was the birth of a new dawn.

Was this the last time she'd see the world in all its majestic glory? Had she reached the end of her journey, her life, her existence? If so, she couldn't think of a more awe-inspiring place to finish it all.

When the first tender shards of golden light crested the snow-capped mountains in the distance, making them sparkle and glow like scattered gems, a sense of anticipation settled over her shoulders. Unable to move, she was transfixed by the warm rays as they swept closer and closer toward her.

The mist rising from the river was bathed in sunlight, creating colorful rainbows for fairies and angels to dance in, or so her grandma had always told her. Seeing nature's gala performance play out before her, Alina was convinced the woman had been right. She'd usually been right about many things.

Her gaze locked onto the river of light pouring through a gap between two mountains. She followed it as it cascaded down the forested hillside and danced with the rushing river, making it look like it was made of gold. Then the torrent swallowed light, throwing it under her feet where she could no longer see.

Swaying forward when vertigo again assailed her sense of balance, she jerked herself upright, and fumbled for the safety of the steel beam behind her, crying out with relief as her fingers found purchase around the sharp edges.

With her chest rising and falling sharply, she scrunched her eyes shut and tried to coax her heart back into its rightful place in her chest after it had lodged itself in her throat. She huffed a small breath. If she'd leaned just a little farther out, she would have fallen into the foaming rapids below.

Is that what I want?

As her heart slowed, a strange sensation spread through her chest. Warmth, hope, and love filled her soul while a shimmer, different from that created by the sunbeams, appeared on one side of her. It billowed, twisted, and twirled as if searching for something.

Alina felt mesmerized by the beauty of its graceful dance and couldn't tear her eyes away. Somehow, the shimmering light spoke to her, to her soul and her heart, but she couldn't understand what it was trying to tell her.

With her breath caught in her throat and her fingers in a death grip around the vertical steel tower, she twisted her body to see better. From behind the next beam, movement caught her eye. She stared without blinking, fearful it would go away if she did, her eyes filling with tears.

With the barest amount of air escaping her aching lungs, a desperate whisper fell from her lips.

"I waited for you."

Thirty-Five

KIRAN, 2017

Kiran kneeled on the ground, his shoulders hunched, groaning from the pain shooting up and down his body. Every inch of him was on fire, and agonizing explosions went off inside his skull in quick succession. Fighting to swallow back the tears of pain, anger, and disappointment, he wrapped his arms around his head as if to hold it together. He knew. He knew without a doubt he'd been catapulted forward again, and this time, the shift had been sheer torture.

He was no longer in St. Louis, that much was certain. The cobbled street had disappeared from beneath his knees, replaced with damp earth, dry leaves, and pine needles. The sounds of the city had faded into a deafening silence.

Why? Why wasn't he allowed to rest, to sleep, to fade into nothingness if he wasn't meant to return to his haven? What had he done? Why was he being punished? Why wouldn't they tell him what heinous crimes he'd committed to spend so long away from his home, where his heart at least used to belong?

Now, he wasn't sure that if they gave him the choice, he'd go back. Not after the way he'd been treated. To be cast out with no explanation, no warning, and no assistance was cruel and unforgivable. If only he could find a way to avoid the shifts, he'd stay on earth and make a life for himself. It might not be much, because, let's face it, he had little going for him. He had no paperwork to back up his skills, even though he was a qualified surgeon, and could only get menial jobs with no references and no training to prove his worth. At least until he'd been able to establish as a legal resident with a social security number. Once he had that, he could consider his career options.

He didn't care what he did. As long as he earned enough to provide for himself, he would be okay. On his own, he didn't need much, and after losing Juliet, he had no wish to get involved with another woman. Unbidden, images of the woman with a smile as bright as the sun drifted into his mind. A warmth in his heart soon followed, and he sighed.

How could he have feelings for a woman he'd only ever seen in his dreams? She wasn't real, was she? *No, it's impossible*, he told himself with an exasperated snort. Yet he'd seen her at Juliet's funeral. That glowing tendril had definitely emanated from her, and when it touched his chest, he'd felt it like an electric shock before her empathy, compassion, and… He hesitated to even think the word, but it was the only one that aptly described it. *Love*. He'd felt her love across the distance — both physical and spiritual.

Love.

That elusive connection to another human being. Once, he thought he may have found it with Juliet, but if he was to believe the romantic literature and cinematic visuals, theirs had been more of a companionship. He'd felt deep affection and warmth for his wife, but he wasn't entirely sure it had been love. Or maybe it was as close to it as he'd ever get? Could he even fall in love? Was his heart capable of such a deep emotion? He had nothing to go on or compare it with, so he couldn't be certain, but he wanted to believe he could love a woman the way she deserved to be loved.

All he knew was that the emotions his chocolate-haired beauty evoked in him were far and beyond what he'd ever felt for Juliet. They were overwhelming and heart-wrenching, and the thought of never seeing her eyes that shined with warmth and desire, or feeling her satin smooth skin again, made his heart scream in agony.

All these thoughts flew through his head at lightning speed while his body focused on dealing with the effects of the shift. A sudden wave of nausea surged from his gut, and he only had time to turn to the side before he emptied his stomach on the muddy ground, adding to the decaying leaves and pine needles already accumulated there.

His stomach cramped over and over until there was nothing left but bile. Catching his breath, he wiped the sweat off his brow with his sleeve and then spat out the last of the vile-tasting fluids. Exhausted, he dragged himself to his feet, using the trunk of a tree to hold him up. He peered around, but his vision swam, and he saw double of everything. The waning light didn't help either.

Staggering toward an opening in the trees, he stumbled onto a blacktop stretching into nothing in one direction and curving between the dark walls of a forest in the other. With the nausea subsiding and the aches in his body fading, he turned his head from left to right and back again, searching for a sign telling him which way to go, but there was nothing except silence around him. Not even a whisper from the gently swaying trees or the cry of a bird.

After several anxious minutes, or maybe it was hours, he took a few tentative steps. In the distance, the road seemed to vanish into thin air. With a whoosh, the ambient sounds rushed back like the popping of a bubble, and he could hear everything. He could also clearly see that the road didn't just vanish but reached toward a soaring structure, somehow reminding him of a pair of wings. How ironic. All he needed now was a glowing light, and a voice whispering in his head.

Staring toward the gleaming metal girders and steel cables, he almost rolled his eyes when he heard a loud whispering, thinking he was definitely going crazy and imagining things. When he got nearer, he barked out a laugh at his own stupidity when he realized it was the sound of a fast-running river far below the wide bridge.

Now what? Was he supposed to wander across this bridge or go in the other direction and hope to find some sign of civilization somewhere? Scratching his head, he retrieved his trusty old duffel bag that had once again survived his time-traveling. Speaking of which, he didn't know when or where he was — again — and he had no means of finding out unless he could find some human habitation somewhere.

Once more, his anger rose over the way he was being treated and manhandled, and he slung the bag over his shoulder, stomping toward the bridge. Walking under the spiring beams, he marveled at the illusion they created with the cables strung tight from the ground up, curving outward when they reached the top before bending back to be bolted onto the heavy steel.

A sharp pain speared through his back at two points on each of his shoulder blades. It was a familiar ache, but this time, the intensity of it made him gasp and falter. Doubled over, he stumbled to a knee, trying to catch his breath. After a long moment, the pain faded to a dull throbbing. Sheer stubbornness made him ignore it, and he trudged forward, step by step.

Darkness descended quickly. Too quickly to be normal. It wasn't long before he could barely see his hand in front of his eyes despite the row of lights along each side of the bridge. Their glow wasn't strong enough to chase away the deepening shadows.

Somewhere in the middle of the crossing, a strange warmth enveloped him, and he hesitated for a few seconds, pivoting to discern where it was coming from, but sensing nothing else, he continued to the other side.

Kiran stopped again, searching the shadows where the opposing bridge tower reached for the darkened sky. He'd expected to feel something, to see someone, but he was completely alone. Not knowing what to do, he sat down by the side of the abutment and thought through his options. Or lack of them.

He was in the middle of nowhere with no town, village, or even a lonely farmhouse within sight, and he had absolutely no sense of what he was supposed to be doing or where to go. All he could do was wait and hope.

Kiran made himself as comfortable as possible and settled in for what he feared would be a long wait. The familiar but unwelcome restlessness had started again in his chest. It ached and burned, and no matter what he did, it wouldn't go away. He tried reasoning with himself, then arguing, and in the end, giving himself a mental knockdown, drag-out knuckle fight, but none of it helped.

Sitting still for so long made his muscles seize, so at some time in the night, he forced himself to amble across the bridge again, listening to the roar of the river and the soughing of the breeze in the trees. The screech of a night bird occasionally tore through the air, and an owl's soft hooting echoed ominously from the towering shadows of the forests.

They were all normal sounds of the sunless hours, but somehow, they sounded more haunting and sinister than he'd ever heard before. Did the owl know what was in store for him and tried to warn him? Did the long finger-like shadows of the trees attempt to hold him back from going the wrong way? Or were they pushing him toward his doom?

The sound of gushing water drew him closer to the parapet with its heavy steel cable railings. It was hypnotic, and he stopped to lean over the void. Thoughts of stepping up on the balustrade and push off, letting himself fall toward oblivion, tugged at his mind as if salvation awaited him at the bottom.

At war with himself, his belief in his home, its strict laws, and strongly held principles and promises fought for dominion over his four-and-a-half thousand years of human experiences. Experience that told him he'd been abandoned and forgotten by everyone. Even Him.

His hands gripped the railing so hard the sharp, braided strands sliced the palms of his hands, blood seeping from the cuts, but he welcomed the pain. It gave him something tangible to focus on instead of his mind's battles with itself.

Close to hyperventilating, he closed his eyes and shoved the thoughts of falling out of his mind. This was not the time for weakness. He had a notion, deep in the pit of his stomach, that *she* should be here and needed to know for sure one way or the other. Once he knew for certain it had all been in his imagination, he would contemplate other options.

A poem by Robert Frost came to mind. Written as a joke for a friend who'd once been undecided about which road to take when out walking, to most readers, it was seen as championing the idea of following your own path in life.

The road not taken.

That was where he always stood —at a crossroads with untold avenues fanning out before him, but he was never allowed the privilege of choosing his own path. Maybe this time the choice would be his and his alone.

Reaching the end of the bridge, he turned on his heel and trudged back toward his perch again. Each time he passed the middle, that comforting warmth swept through his soul, and he felt strangely bereft when it drained out of him the closer to the end he got.

As he settled back down with his duffel as a cushion, a deep sadness gripped his heart. Was this how his life would always be? Going from one time period to another with no goal, no direction, and no companion? He was tired and needed respite from it all, to rest, recuperate, rebalance, and breathe.

He always felt as if he were waiting for the next shift, never able to relax and enjoy what life afforded him. His time with Juliet had been so full of joy and affection, and he'd be happy with having that again even though he longed to experience true, overwhelming, blisteringly hot, and passionate love. The kind he'd felt in his dreams with his soul mate.

His soul mate. How easily that word had slipped into his mind, and now that it had, he felt the truth of it. Somehow, this sensual, passionate woman with eyes the shade of slate and cocoa-colored waves of shoulder-length tresses, who he'd only touched in his dreams, was his soulmate.

Their encounters had affected him in a way no other woman had, not even Juliet. While he hadn't lived like a monk, he also hadn't been with that many, but he'd certainly met and spent time with scores of them during his many years on earth.

None had touched his heart like she had, and he'd never even seen her face, only her eyes and enigmatic smile. How was this possible? Was it yet another test of his loyalties? In that case, it wasn't only a callous act toward him, but to her as well. She hadn't Fallen or been cast out, of that much he was certain. He'd know if she was one of his siblings. No, she was a human, or mostly human, at least.

Unless she was— No, that was too farfetched even for him, who'd seen much of what had occurred between Heaven and Hell and throughout the universe. She couldn't be one of them, could she? Legends abound among his kind of children infused with some of their energy and sent to be born on Earth. They were meant to share their love and kindness to counteract the evil that was always trying to gain a foothold in the hearts of humans.

Was it possible? It was said they would suffer great tragedy and from that, their capacity for love, compassion, and empathy would be released and passed on to all those who they came into contact with. Anyone with less than an open heart would react violently and seek to dominate and possess them.

Kiran's chest ached at the thought because the legend also told that after suffering their traumatic event, the person was destined to always be alone and only experience friendship and companionship but never love again.

Inside, his soul crumbled. It all made sense. His woman wasn't really his. She was out of his reach, and he'd never find the kind of love he wanted with her. She was beyond him now. So why was he still dreaming of her, and why did he feel as if he had to find her? None of this fitted the puzzle.

Kiran's lungs seized, and his heart stuttered in his chest.

He was done.

Done with the endless wandering, done with the shifts, done with the loneliness, done with the constant longing and endless disappointments. He was just done.

A sob caught in his throat, but he swallowed it back. Remaining still for a long time, he finally came to a decision. This ended now.

Pushing to his feet, he left the duffel behind on the ground. Where he was going, he'd have no need for it. He only hoped it would work the way he wanted.

As the silvery shimmer of dawn lightened the skies, he slowly made his way back to the center of the bridge, thinking everything through not once, but a hundred times, to ensure he was making the right decision.

His heart beat so hard in his chest he was sure he could hear it over the pounding of his pulse in his ears. Despair and agony interchanged with one another like a relay race at dizzying speeds until they merged to become one. The hurricane they created blasted through his head, causing him to cry out and fall to his knees.

With the last of his strength, he found the spot where the unusual warmth wrapped around him once more, and he climbed onto the parapet. Using the steel beam for support on his right, he stood facing the chasm below and its violent rush of water. On the far horizon, the sun sent pastel-hued tendrils of light over the distant mountain, creating a waterfall of golds and pinks cascading down toward the sparkling river.

He felt the pull of the sun and the sky on his soul, but he resisted. That wasn't where he was going. Not this time. The comforting warmth still held him in its embrace, and he drew strength from it. It felt like the tender caress of a familiar yet exciting lover.

His heart ripped to shreds, knowing he'd never get to have that. He'd never be allowed to feel secure in someone else's love and acceptance. Was it really too much to ask, after all these millennia, to be free to find that one person who always lit up when he walked into the room, who gave their love unconditionally, and who wanted his in return?

For the last time, he sent a prayer, asking for guidance, an explanation, a reason for his existence. Like every time previously, he was met with a deafening silence. He'd been discarded, forgotten, ignored, and he would take it no longer.

As he gazed over the chasm, the mist from the waters below sparkled and shimmered, and he knew otherworldly beings in the shards of light were dancing with wild abandon. He suspected one or two of his siblings were likely there, enjoying the glittering gala with music provided by the white rapids and swirling eddies.

Would they see him as he embraced the water? Would they resent the interruption and turn their backs on his fading light? Or would they dance farther away in the mists before returning home, never to have felt his presence at all?

Over and over, he beat himself up with the constant questions. Ones to which he'd never receive an answer. He was no longer one of them. He'd lost his family, his friends, his reason for being, and the pain was becoming unbearable.

Kiran edged farther out, grasping the steel beam in a tight grip. A narrow ledge ran along the outside, and he shuffled out until his back was pressed against the cold metal. With his eyes closed, he stood there, breathing deeply to imprint the scent of fresh air in his mind.

The warm glow from before intensified, and a scuffling noise interrupted the serenity that had taken hold in his chest. Slowly opening his eyes, he held his breath and listened. With fear, anticipation, and excitement warring in his soul, he swung his head to the right.

She is here.
My woman.
My soul mate.

She was as beautiful as he'd imagined, with a heart-shaped face, straight nose, and full lips. Her body was slender, with a narrow waist, graceful hips, and perfectly sized breasts. He knew every nook, every crease, every dip, and every fall of her luscious curves, but he'd never seen her full and beautifully formed figure before. Even her face had been a mystery until now, but suddenly, he felt as if he'd always known what she looked like.

He'd seen her in all the women he'd met over the eons. One had her nose, another had her legs, and yet another her hands, but only now did he get the full effect. He was overwhelmed and deliriously happy.

Her gray eyes widened when she took in his sudden appearance, and he could sense the rapid flutter of her pulse in her throat. His own pulse chased hers in a wild dance, and his heart synchronized with the rapid acceleration of the beats inside her ribcage. With his gaze transfixed on hers, he felt his soul reach out and saw the ribbons of light and energy wrap around each other, twirling and twisting, as if overjoyed to have finally become one.

When her eyes filled with tears, it felt like a punch in the gut, and his mind short-circuited as her mouth opened as if to speak.

Please, don't reject me. Don't say you don't know who I am, because I know who you are. I couldn't bear the rejection. Not from you. Not now. Not after all this time. I need you to make me whole, to give my life purpose and worth. I. Need. You.

His pleas tumbled silently through the void that opened in his soul, and he prepared the best he could for her rejection.

Like a whisper on the wind, her voice and her words floated toward him.

"I waited for you."

Thirty-Six

ALINA, 2017

Rooted to the spot, Alina stared at the man who'd suddenly appeared by her side as if he'd materialized out of thin air. His golden hair shimmered faintly in the rays of the rising sun. His ice-blue eyes held her gaze with as much wonderment and awe as she knew were shining from hers. Recognition flared in their depths, and a smile tugged at his lips.

Deep inside her, a heat blossomed when her heart responded to the emotions flowing off him in waves. Her pulse quickened, and her breath caught in her throat as she took in his god-like features. With an angular jaw, chiseled cheekbones, and refined nose, he could have been mistaken for Adonis. Add to that his cut muscles, bulging biceps barely contained by the shirt he wore, sculpted chest, and broad shoulders, and the effect was mouthwatering. More than all of that, though, it was his heart, full of love and adoration, that drew her in like a magnet.

"You're here. I was losing faith," she breathed.

He smiled hesitantly. "I still had hope, but it was waning. I'm grateful you didn't give up."

"Is this real?"

"Yes, I believe it is."

Alina was unsure what to say or do. She felt so much for this man who she'd never met. Yet she knew him intimately. The touch of his fingers on her flushed skin, his mouth against hers, nipping, tugging, and licking, his scent in her nose, and his body wrapped around hers, was all so familiar, comfortable, exciting, and very thrilling.

From far away, she heard a voice telling her to let go and be with the man in front of her. It was Jonas. She was sure of it. He was giving her permission to be happy, and to love and be loved again. His voice made her smile, an immense weight lifting off her shoulders.

She was free.

Jonas and their children would always be a part of her life and her heart, but they were gone, and she deserved a new chance at life. Would this man be that new chance? She didn't know yet, but she wanted him to be. It felt right. It was as if they were two halves of a whole and were meant for each other.

Swaying on her precarious perch, she reached for her soul mate. With a gentle smile and loving warmth in his eyes, he stretched his hand to meet hers. When their fingers connected, a warm glow enveloped them, with silent starbursts exploding around them.

For a second, Alina's vision went blank, and she began spinning, tumbling, until she found herself in an unfamiliar space. She was sitting on a comfortable chair, or cushion, she couldn't quite decide. For a heart-stopping moment, she thought she'd lost him, but he sat right opposite her in a similar seat.

"Where are we?" She looked around but couldn't see anything except for a golden glow and floating ribbons of mist.

"I'm not certain, but we're safe. I know that much."

Alina's hands twisted in her lap. She wasn't sure what to say or do now that they'd found each other.

"Do you know who I am?" he asked her.

She nodded. The knowledge seemed to trickle in as she needed it.

"Your name is Kiran. She tilted her head to the side and studied him closer. You have been wandering among us for a long time. Alone. You've suffered so much. Too much." Her heart broke for his suffering.

"You're right." He nodded. "I have been wandering alone, but maybe just long enough to find you." Leaning forward, he took her hands in his.

Alina looked down at their intertwined fingers, where he stroked the tops of her palms with his thumbs. Letting go of one hand, he put his knuckles gently under her chin and tipped her head up. Her gaze followed and settled on his.

"Do you know what I am?" he asked.

She thought for a moment and then nodded.

"Yes, I know what you are. If you're one of *them*, why are you here and not... up there?" Her gaze rose momentarily to the ceiling.

His voice held a note of wonder. "I don't know yet, but I believe I was meant to find you."

"What's it like up there?"

Kiran closed his eyes briefly before opening them again. "It's serene. Quiet. Friendly, I guess you could say."

"Is Jonas up there? And Theo and Daisy?" Tears gathered in her eyes at the thought of her family.

"Yes, they're all there. They're together and live a happy life. Of course, they're waiting for you to join them."

"Does he... watch over me? Can he see what I do and what happens in my life?" Alina chewed her lip as if afraid of the answer.

"He can, but it's a different consciousness than the one where he's with your children. It's hard to explain" — Kiran furrowed his brow — "but up there, you can be many different versions of yourself, all existing happily in their own realities. He'll always be with you, and not just watching from above, but also in your heart. You carry his love with you forever."

Alina tried to process Kiran's revelations. Knowing Jonas and their babies were happy and together filled her with joy as well as longing.

She missed them desperately, but suddenly, the pain was no longer as sharp. It was more of a distant, dull ache.

"So, what happens when I die? If I'm with someone, married or... you know." She chewed on her lip. "What happens with Jonas and him waiting for me?"

"As I said, you can be with Jonas, or with whomever you may fall in love with in the future." Kiran looked down, and Alina thought she caught a slight blush on his face.

She scooted closer and pressed a hand to his cheek. His gaze flipped up at her touch.

"So I can be with Jonas or with you? I just have to choose?"

"Do you want to be with me?" Kiran asked, hope coloring his words.

"Yes, I do." She nodded thoughtfully. "At least, I think so. Isn't that what all this has been about? For the last couple of years, I've been chasing after something, or someone, without understanding why or how." She looked into his eyes, holding his gaze with her own. "Now, I know it was you all along. I was meant to meet you and be with you. Don't ask me how I know because I couldn't tell you." Alina shrugged.

Kiran leaned into her hand on his cheek and closed his eyes.

"Was it you at the funeral?" he asked, pain crossing his handsome features.

"You mean the one you attended? Where you stood on your own for a long time? I saw you across the meadow," she replied. "Somehow, we connected, didn't we?"

He nodded. "Yes, we did. I saw this ribbon of light reach out to me. It touched my heart, and the sensation was overwhelming. I've felt nothing like it."

"Who was it? In the casket, I mean?"

Kiran inhaled deeply and bowed his head. "My wife, Juliet. She passed from cancer, and I couldn't save her." A deep sigh shuddered through him. "I was a doctor back then and should have been able to do something about it."

"I'm so sorry. You must have been devastated."

"I was. Juliet was the only woman I'd had a genuine relationship with since I Fell. She was warm, kind, and loving."

Alina whispered, "You must have loved her very much."

His eyes snapped to hers while he pressed her hand closer to his cheeks. Then he moved her palm to his lips and placed a soft kiss on it. A shiver ran down her spine, and heat furled in her stomach from the tingling it elicited. His eyes darkened to a midnight blue, and Alina's breath caught in her throat from the onslaught of emotions.

Kiran pulled her tight into his embrace. She hadn't even realized he'd moved from his seat to her. Effortlessly, he lifted her enough to slide in underneath her and settle her in his lap. She snuggled into him, resting her cheek against the hard plates of his chest. A sigh slipped from her lips as a small piece of her heart slid back into place.

His muscular arms made her feel secure... and loved.

"Kiran?"

"Mmhmm?" He'd buried his nose in her hair, and his reply was slightly muffled.

"Tell me about Juliet?"

"What do you want to know?"

"How did you two meet?"

Kiran settled into the cushioned chair and made sure Alina was comfortable before he told her the story of how he'd shifted into 1948 and eventually met his wife.

"Her dying set me adrift in a way I hadn't experienced before, and I couldn't handle it," he explained. "I needed to get away, but I had no way of knowing if or when I'd shift again. That's when I signed up for the Vietnam War as a field surgeon."

Alina looked up at him, compassion and empathy filling her chest.

"You volunteered? How long were you there for?"

His arms tightened around her, and she could only imagine what kind of horrific memories of that time were ripping through his mind.

Alina frowned. "Wait, you said there was an Australian called Geoff there? I met a young woman in Atlanta who said her grandfather had been killed in Vietnam," she said. "She was Australian, and his name was Geoff. Another man who'd been held prisoner with her grandfather visited her grandma to tell her how he'd died and how he'd wanted a message relayed to her." She tilted her head to peer at him, a strange expression sweeping across his face. "The soldier also spoke about a doctor in the camp who'd been of great help to many of the prisoners, but he wasn't among the ones who were freed in 1973. That was you, wasn't it?"

Kiran's eyes widened, his eyebrows rising as if in disbelief. Alina couldn't blame him. Life was full of coincidences, but this one must be the biggest one of all.

"I was there," he said. "Geoff was a good friend, but he died from dysentery in February 1973. I succumbed to it only a week or so later."

The more they talked, the more she realized how their paths had crossed over the years. When Alina told him about Clara Miller and how she'd looked for Junior Mints in the grocery store, a soft smile spread across his face.

"So, he's still alive." Kiran's eyes misted over as he seemed to lose himself in his memories for a moment. "Edward was a magician at improving and developing any medical instrument. The ideas he came up with were absolutely genius."

"He invented something that revolutionized keyhole surgery," Alina said quietly. "My son, Theo, had to have heart surgery after he was born, and they used the equipment with the part Joseph invented. He helped save my son's life."

One by one, they worked their way through as many of the people Kiran had met that he could remember and who could still be alive or have close relatives. He mentioned those he thought he'd affected most and eventually, they connected some to a few that Alina had encountered in the years since she left California. They found six in all that Alina had either met or at least spoken to someone connected to them, like Ellen's son and daughter-in-law.

Kiran told Alina that hearing how he'd impacted so many in such varied but positive ways filled him with warmth, and his many lifetimes didn't feel quite so wasted to him. After all, if he'd managed to change those people's lives for the better in only the last few years, there was no telling how much good he'd done since he first began his wanderings.

"So, Evie is now working on experiments that will be sent to another planet. Shannon is back with her parents, and Tyler is working hard on his degree. Wait, his focus is on bridge construction?" Kiran's brows shot up to his hairline.

Alina smiled and nodded.

"Yep, and he was immensely grateful for you helping that time and wanted to pay it forward, which is why he gave me the bottle. I still have it in my bag back at the inn. You've done so much for so many people." She placed a hand over his heart, feeling its rhythmic thudding. "Much more than you'll ever know. The butterfly effect is in full swing, and those ripples will just continue to spread outward in never-ending circles. It's your legacy to the world — to all of humankind."

Thirty-Seven

KIRAN, 2017

Alina shifted on his lap so he could see her face, and she threaded her fingers through his hair. He nearly groaned at the sensation. Her closeness had certain parts of his body responding, and he had to push down on the reactions. This was neither the time nor the place. He couldn't deny his feelings for her, though, including the physical ones. What he'd had with Juliet had been beautiful, but the feelings Alina evoked in him were passionate, raw, and so much more intense. They took his breath away and made his heart beat wildly. With effort, he pushed them to the back of his mind to be let loose later, he hoped.

Alina let out a tiny laugh, letting him know she knew exactly what effect she was having on him. When she wriggled her backside against his groin and the growing hardness there, he growled, and swatted her ass, making her yelp and then laugh harder. He rolled his eyes and shifted in the seat to give himself more space.

She stilled in his arms, her eyes riveted on his. He could have sworn he heard her heartbeat pick up pace when he swelled even further underneath her. He closed his eyes for a moment and swallowed hard, then opened them again, only to find hers still fixed on him, her teeth nibbling the inside of her cheek. Then her tongue darted out to wet her lips, and his control snapped.

Crushing her to him, his mouth sought control, sucking and licking at hers while a hand slipped down her side, cupping a breast. A sexy little moan escaped her mouth and stoked the fire already burning in his gut.

He threaded his fingers through her hair and tugged gently, tilting her head to the side to expose her neck. The creamy skin begged for him to lick it, and he planted wet kisses all the way down to her clavicle where he nipped gently, soothing the biting sting with his tongue.

Alina pressed his hand harder against her breast, melding into him as her breathing grew heavier.

"Please, Kiran. Touch me. Everywhere."

Her pleas spurred him on, and his hand slipped under the shirt she wore, tugging the cup of her bra down until her soft flesh was bared to his touch. She yanked at the fabric until it was over her head and then disappeared somewhere beneath them. Kiran pulled back slightly so he could see her properly. With one breast bared and the other still in its lacy cup, she looked wanton and lustful.

"You are the most beautiful woman I have ever seen. I love you, Alina. No matter what happens, don't forget that," Kiran breathed, the desire for her setting off bolts of lightning in his mind.

If he wasn't careful, he'd pass out from the sheer pleasure of finally having her in his arms. Not just in a dream, but skin to skin, heartbeat to heartbeat.

Alina just looked at him, her fingers busy undoing the fastenings on his shirt until she got too impatient and tore the two pieces of fabric apart, buttons popping in every direction. Kiran couldn't help the laugh that burst from his chest. She was so adorable with her kissable lips all pouty.

She shoved the shirt down his arms, and he shook it free to join hers somewhere on the floor. In one swift move, he had her stretched out on the cushions beneath them. Supporting himself on one arm, he took in all the little details of her face. The tiny dimple in her cheek, a smattering of freckles across the bridge of her nose, and the little creases at the corners of her expressive eyes.

He quickly relieved her of her remaining clothes before shucking his own and returning to his place by her side. Propped up on his elbow, he traced the contours of her face and neck down to her shoulders, brushing over her collarbones and back up again. Little trembles raced through her at his touch. He could see them in the way her hands shook and how her breathing shuddered.

Then it was his turn to shiver when her hands went on an exploration of their own. Tracing the planes of his chest, she explored every ridge and valley of his abs, making them contract involuntarily. When her fingers grazed his painfully hard erection, he hissed, his whole body tensing with the effort of not exploding like an immature adolescent.

Alina's hands closed around his hard flesh, making him grit his teeth, his lungs seizing up behind his ribs. Needing to feel all of her, he filled his hands with her breasts, pulling and twirling her rosy nipples as she writhed beside him, her chest rising sharply in tune with his.

Moving one hand down her body, he found her slick folds and parted them with his fingers, making Alina cry out. She was hot, wet, and swollen, and he could no longer hold back. As he centered himself over her, the crown of his cock nudged at her entrance and he stilled, catching her gaze with his questioning one. She nodded, giving him the permission he sought, and slowly, he slid home.

Being inside her for real suddenly became his new heaven. It was where he belonged and wanted to stay forever. Her eyes never left his as he surged forward and then pulled out again. He saw so much desire, passion, and love in those gray orbs that the emotional connection overwhelmed him. He never knew how much he'd craved that kind of bond with another being. Now he had found it, he could never give it up.

Together, they found the cadence that bound their bodies together, and he spiraled ever higher from the sensation of being inside her glorious body. Electricity crackled between them, sending jolts of lust through his nerve endings. Soaring on the winds of ecstasy, he knew he was approaching the peak of his desire for the woman in his arms. She was a shimmering vision of fire and lust.

He changed the angle of his hips, and a keening wail immediately erupted from her mouth. Her inner walls rippled around him, squeezing rhythmically, making his own climax race through him with blinding speed, and he exploded in a tidal wave of fiery sensations. Collapsing to her side, he drew her close, his breath coming in rapid gasps, mingling with her sharp puffs. They lay quietly, basking in the afterglow, and he reveled in the deep sense of physical satisfaction he felt with Alina. It was something he'd never experienced before. It was soul-deep and life changing. He knew in his heart he could never live in any world where Alina didn't exist.

Alina's hand on his face broke the somber path his thoughts had suddenly veered onto, and he looked down into her eyes, which widened with worry.

"Kiran, what happens now? Will they rip you away again? Push you forward in time like before? Will I" — Alina took a shuddering breath — "lose you now when I've just found you? I couldn't bear losing another man I love." Her words finished with a sob.

It was the first time she'd acknowledged out loud the feelings she had for him.

Kiran's arms tightened around her. Nuzzling her neck, he planted tender kisses against her skin.

"I don't know, my love. I hope I'm done with the shifting."

"And if you're not? What then?"

Kiran's mouth thinned at her questions. He didn't want to shift again, ever. It tore at his body and his mind each time it happened, and he'd had enough. He'd been compliant, patient, and understanding of it all, but now he needed some answers. The more he thought about it, the clearer the solution became, but Alina had to do it with him, or it wouldn't work. Would she trust him enough to risk it all? With him? For him?

"How is any of this possible?" Alina breathed.

"I think — I think you may have some celestial blood in you. It's the only thing that makes any sense."

"But how?" She sat up and looked at him.

Kiran pushed up to eye level with her. "There are plenty of stories where I come from that tell of some of us who have been with humans. It's not supposed to happen, but I'm not the first who's been cast out. And if others have endured the same as I have, then it doesn't surprise me." He reached for her hand, lacing his fingers with hers. "We're no different from you. We have the same emotions, the same needs, and we are just as capable of falling in love. Up there, it's much more muted and reserved, but down here, it seems our senses are heightened and our emotions with them." His lips pursed. "God knows it wasn't for lack of trying that Juliet and I never had children. But after she passed, I felt it was a blessing that we didn't."

In comfortable silence, they both pulled their clothes back on. Kiran's mind worked furiously at what he believed was the only way out of their situation. It was something he'd never contemplated before since he found it abhorrent, but for Alina, he would do whatever it took to stay with her.

His mind made up, he cradled her head in his hands, and brushed a soft kiss against her full lips before deepening it and taking possession of her mouth. Savoring her taste, scent, and touch, his tongue plunged deep and tangled with hers. Stroking, licking, and tasting her like a man possessed, he kissed them both breathless. If what he had in mind didn't work, he wanted to have this one kiss to hold on to forever and leave a little of himself for her to remember as well.

As they broke apart, the shimmering space they'd been sheltered in faded, and they found themselves back on the bridge, arms entwined around each other, and lips still touching. Kiran could feel her warm breath on his face and inhaled her smell one last time before stepping back.

The familiar sharp pain in his back broke out again. Two searing points, one on each shoulder blade. Beside him, he heard Alina let out a small cry and twist her back, as if uncomfortable or in pain. He squeezed her hand reassuringly.

"Alina, my love. Do you trust me?" He searched her face for the answer.

She gazed up at him, a gentle smile on her lips. "Yes, I trust you with my life."

He took her hand and turned them to face the sunrise. Far below, the river churned and danced, mists still swirling above the surface in all the colors of the rainbow.

Kiran looked up to the heavens, closed his eyes, and whispered, "I'm ready."

With Alina's hand in his, they took one small step.

Falling, tumbling, plummeting.

Behind them, the flutter of two pairs of wings danced on the breeze.

Thirty-Eight

KIRAN, 2017

"Where the hell am I?" Kiran knew full well where he was but asked anyway.

"Seriously, brother? That's the kind of language you want to use here?" someone spoke behind him.

Michael.

Kiran spun to face the person to whom the voice belonged. It had been a long time since he'd heard his oldest brother speak. He wasn't sure how he felt about it.

"Where is she?" he demanded, anger putting razor-thin edges to his words.

Michael raised his hands palms up to placate him, but Kiran didn't want to be appeased. He wanted answers.

"Tell me where she is, you son of a bi—"

"Kiran! Enough!" Michael demanded. "You know better than that."

"Do I?" He growled, arching a brow. "It's been a very long time since I was last here. I doubt anyone even remembers who I am. I sure as hell didn't hear from anyone the entire time I was down there." He folded his arms over his chest and stared at Michael.

Michael sighed. "I know, brother, but I was watching over you, I promise." He gestured to a chair by Kiran's side. "Please, let's sit down. I've missed you."

Kiran refused to move at first but relented and sat stiffly on the edge of an armchair that seemed to appear out of thin air. Michael steepled his fingers and tapped them on his lips while studying him. Kiran felt his ire rise again and tamped it down, but not without effort.

"If you don't tell me where Alina is, I'll walk out of here right now," he grunted. "And I won't return. Ever."

Michael sat impassively. "Your human is fine. She's just in another space being taken care of. She has some questions of her own that she's demanding answers to," he said with a wry smile. "Gabe is with her."

Kiran ran his hands down his face, his anxiety easing, knowing Alina was in good hands. Gabe was one of the kindest and most compassionate of them all, and that was saying something, considering who they were. Crossing his legs with an ankle on the opposite knee, he gestured for Michael to go on.

"First of all, it's great to see you. You have no idea how hard it's been for me to know what you've gone through." Michael leaned forward, arms braced on his knees. "I hated for you to have to suffer that way, but you knew there was a good reason for it. You're my brother," he said, "and if I could have helped more, I would have done so in a heartbeat, but I wasn't allowed to interfere. So, I did what I could."

"It was hard for you?" Kiran blurted mockingly. "Try enduring breaking every bone in your body falling from the top of a pyramid, or being skewered by a short sword from front to back while the citizens of Rome cheer and bay for blood, or being burned alive by a volcano!" He shot to his feet, unable to sit still, and started striding back and forth behind Michael. "Or how about finding an arrow in your chest and slowly bleeding out, or drowning in the bowels of a ship? Or the best one yet" — he barked a humorless laugh — "suffering years of the most vicious torture known to man, only to die from a parasite mere days away from rescue? And yet, none of that compares to watching someone you hold dear waste away to nothing." His voice sharpened enough to slice glass. "To see her change from a vivacious, happy, and loving woman to a gray, skeleton-like shell of her former self, knowing there is nothing you can do to stop the disease from ravaging her body...

That is the purest form of horror anyone can be subjected to. And someone thought it would be fun to put me through that!" Kiran shouted the last bit, his emotions savage and irrepressible. "What did I do, Michael?"

"What do you mean?" Michael frowned, confusion narrowing his eyes.

Kiran leaned on the back of the white armchair, hands gripping the edge hard enough to whiten his knuckles. "What did I do that was so heinous that I needed to be punished that way? Over and over and over. I could see no end in sight, didn't know if I would have to endure death and terror in all its forms and new personas for the rest of my existence. What did I do to deserve that?" He slumped back in the chair, hands clenching into tight fists.

For a brief second, the look of horror on Michael's face registered in his mind but was soon overridden by the storm gathering in his chest. His palms burned from digging his fingernails into them. It was the only thing keeping him from dissolving into a chaotic mess of rage, fear, grief, and despair.

"I could have learned my lesson had I only been told of my missteps, but I Fell with no warning. Cast out from everything I'd ever known and everyone I loved. For what?" he choked out.

"Oh, my... You weren't told? Not once while you were among the humans? While you walked... I can't... I don't... *Kiran*." Michael's eyes widened, his voice full of anguish. "Brother, I don't know what to say. You were supposed to have had that knowledge with you from the very beginning. I don't know why it wasn't given to you. I can't even begin to imagine—" Michael buried his head in his hands, his shoulders shaking.

Kiran stared in disbelief at his oldest brother, his chest heaving up and down as if he'd run a marathon.

With a ragged breath, Michael continued, "It should have been passed on to you when you first regained consciousness. I will find out who neglected to do so." His eyes connected with Kiran's. "Dearest brother, you Fell, yes, but we did not cast you out. We would *never* cast you out. You were always the best of us," he said, with quiet, desperate firmness. "Which is exactly why He felt you were the best man for the job. He considered sending Eos, but she claimed she'd be better suited giving you glorious sunrises to lift your spirit. We could only hope you'd receive her messages."

The rage in Kiran's chest subsided, replaced with bewilderment and a new worry. "If I wasn't cast out, and I'd done nothing wrong, then why? Why in His name would you subject me to this soul-breaking hardship?"

Had he done something to displease Him? It was the last thing he'd ever want to do, and he'd rather spend an eternity wandering the earth, living life after life, suffering whatever was thrown at him, than live with the knowledge he'd somehow upset Him.

Michael straightened. "He needed someone who could bear the challenges of learning humankind's triumphs, trials, loves, and hates. You were the only one, besides Eos, who was deemed worthy and capable," he said. "Everything you've been through has been passed on to your siblings. Unaware, they've learned from all the trials to which you were subjected. And I think you've learned something as well, haven't you? Something that pertains to your position with us, I mean." Michael cocked a brow and tilted his head, closely studying Kiran, who almost squirmed under the scrutiny.

Some of the weight lifted from Kiran's shoulders as another link in the chains binding him broke and fell from the knowledge he hadn't made a grave error or failed to live up to His expectations. He never wanted to fail His mission, and if he was completely honest with himself, he had learned so much, all of which he'd put to good use if he resumed his position.

The all-encompassing picture was paramount in the creation of life in the universe, but he now knew what all the little swipes of his fingers could mean for the people on earth. The flicks, nudges, and taps had far-reaching, and sometimes devastating consequences, and he could no longer add a war here, a natural disaster there, or an end-of-life event like the meteorite that crashed into the ocean near what was now called the Yucatan Peninsula, wiping out an entire dominant species. At least not without stopping to consider the effects on individuals.

Nevertheless, he'd spent the better part of four-and-a-half thousand years living, suffering, and dying in an endless cycle. All for the benefit of his siblings and the universe as a whole. So much of his bottled-up emotions surged to the surface that he struggled to push them back, to keep his head straight, but not all of it could be contained.

"Did they have to watch what I went through as well?" He spat bitterly. "Was I some kind of lab experiment, stuck under a microscope for everyone to gawk at and pity?"

Michael sighed. "No, He blocked their minds from noticing your absence. As far as they knew, you were still with them, only they were prevented from seeking you out, or even thinking too closely about you." He leaned forward again, holding Kiran's gaze. "But they learned, Kiran. They learned so much from all that you saw, heard, felt, and experienced. They are all more aware of what the humans go through when we alter the course of their lives, and do their utmost to limit their suffering. Of course," he muttered, exasperation creeping into his voice, "there is still only so much they can do, and we can't forget the scrapes the humans get themselves in. You know our directive. If it doesn't have an adverse effect on the tapestry, we do nothing."

Unable to contain his restlessness, the intense crackling under his skin, which had been present before he found Alina, made itself known, and Kiran began pacing the room again.

"Let me get this straight," he said. "I Fell but wasn't cast out. My experiences were necessary for the fabric of life, and I've had my eyes and mind opened, so I can perform my duties better. But it was never a punishment for a crime. I did nothing wrong." He repeated the statements to himself as if he were ticking items off a list.

He halted his march back and forth on the plain, faintly shimmering floor, and pivoted to face his brother, without really looking at him. Instead, he began treading a new path around the white room they were in. Then he stopped again, as if he were seeing the space for the first time. His gaze traveled along the soft white walls and the ceiling, which had a slight gray tone to it. Michael sat quietly, watching him with an inscrutable expression.

It was the same style of room you'd find anywhere around here. If you needed a private space, all you had to do was think about it, open a door, and it was there. The dimensions, appearance, layout, and any furniture could be changed at the briefest of thoughts, all to suit whatever needs the occupier had at that moment.

This room was plain, with only the two chairs in the middle. Michael had clearly not thought out anything specific for the area as the corners were diffused, and all edges undefined. It had no decorations of any kind, not even a window, despite him being able to conjure the most beautiful scenery imaginable outside.

Kiran could only guess it was either because his brother didn't deem it important, or Kiran's sudden appearance had taken him by surprise. He had a feeling it was the latter, as the normally so unflappable Michael would have had a comfortable room ready with everything they might need ready at hand.

"Were you watching the entire time?" he murmured, twisting his head to glance at the other man.

Michael turned his gaze to the ceiling, clearly uncomfortable with the question. Then he drew a sharp breath and nodded, his lips drawn into a thin line.

"Yes, I saw everything. I kept a part of my mind fixed on you at all times. I'm so sorry, Kiran. I did what I could to ease your burden. I'm the one who sent you Juliet, although I had no way of preventing what happened to her, and I also sent you Geoff, Margaret, and countless others to give you comfort, however small it may have been." Michael went to him, and placed his hand on Kiran's arm, gripping it gently. "It was honestly all I could sneak past His watchful eye. You know how He is. I even sent the most obvious sign ever that I was watching." He chuckled. "I mean, come on, to borrow a human term, don't be a knucklehead. I gave you your last name."

"What do you mean?" A crease appeared on Kiran's forehead. "It was Mitchell. Mitch—Oh, I see. Mitchell, Michael. Damn, I should have worked that out sooner." Kiran shook his head at his own stupidity.

It had been there, right in front of him, all this time. He could see Michael's efforts now. His admission made them quite obvious even if he'd been unable to notice them before while toiling under such heavy burdens.

"I saw one of your signs. I knew it had to be you who was sending me that sign — at least I prayed it was. For that, I thank you, my brother. It gave me hope at a time when life was quite literally flowing out of me."

Michael nodded.

The thoughts Kiran had had had about the five stars — the ones Ghengis had claimed were a sign of triumph — while he lay under the vaulted heavens by his Khan's side, life fading from them both, had been right.

Kiran and Michael both returned to their seats.

"So, what happens now?" Kiran asked. "What will happen to Alina? I can't lose her, Michael. Please, for the love of everything that is holy, don't make me give her up."

Michael's eyes filled with love and compassion. "No, Kiran. We wouldn't do that to you. It was part of both of your journeys. Your other mission was to encounter humans who needed your help in some way or other. As you already know, Alina has met several of them as well. I arranged that for her as a way of letting you know your efforts had a significant impact on their lives," he explained.

Kiran nodded, drawing in his lips thoughtfully, but said nothing.

Michael continued, "My belief was that it would also help her deal with her grief and desolation. Take your Tyler, for instance. As young as he was, he was already on a downward slope after losing his family so brutally." Michael's mouth twisted with sympathy for the boy's hardships. "Your words and wisdom ignited a strong desire in him to live the best life he could and make his parents proud. And they are proud. More than Tyler could ever fathom," he said emphatically. "The bottle he passed onto her — your bottle — was something tangible for your soul to latch onto. Something she felt and took comfort from, even if she didn't know at the time."

Kiran considered his words. It was a comforting thought to know he'd had a positive influence on at least some of the people he'd known and loved.

Michael shifted in his seat. "But to answer your question, you now have a choice to make. You can come back to us, resume your old life, and live happily with us, your family, or... you can go back to earth with Alina." He raised a hand to stay Kiran's question. "I promise nothing will happen to destroy your happiness, and be as happy as you two can make each other. If she chooses you, of course." He paused for a moment, palming his jaw. "If that's your choice, when you finally depart your earthly life, you will again be given a choice. You and Alina stay together in your chosen forms and take your place here the same as all humans, or you come back to us and let Alina fully join her husband and children and forget everything about you. The two opportunities to choose are His reward to you for your sacrifices."

"What if I choose Alina, but she chooses Jonas and the children?" Kiran asked, fear twisting his gut. "What happens to me then?" His head spun from the implications of each alternative.

"You will return to us." Michael shrugged. "You won't ever have to wander the earth again, but you will always remember what you went through, including your life with Alina. I'm sorry, but there's no way of erasing only some memories and not all of them. It's how it has to be." Michael's voice was tinged with concern and empathy. "We need you to remember what happened or your brothers will lose what they've learned from you. Your achievements and sufferings will all have been wasted."

Kiran closed his eyes while contemplating his options. In the end, he could make only one choice. He opened his eyes again, finding Michael's identical ones fixed on him. "I choose her. I choose Alina," he stated without hesitation. "It's the only decision I could possibly make. Her soul is entwined with mine, and I need her like I need air to breathe. She is my life." The sound of chains breaking and clattering to the floor crashed through his mind, and he suddenly felt free.

The heavy burden he'd carried for so many millennia was gone. From his back, a pair of snowy white wings unfolded, but it was no longer a painful transformation. With a touch of his mind, they gently fluttered, shimmering brightly for a fleeting moment before they disappeared again.

Michael nodded, sorrow joining the theater of emotions in his gaze.

"I expected that, and I can't say that I blame you. I will try to visit you if I can. And I will always watch over the two of you. As long as she chooses you, of course." He dragged a hand over his eyes. "You are my brother, and my love for you cannot be contained by the restraints of our environment. Remember that."

Kiran dipped his head, the enormity of his decision causing his heart to ache. He knew there was a possibility Alina would decide to join her husband and children, but he couldn't allow himself to even consider it. "You know I feel the same. I will look out for you. Don't make it too hard for me to spot you," he entreated. "And I will neither forget nor cast you out from my heart. We will always be bonded."

The two brothers embraced, both with tears glistening in their eyes. Behind them, the door opened, and his other brother and two sisters joined them. They were the Valence of Five, the Pentarchy, and he would always carry them in his soul. His other siblings would remain with their minds blinded to his absence. It was how it had to be.

"Oh, Kiran," Eos murmured. "I'm so sorry. If I'd known, I would have taken your place when it was presented to me. But I tried to give you as many graceful dawns as I could. I love you, my brother. I will be watching every sunrise. I hope you will join me as often as you can. And Alina, too. She is perfect for you, and I know you will be so happy together. Your love for her is making your aura sparkle like diamonds." She clapped her hands in delight. "You've always had the strongest glow, but now you're positively aflame. Love and be loved, my dearest brother." Eos rose on her tiptoes and kissed his cheek.

Kiran swept her into his embrace and whispered in her ear that he would gaze at as many dawns as he could. Stepping back from his sister, he turned to face his four closest siblings. The Five together one final time.

"All that remains is to find out Alina's decision. Pray for me, my family." Kiran bowed his head, his hands clasped, his eyes slamming shut as the possibility of Alina making a different choice weighed heavily on his already burdened mind.

Thirty-Nine

ALINA, 2017

Curled up on billowy cushions, Alina kept her eyes shut tight.

"Alina?" a gentle voice spoke. "Please, don't be afraid. No one is going to hurt you. Kiran is fine. You'll see him soon, if that's your choice."

Pushing her fear aside, Alina pried her eyes open. The mention of Kiran made her heart sing, and she needed to know more about what was happening. Without moving, she observed as much of the space around her as she could manage. A first glance revealed muted pastel colors and soft furnishings. She pushed herself up, noticing she'd been reclining on a dainty loveseat with a velvet cushion under her head. To her left was an open picture window with a gauzy drape billowing in a warm breeze.

Swiveling her head slowly from side to side, she took in the feminine touches in the room. Paintings of sweeping landscapes graced the walls, and on the table in front of her, a carafe of iced water rested on a delicate cloth. The condensation on the cut glass obscured the sparkling ice cubes, and large drops of water dripped down the sides. She felt thirsty just looking at it.

"Please, help yourself to the water. If there's anything else you need, just ask." It was a woman's voice, low and slightly husky.

Startled, Alina lifted her eyes, taking in the beautiful woman sitting in a chair across from her.

Where did she come from? She wasn't sitting there a few seconds ago!

"Where am I?" she croaked.

The woman smiled warmly. She wore a midnight black dress that sparkled with the slightest movement. It was like the sky on a clear night, with all the stars twinkling like the brightest jewels.

"You're in a... waiting room, for want of a better word," the woman said kindly. "We thought you'd be more comfortable here than in the void."

Alina's forehead scrunched. "The void?" It didn't sound like a place anyone would want to be in.

"Yes, but it's not as terrible as it sounds. It's just a place where spirits go before He knows where they belong — where their souls belong."

Alina's head spun. Spirits? Souls? What was happening? She closed her eyes tight and tried to think what could have happened.

The last thing she remembered was stepping off the bridge with Kiran, and the heavy beat of something akin to wings behind them!

They'd stepped off the parapet! Together! The recollections of what had happened since she reached the bridge flooded back into her mind.

Kiran.

Where was he? She already knew he wasn't nearby. And where was *here*? Fear and worry burned in her chest.

"I'm sorry, I forgot to introduce myself. I'm Nyx." The woman leaned forward with her hand outstretched.

Alina stared at it for a moment. Then she took it in hers, surprised at the cool touch of Nyx's skin, and gently shook it. It seemed a little formal, but since she didn't know the formalities around here, she rolled with it.

Wait, where am I again?

"Can you tell—"

"Have you seen the view from here?" Nyx asked, rising to her feet. "It's rather gorgeous." She crossed to the window, pushing the drape aside, and gestured for Alina to join her.

Hesitantly, she went to stand next to the mysterious woman. The view was wonderful, almost magical. Rolling hills spread out before her, the closest ones covered in an abundance of colorful flowers, with trees dotted here and there. A small river meandered away from the bottom of a waterfall that cascaded down from tall mountains in the distance. Birds sang, bees hummed, and butterflies flitted between the flowers. It looked like something out of a fairytale.

She drew in a deep breath of the fresh air. It was scented with the sweet perfume of the flowers and something citrusy. It helped clear her head a little.

She turned to Nyx and asked, "Please, tell me—"

"Oh, look!" Nyx exclaimed. "A rainbow."

Alina looked to where the woman pointed. Above the waterfall, a shimmering rainbow had appeared, its colors deep and vibrant. It arched above the flowing water with the peaks of the mountains behind it. The whole scene was breathtaking, and Alina couldn't help staring, her lips parted in wonder.

She shook her head, nearly forgetting what was pressing on her mind.

"Please," she begged. "Tell me where—"

Nyx took her hands, looking deep into her eyes for a moment. A warmth spread up Alina's arms and into her chest from the touch, and Nyx led her back to the chairs. A languid feeling washed through her limbs, her mind relaxing as if nothing could worry her, and she curled up on the soft cushions. She'd been about to ask a question but couldn't for the life of her remember what it was. It couldn't have been that important.

Nyx crossed one leg over the other, her hands clasped in her lap. "Tell me about Jonas. How did you two meet?"

Alina sighed contentedly. She loved talking about her husband.

"I had just finished college and was taking some time over the summer to relax and think of what to do next. I had a few job offers, but none that I was really interested in. Then my friend Katie called to ask if I wanted to spend a few weeks with her in Santa Barbara. Her parents had rented a villa there, and of course, I said yes." Her eyes lost focus as the memories danced through her mind. "The people next door organized a party one weekend, inviting us all, and when we arrived, Jonas was playing around in the pool with some buddies. As soon as our eyes connected, I knew he was someone special. He immediately got out of the pool and came over to me."

She smiled at the images conjuring in front of her eyes. "That night, we went for a walk on the beach, and before he escorted me to my door, we kissed. It was one of those perfect, toe-curling, heart-stopping, breathtaking kisses that you remember forever. After that, we were inseparable. Fortunately, he didn't live far from me, so we could keep seeing each other once we left Santa Barbara. Jonas was so kind, funny, and never hesitated to show how much he loved me." She laughed. "He could be very bossy and protective, but he was never overbearing. You know" — she swung her gaze to Nyx — "we rarely argued, and if we did, it never lasted long before we dissolved in laughter at our own stupidity. We kissed and made up, forgetting it had ever happened."

"Oh, my," Nyx murmured, her hand on the base of her throat. "That sounds so beautiful. You must have been so in love."

Alina nodded. "Yes, we were."

Nyx put her hand on Alina's arm, sending another rush of warmth and languor through her core, making her feel like she was floating in a dream where everything was diffused and blurry. "And what about your children? Theo and Daisy?"

Once again, Alina lost herself in memories of her babies. "When Theo was born, things were... difficult, and I would never have made it through without Jonas. It took me a couple of years to let go of the anxiety I'd carried since we found out Theo needed surgery, even after it was successfully completed."

Nyx tilted her head. "What was Theo like as a toddler?"

"He was so bright," Alina gushed, "and inquisitive. Full of energy, of course, like most children his age, and when Daisy came along, he was the best big brother you could imagine. She was a dream baby. Sweet, always smiling, and never fussed. She slept through the night from six weeks old and ate anything you put in front of her from the moment she went onto solid foods." Alina fell quiet, staring out the window for a moment. "She was also a very determined and strong-willed young lady who knew what she wanted and quickly learned how to wrap both her daddy and her brother around her little fingers to get it."

Nyx giggled. "Sounds like an amazing little girl."

Alina dropped her gaze to her lap. A sense of sorrow rang like a delicate bell in the far reaches of her mind. She didn't like it.

"Is there anything you want to ask me?" Nyx's brow creased slightly, her dark eyes studying Alina closely.

"I guess... Well, I'm a little confused," Alina began. "You say you are Nyx, but I thought she was a Greek goddess?"

Nyx laughed. It sounded like a gentle, babbling spring brook — light and joyful.

"Those different pantheons, like the Greek, Roman, and Norse, are a human construct. We are all the same, but with different names and attributes according to each faith," she explained. "My sister, Eos, is also thought of as my daughter. She's also known as Aurora, and I as Nox among the ancient Romans."

"I see," Alina murmured, her forehead wrinkling.

"Would you like me to explain the basics of the hierarchy here?" Nyx asked.

"Would you? I mean, are you allowed?" Alina pursed her lips.

Nyx laughed again. "Of course, it's no secret. To begin with, it's not a hierarchy the way humans see it. No one is above anyone else. We all have our areas of concern, and each is as important as the next. Those with the overarching responsibilities, the Five or the Pentarchy, are usually deferred to by those on other levels since they oversee the universe — the fabric of life, time, and space. Anything they do affects humankind somehow, either now, in the past, or so far into the distant eons of time that humans of today will be seen as primordial beings by those who will exist then."

Alina listened, fascinated. She'd never given much thought to religious construct after the few times she went to Sunday school with her grandmother as a child.

Nyx continued, "Then we have those who care for your immediate future — the next few millions of years or so — and who guide your future evolution in the right direction. I know" — she waved away Alina's protest before it left her lips — "it's not immediate from a human perspective, but around here, things work a little differently."

"Yeah, I guess. A few million years is way beyond what anyone I know would call 'immediate future'," Alina said, biting her lip. "What comes next?"

"Well," Nyx said, resting her arms on her knees, her hands clasped. "Next come world events. You know, the ones that affect large parts of the world at the same time. Like wars, plagues, celebrations, major breakthroughs in science and technology, that kind of thing. Some of them are difficult to administer, but they're always performed because, for some reason or another, they are necessary. Those who are in charge of these events are our most strategic and logical siblings."

"I can't even imagine having to send a deadly disease around the world. So many deaths…"Alina's heart clenched at the thought. "How many more are there?" she asked. "Levels, areas, or whatever they are."

"Only two more. We have Faiths and Guardians. The first one is where the world's different faiths are guided and assisted in a way not to become too powerful, so they squash all the others or lose sight of their principal tenets." She grimaced. "I must admit, I'm relieved it is not one of my assignments. It has to be directed with an immensely diplomatic hand."

"And the Guardians?" Alina wrapped her arms around her middle, the warmth that had coursed through her fading. "What do they do?"

Nyx's eyes took on a faraway look. "They're the ones that walk among you humans, at least from time to time, depending on who they're looking after. Some need them closer than others. The Guardian Angels usually focus on only one individual at a time. They can sometimes have more than one if they've been blessed with a few that are going through happy times in their lives." She fell quiet, her thoughts somewhere else. "The Guardians are bound to their charges in a way that allows them to feel, hear, and see everything they do. They are there to support them in difficult times, to give comfort, and to help them move forward. They're also present for all the joyful occasions, but tend to stay in the background for those since they're not really needed. It's more to make sure they always have a full picture of what's happening in their human's life." She took a deep breath, a hand sweeping across her brow as if to wipe away a fine mist. "What they do requires an incredibly strong mind. I don't know how they cope. The mental strain is enormous."

Alina shifted in her seat, sensing a sadness in Nyx.

"Can you say no to your assignments? Or move to a different one?"

"Yes, we can. It doesn't happen too often because we're usually exactly where we're meant to be. He can move someone if they seem particularly suited for something other than what they're already doing." Nyx paused, her dark eyes fixed on Alina, swirling with some emotion she could only describe as deep sorrow. "The Pentarchy hasn't changed since the beginning of time, but even one of them can leave if they want to do so."

Alina felt uncomfortable with the sadness flowing off Nyx. She didn't understand it and wasn't sure she wanted to either, so she decided to change the subject.

"Is my family here? I mean, are they close by?"

Nyx seemed to relax, and the smile was back on her face.

"Alina, it's lovely to finally meet you, even if the circumstances aren't what I had expected," a man's voice sounded to her side, making her jump.

She turned toward the new voice and found a man, close to her own age, in the armchair on the other side of the table. Glancing at the chair Nyx had occupied, she was disturbed to see it empty. Where had Nyx gone? Who was this man? Had he been here the entire time? No, that was impossible. And yet, it felt as if they were acquainted.

Dressed in an elegant suit that looked like something out of the nineteen-twenties, he had the same ethereal beauty as Kiran and also his masculinity and strength, but that's where the similarities ended. This man was as dark as Kiran was light. A slight shimmer still surrounded him, but it was more amber than gold, though his eyes were the same sapphire blue.

Kiran! Where was he? How long had they been separated? Alina went cold, her mind flooding with the recollections of everything that had occurred and what had led to her being where she was. Why did she only just now remember him? She didn't understand what was happening. One second, they'd been on the bridge, and now— Alina wasn't even sure what had gone on since then.

Had someone else been here? A vague sense of having had a long conversation with someone echoed in her mind. A woman? What had they been talking about? Why hadn't she asked about Kiran before now? Unease slithered into her stomach. Something wasn't right. She would never forget Kiran unless she was made to do so. Maybe she'd been drugged, somehow. For some strange reason, that thought made her feel a little better. Having been drugged was the much-preferred alternative to having completely forgotten about her love, no matter how fleeting.

"Where am I? Where's Kiran?" The rising panic in her chest made her voice break into a husky whisper.

"Please, don't worry. Kiran is just fine." The man waved toward something behind him. "He's meeting with our brother next door. He can be with you soon."

"His brother? Then this is —"

"His home. Yes. He's been gone a long time, and we've all missed him." The man rubbed his chin, his gaze fixed on her face. "But more importantly, how are you? Did Nyx look after you?"

Alina dragged her eyes away from the gorgeous man watching her.

Nyx.

That's who she'd been speaking with. How could she have forgotten? She swatted the question away and concentrated on the man before her. As beautiful as he was, he wasn't the man her heart called out for, and yet, the more she looked at him, the more he resembled Kiran..

"I'm... all right. I think. When can I see him?"

The man sighed briefly but smiled and poured her a glass of water.

"He just needs to have a conversation with Mike." He passed her the glass, looking pleased when she accepted it. "I'm Gabe, by the way. Any questions, please ask, and I'll do my best to answer them."

Her eyes narrowed. "Why am I here?"

Gabe leaned forward and propped his elbows on his knees.

"You remember stepping off that bridge?" he asked.

When Alina nodded, he continued, "Well, He doesn't like any of his sons or daughters taking matters into their own hands, and He needs to know why. So, Michael is having the unenviable task" — a wry grin tugged at Gabe's mouth — "of seeing our brother for the first time in a very long time, while also trying to figure out what drove him, and you, to step off a very high bridge. Care to enlighten me?" Gabe leaned back in his armchair and clasped his hands behind his head, looking relaxed and disarming.

Alina dropped her gaze to the floor, desperately trying to gather her thoughts. The handsome man facing her didn't make it easy. He looked too much like Kiran for that. As the image of her lover crashed through her mind, all thoughts of Gabe were swept clean, and only Kiran remained.

A shuddering breath shook her shoulders. "Desperation, I guess." She shrugged. "And needing an end to it all. We've both been through the wringer in more ways than one, and all we want is to be together. Is that too much to ask?" Her voice faltered at the thought of losing the man she loved. "Will Kiran be allowed…" It would be too much for her. Once was heartbreaking, twice would be soul-destroying.

"Well, I'm here to give you some options. I'm guessing Kiran has already explained how things work when you… pass away?" Gabe cocked a brow.

She nodded. "Yes, he did. He said Jonas and my babies are together and waiting for me. And I can join them if I want. But I have to choose. Kiran or Jonas and our children."

Gabriel nodded and leaned back again, looking every bit a debonair nobleman out of the early twentieth century. Alina knew better. This man had never lived among her kind.

"That's true. You can be with your husband and children. Forever. Or you can be with Kiran." His gaze was fixed on her. "I wish we could somehow split you in two and give you both alternatives, but that's beyond even our capabilities. It's possible He could do it, but He rarely gets involved in such minor matters. Minor for Him, that is." Humor danced briefly in his voice before it became serious again. "It could cause more complications, rips in the fabric of existence, than we can handle. I'm truly sorry. What we really need to decide now is what you're going to do for the immediate future."

Alina scrunched her face, unsure of what Gabe meant. Who was He? And who was Gabe? Short for Gabriel, usually. *Gabriel*. Holy heck! Her stomach dropped with the realization. He was an Archangel and God's messenger. Did that mean —? Alina couldn't finish that thought process, but she'd distinctly heard Gabe saying Kiran was with Michael.

As in the Chief of all Archangels? The strongest, most powerful of them all, if she remembered her Sunday school teachings correctly?

Oh.

Alina leaned forward, her head spinning. Breathing deeply, she slowly regained her equilibrium and sat up. Gabe was watching her with concern in his blue eyes, and her longing for her man increased tenfold.

She lifted her head. "You said I have options?"

"Of course, you do." Gabriel's hand flicked out.

Alina listened hard as Gabriel laid out her choices in more detail. Jonas, Theo, and Daisy for an eternity. Or Kiran for a lifetime — what would happen once she finally passed away was unclear and depended on several circumstances, but Gabe didn't go into them too closely. Alina barely heard anything after the first two alternatives, anyway. The thought of being with her husband and children again exploded in her heart.

They could be together forever. It would be as if they'd never been apart, and she could hug and kiss her babies whenever she wanted. She could bask in her husband's adoration again. Make love to him. Resurrect their hopes and dreams. Make them a reality. Or as real as was possible in the afterlife. She and Jonas had been the perfect couple. Their love had been the beacon of hope for so many of their friends who'd struggled in their relationships.

Okay, so they wouldn't be that again since all of their friends were still alive, as far as she knew, but to feel Jonas' arms around her again, his tender kisses and caresses, hear his whispered sweet nothings. It would be her own private paradise, and it was all hers for the taking. She just had to be brave enough to reach out and say yes.

Images of Jonas and their life together, and of Theo and Daisy, flashed before her eyes. Jonas' smile that could light up a room. Theo's curiosity and intelligent questions, his arms around her neck whispering how much he loved his mommy. Daisy's wide-eyed assessment of the world around her, her patience, her soft little grunts when she snuggled into her mom or dad's arms for some comfort and security. All of it. She could have all of it.

Alina stood. Gabriel got to his feet as well, catlike and smooth in his movements.

"I've made my choice. There's only one decision I can make."

Gabriel nodded, his face somber. "It's what I expected." His shoulders slumped. "I will make sure Kiran is informed. Will you please wait here?"

Alina watched as he walked out and closed the door behind him.

From far away, the muted sound of chains breaking and falling to the ground reverberated through the room.

Epilogue

KIRAN, 2023

Kiran smiled as he looked over the backyard. The summer sunshine filtered through the trees, making the ocean just past the boundary sparkle. Two children, a girl and a boy, squealed with laughter while their colorful kites rose and fell in the fresh breeze. Their mom guided their little hands on the strings, and they all laughed as the white-winged pieces of nylon caught the warm currents and soared into the skies.

Kiran's heart was full of love, and he couldn't think of a better existence than what he had right now. He had a woman by his side who he worshiped and adored, and two children who were the light of his life. It was all he'd ever wanted, even if he hadn't known it until it was within his grasp.

He finished washing the dishes and prepared vegetables for lunch. His little munchkins loved everything green and healthy, and scrunched their noses at potato chips and candy. It wasn't natural, they said. He couldn't agree more but secretly enjoyed the occasional bowl of chips with a sour cream or guacamole dip.

Keeping his eyes on his family, he smiled as Alina's laughter rang like silver bells in the clear air outside. A wave of love and gratitude for the woman who made his life complete washed through his soul.

Thinking back to the time right after they stepped off the bridge, he realized how worried he'd been she wouldn't choose him. His brother, Gabe, was an expert at making people see their options. Everything that was and everything that could be.

Alina had lost her husband and children in a horrific accident, and the prospect of being with them again would inevitably have been an enormous temptation for her. Kiran knew that, and so did Gabe. His very presence could make the most steadfast person doubt their choices, but that was his job. To make each and every one who came through their gates consider their past and their future.

Kiran could only be grateful that Alina had ultimately chosen him instead of staying with the family she'd once lost. He would forever be in Gabe's debt that he'd presented her options so clearly and unbiased.

A deep shudder went through his core. He couldn't ever forget hanging around in that empty, indistinct room where everything seemed shrouded in indecisions and uncertainty. That's how it had appeared to him, at least. The waiting had been torture. Not that he'd waited very long. Michael had made sure of that, but every second had felt like a death sentence.

He'd never wanted to believe Alina would choose her family over him, but as the minutes ticked by, it was exactly what had gone through his head. It had been more agonizing and torturous than anything he'd experienced on earth. The doubt had amplified tenfold. Who was he compared to the man she'd loved and lost, and the children she'd borne and adored? He came second best at most.

When Gabe had walked through the door, alone, Kiran's heart had sunk, and a black cloud engulfed his mind, chasing all the light away. Then Gabe had stepped aside, and Alina appeared behind him. When her worried eyes had captured his, she'd flown through the room and flung herself into his arms.

His soul had burst into flames and merged with hers in a blaze so fierce it stole the breaths from their bodies.

She had chosen him.

He would never let that slip from his mind and had resolved there and then never to disappoint her. He would spend the rest of his life worshiping, adoring, and cherishing her.

As he put the flatware in the cupboard and wiped the countertops, he heard the love of his life calling for the children to come in. It was time for them to have lunch and then take a nap. They were still young enough to need a rest during the day. Especially since they'd all been up shortly before dawn to greet Eos and her mesmerizing show of light and color.

When the sun crested the horizon, he'd gone to meet his sister and thanked her, as always, for bringing a new day to his life. It was another opportunity to show his sister how much he appreciated her. Eos had been her usual graceful self and brought greetings from Michael, Gabriel, Nyx, and their other sister, Tien — the Five. As always, Kiran sent his love back to them all.

Nyx had taken Kiran's place in the Pentarchy, but not without a lot of grumbling and sending Kiran dirty looks when he passed his mantle to her. It was mostly for show, they all knew. Nyx would seamlessly slip into her new role, performing her duties to perfection, and the Five would carry on directing and aiding the weaving of the tapestry of the universe, life, time, and space the way they had done from the beginning of everything. They were the Protectors of all.

He would occasionally glimpse Michael or Gabriel when they had reason to descend to Earth, but they never stayed long. For Kiran, however, it was enough to know they hadn't forgotten about him and still watched over him and his little family.

Never in his eternal life had he thought he'd end up on earth with the humans, loving a human being, and cherishing every second. Alina and their children were everything to him.

Her parents had welcomed him with open arms, and even her sister, Sophia, had been gracious and kind. She had finally found a man who made her happy and who brought out the best in her. She and Alina now had a warm and respectful relationship, and in time, it would hopefully become a close bond the way sisters should be connected.

A smile tugged at his lips when he thought of the trip they'd taken to New York before the twins were born. They'd stayed with Alina's friends, Stephen and Carl, and had cooed and 'awwd' over their six-month-old little boy. They'd named him Gabriel, which he'd found rather amusing, but when his brother found out, the joy and happiness exuding from Gabe that had washed over Kiran had settled in his heart, and both he and Alina thought the name was perfect.

The backdoor opening had Kiran switch his attention to Alina and their own little bundles of joy, Cleo and Joshua. They were the light of their lives, and soon they hoped to have more. Last night, Alina had shared she believed she was expecting again, and Kiran couldn't have been happier.

If it was up to him, they'd have enough to create their own choir of cherubs, but he knew it was unrealistic and waited for Alina to give him the slightest sign she'd had enough of putting her life aside to carry the light of someone new.

"Come on, you two," Alina urged the children.

She waved for them to come inside, and after their usual protests, they came running.

Kiran couldn't help but feel incredibly fortunate to have his growing family. He watched while Alina enticed the children in. As young as they were, they loved nothing more than to play out in the fresh air. They had an unobstructed view of the ocean toward the east, which was one of the reasons they'd bought the house.

He stepped forward to help his family inside, even though he knew Alina could do it all blindfolded and with one hand tied behind her back. She was one of the most capable women he'd ever known. And she was all his.

"You must be hungry. I bet Daddy has something yummy ready for you. How about pancakes with fresh strawberries?"

Kiran laughed. She knew him so well. It was one of his favorites, and he served it most Saturdays for lunch, since breakfast usually comprised cereal and toast.

Kiran met them at the door, giving Alina a passionate kiss, and took his children's chubby little hands in his.

"Be careful now. Just take one small step."

THE END

Also By Cassidy Reyne

THE BOUND BY CONVICTION SERIES

The Sentinels — Saving Innocence, a Prequel

The Sentinels — Saving Her

The Sentinels 2 — Saving Him

The Sentinels 3 — Saving Lives

The Sentinels 4 — Saving Dignity

The Sentinels 5 — Saving Sanity

THE AGENT OF HONOR SERIES

Agent: Undone

STATE OF GRACE SERIES

Angel Unchained

A Note From Cassidy

Dear Reader,

Thank you so much for reading Kiran and Alina's story.

From the moment his story crashed into my head, Kiran stood before me with such heavy weights on his shoulders, in his heart, and in his soul, and he was begging me to tell his earthly life's story. Once I started listening, the events and challenges he'd faced came pouring out, and in the end, I had to choose the ones that had had the most impact on him and later, on Alina. At his request, I mentioned a few others, such as the eruption of Krakatoa. I could almost feel the crackling heat.

Alina was a little more reluctant. The beginning of her story was centered around the most traumatic event in her life, and she felt as if there was no substance to her as a person after that. She was an empty shell. Of course, her life began to fill again as she processed her trauma. Her grief was palpable to me, and I was in tears more than once while writing it.

I know they're not real people. But when you live with them in your head for so long, they become fully fleshed-out characters with personalities and minds of their own.

This was not an easy book to write. Giving them both valid reasons

A NOTE FROM CASSIDY

to be where they were, together with natural ways of meeting the other characters, was tricky to say the least, but so much fun to work out.

Their individual timelines needed to be simple to follow, but they also had to meet romantically before the last few chapters. Separated by decades and hundreds of miles, the only way for them to do that was in dream sequences. Or maybe they weren't dreams? Only they can answer that.

Creating the world of Kiran and Alina was a fun, thrilling, but also heartbreaking experience. Writing stories like this is often a labor of love, and as a writer, I expect times when the words won't flow, so when inspiration strikes, I sit down and let it rush through me. It takes on a life of its own, and sometimes, all I can do is hang on and let my fingers fly across the keyboard as fast as I can.

As an author, I often get asked how I began my journey. Well, let me tell you. A sudden case of empty-nest syndrome was my catalyst for jumping off the self-publishing cliff, and it has also been my salvation. One day, my life was full of supporting my children through school and co-curricular endeavors, and the next it wasn't. I still had my work with our family business, and my one-day-a-week as an administrator at a local dance school, but none of that appeased a craving in me for something even I couldn't explain. I decided to the scariest thing I could think of and began to write down something that had been spinning in my head for nearly ten years. That was the birth of the Bound by Conviction Series.

Having my amazing readers along for the ride is an incredibly thrilling adventure, and I hope you'll stick with me for all the other stories I have planned for the future.

If you'd like to grab a FREE novel, head over to my website and sign up for my newsletter. You get the prequel to the Bound by Conviction Series, The Sentinels — Saving Innocence, as a thank you from me.

Would you mind taking a minute or two out of your time and leave a short review by following one of the links below? It would mean the world to me. It doesn't have to be long — a few sentences will do or a simple star rating.

Reviews are incredibly important for authors, especially indie ones

A NOTE FROM CASSIDY

like me, and more than that, I would love to hear what you think of the book.

Amazon US
Amazon UK
Goodreads
BookBub

If you'd like to get in touch, send me a message via my website or on social media.

Thank you so much!
Cassidy x.
Website
Instagram
Facebook
Threads

About the Author

Cassidy Reyne is the Alter Ego of a Swedish girl living in England. She's been happily married for over 30 years and has two grown up children.

She writes steamy, contemporary romance with some suspense thrown in for fun and excitement. Her current books, The Bound by Conviction Series and the Agent of Honor Series are available in Kindle E-books, Paperbacks and Kindle Unlimited.

Currently residing in South London, she fits her writing in with the family property business. When she isn't writing, she enjoys photography, spending time with friends, visiting her family on an island in Sweden and drinking a glass or two of a good wine. Sometimes the wine is replaced with vodka or rum.

Cocktails anyone?

If you would like to connect with Cassidy, you can find her on several social media sites.

Website
Instagram
Facebook
Threads

facebook.com/cassidyreyne
instagram.com/cassidyreyne
threads.net/@cassidyreyne

Acknowledgments

How do you write a romance where the two main characters don't actually meet until the end?

That conundrum is what I was facing when I started writing this book, but the story had come to me in a flash of inspiration and within a few hours, was all outlined. Kiran's time jumps, coinciding with events in Alina's life, seemed logical, straightforward and easy to write. Until I started writing...

I'm fortunate enough to have the same tribe of friends dancing crazily along with me in my writing journey. We stand by each other in thick and thin, and offer unwavering support at all times of day and night.

Jodie and Kara, I thank you from the bottom of my heart. The insightful advice and creative suggestions you readily impart with are invaluable, and my sanity is still somewhat intact thanks to you. Your encouragement, laughter, virtual hugs, and the endless exchanges of silly gifs are a constant light in my life, and I'm forever grateful.

You are my partners in crime, my fellow crown-bearers, and my sisters by choice. My days would be so much duller without you, and just so you know, you're stuck with me. I will hang onto our friendship like a koala in a storm.

I love you both.

Michelle, you are the warmest, most kind-hearted, and honest person I know. Having you in my life has become essential. You're always there for me with love and support, some wise words, a few blunt truths, or silent companionship when life gets me down. You have become one of the most important people in my life, and I can't tell you how much you mean to me.

Heather, we are so alike in so many ways I'm sure we must be related somehow, somewhere in the far, or maybe near, reaches of our ancestries. The similarities we find are often hilarious, and it's not just the blonde hair. I love our giggly chats over a glass of wine, the fun we have with our joint projects, and the entertaining text conversations that occur on a daily basis. I'm so excited to get to hug you for real when you come over for a visit.

Valika, you are the twin to my heart. You always cheer me on, listen to me ramble about plots, timelines, characters, and HEAs and never fail to make me laugh. When we grow up, we'll be causing mischief and mayhem, drinking large glasses of wine, and laughing until the tears stream down our faces. Oh, wait. We're already doing that. But we're leaving the growing up for a few more years, right?

Nat, thank you for all your advice, tips, and ideas on everything from editing to marketing and publishing.

You alpha read, check for inconsistencies in my writing and story building, and point out the British expressions that inevitably make their way past my best effort to keep them out. You give my manuscript a good run-through with your eagle eyes and attention to detail. I always listen when you tell me things.

The editing was done by the wonderful **Kelly** of Spirit Editorial who very patiently points out the mistakes I make, suggests improvements, and calls out when something jars or just doesn't fit in the story. It's thanks to her the story flows the way it does. This book wouldn't be anywhere near as good without her expertise.

I also need to say a huge thank you to **Natalie** from NMT Design Studio. I spotted one of her pre-made covers in her Facebook group and instantly, the image made the story flash in my head like a lightning strike. I only had to write it down.

Natalie's covers tell a story all of their own. They are beautifully created, imaginative, all original, and with no AI.

You want to judge my book by its cover? Please, be my guest. It won't ever disappoint with one of Natalie's creations.

Finally, I thank my family. Last year was marred by a huge loss, and I would never have made it through without the support of my amazing and devoted husband. My two wonderful children were also like rocks in a raging storm. They supported me with their love and care while dealing with their own grief. They may live on opposite ends of the earth from me now, but the distance will never diminish the bonds we have created as a close-knit family

Lastly, but by no means the least, I want to thank my fabulous readers who take the time to live with my characters for a little while, cheering them on, reaching for tissues, or wanting to give them a swift kick when they're being idiots. I appreciate and thank you for your continued support.

Cassidy xxx.

Printed in Great Britain
by Amazon